KING NYX

ALSO BY KIRSTEN BAKIS

Lives of the Monster Dogs

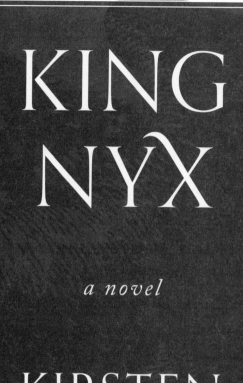

KING NYX

a novel

KIRSTEN BAKIS

LIVERIGHT PUBLISHING CORPORATION
A Division of W. W. Norton & Company
Independent Publishers Since 1923

Copyright © 2024 by Kirsten Bakis

Title Page: Ivan Bilbin, illustration for the poem "Two Crows" (Два ворона) by Alexander Pushkin (1910). Courtesy of Art Heritage / Alamy Stock Photo.

For information about permission to reproduce selections from this book, write to Permissions, Liveright Publishing Corporation, a division of W. W. Norton & Company, Inc., 500 Fifth Avenue, New York, NY 10110

For information about special discounts for bulk purchases, please contact W. W. Norton Special Sales atspecialsales@wwnorton.com or 800-233-4830

Manufacturing by Lakeside Book Company
Book design by Beth Steidle
Production manager: Julia Druskin

ISBN 978-1-324-09353-4

Liveright Publishing Corporation, 500 Fifth Avenue, New York, N.Y. 10110
www.wwnorton.com

W. W. Norton & Company Ltd., 15 Carlisle Street, London W1D 3BS

1 2 3 4 5 6 7 8 9 0

For Theo and Charlotte

This one datum:
The fall of blood from the sky—

—CHARLES FORT,
The Book of the Damned

KING NYX

PROLOGUE

June 9, 1933

LAST NIGHT I DREAMED MY husband came back. He was blurry, like an old sepia photograph, but otherwise looked the way he had in life: tall and pale, with that shy smile hiding under his mustache, happy with some private thought.

"Charlie," I said. He looked up, first surprised to see me, then glad, a little of his smile appearing, like sun peeking from behind a cloud. He tried to move toward me, but didn't seem able to get his feet off the ground.

Then a drop of something splashed on his oval wire-rimmed glasses. Another slid down the side of his forehead. Liquid ran through his hair. The sepia streaks were dark on his skin. Darker than water.

"It's blood, isn't it?" I asked in the dream.

He ran a finger along his wet cheek, then held it up to look. A whole, bright smile came out from under his mustache. "Why, so it is!" he said. "Isn't it wonderful, Annie?"

Charles spread his arms and turned his round, soft face up to the sky. When he looked back at me, the lenses of his glasses were covered with dark droplets, almost hiding his eyes.

Something bounced off his shoulder. It was a small, surprised-looking frog. Then another, and another. An eel wriggled down the front of his suit jacket and slid into the puddle that was forming at his feet. Walnut-sized hailstones sent ripples radiating outward, and long, thick drops of an oily substance created wriggling, shiny streaks, which intersected with the ripples, making patterns on the surface of the puddle that shone in faint rainbow colors.

Yes—colors. The sepia tint was fading, and the frogs became a muddy green, the puddle brownish red. It was like the time just before dawn, when sunlight begins to fill the gray world with color.

Charles looked so happy.

"Everything will be all right now, Annie, won't it?" He stood with his arms spread, a mix of blood and something fatty like melted butter pooling in his upturned hands.

I wanted to say yes, everything would be all right. I sensed that it was my last chance to say anything to him, that I would never see him again.

"Won't it be, Annie?" he said. "Everyone will believe now."

The strange rain came harder, fish struggling through his hair, gouts of blood and wet, ragged pieces of flesh splashing into the puddle, which had now risen over the tops of his shoes. It was harder to see him. He was still waiting for my answer when he was completely lost to view, the expectant smile still on his face.

As I sit at my desk this morning, I wonder: What, exactly, did he want everyone to believe?

Was it the thousands of odd occurrences he cataloged in his books: the rains of blood and fish, cryptic footprints in the snow? The mysterious clustered lights at night that drifted along a ravine outside St. Petersburg, or the colored orbs above the Dysynni River, or the flares that stood like beacons on the coast of Durham, luring sailors to their deaths?

No: those and all the other anomalies were accepted, noted by credible observers, even documented in scientific journals throughout the world, throughout history. But they were always given cursory explanations, and shrugged off.

What Charlie wanted everyone to believe were his Grand Theories explaining *why* these things happened. He had several, all hard to parse and harder to swallow. Martians beaming energy through outer space. A powerful race in a secret city at the North Pole, controlling our perceptions. An invisible body of water, a "Super-Sargasso Sea" that hovered above the clouds, repository for all things lost or rejected on earth. In its storms, unseen ships capsized, spilling cargos of eels, or butter, or silk— all those things that fell mysteriously to earth and were cataloged in the scientific journals he studied year after year.

He claimed he didn't believe his own theories. But I always thought that really, deep down, he needed to think they *could* be true. Their flaw was that they made no sense; but their appeal was that they were all-inclusive, and he needed that. Nothing was written off; nothing was rejected or excluded.

They were to scientific thought what Frankenstein's monster was to humanity: lumpy, clumsy imitations, stitched together from mismatched scraps. If an occurrence didn't fit elegantly into the body of his theory, it didn't matter; he added it anyway.

For example, mysterious footprints in the snow reported in Devonshire in 1855 couldn't be explained by his Super-Sargasso Sea or beams from Mars—so maybe they were left by massive goats who roamed frozen hillsides in the night. Why not?

The unexplained mass of lights seen by Monsieur Trouvelot from the Meudon Observatory in 1885? Angels? Yes, why not?

The scientists wanted to write off those lights as a trick of tired eyes. But Charlie didn't want to write anything off. In his world, they *were* angels: winged bodies lifted by celestial winds from their home on the sun, drifting across the evening sky, scattering like glittering dandelion seeds through outer space.

I never discouraged him from spinning out these ideas, no matter how bizarre. In all our thirty-six years of marriage, all I ever did was encourage him. I thought that was my job. When I suspected he was wrong, I kept my mouth shut. When I knew he was wrong, I kept my mouth shut.

He was a kind man, and if I had ever spoken up, he wouldn't have expressed anger; he would only have retreated to his desk, surrounded by shoeboxes full of notes, and said nothing. But I would have known I'd hurt him.

Yet, looking back, I wonder if the temporary sting could have benefited him in the long run. Maybe he'd have changed course. Maybe he could have gotten the respect of the public, instead of notoriety.

Anyway, it's too late now. The name of Charles Fort will always be associated with those rambling books in which he asked us to believe in swarms of luminous beings, and visitors from Mars, and invisible ships sailing across the clouds.

And when I think about it, what are the chances he would have changed any of that for me? Maybe I shouldn't blame myself. I knew my choice: support him or leave. And I couldn't imagine my life without him. I loved him.

Though once, in the fall of 1918, a strange gift was given to me and I could have left . . .

June 10, 1933

I LIKE TO LET THE telephone on my desk ring a few times before I pick it up. I'm sitting right next to it, and I could answer, but I like the sound of the bell. Heavy, yet bright; mechanical, but also—what would be a good word? "Fruity," maybe. Or even better: "ripe."

Yes, I like those words. "Ripe" is good because it suggests

a sense of imminence, readiness. Soon I'll know who's on the other end.

The instrument is solid and black, and it vibrates slightly as each ring shivers through it. The late spring sunlight from the windows makes gold-white highlights on the dark Bakelite surface. Outside the windows, a flurry of poplar fluff drifts sideways past the green hayfields.

Charles wouldn't have a telephone. He was too shy to use one. I promised I'd answer it, but he said any caller would be asking for *him*, and he was right. It's only in the year since he died that I've had my own desk, and telephone.

Ginger shouts from downstairs, asking if I want her to get it.

"No!" I shout back. The pleasure will be mine.

THE RUMBLING VOICE ON THE other end was immediately familiar, but I couldn't place it.

"Theodore Dreiser."

Ah. How could I forget Charlie's most famous friend?

"That you, Anna? I was surprised you asked me to telephone," he said brusquely. "I didn't know you had one."

"I do now."

He'd sent me a letter last week, and instead of writing a response, I'd sent my number. Maybe I wanted to show off.

But Mr. Dreiser didn't seem impressed. He grunted. Then he said, "Well-ah, look: as I wrote to you, I'm working on a biography of your husband, and I want to ask you some questions. When can you come for an interview?" I started to answer, but he wasn't done. "Charles was a brilliant man. He deserved more recognition. You, of all people, must know that. When my biography is done, *everyone* will believe."

I remembered Charlie's words from the dream, then. *Everyone will believe.*

"Believe what, exactly?" I asked.

"That he was right."

"About what?" I pressed.

"You know all the phenomena in his books were from documented sources: scientific journals and so on."

"But that isn't what you mean when you say he was a genius, is it? That he collected facts out of magazines."

"Well-ah, no," said Mr. Dreiser, "you're right. Other people could have collected those." In fact, I had collected some of them, but I had never made a fuss about that, and I didn't say anything now. "But," Dreiser went on, "no one else could have used them as he did to critique the scientific establishment, the whole lot of stiff, hidebound old men who put themselves in charge of what is and isn't true."

"So you believe his theories?" I'd always meant to ask that, but the few times we'd met, Charles was always there, and I didn't know how without hurting his feelings. "Invisible ships capsizing and dropping frogs on us, living organisms the size of continents drifting across the night sky, and all those other things?"

"It sounds ridiculous when you put it like *that*," Mr. Dreiser said, as if it was my fault.

"I guess I don't have Charlie's way with words."

"But the fact of the matter is, why not. Why couldn't it be true? You know *he* didn't believe it all himself. You understand that about your husband, don't you? But the point is, is it any less likely than what the scientists tell us to believe? That's the point he was making: Why should they choose what truth is? Why shouldn't *we*?"

"I guess it always was all rather hard for me to grasp," I said, feeling tired.

Mr. Dreiser grunted sympathetically. "You can't expect to. Few people have a mind like his. But you served him well, even when you didn't understand him." When I didn't reply, he went on: "Look, when can you come up to Westchester and talk?"

I remembered then that his letter had been forwarded from

our old home in the Bronx. He didn't know I also lived in Westchester now, outside a little town, surrounded by six acres of hay, pasture, and woods.

I wondered whether to tell him. I'd given my telephone number as "Croton 6612," but he must not have recognized the name of the town.

In a way, I was relieved that he thought I was still in the Bronx. I had gotten used to keeping the farm a secret. That had begun as a way of keeping Charles happy. We pretended to each other that it didn't exist, that my only life was with him.

It wasn't that he was an ungenerous person. He just needed me so much.

"I can come up early next week if that suits you," I told Mr. Dreiser.

"Good," he said.

After he hung up, I sat by the telephone, thinking.

"Why should those hidebound old scientists be in charge of the truth," he had said. "Why shouldn't *we*?"

I think he really meant "Why shouldn't I, Theodore Dreiser, be in charge of it?" I'm sure he didn't mean *me*.

But I don't need to own the truth. I have my farm, and that's enough. A desk and a telephone, windows and the light of June, green birds chattering in the apple trees, and poplar fluff floating sideways over the bright green fields. I couldn't ask for more.

June 12, 1933

IT'S AWKWARD GETTING FROM CROTON to Mount Kisco by train—I had to go all the way south into the city and take a different one back up. As far as Mr. Dreiser knew, I might have been coming from the Bronx. I felt relief that I didn't have to mention the farm.

He met me at the station in a big black Cadillac with the

top down. He looked the same as when he last visited us, when Charles was alive. The big important-looking forehead. The permanently dissatisfied expression.

I'd seen him smile at Charles, and also at his mistresses. I think he liked best visiting with Charles alone, but when he wanted to show off one of his lovers, he'd invite me along, too, so she'd have someone to talk to. Today, however, it was only me, an unimportant person, and there was no smile.

Sitting beside him in the car, I ran my fingers over the smooth, expensive leather seat. The responsibility of talking about my husband's work was all mine today. A much younger me might have been anxious. God, the hornet swarms of panic that used to chase me . . . but it had been a long time now. Since I bought the farm, much that used to frighten me had lost its power.

I studied his face as we drove out to his house. I remembered how I used to wonder if he looked in the mirror and pushed his eyebrows around with his fingertips until he had the perfect craggy brow. Then I pictured him ruffling his short gray hair just so everyone could see he didn't comb it. *Important novelists don't have time to comb their hair,* I imagined him thinking as he stood over the sink, *and the world must accept it—accept it or be damned!*

He always claimed to be against things like "propriety" and "morals," which he said were only for stuffy prudes, but I sometimes wondered if that was all just an excuse to cheat on his wife. You can't say something like that out loud, though, can you?

He noticed me looking at him and glanced sideways as we drove along the leafy road out of town. "Lovely day, isn't it?" I said. He grunted.

A long driveway wound through trees to his house. It was a dark and heavy-looking place, with one section that resembled an old hunting lodge, and others that didn't quite match, as if they'd been added more recently. There were fieldstone walls and big rough-hewn beams.

"I call this place Iroki. It means 'spirit of color' in Japanese," Mr. Dreiser said.

"Oh, do you speak Japanese?" I asked.

"No," he said shortly.

As we walked up the path to the front door, a beautiful shaggy white dog with an extremely long, narrow head came down the path to meet us.

"That's Nick," said Mr. Dreiser, patting him. He smiled then. "He's a borzoi." Nick touched me with his cool nose and gave my hand a feather-light lick, like a blessing, before he went away again into the lush garden at the side of the house.

MR. DREISER'S STUDY HAD A big window that looked out over the garden. A fly buzzed against it. Outside, I could see daylilies and daisies and foxgloves. There were some big, wild-looking roses, and pink and purple hydrangeas blooming, too.

Inside, he had a huge rolltop desk—much bigger than my own desk back home, which was only a plank built into the wall—and also a table scattered with books and with papers covered in his looping, impatient handwriting.

"Helen's out today," he said, "but the housekeeper makes acceptable coffee and sandwiches."

I tried to remember whether Helen was one of the lovers I'd met, but I couldn't.

"Sit there." He pointed to a heavy chair. "Now-ah, let's see, what did I want to ask you?" He rummaged through some papers. "When did you first realize your husband was a genius?"

I hesitated. The truth of what I thought about Charlie's work was more than I could capture in a few sentences. I believed him brilliant when I married him at twenty-four, but a lot had happened since then. Finally I said, "I don't rightly know."

"Of course you don't," said Dreiser sympathetically. "He was complicated. Perhaps you even doubted him at times."

"Oh, no, no." I said it automatically. Of course I had doubted him. But it would have broken his heart for me to say it. If I had any job in this life, I believed, it was to keep his heart from ever breaking.

"People thought he was a crackpot. Writing out all those crazy theories about angels and monsters and visitors from other worlds," Dreiser said. "Of course, *I* could see it was all tongue-in-cheek."

"Was it?"

Even though Mr. Dreiser had asked me to sit, I drifted back up from my chair, and over to his bookshelves.

He didn't seem to notice. "The point was to *question* the prevailing dogma," he continued, as if talking to himself. "To question the Victorian certainty we still cling to as a society. A place for everything and everything in its place. Respectable men of science in charge of truth. He asked us to question all that, look at the facts ourselves. That made people uncomfortable."

"This was your first big novel, wasn't it?" I asked, pulling a solid red brick of a book from the shelf. In plain black letters on the cover it said SISTER CARRIE.

Mr. Dreiser looked over at me and grunted. "It took a while for me to get recognition. Those stale old Victorians tried to keep *me* down, too. They wanted to look at young girls and see pretty, innocent flowers. They called me immoral for telling the truth, but I told it. I know women and I told the truth."

I opened the book and read aloud, "'Carrie . . . was possessed of a mind rudimentary in its power of observation and analysis.'"

Dreiser chuckled appreciatively.

I went on: "'Books were beyond her interest—knowledge a sealed book.' You used the word 'book' twice in one sentence, there."

What was I thinking, criticizing the likes of him? But when I looked up, he was smiling. "Ha. So I did."

"Not that it matters!" I said.

He kept smiling. "In the end, I won. People understood the importance of my work. And they will understand the importance of Charles Fort's, too, when I'm done with this biography. Do you know the story behind Boni and Liveright publishing *The Book of the Damned*?" Of course I did, but Dreiser didn't wait for me to answer. "They thought he was a crackpot, they thought it was rubbish. But by then it was 1919, *Sister Carrie* had been out in the world almost twenty years, and I had a name. I told them, I told Boni and Liveright, 'You must publish this book.' 'But it doesn't make sense,' they said." Dreiser did a whining voice: "'Why's it called *The Book of the Damned*? What does that mean? We'll be laughed out of town.' This is what I told them: 'The damned are facts science wants us to ignore! The anomalies that prove it's a flawed system! It's not my fault if you're too dull to see that, but I'll tell you one thing: if you won't print it, I'll leave you. I'll find a different publisher for my own books.'" He laughed. "'Oh no, Mr. Dreiser, don't do that,'" he said, doing the whining voice again. "'We'll publish it, Mr. Dreiser.' And they did. That's how your husband's career started."

I was familiar with these facts, but I just smiled. "I can't thank you enough."

Still, looking back, all these years later—looking back now, from my kitchen table, with the clock ticking on the wall, inching forward into the small hours, and my own life slipping into the small years, the ones that go fast—I wonder: What if he *hadn't* talked those men into publishing Charlie's first book? Maybe Charlie wouldn't have kept going in that direction; maybe . . .

. . . what? Maybe he could have done something better?

I remember him telling me how, years ago, when they were both young, his brother Clarence had been sent to a horrible, cruel reform school. Charlie dreamed of getting him out of there, giving him a better life. If he'd gone into business, maybe he could have. But his writing called to him. That was his destiny. He never did get Clarence out, and later the young man drank himself to death. But I doubt anything could have changed that.

"You're responsible for his whole writing career," I said to Mr. Dreiser there in his sunny study.

Dreiser paused then, and looked at me with something like appreciation. "So are you," he said. "Do sit down." He pointed again to the heavy chair. "Charles always said he couldn't have done it without you."

As Mr. Dreiser ticked off mundane questions about where we'd lived and when, my mind kept going back to those words: "He couldn't have done it without you."

It was when he got up to go to the bathroom down the hall that I decided, for some reason, to snoop among the handwritten papers scattered on the table. The big, fat, shiny fly kept bumbling against the windows, trying to get out into the garden. I don't know what I was looking for. Maybe something secret and scandalous about Dreiser's lovers, a shiny bit of truth I could tuck into my mind and take home, like a souvenir.

Instead, I found my eyes drawn to a page with the words "tenement," "winter," and "chicken fricassee." And I realized I was reading a description of the cold night in New York City twenty-five years ago when I had first met Mr. Dreiser.

I remembered that day: coming home in the morning from the weeks-long stint at the hotel where I'd bunked with other women, putting in sixteen-hour days in the hot basement laundry so Charles didn't have to work, so he could write—he always needed more time to write—I opened the door of our run-down apartment in the neighborhood known as Hell's Kitchen to find Charlie in his bathrobe asleep at the kitchen table. A spot of drool stained the scribbled manuscript under his head, and empty tin cans and beer bottles littered the table and floor.

He didn't hear me come in, and I had to shake him. The first thing he said when he opened his eyes was: "Theodore Dreiser is coming to dinner."

I knew he and Charlie were slightly acquainted, but— "*Dinner?*" I repeated.

"At eight," Charlie said. "Tonight."

Mr. Dreiser wasn't a famous novelist then, but he was a magazine editor, and that was plenty. I looked around the place in despair, then back to Charlie. I straightened his crooked glasses, licked a fingertip to tame his eyebrows. "You'll have to shave and wash your face and *please* don't wipe your mouth on your sleeve tonight, Charlie," I begged.

"Yes, dear." He smiled as if indulging me, as if he really did not comprehend how much this dinner could mean for us.

Oh, the work I did to get that place presentable, and Charlie in a clean shirt, and something on the table. Then our guest arrived, and Charles didn't speak at all. I had to fill the silence with whatever came into my exhausted head: the pigeons and sparrows I fed out on the fire escape. I'd gone on and on about them—clearly I had, because here were Mr. Dreiser's own words describing my chatter and how, when Charles finally did speak, and their conversation got going, I sat back and looked uncomprehending, but satisfied.

"This woman cannot think," said the words in Mr. Dreiser's handwriting, "she feels. Yet she does seem to grasp that she is part of something magnificent."

The loud flush of a toilet down the corridor brought me back to the sunny study, and I quickly pushed the papers back into place. I heard footsteps as Mr. Dreiser approached. I was sitting down innocently by the time he came through the door.

He asked more questions—when had Charlie's eyesight begun to fail? (Several years ago.) What did he do when he could no longer see well enough to write? (He dictated his thoughts to me and I typed them.)

As I was leaving, and Dreiser was getting ready to drive me

to the station, I suddenly asked him to call me a cab. "A cab?" he said. "All the way to the Bronx?"

"I don't live in the Bronx anymore."

I just let it hang there. I thought he might be surprised. I even worried for half a second: maybe I should have gone on keeping the farm a secret.

But, after a pause, he only said, "Oh." He turned away from the door with that irritated manner he always had and went and called me a cab. He didn't even ask where I lived now.

As we were waiting for the car to come, sitting in his parlor, him done with me and impatient for our meeting to be over, I blurted out: "I live outside the town of Croton-on-Hudson now. It's a nice place—a farmhouse, and there's an orchard and a barn."

"Huh."

"I bought it years ago, actually. Just before you got his book published, I had an unexpected windfall."

What was I doing, spilling things I hadn't spoken of in all those years?

He wasn't really listening anyway. I stopped talking, and we sat in silence.

FUNNY, I WAS GLAD WHEN I first got the letter saying Dreiser wanted to write the biography. I assume his works will be read long after Charlie's have gone out of print. If Dreiser was his biographer, I thought, then his version of Charles—the misunderstood genius—would be the one to survive.

I was glad for him to be recognized, knowing his work could not have existed without me helping with his notes, feeding him, taking care of him, putting in grueling workdays with washboards and scrub brushes, so he could sit at the kitchen table and write. I thought Dreiser's glowing biography would be a testament to my hard work as much as my husband's.

But after I read the notes on the table, I understood that the version of me that would be in that book was this:

This woman cannot think, she feels.

As he'd said, he *knew* women. I guess when the public finally accepted that novel of his as a masterpiece, they accepted his authority on the subject of us. And they would accept his authority on the subject of me.

June 13, 1933

IT'S ANOTHER BRIGHT DAY, and outside I can see the hay-fields, the green grass tall and almost ready for cutting. The summer is still new and all the leaves are fresh and bright; they haven't matured into the deeper greens of July and August.

I will never tire of this view.

The smell of coffee drifts up from downstairs, where Ginger is working in the kitchen. Her daughter, Lois, is walking out across the field, zigzagging through the tall grass—going where? She has a book in her hand. It's an ordinary Tuesday, she's fifteen, school is out, and she's going somewhere to read—maybe out by the brook.

What am I doing? Why am I recording all these small, unimportant thoughts in my notebook? No one cares. My thoughts are between me and the field, the sky, the trees. I've never had anything of value to say.

Ah, no, that isn't true, and I know it.

It's an old reflex, to tell myself that what's in my mind is unimportant. It was always easier that way.

But imagine if I told the story that's been tucked away in the back of my memory all these years. The events that happened a decade and a half ago, in 1918, a year before *The Book of the Damned* was published. The strangest week of my life.

I've never written a word about it. I've never told. Long ago, I decided to be part of Charlie's story.

Not that it was an easy decision. We fought about it many times.

I remember ten years ago or so, complaining I was always cooking and cleaning and I never had any time for my own—

"Your own what?" Charles demanded.

"My own story," I said, but he was talking over me and didn't hear.

"It doesn't matter what, Annie," he shouted, "because we'd be flat busted without you doing what you do, we'd have died sleeping in the park with newspapers wrapped around us trying to keep warm, and not keeping warm, and freezing to death. One damn genius in the family," he said, "is too damn much."

I knew he was right. That fight ended the same as all the others, with a bottle of beer in my hand, and later we were singing together. We did a nice harmony for "On the Banks of the Wabash," not minding how loud we were, and I hoped the neighbors were listening, because we were pretty good when we sang together.

Oh, Charlie.

I don't think Dreiser will finish your biography. He said he had six hundred pages already, and I sensed it was going to be one of those projects that never end.

As he said, few people share his opinion that you were a genius, and if I'm honest, I don't think the biography would change that.

I reach out and open my own small window, and the breeze comes in, carrying the sweet young smells of early summer, of honeysuckle and sunshine. Poplar fluff is still in the air, and it drifts in and dots my plain bare desk and the notebook I'm writing in, a cheap composition book because that's still the kind I like best.

Years ago—close to forty now, back before I was married—a

friend gave me the first one. For a long time I didn't write in it, because I thought I didn't have anything to say; and then later, when I did have a story to tell, I made the decision not to tell it.

But since moving to the farmhouse last year, I've filled two, almost three, with small thoughts and observations. Nothing important. Yet it feels good to set these things down, and reminds me a little bit of when I was a child: the pure pleasure of telling myself long, plotless stories about a black bird I called King Nyx, stories I whispered to myself as I walked along the sidewalks of Albany.

In real life, King Nyx was a toy, a black tin bird that, when wound up, rolled on wobbly wheels, her wings moving up and down. For subjects she had a handful of cheap penny dolls, half naked, with chipped faces and broken limbs, which I kept with her in a cigar box under my bed. In my imagination they traveled on long journeys through the woods, always looking for something . . .

I used to talk to her, too, sometimes, between waking and sleep. Her voice was calm and knowing. But somewhere over the years, I lost the ability to hear it. Or was it that I stopped trying?

I did hear it again during that one week in 1918.

I WATCH THE SHADOW OF the fluff tumbling across the lined paper now, and I think back to those days that Dreiser will never know about.

One version of me exists on the page in a famous man's study, in his handwriting: a chattering, simpleminded servant to a brilliant husband.

This woman cannot think, she feels.

I pause and look at the tortoiseshell pattern on the pen in my hand, and I think . . .

I think, Charlie, maybe I will write about that week after all.

ONE

I HUGGED THE QUILT-COVERED BIRDCAGE HARD AGAINST my body as we stood by the docks in Clayton, waiting for the boat. The dark choppy waters of the St. Lawrence River shone like liquid steel. Above us, in the distance, large birds circled, gliding, black against the sky, which was overcast but bright from the cold sun that hid somewhere behind it.

I couldn't tell whether my parakeets were moving inside the cage. On the last leg of the train ride, the local from Albany, I had held it on my lap and hadn't lifted the cover at all, knowing they'd be calmer in the dark. As the train rocked and clattered, I whispered the names of the towns we passed—*Herkimer, Deer River, Carthage*—hoping they'd be comforted by my familiar voice, even though the words could mean nothing to them, an indecipherable report from the unseen realm outside their tiny world.

We'd gotten off in Clayton and had lunch at a restaurant, where I flipped up the quilt quickly, just enough to glimpse them. They looked dazed and uncomfortable. That had been over an hour ago; now we'd been standing out in the cold wind for twenty minutes. I was afraid they'd freeze to death before the boat arrived, that they might have already, but I didn't dare lift the quilt to check and risk exposing them to the November wind.

I closed my eyes and tried to imagine myself into the cage, to feel the beating of their tiny hearts, but I was distracted by Charles, who put his arm across my shoulders.

"Are you cold, darling?" he asked.

"Just worried about the birds."

He gave me a sympathetic smile that had an edge of pity. He had urged me to leave them with Mrs. Binns, who was watching the others while we were away. He was too nice to bring it up now, but I was sure he was thinking it.

"You were right, Charlie, I should have left them. Two more wouldn't have made a difference when she's already watching the other nineteen. It's just, they're my favorites." A chilly gust pushed at my hat. I thought, *And now my favorites are going to freeze.*

"They'll be all right."

"But you know they're native to South America, and the temperatures up here . . . "

He squeezed my shoulders, a warm, familiar gesture. "Soon we'll be in Mr. Arkel's house. It won't be cold there, you can bet on that!"

"I'm sure you're right," I said. I tried to calm myself with the thought of the mansion he must own, big rooms full of light and warmed by steam heat. "Not that the birds will really be able to enjoy it," I said out loud. "They can't fly around like at home."

"No, we can't have droppings on my esteemed patron's furniture! But they only have to get through the winter. Then, when I get done with my book, I'll build you a whole aviary." He smiled.

Though I wanted to, I did not feel reassured. "We'll be locked in, too, in a way," I pointed out. "They say the river's icebound from December to May."

"It'll be a good rest for you. No housework. Absolutely nothing to do."

In the town behind us, I could see a closed souvenir shop and an ice cream parlor. The curving, gold-edged letters spelling out *Ice Cream — Candies — Fudge* looked cheerful, but the place was dark and the planters out front were full of dry, brown, weedy-looking stalks still holding a few dead flower heads. Pieces of a broken crate, which no one had bothered to dispose of, were piled against the wall under the big window. It was a summer town, and now it looked empty and unreal, like scenery from a play that had been put away in a basement. "Why do you think Mr. Arkel lives here all year?"

"He's a very private person. Isn't that what you read?" Charles asked.

The letter containing the invitation had come out of the blue, from a man we knew nothing about, except that he shared a family name with the famously wealthy shipping baron from whom he was descended. In the few days before we left home, I'd gone to the library and searched old magazine articles, but had not found much.

"There was lots to read about the family, but hardly anything about Claude Arkel. The one article that did mention him just called him 'reclusive,'" I said.

"'Reclusive' is just an unflattering way of saying he likes privacy," Charles said.

The article had also said he was "building an empire from canned fruit," and mentioned a very large and impressive house. There had been a picture of him looking steely-eyed, with a tightly trimmed, brushy mustache. That was all I knew.

I felt Charlie's hand on my arm. "Don't look now, but there're some women coming around with a petition or something. If we ignore them, maybe they'll leave us alone."

"What if it's a worthwhile petition?"

Charles was usually sympathetic to whatever I wanted to sign, but now he puffed air out impatiently through his mustache. "We can't get distracted. We must be ready when the boat comes. A man like Mr. Arkel can't be kept waiting."

"It's not as if he's coming to get us himself."

"You know what I mean. Anything we do or say around his employees could get back to him."

I stole a glance toward the street, where three women were trying to talk to a lone man in a tweed jacket. He waved them away.

"Did you *have* to look?" asked Charles, exasperated. "Now they'll think we're interested and come over. It's probably just some old suffragettes anyway."

He was right; the women were heading straight for us. The one in front, whose hair was iron gray mixed with black, held a clipboard. "There's no one else here at the docks," I said. "Who else would they talk to?"

"What can they want? The voting thing already passed, didn't it?"

"In New York State. They want an amendment to the Constitution so it will be nationwide."

"But you've already signed plenty of their petitions back home."

Annoyance rose in me, but I pushed it down. Charles was a good husband. He'd given up a lot for me—his whole inheritance, in fact, because his father didn't approve of his marrying one of their maids.

"It'll take just a minute," I promised.

Charles turned away, shaded his eyes with his hand, and pointedly looked out over the river so no one would start talking to him. I put on a friendly, cheerful face as the women got closer.

The one in the lead had a purposeful stride. "I'm Mrs. Laches," she said, holding out the clipboard. "We're petitioning Governor Whitman to send the state police up to the Thousand Islands. Three young girls have gone missing, and the local police won't do anything. Will you sign?"

That was not what I had been expecting. "Why won't the police do anything?" I asked.

"Well, because of where they're missing *from*," said one of the woman's companions; she had a motherly look, with auburn hair pinned up in a soft, old-fashioned style.

"Which is where?" asked Charles, who had been listening despite pretending to ignore us.

"The Arkel School for Domestic Service," said Mrs. Laches. She nodded toward the river. "Over on Prosper Island."

Prosper Island! That's where we were headed. Charlie and I exchanged a startled glance.

"I didn't know there was a school there," I said.

"It's run out of the estate," Mrs. Laches said. "We worked with the late Mrs. Arkel to establish it. Eight girls at a time, the most promising that can be rescued from the New York penal system. They get excellent training and become highly employable."

"And the Arkels get a lot of free work out of them," said the third woman. Her frizzled gray hair seemed to have been pulled back impatiently under a black winter hat that looked expensive but out of date, with a single black bird wing fanning up from one side. Her eyes were small and blue, like chips of ice.

"In exchange for training and room and board," Mrs. Laches said.

"That's how it was *supposed* to be," said the motherly-looking lady, quietly.

The oldest spoke up again: "I said from the beginning, I told you, something's not right over there."

"It did work for more than twenty years, Aisa," Mrs. Laches replied firmly. "Please don't mind Mrs. Morton," she said, turning back to me. "It's only in the last six months I've been worried. Since I got this."

She lifted the petition to show a letter fastened to the clipboard underneath it. I read it over the top of the birdcage I was still holding close to my body. In large, careful handwriting, it read:

Dear Mrs. Laches,

I know you are one of the trustees of the School.
I wanted you to know things are going on here
which are not right. We have nowhere to turn and
need your help. I can say more in person. Please
come immediately.

Signed,
A Concerned Girl

I saw Charles reading it, too.

"It arrived the same week Mrs. Arkel died. For six months
I've been asking Mr. Arkel for permission to go talk to the girls,"
said Mrs. Laches. "He won't give it."

"The letter doesn't say anybody's missing, though, mind you,"
Charles pointed out.

"No," Mrs. Laches said. "But that's what I found when I
finally gave up asking and went over last week."

"Took a boat and rowed herself right over," the oldest lady
said.

Charlie's eyebrows contracted and his mustache got the slight
bushiness that meant he was worried and his mouth was pucker-
ing underneath it.

I could tell he didn't want us to align ourselves with people our host might consider a nuisance, or worse. Our future
depended on staying in Mr. Arkel's good graces so he could finish his book.

"It had to be done," Mrs. Laches said matter-of-factly. "And
it's a good thing I did go, because instead of eight girls at the
school, I found five. When I asked where the others were, no one
would say. They only said they had 'gone away.'"

"What does that mean?" I asked.

"That's what we want to know," said the maternal-looking
woman.

"The local police won't even take a statement," said Mrs. Laches. "They say it's Mr. Arkel's private business."

"And maybe it is," Charles interrupted.

The ladies ignored him. "These girls have no one looking out for them," said the auburn-haired woman to me. "They're poor and alone."

"I'm sure you must be overlooking some reasonable explanation," Charles said.

The elderly lady turned to him sharply, the blackbird's wing trembling on her hat. "Nothing *reasonable* would make those girls too scared to say where their friends are."

"That's right," said Mrs. Laches. "And what Mrs. Cloake says is true: there's no one else looking out for them. No one wants to get mixed up with him because of the family name."

"Look," he said, "the man likes to be by himself. It doesn't do to foster rumors just because he's a bit . . . removed."

"*Removed.* That's a word for it," the old lady muttered.

"You're afraid the girls are in danger," I said.

The ladies glanced at one another and seemed reluctant to elaborate. "We just want the police to have a look," Mrs. Laches said.

I saw that the petition, which had three columns of maybe thirty lines each, had only three signatures on it already, those of Mrs. Laches, Mrs. Cloake, and Mrs. Morton. "No one's signed this but you," I said.

"The Thousand Islands," said Mrs. Laches, "are ruled by some extremely wealthy men. Mr. Arkel is the wealthiest. The townspeople don't want to antagonize him."

"Nor do we," said Charles quickly, putting his hand gently on mine.

"The fact is," I explained, "Mr. Arkel has invited Charles to spend the winter, to finish a book he's working on."

Mrs. Morton looked at the other two. "He hasn't had house-guests in years," she said. "I tell you, he's up to something."

"Having guests," said Charles. "That's what he's up to."

"I don't think the police would do a damn thing unless the body of Mr. Arkel himself washed ashore," Mrs. Morton spat.

I pulled my hand away from my husband's warm grip. "I don't like it, Charlie," I said.

For a few seconds he was silent, the air heavy with disappointment. I had tried so hard to stay enthusiastic up till now. "You could turn around and go back right now if you want," he said. "I won't force you to go."

"You mean you'd come home with me?"

"No. I'm sorry, Annie. Dreiser said the name of Arkel could be the thing that finally gets me published. A stamp of approval. And besides, now that I don't have a job, how else can I finish my book? I won't have you go back to working in that hotel laundry." He held my gaze. "Please, Annie. Maybe he has some peculiarities. But this is my chance. It's *our* chance."

"But three girls are missing."

Charles glanced sideways at the women, then back to me. "The police have already been notified," he said finally. "It's in their hands."

"But they're not doing anything," I said.

The three women watched us.

"Look," Charles said, almost under his breath. "These ladies are well-intentioned, I'm sure, but they may be mistaken in thinking there's anything sinister going on. The three girls might just have been . . . I don't know . . . sent somewhere, and the others didn't want to talk about it. There may be nothing *to* do."

"You can sign the petition," said Mrs. Laches, holding it out to me. "That's something you can do."

I reached awkwardly for the pen, my arms still wrapped around the birdcage.

"Shall I hold that?" she asked.

"No." I couldn't trust anyone else with the twins' cage. What if the quilt slipped off while she was taking it, exposing them to the freezing air? That might be all it took to kill them.

I scrawled my name as best I could.

"Thank you," she said, taking the pen back.

I watched the women as they walked away. "All right?" said Charles, patting my arm. "You ought to stop thinking about it now, Annie. You signed. Under the circumstances, there's no more you can do. It's not our responsibility or even our business."

Before I could reply, we heard the sound of a motor. Charles glanced out over the water. "Look," he said, "there's the boat."

TWO

IT WAS A SMALL YACHT, WELL KEPT, ITS BRASS AND wood polished and gleaming. The name *Yo-Ho* was painted in gold letters on the hull. A gruff man with a short-trimmed beard and a weathered face got out and loaded our luggage on.

The noise of the boat's motor was loud, and for a few minutes after we were underway, Charlie and I did not try to talk. The wind was strong in our faces as we stood at the railing. I stayed a step back, my arms tight around Castor and Pollux's cage, looking down at the choppy gray surface of the river. I could not stop thinking about the missing girls.

The most promising that can be rescued from the New York penal system, Mrs. Laches had said. So they'd already been lost girls, in a way, before they arrived at the Arkels' estate.

Like Mary.

The thought of my friend seemed to open up an old darkness below me, turbulent and inhospitable as the water under the boat. It was not liquid, though it heaved and moved like the river; it was more like a bramble patch, and if you fell in, it closed around you and held you with sharp thorns from every direction till you couldn't do anything, couldn't even breathe—

I felt the weight of Charlie's big, soft hand on my shoulder. "All right, Annie?" he asked, raising his voice to be heard over the boat's motor. I looked away, afraid he would see in my face what I had been thinking about.

"I'm fine."

"Really?" When I turned back to him, he had an expression of concern I hadn't seen in a long time—years, actually. He did know. There was no point trying to hide it.

"Something made me think about Mary for a minute," I said. "I'm okay now."

He squeezed my shoulder. I did my best to smile. But I saw the worry in his face.

It wasn't exactly that I hadn't thought of Mary lately. Even though I hadn't seen her in over twenty years, and even though our friendship had lasted only a summer, she was woven into the fabric of my consciousness, so that an awareness of her was often present, but in small ways: the memory of her raggedly chopped hair coming loose from its pins and falling over one ear; a dismissive gesture as she threw the dustpan into the corner of the closet. Small things.

But I was usually careful not to let it go any further than that. To only think of her, and not the events around her disappearance.

Mary, too, had been a lost girl. A runaway who'd talked her way into a job at the Forts' house when I was the head housemaid, twenty-three years ago. She'd stayed for a few short months, then disappeared back into the chaotic world she'd come from.

It had been her leaving—and the events surrounding it—that had first thrown me into that darkness, and it had been Charlie who'd gotten me out, by paying for a month at Dr. Jacobson's private sanatorium. He'd spent all his money on it and then proposed marriage as soon as I got out, cutting himself off from the possibility of any financial help from his father.

That, I reminded myself, was why we were here now. That was why we'd been on the verge of having to move out of our nice apartment in the Bronx, before he got the offer from Mr. Arkel. Because he'd given up a comfortable life for me.

His hand was still on my shoulder. I couldn't reach it with mine because I was holding the birdcage, so I turned my head and pressed it affectionately with my cheek, feeling momentarily better.

But when I looked down at the river again, I saw that heaving, dark thicket. It was right there, beneath us.

I squeezed the quilt-covered cage as hard as I could to calm myself. "Are we almost there?"

"Yes, look!" he said, and I realized I'd been staring at the water for so long that I hadn't seen the island coming into view.

It was hunched, and bristling with tall pines, like a hedgehog. Above the treetops rose a big pile of a mansion, with turrets and spires everywhere.

Just then there was the sound of a cough from the red-faced captain, who stood nearby us at the wheel. For the past month, since the resurgence of the influenza, we'd avoided movie theaters, I'd done my shopping quickly with a scarf tied over my mouth, and we'd given others a wide berth on the sidewalks. We'd heard awful stories. Little children found alone with the bodies of their parents. A neighbor's daughter coughing in the morning and dead by bedtime. Charles and I glanced at each other, and I saw the fear in his eyes for a split second before he blinked it away. "Cold air is hard on the lungs," he said, his voice just loud enough to be heard by me, but not the captain. "There won't be influenza out here in the country. Besides, the letter said no one the least bit sick is allowed on the island."

I tried to pick up on his optimism. "No one sick would be allowed near you, anyway, I'm sure," I said. "The guest of honor."

I said it to make him feel better, and it worked; Charlie's back straightened and he adjusted his coat collar. "Very kind of Mr. Arkel to say so, don't you think?" he asked. "*Very* generous to invite me to stay the whole winter just because of a little thing he saw in the newspaper. Very kind man."

I smiled. "The guest of honor of the Canned Fruit King," I said.

Charles looked at the captain as if he might have heard, though he showed no sign of listening. "Do you mind not calling him that?" he said in a hoarse, loud whisper. "It sounds disrespectful."

It was what the magazine had called him. "But he is—I mean, his fruit is everywhere. Arkel's Canned Fruit. Pineapple, tomatoes, peaches. Tomatoes are fruit, too, you know. I wonder what it would be like if you made a sauce out of peaches and tomatoes . . . "

I was chattering because of nerves; Charles wasn't really listening.

Of course he wanted to make a good impression. Even though Mr. Dreiser had been so encouraging in his occasional visits throughout the years, he was Charlie's only acquaintance with any standing, and mostly Charlie was keenly aware of his work *not fitting in*, as he always said. But now, by some miracle, he had a patron.

"That is quite a house," I admitted as we approached the island.

"It's modeled on the *Château de Chambord* in the *Val de Loire.*" Charles enunciated the French names dramatically.

"I know, I'm the one who showed you the article."

"But Mr. Arkel expanded it, made it even better." Charles put his thumbs under the lapels of his wool coat and tucked in his chin approvingly. "It's magnificent."

"You don't think it's a little excessive?" It seemed rambling and jumbled to me, as if it had been built by someone who didn't know when to stop.

Charles looked at me with a hint of disappointment.

"At least it'll be warm," I said, thinking of Castor and Pollux.

"I daresay it will!" he said, cheering up a little.

As the boat came close to the island, I saw that the path leading away from the dock was flanked by two stone columns that supported an arch in which letters made of wrought iron spelled out some Latin words. The engines shut down as Charles read them out loud: *"Non est potestas, Super Terram quae . . . Comparetur ei."*

"What does it mean?" I asked.

"If I remember my high school Latin," Charles said, "There is not . . . power . . ."

"There is no power on earth that compares to him," said the captain's gruff voice. We both turned our heads at the same moment to see him standing behind us, closer than we'd realized. "It's Mr. Arkel's motto." Not waiting for a reply, he went and began to do something with the ropes.

"Yes, that's right," said Charles. "That's what I was starting to say."

"Is it a quote from somewhere?"

"It must be. We'll ask him."

The captain put the short gangplank down for us. I stepped on it nervously, suddenly overcome by an image of the birds' cage tumbling into the water. I squeezed it almost hard enough to dent the thin steel bars under the quilt. My breath came shallow and quick as we stepped onto the dock. Charles was giving me that concerned look again.

I watched the captain heaving our luggage off the boat, one piece after another, his face growing redder with each trip. I was worried he'd strain himself, and he seemed angry, too.

"Did we have to bring so much?" I whispered.

But Charles didn't seem to notice. "Careful, those are my notes. They're irreplaceable!" he called, as the man threw our largest trunk onto the dock. When the captain stomped back toward us, Charlie said, "And who's taking us up to the house, my good man? I don't see any means of conveyance."

It was then that I realized that Charles was not calm. *Good man. Means of conveyance.* It was a habit he fell into when he was nervous. He didn't even know anyone who spoke like that—it was his imagined version of how English gentry would sound. His family was wealthy and Dutch, not Irish and German peasants, like mine, so he shouldn't have felt the need to put on airs, but he did.

"Your *means of conveyance* will be along," the captain answered, getting back on the boat.

"I say, are you leaving?" Charles asked.

"I said, someone'll be by to get you," he yelled, starting the engines.

"I say, my wife is cold!" Charles shouted back.

But it was no good. The boat pulled away.

"Don't be nervous," Charlie said, looking at me. "I'm sure Mr. Arkel knows we're here." I saw the uncertainty in his eyes but pretended not to.

"I'm glad we're together," I said, wanting to make him feel better. "I'm sure I'd be scared to death if I were here alone without you." It was the type of small white lie I'd told a million times, only this time, I couldn't get the fake sound of it out of my head—it seemed to echo around in there. I wouldn't be here at all if it weren't for him. I should have turned back on the other side of the river when I'd had the chance. The birds might be frozen to death after that windy boat ride. In spite of the cover, slices of cold air must have worked their way into the cage. I recalled reading in a magazine article about an explorer in the Klondike that freezing to death was like going to sleep, that one didn't even feel cold, just drowsy. Maybe they'd be better off if they did die.

But even as I thought it, I realized I was squeezing the cage again. They couldn't die, they couldn't. My miracles, hatched from a single egg, impossibly tiny. I'd fed them by hand, slept on the floor next to the shoebox lined with flannel.

I was aware of that prickly darkness again, only this time it wasn't beneath me, but around me, pressing in. I turned my head back and forth, as if I could find a place among the thick brambles where there was more air.

"Annie, Anna." Charles was gripping my shoulder. I looked at him with surprise. His expression of concern should have been comforting, but it had the opposite effect. I knew what he was thinking. He was thinking the old darkness was coming back, the thing I was supposed to have been cured of twenty-odd years ago.

"You don't understand." I pulled away. "The birds can't live, I'm *not* making too much of it!"

I heard the hysterical edge in my voice. I remembered that I could calm down by taking a deep breath and holding it for a count of five, as Dr. Jacobson had taught me. But not this time. I gulped air, but my lungs refused to fill.

"Okay," Charlie said, holding his hands up, as if I was a scared animal. "It's all right."

"Oh, God," I gasped. "It's coming back. It's because I thought about Mary."

"Best not to talk about it too much right now," he said. The worry in his voice was worse than anything he could have said.

It *was* coming back. I felt the realization sink slowly through my body like a stone through mud. I sat down on the big trunk, trying to breathe.

"The journey is straining your nerves, that's all," Charlie said, without as much certainty as I wanted to hear. Seeing my face, he added, "Maybe there'll be a doctor on the island."

"But the kind I'd need?"

"We could write Dr. Jacobson a letter." Charles pushed the sleeve of my coat back to leave a gap between it and my glove. "You still have this," he said, touching my bracelet. It was a gold-plated chain. Some of the plating had rubbed off, so the steel underneath showed through. The clasp was made to look like a heart-shaped padlock, but it wasn't really a lock; it opened with a small lever. I could take it off easily, but I never did. Charles had given it to me when I'd gotten out of the sanatorium. It was a symbol of his love, and even after twenty-three years, it gave me a feeling of security that I sometimes needed more than air.

"You see, now," Charles was saying, "I'll be able to finish my book here, and when I sell it, I'll buy you one that's real solid gold."

"You got this one because you chose marrying me over your family money. That means more to me than gold."

"It wasn't right of them to cut us off," he said. "You deserved so much more."

Charlie's mother was dead, but he always called his father "them." Never "Papa" or even "him"; always "them."

I looked at my husband's face, round and pale above his dark coat collar. He was tall, doughy, comforting. "You've given me a good life," I said.

"We could have had a big house. Could have seen a good city doctor about your infertility. You'd have had all the children you wanted instead of . . . not that I dislike the birds . . . "

I found myself smiling. I'd never been disappointed—not really—that children didn't come. It was enough trouble taking care of him, and anyway, neither of us had much in the way of parental examples. His father had been too strict, his mother helpless; and my mother had died when I was too young to remember, leaving me with a papa who could hardly take care of himself, let alone a little girl. Besides, I liked my birds.

"I'd rather have had you than all that," I said. "Anyway, we have other things to worry about right now. For example—"

"Yes, where the bloody hell is the fellow who's supposed to pick us up," Charles finished, looking out at the road that led from the dock.

His words died away, and a chill silence settled around us. I found my eyes searching the trees across the road, as if I might see some evidence of the missing students the women had told us about.

"Charlie," I said. "About those girls who disappeared—don't you think maybe we should try to do something?"

"Like what?"

"I don't know."

"Listen, I didn't want to make too big a fuss when they were there," Charles said, "but those women were probably crackpots. You know that, don't you?"

"What do you mean?"

"You saw there were no signatures on the petition but their own. Powerful men like Mr. Arkel, you know . . . they attract crazies."

"But they showed me the letter from the girl—"

"Anna. Anyone could have written that. *They* could have written it." He saw that this gave me pause. "They said they reported it to the police, who ignored them. Do you think if there were really anything to worry about, the police would have ignored them?"

Everything Charles was saying sounded reasonable, and yet . . .

A memory came to my mind: a policeman standing outside the Forts' house twenty-odd years ago. A bad feeling: fear and dread and the sense that I could not speak.

That was all. I couldn't remember why he had been there or what it was about.

A rumbling became audible from beyond the trees on our right, and we both turned. From around the bend, a large black automobile came into view. At the wheel was a man in a cap and driving goggles.

At the sight of the motorcar, I felt relief run through both Charles and myself, as if we shared a body. "Hello!" Charles said as the machine pulled up near the dock.

It was grand: a long, sleek black Packard with maroon leather seats, its brass wheel spokes and headlamps polished to a spotless, bright shine. It was quieter than any motorcar I'd ever heard; it emitted a big, smooth, low rumble like a panther.

I thought the driver said something as he got out, but his mouth was muffled by the thick scarf wound around his neck, and I couldn't make out his words. The large green-tinted lenses of the driving goggles hid his eyes. He strode over to the luggage and began to load it onto the back of the machine with a good servant's silent efficiency. He wore a black oilskin coat that had a slight shine to it, and black gloves. Something about this odd, taciturn, muffled man made us both uncomfortable. I could see it in Charlie's eyes when he turned to me. There were no words of welcome or apologies for making us wait. The man gestured to us to come toward the automobile and held the door open. We got in silently, and he seemed to stare at us as we did, though it was hard to see his eyes behind the goggles, which barely showed above the gray-and-black checkered scarf wrapped from his neck to under his eyes.

The side curtains were drawn and the car started. As we drove on, I caught a glimpse of flames through the trees. I saw someone moving, and—was it possible?—a body hanging from a tree, skinless, shining wet and pink in the firelight.

I grasped Charlie's knee convulsively.

"They're butchering deer," he said, putting his hand on mine. "They do that in the fall. It's hunting season."

"It didn't look like a deer." Hadn't the limbs been too thick?

"Well, it was."

I closed my eyes. "I don't like it," I said. I heard a fragile sharpness in my voice, like the edge of a broken wineglass.

Charlie squeezed my hand. Then he sat up straight, changing the subject. "Well, sir!" he said to the driver, a little too loudly. "I'm certainly looking forward to a good warm dinner!"

The man must have heard, but didn't acknowledge him.

"I say, old chap," Charles said, touching him on the shoulder, "can't you speak?"

Suddenly the goggled head turned away from the road to face us, the big round lenses giving the man an eerie, insect-like appearance. Then he faced forward again. I saw one hand reach to tug at the scarf that hid his features before he turned back to us.

We both jumped when we saw his face, which at first looked crumpled and misshapen—but no, we realized, it was a canvas hood, ending in a blunt point from which a rubber hose extended down into the opening of his coat collar. He gestured at it with a black-gloved finger. Then he turned back to the road.

"It's a gas mask," Charles said. He looked pale.

"I know. I've seen them in the paper too. Why is he wearing it?"

"Damned if I know," Charles said.

Possibilities raced through my mind: Was there, somehow, poison mustard gas on the island? Or was he a former soldier, shell-shocked, still believing himself to be in the trenches in France? Or maybe the mask hid something shrapnel had done to his face?

We rode on in silence. Charles must have been thinking the same things, as the big automobile rounded a bend, drove through a stand of tall pines, then past twisted black trees to which a few brown leaves still clung.

Something was wrong.

"Charlie," I said, leaning close, "I don't think we're going toward the house anymore."

"I see that," he said between his teeth.

"What should we do?"

He looked at the driver, set his jaw, and tapped him firmly on the shoulder. "You there!" he said. "Where are you taking us? The house is back that way."

The driver turned his uncanny face to us again for a second, as if to remind us why he couldn't answer, and drove on.

THREE

"YOU OUGHT TO TELL US EXACTLY WHERE YOU'RE TAK-ing us," Charles said indignantly, as the automobile continued driving away from the mansion. "Gas mask or no." But it was clear there was no point in talking, because the driver wouldn't respond.

"Will we be all right?" I asked.

"Well, he can't be kidnapping us—we're on a private island," Charles said. I sensed he was trying to reassure himself as much as me. I wondered, though: Might there be secluded places on the island where bandits could hide? What if the man wasn't an employee of Mr. Arkel's at all?

"It would be damned thoughtful of him to tell us where we're going," Charles continued.

"Yes, I wish Mr. Arkel—"

"Whatever's going on, it isn't *his* fault."

"But isn't he in charge of everyth—"

Charles cleared his throat loudly, cutting me off with a gentle elbow bump. I didn't think the driver could have heard me, as we were talking in low voices, and his ears seemed to be covered by the canvas hood and scarf, but I shut my mouth anyway. "I couldn't agree more. Very grateful to Mr. Arkel, indeed," Charles said loudly.

The Packard began to climb a slope, and an old apple orchard appeared, full of short, gnarled trees that looked untended. A few small, rustic cabins were spaced loosely at the edge of the orchard. As we got closer, I saw brown misshapen apples lying on the ground among the dead leaves. "It doesn't look like anyone ever came to pick those, does it?" I asked.

"I say, is this where you're taking us!" Charles said.

Evidently it was, because the automobile stopped in front of one of the cabins. A dim light shone from its windows. The sun had begun to dip below the horizon. The cabin next door was dark, but the one next to that was lit brightly.

The driver got out, silent in the fading light, and began taking our luggage out of the car and putting it on the grass.

"You can't just leave it on the ground," Charles said. "Surely that's not what—" He stopped himself before saying "what Mr. Arkel told you to do." I knew that's what he had been about to say, and I knew that the reason he didn't was that in all likelihood, it was exactly what Mr. Arkel had told him to do, and he didn't want anything that sounded rude to get back to our host.

One thing was clear: whatever unusual ideas Mr. Arkel had about how he would host us, the main thing for us to do, if we didn't want to lose the chance for Charles to write his book, was to avoid offending him.

It was our only job. I knew this from being in service. The dusting, sweeping, laundry, and everything else was incidental. The real job was keeping the employer happy.

We watched helplessly as the driver put the last of our luggage on the grass. When that was done, there was still a large steamer trunk strapped to the back of the Packard. He pulled this off with some effort—he was not a large man—and dragged it across the frosty green-and-brown grass to where our bags were.

"That one's not ours," Charles objected.

The driver paused before opening the door of the automobile to get in, turned his eerie face to us, politely lifted his cap off his big, crumpled canvas head, and left.

"It's not even ours," Charles repeated, to the darkening air, as the motorcar drove away.

"Oh, that's from the host," said a bored, slightly slurred voice close behind us. We both turned to see a slender woman, her jet-black hair cut shockingly and fashionably short. She was wearing some sort of opera coat of silk brocade, which looked out of place in the rustic surroundings. It was dove gray and matched her large, rather cold eyes. In one of her elegantly gloved hands was a tumbler with ice and what smelled like whiskey. In the other was an unlit cigarette in a short, masculine holder. "Welcome to hell, by the way. I'm Mrs. Bixby. You can call me Stella."

She looked at her right hand as if deciding whether to bother transferring the cigarette so she could extend the hand for us to shake and seemed to decide against it. I wouldn't have been able to shake her hand anyway because of the birdcage.

A slender man with sandy hair and circles under his eyes appeared beside her. "Darling," he said with barely restrained patience, "I really wish you wouldn't—"

"All right—not hell," said Stella, irritated. She was clearly not on her first drink. "Purgatory. Is that better?"

"Frank Bixby," said the man, ignoring her, and ignoring me as he held his hand out to Charles. "How do you do."

"Charles Fort."

Stella turned to me. "Well, they're getting along. You come with me." She hooked her arm through mine. "I'll show you the digs."

I glanced back at Charles, but he was not looking at me.

"What's going on? Why are we all here?" I asked as Stella led me to the porch of the nearest cabin.

She gave an exasperated sigh. "Apparently we have to quarantine first," she said. "For two weeks. As a matter of fact, Frank and I have to extend our stay to two weeks from today, even though we arrived the day before yesterday. Your arrival resets the clock. Well, we didn't have to. We were asked if we wanted to move to some even more miserable place far away from anyone, instead of meeting you, but I didn't. I'd rather get the extra days. I desperately need someone to talk to. Anyhow, this is where you'll be staying, you and your husband. They had people come out and put furniture in it today. They swept out the cobwebs, too." A cut-glass kerosene lamp burned on a table inside, and a faint glow came from a potbellied woodstove. "You can put your thing down now, whatever it is," Stella said.

"It's a birdcage." I set it gently on the floor about six feet from the stove, then carefully lifted one corner of the quilt, holding my breath, afraid of what I would find. Stella crouched beside me.

Castor and Pollux were still alive, but sitting in little puffed-up lumps on the bottom of the cage. At Clayton only their heads had looked ruffled, and they'd still been on their perches. I unlatched the door and stroked Castor's head with my fingertip. He opened his eyes briefly and then closed them again with a small, pathetic shiver.

"Are they all right?" Stella asked.

"They're chilled," I said, trying to stay calm. "I'll leave them here to catch the heat from the stove."

"Good idea," Stella said. "You stay there, little birdies." We stood up. "How do you like your cabin?"

I looked around. Stella said it had been swept, but it didn't look like it ever could be truly clean, not like our current quite decent apartment in the Bronx—the one we stood to lose, I reminded myself, if Charles couldn't finish his book. Two weeks in this place, and then we'd be in better lodgings.

The walls of the cabin were rough-hewn planks, and the spaces where the boards met were packed with mud daub. The place was partly *made* of dirt. The stove was old and had spots of rust; the window curtains were faded, cheap cotton. Yet the few furnishings looked out of keeping with the hunting-cabin-like atmosphere. There was a table of dark polished oak with slender, elegantly turned legs, and four matching chairs upholstered in yellow. By the stove sat a brown leather wing chair that would have looked more at home in a well-off family's parlor. The bed I glimpsed through an open door was covered with a green damask bedspread, and I saw a small chair near it upholstered with matching fabric.

I wasn't sure Stella was right about the basic cleaning having been done, though. Darkness lingered in the dusty-looking corners.

"I don't think much of it at all," I said. "I don't understand Mr. Arkel inviting Charles to be his guest, only to put us here."

"I agree," said Stella. The two of us were sitting at the table now, across from each other, and she leaned toward me. "Thank God he sends us plenty of alcohol." She lifted her glass to her lips, then seemed to notice the unlit cigarette in her hand. "Be a dear and light that from the lamp," she said, handing it to me. "I've been drinking on an empty stomach and I don't trust myself not to singe my eyebrows off."

"Oh, I've never smoked," I said, pushing it back toward her. "I wouldn't know how."

"Ah, an innocent," she said, although she looked to be a few years younger than I was. She took the glass chimney off the lamp and leaned toward it. As her sleek hair swung forward, I reached out quickly and pushed it back before it touched the flame. "You're an angel," she said, leaning back and blowing smoke toward the ceiling.

"There are still so many things that don't make sense," I said. "Did you see the driver wearing a gas mask?"

She waved her hand. "It's the same thing. Mr. Arkel is petrified of germs and determined to keep the epidemic off his island."

"But how do you know all this? No one has told us a thing."

"It was all in the letter we got on the first day. You'll probably get one, too. It'll be in tonight's trunk." She put her cigarette to her lips.

"What *is* that huge trunk?"

"It's full of supplies and dinner. We get one every evening. And it's decent food really, and wine . . . We just aren't allowed to go near the house."

Stella looked around for a place to tap her cigarette ash and, not finding one, said, "Let's have the boys set up dinner in your cabin tonight, since it's bigger." She stood up and made her way to the door. Leaning out, she tapped her ashes onto the porch. I saw beyond her that Frank and Charles were deep in conversation in the fading November light. Charles seemed animated and happy. If I was having doubts about this whole enterprise, it seemed he wasn't.

"Frank, dear," said Stella. At the sound of his name, Frank's expression changed, and he looked up with a haggard face, almost with fear. "Could we set up the dinner trunk in the Forts' cabin tonight?"

"Yes, darling," he said right away.

IT TURNED OUT THE TRUNK was cleverly designed. It stood on its short end, so it was taller than it was wide, and when the top was lifted, it brought the front panel along with it, revealing a chest of drawers. The aroma of hot food filled the room. When the top was fully opened, a bouquet of flowers that was attached to the inside popped up and spread out. It made me think of the trick where a magician makes flowers come out of the end of his wand. They looked real, but as I reached out to touch a huge orange lily, Stella said, "Silk."

"They're impressive," I admitted.

"We get them every night."

"The same ones, in the same trunk?"

"Oh no. He won't take the trunks back to his house till they've quarantined as well. Look." Stella walked to the window at the back of the cabin and pushed up the sash. "Lean out and look to the right, toward our place," she said. I could just see, in the light cast from their window, two big trunks like the one we'd just opened, sitting abandoned on the weedy margin between the cabin and the woods.

"There they sit, full of enough leftovers to feed a band of pirates. I keep telling Frank we're lucky a bear hasn't come by. He says there aren't any bears." Stella shrugged and closed the window.

As someone with plenty of experience trying to figure out how to turn a lump of lard, a day-old loaf of bread, and half an onion into some kind of dinner for Charlie, this shocked me as much as anything that had happened since we'd gotten off the train back in Clayton. I had understood that Mr. Arkel was wealthy, but this brought it home in a different way.

"What extravagance," I said.

"He doesn't care."

Frank was unpacking. There was a white tablecloth. There were linen napkins with silver napkin rings. There was china, and wineglasses, all stored in carefully designed compartments.

Watching Frank begin to set the places, Charles looked bored. "I think the girls can do this, can't they?" he asked.

Frank glanced nervously at Stella, who looked back, expressionless. I couldn't tell what passed between them. "It's all right, darling," he said to her. "I'll just set the table, why don't I?"

"Thank you," she said. She took my elbow and led me to the door. "Mrs. Fort and I will get that big decanter of whiskey from our cabin."

But once there, she sat down with a sigh in the front room near the woodstove, on a sofa covered with green velvet that, like so many of the things here, including Stella herself in her opera coat, looked out of place among the rough-hewn, mud-packed walls.

"Where's the decanter?" I asked, wanting to be helpful.

"I'll get it. I just need to sit down a minute."

I sat, too, in an aggressive-looking red chair that was all right angles and ebony and brass studs. The furniture seemed expensive but mismatched, as if it had been pulled out of packed storage rooms. This added to my sense of discomfort, of being in a strange, marginal place.

"What do you know about Mr. Arkel?" I asked. "I don't know anything at all. We got our invitation out of the blue. But I thought at least I'd meet him before the end of today—not have to wait two weeks to even see what he looks like."

"You might be lucky and see him from a distance," Stella said. "We did, the first day. Being driven in that big automobile with his brand-new wife, by that creepy chauffeur. Imagine having an estate so big you had to be chauffeured around it like a sightseer."

"He has a brand-new wife?" I remembered Mrs. Laches saying Mrs. Arkel had died this past spring, not long after she received the mysterious letter.

Stella nodded. "Going from her general shape and what she was wearing, she looked young and fashionable. But that's typical of his kind."

"What *is* his kind?" I asked.

"Oh, I hardly know anything about him, either," said Stella. "I just meant . . . you know, wealthy."

"Don't you know anything at all? You were invited out of the blue, too, just like us?"

"More or less."

"How do you know it's not some kind of . . . joke, or trap? We've volunteered to stay for the whole winter . . . nobody would even miss us until May."

Stella waved her gloved hand, dissipating a thin cloud of smoke. "We do know a bit about him. You ought to have a drink. It makes everything so much more bearable." She glanced at her glass, finished what was in it, and went over to a side table in the corner I hadn't noticed; it held a tray with a decanter of whiskey and a few more tumblers like hers made of elegant crystal. "Will you have some?" she asked, turning to me.

I wasn't used to drinking more than a couple of bottles of beer now and then with Charlie. We did like our beer. But usually when he brought home anything harder than that, I left it for him. "Just a little," I said.

"There's an icebox under this table with ice for our drinks. So many thoughtful details."

"You said you know 'a bit' about Mr. Arkel. What do you know?"

Instead of answering, she refilled her glass and poured a generous amount for me, more than I wanted.

"Stella," I said, as she handed me the glass. "Something happened when we were at the docks in Clayton, waiting for the boat. Three ladies were collecting signatures for a petition to have the state police come out here and investigate."

"Oh, I know," said Stella. "They came to us, too. We didn't sign. Some girls supposedly missing from the School for Domestic Service, right? Nobody is going to sign that. It's the Arkels' pet charity project. It's been going for decades. We don't want people like them to stop doing charity." She raised her glass toward me. "*We're* charity, in a way. All of us being allowed to stay here for the winter. I'm sure the Arkels have done their level best with those girls. I mean, it's a reform operation to turn criminals into model citizens. One wonders if those really work."

"But one of the girls was asking for help. Three are missing."

"Well," said Stella. I waited for her to say more, but she didn't.

I took a sip of the whiskey, which burned my throat. "Is it that you don't think it's important because they're servants?" I said suddenly.

Stella looked at me with surprise. "I have nothing against servants," she said. "Good heavens, what would we do without them? It's more that I wonder if you get a group of delinquents together, whether they might get up to things. Maybe run away, cover for each other. No matter how good the school is, one can't *force* criminals to reform."

I noticed a bag dangling from Stella's wrist, its elaborate beadwork glinting in the lamplight. I wondered how much it had cost. I still had not taken off my plain black wool coat, linty from traveling. "Why are you all dressed up?" I asked.

"For *company*," she said, not looking at me as she concentrated on bringing her cigarette to her lips. Then she blew smoke out and looked up, meeting my eyes. "For you."

I felt myself blush and laughed nervously, flattered in spite of myself.

"Not me," I said. "I'm nobody."

"Says who?"

"No one has to say it. I just know."

Stella smiled tipsily. "Nonsense."

Of course, she didn't know I was a housemaid. Not that I did that anymore—since Charlie had gotten the steady newspaper job, anyway—but I always felt, without actually thinking about it, or meaning to, that deep down, a housemaid was what I was.

And then, of course, I reminded myself, he didn't have that newspaper job anymore. I took another, larger sip from my glass. That was why he had to finish his book if we wanted to keep our apartment. That was why we were here.

He'd finish his book, or I'd go back to the basement laundry in the Beekman Hotel, where the steam was so thick you could hardly see the other sweating, gray-faced women in there, and only a few small, high windows that hardly let in any light . . . If there was a hell, I always imagined, it would look like that.

A third sip from my glass made me feel a pleasant numbness, a sensation of being slightly lifted out of my body.

"I guess this isn't such an awful place," I said. "We can stand it for the winter."

Stella smiled and clinked her glass against mine. "It's a *fantastic* place," she said. "Once we're out of these cabins . . . Do you know Mr. Arkel's house has two hundred rooms and covers an entire acre? We can't go there yet, but if we're sneaky enough we might be able to get a glimpse of the greenhouses out back tomorrow. They're . . . " She lifted a hand vaguely.

"Big?"

"You have to see. Apparently he's experimenting with growing fruit in cold climates: peaches and apricots and pineapples. So he doesn't have to import them. He's got whole orchards and . . . streams, and things . . . all under glass. We can see them if we just don't"—she lowered her voice as if there was someone to overhear us—"get caught by the detectives."

"The what?"

"The house detectives. His private security guards. The ones who prowl around making sure we don't go out of the quarantine area. Don't worry, though, they won't shoot us."

"Shoot us!"

"They won't." She held up her glass and saw that it was empty. "I'm drunk, aren't I? Time to eat," she said. "Let's go and join the boys for dinner."

FOUR

"THE BOYS" HAD SET THE TABLE, AND THE COVERED dishes of food were displayed in the chest of drawers that the trunk had converted into, with the drawers pulled out in such a way that their contents were visible, the lower ones pulled out farther. As we approached, Frank was folding the last of the napkins into a fan shape to be tucked into a silver napkin ring. He seemed absorbed in the task and was laughing at something Charles had just said. When he saw us, his expression changed—it flattened, became resentful. Stella didn't seem to notice, or if she did, maybe she was too drunk to care.

She got to an empty chair before either of the men, on the opposite side of the narrow table, could rise, and held it out for me. As she did this, she gave a glance at Charles that I couldn't read. But I could perfectly read his almost imperceptible shrug, which meant, *Most women would have waited for me to pull out my own wife's chair, but all right, have it your odd way.*

Charlie turned his attention to the dishes displayed on the open trunk. "Look at this feast," he said. I wondered if I should get up and serve it, but before I could say anything,

Stella said, "Frank, dear, would you serve us? They're our guests tonight—they're new."

"Of course, darling," he said.

When Frank poured water into my glass from a decanter, I excused myself. "I just want to take some water to the birds," I said.

Charlie looked over at me with gentle exasperation. He seemed happy overall now that he'd talked to Frank and sipped some whiskey. "My wife keeps parakeets," he explained to the others. "She insisted on bringing two with us. And now they must have water from a crystal glass."

I resented his indulgent smile but returned it. "I'll be right back," I said, taking my water glass. There was no kitchen in the cabin; there was an indoor bathroom, which looked to have been recently installed and had running water, but I didn't trust it to be as clean as the drinking water that had come with the trunk.

I went over to the cage, across the room from the dinner table. The birds were still sitting in the chopped straw on the bottom, not on their perches, but they looked a little less ruffled, and as they watched me open the door, they blinked at me with simpleminded curiosity that made my heart ache.

I unhooked the empty tin water dish from the side of the cage and blew into it to get out the straw dust. I poured the water in, repositioned it, and gently lifted Pollux and then Castor onto the lower perch so they could reach it. Before too long, first one, then the other drank some water. They both shook themselves, and Castor began grooming one of his wings, which made me feel much better.

I rejoined everyone at the dinner table. Frank was pouring the wine. "Do you know what Frank does for a living?" Charles asked. "He's a psychologist in Boston."

I stiffened, remembering our conversation at the dock about my problems of years ago, and how they might be returning. For half an hour or so, I'd forgotten, and I wished it could have stayed forgotten. When Charles had said, *Maybe there'll be a doctor on the island,* it had never occurred to me we'd actually run into a psychologist. Maybe I should have been glad to find myself across the table from one, but instead I was uncomfortable.

"He's very well-known," Charlie went on. "He studied at Harvard under William James, and he's going to use his time here to finish his monograph on dreams."

"Oh," I said. "How interesting."

Frank came to the table with a napkin over his arm, holding a soup tureen. He glanced at Stella, as if looking for her approval. She seemed not to notice him, for the most part, but when her gaze did fall on him, her face became expressionless.

"I doubt my research is nearly as fascinating as your husband's," Frank said, ladling soup into my dish.

I looked at Charles, surprised. He wasn't a very social person in general, and in particular it usually took him a long time to let anyone know about his book. This was good, because when he did, it tended to make the conversation awkward. Like that night we had dinner at the newspaper editor's house, shortly before he was fired.

Stella raised her eyebrows. "Do tell," she said.

There was no getting out of it now, I realized. Somehow— maybe the whiskey had something to do with it—I decided to jump in. Maybe I could keep things from getting too awkward. "My husband is a crypto-scientist," I told Stella. "He's writing a book about it."

"That's the term I coined for it," Charles said, settling his napkin comfortably in his lap. The thought flickered through my mind that I'd been the one to suggest it. Not that it should matter.

Stella leaned forward, "Crypto-scientist. Tell me what that means," she said.

"'Crypto'—it's from the Greek for 'hidden,' 'secret,'" Charles said. "I study the data that Science has excluded." I could hear the capitalization in the resentful weight he gave the word. "You see," he went on, "Science is an incomplete system, because it excludes that which the Scientists don't want to see."

"But aren't you a *kind* of scientist?" Stella asked. "You just said so."

"Self-taught," Charles said proudly. "An outsider—a maverick, if you will."

I worried that I would feel embarrassed when he launched into his usual speech about how he'd eschewed college to get a "real" education traveling in boxcars and on cattle ships, learning the ways of the world and mankind. But before he could, Stella interrupted him.

"Well!" she said. She reached for her wineglass, and we all did the same. "Here's to a very productive winter of writing for both of you, Charles and Frank."

Before we could drink, Charles said, "And what about you ladies? Here's to a good winter for you as well! Doing just as much of nothing as you please. No housework, no—"

"Oh, yes," said Stella, thrusting out her glass again, clinking it a little too hard against the others. "Here's to all of that, too." She took a good sip of wine, then picked up one of the three spoons that had been laid by the plate. Which one? I was so anxious to get it right that I forgot to taste the wine as I watched Frank and Charlie carefully and then, following their example, picked up the large outermost spoon and dipped it into the clear soup. It looked like the broth you'd make for a sick person and I didn't expect it to taste like much, so I was surprised by the complex flavors. They were *vivid*, evoking pictures, experiences I'd never had—walking at night through some European forest where ankle-deep leaves hid dark mushrooms, sharp green herbs, secret pockets of animal warmth.

"Now, go on talking, Charles," Stella said. "Give me an example of your cryptic . . ."

"Crypto-science, yes," Charlie said.

I took another sip, trying to keep my face neutral, as if it was normal for me to be eating the sort of soup they must serve at the Ritz.

Stella nodded. "Example."

I'd been so lost in the soup I hadn't realized what was about to happen, and now I tensed. It was obviously too late to turn back.

But maybe we'd never met the right people before. Maybe everyone he'd told before was too unsophisticated to really understand, and now he was finally about to find his audience.

"For example, I write about unexplained things falling from the sky. Like fish, or blood, or rotten flesh."

I looked anxiously at Stella. Her face was perfectly expressionless. After a pause, she said, "Rotten . . . ?"

"Flesh," Charlie finished confidently.

The table was silent. I glanced at the clear soup, glinting reddish-brown in the lamplight. Then I made myself look up. "Maybe we'd better discuss it *after* dinner, Charlie," I said.

Frank cleared his throat. "Well, that's, that's fascinating," he said. "I didn't realize that's what you meant, Charles, when you said you studied anomalous weather events."

The skepticism in his tone, almost disdain, made me feel defensive of Charlie. "Those things *do* really happen," I said.

"Yes," said Charlie. "They've been reported in every major science magazine throughout history. The irritating thing is, the Scientists just shrug them off. Offer a half-plausible explanation and never talk about them again."

"Is that so," said Frank.

"For example," said Charles, seemingly unaware of Frank's tone, "the last thing I wrote for the New York *Sun* was about stiff dead eels falling out of the sky."

"So they printed it," said Frank, cautiously. "It was verified."

Nervous, I found myself filling the quiet with words: "Yes, completely verified! It was an outrage that they fired Charles for it, really it was."

I sensed an even deeper silence than had occurred at the mention of rotten flesh a few minutes ago. Now Charlie was unhappy, too. He hadn't mentioned that yet to our new friends, I realized—that he had been fired recently. Why would he?

I looked at my wineglass. I had no experience mixing whiskey and wine, or drinking whiskey at all. But my hand was already on it, and in the seemingly endless pause, I took a large sip. The taste was light, it was cold, it made me think of an underground stream tumbling over ancient stones, its surface glinting with torch light. I felt it could have told me an entire story if I hadn't downed it in one nervous, uncultured gulp.

When I looked up to meet Frank's eyes, his expression was carefully neutral. A familiar expression I had seen often on the face of Dr. Jacobson at the sanatorium.

"If it was verified," he said mildly, "then why do you think they fired him for it?"

"It was, it came from an article in the scientific journal *Nature*. You've heard of that." My voice had a plaintive edge that I didn't like.

I'd been doubting Charlie's theories for years, but seeing Frank disbelieve the one part of his work that *was* undeniably true—that scientific writers throughout history have documented anomalous events—made me feel defensive.

There was something penetrating in Frank's gaze, too, as if he knew something about me, knew about the sanatorium years ago, even the frightening, prickly darkness I'd sensed below me when I'd looked over the railing of the ferry.

"Of course I've heard of the journal *Nature*. You say it was in an article there?" Frank asked.

"September 1918, volume one hundred and two," Charles said, with the complete, impenetrable confidence that came over him when he discussed his favorite subjects. "They were called sand eels. The town is called Hindon, and it's a suburb of—"

Fearing that Charlie would lose them in a forest of details, I cut in, a little too loudly: "But the *point* is, the fall of fish was documented—"

"Eels," said Charles.

"Eels *are* a type of fish . . . aren't they?" Why did I ask that? I happened to know they were.

"It's important to be precise," said Charles. "It was in the article," he went on, "and I cited my source, and anyone can go and look it up if they want to."

This, I knew, was true. As far as his sources were concerned, he was meticulous.

Frank said, gently but firmly, "I think you know very well that we can't look it up to verify it. We're in a cabin in the middle of the woods."

"Well—you know what I mean," Charles said, a little disgruntled.

"But now, help me understand," said Frank. "You said they fired you for writing it? Why?"

"Because people don't want to know the truth," Charles said.

"They don't?" asked Stella. "Why ever not?" She now seemed somewhat less skeptical than Frank, and more drunkenly interested.

"They're afraid," said Charles. His tone suggested that he was delivering unpleasant but important news.

"Afraid of what?"

"Of angering the Scientists. The men who put themselves in charge of our reality."

I looked worriedly at Frank's face. I saw his eyebrow twitch.

"In charge of our reality," he repeated.

I winced as Charles continued barreling headlong toward his current favorite Grand Theory. This was where I could not follow him, could not defend him.

The last time he'd done it was when the Strakes had had us to dinner, shortly before the incident that caused Mr. Strake to fire him. Their discomfort had been clear, and dinner had ended early. In the cab on the way home, Charles had complained that they didn't have a sense of humor. It was often hard to tell where Charlie's joking began and ended. Sometimes I thought he himself wasn't quite sure.

But that night it dawned on me that this ambiguity might be hiding the fact that he believed, or wanted to believe, things that sounded ridiculous, so he retreated into saying he wasn't serious, unless someone else showed a willingness to believe.

None of that was going to make his Grand Theory palatable to the Bixbys.

The thought of the Strakes, of Charlie being fired, of the dismal future that loomed for us if he didn't succeed with his book this winter cut through the fog of alcohol like a sharp gust through a loose window frame.

"Maybe that's enough shoptalk for now," I suggested, pushing my wineglass away. "Maybe we should talk about something else."

I lifted another spoonful of the soup to my lips, but it had cooled, its magic dulled.

"You see," Charles went on, as if he hadn't heard me, "the Scientists can't suppress *facts*. They'd like to, but they can't. People see things with their own eyes. Mr. Strake couldn't fire me for simply publishing the facts in the paper. No, my crime, in his eyes, was to go beyond that and question the Establishment."

Stella's eyebrows lifted questioningly, and that was enough to make Charles continue talking. "The problem, you see, is this: When Science fails to repress a fact, it makes up an explanation, which, however nonsensical, is declared the most plausible *inasmuch as it doesn't disrupt the accepted worldview*. Do you see?"

"No," laughed Stella. She had hardly touched her soup, but she glanced at Frank, who put his napkin down and began to clear the bowls away.

"For example," Charles said, getting more animated, "the

Scientists say the sand eels that fell from the sky must have been swept up by a tornado over the sea, taken twenty miles inland, then dropped."

"Mightn't that be true?" Stella asked. A slight wobble as she turned her head suggested that she was too drunk to calculate whether this was supposed to be plausible.

"Twenty *miles*," Charles repeated. "A wind carrying bucketfuls of eels, and only eels, nothing else—no seaweed, other fishes, or anything else—twenty miles from the sea." Stella looked like she was about to say something, but Charles went on: "And it gets worse! They said a tornado carried the eels—but no tornado was seen that day. The sky was cloudless. Cloudless. You might well ask yourself, How would the Scientists answer *that*?"

"How would they?" Stella asked.

"They say, 'Well, the tornado must have been in the upper atmosphere, too far away to see.' They think we're as gullible as little children. If the sky is cloudless, you can see everything. The sun and the moon. The tornado would have been seen even if it were in outer space! Of course there was no tornado. But it doesn't even end there," Charles continued, not giving anyone else a chance to speak. "Do you know what the most extraordinary thing was?" He didn't wait for an answer. "The eels were dry. *Dry*. Desiccated. Like salt fish. But Science has an answer for that, too, of course. 'Oh, they must have dried in the upper atmosphere, up there where the invisible tornado was. A fish would shrivel up instantly, up there.' But do you want to know something? Fish don't shrivel up and get hard in the upper atmosphere. If, for example, you send a fish up in a balloon, as high as it will go, the fish will come down dry to the touch, but not hard and stiff, like those eels were."

Stella laughed. "A fish up in a balloon!"

"I'm quite serious," Charles said, picking up his fork to try the next course, which Frank had set in front of us. It was, in fact, fish.

"But who's done that to find out?" Stella asked.

"I have," Charles said, putting the forkful in his mouth. He was silent for a moment, chewing appreciatively. "Now this fellow here," he said, "Mr. Arkel, he understands. He believes in my book. That's why he invited me. And he keeps a good cook, too—wouldn't you say, Annie?" He glanced at me. He didn't seem to notice I was not eating.

I hadn't liked seeing the little goldfish flopping and gasping on the bottom of the small basket of the toy hot-air balloon as Charles lit the candle and sent it into the sky, with a thin silk string attached. Nor had I been convinced that the experiment for which it was being sacrificed was very scientific. How high would the thing actually go? Charles had said I was too softhearted.

"What is the explanation, then?" Frank asked quietly. He'd spoken so little recently that we all turned to him, and he raised his sandy eyebrows. He looked just the way I imagined someone who'd gone to Harvard would, with sharp, aristocratic blue eyes and an air of just having come from a tennis court, or some other place much more pleasant than where he was now.

Charles cleared his throat. I looked down at the pool of sauce in which the lump of fish sat on my plate. I tensed. He was going to tell it now. The Grand Theory. He began in a patient voice, as if he were explaining something to a child.

"The things I study are things that fall to the ground," he said. "Now, when something falls onto the ground, where must it have come from?"

Frank was silent, as if waiting for Charles to answer the question himself. Finally, Stella said: "The sky?"

"That's right," said Charles. "And from where in the sky?"

"Clouds?"

"And if there are none?"

"*Birds*," said Stella with finality, as she told Frank with her eyes to refill her glass.

"Ah, but suppose there are no birds," Charles said.

"Don't say that. There are always birds," Stella answered distractedly, watching the wine as Frank poured it.

"Sometimes there aren't," said Charles, as if he was dispensing wisdom.

"Just tell them, Charlie," I said, dreading it but wanting to get it over with.

"To the naked eye," he began, "there is nothing there. Therefore, logically, it must be something we can't see. Simple deduction tells us that."

"That's inference," I said under my breath. Not that it mattered.

"But," Charles went on, ignoring me, "every now and then, our visitors betray their presence, when something falls . . . off the edge." He said this with satisfaction, as if he had proven something.

Stella and Frank sat in uncomprehending silence. I felt heat creep up my neck, hating that I was embarrassed for Charlie.

Invisible people in the sky was his Grand Theory of the moment. Others he'd had over the years—people controlling us from Mars, energy beaming over the planet from the North Pole—were no better. They'd all developed after our marriage. At first, I'd written off his occasional odd comment. Later, when he began to talk incessantly about them, I'd accepted his claim not to believe the theories himself. He said he put them out there in a spirit of experimentation, to get reactions. But at the dinner with the Strakes, his passion had felt very real. As it did now.

And so I felt shame. For my own husband. Even worse was my own sense of disloyalty.

"Who are these . . . visitors?" Frank asked after a moment. His carefully neutral expression had returned.

"Oh, now," said Charles, waving his finger and smiling, "I won't fall into that trap. I won't speculate. That would only force me to make up fantastical stories, which would sound ridiculous. I'll stick to what is indisputable: These objects are falling from somewhere we can't see. It's not a natural phenomenon, because the things don't fall regularly, or everywhere within a particular climate, as naturally occurring things do—say, rain. You get dried fish in England one year, then small frogs in Bombay half a century later—*not* dry. In Kentucky, flakes of raw meat turn up in a farmer's yard; in Alaska, an oily yellow liquid drips down from nowhere. I think anyone would agree that this is not natural weather. Therefore, if it's not natural, there's necessarily an intelligence behind it. Ergo, 'the visitors.' Intelligent, conscious, invisible entities that—as we can see now by simple logic—*must* live in the sky, and drop things on us."

"But why do they drop them?" Stella asked.

"That we cannot know. For their own reasons, or for no reason at all. Maybe we ground dwellers live in what they think of as, essentially, a trash heap, and it's the leftover bits from their lunches, their floor sweepings." He raised his finger again. "But there again, I'd be speculating. You won't catch me speculating."

There was an awkward silence. "It makes sense." My words came a bit too late, and sounded thin and unconvincing.

Stella sat back in her chair, nursing the whiskey tumbler she had brought with her to the dinner table, her eyes searching for Frank's for the first time since we had all met, a moment of connection as they dismissed Charlie. How, I wondered, watching him pat his mouth with his napkin, did he manage to look so confident, with the party once again turning against him?

"Our host believes it, too," I said. "That's why he invited Charlie here to finish his book."

Stella cleared her throat and glanced briefly up at the spiderwebby-looking rafters lost in the darkness above the circle of light from the kerosene lamp. I wondered if she was thinking that, given how eccentric our host was, this wasn't much of an endorsement.

"Why don't we talk about Frank's book?" I said. "You mentioned that Mr. Arkel invited him here to write, too."

"Oh, it's nothing very interesting," said Frank. "Not compared to . . . what was it you called it? Crypto-science." His expression of neutrality was gone, and he looked uncomfortable at the mention of discussing his work. I wondered if he felt devalued, realizing he'd been lumped with a man he obviously considered eccentric at best, at worst a lunatic. Maybe Mr. Arkel's patronage had seemed an important endorsement at first, and now the rug had been yanked from underneath him. My cheeks heated and itched.

"Frank studies patients with recurring nightmares," Charlie said. "And he's researching an experimental cure. Sounds fascinating to me. He has the patients reenacting their dreams—isn't that right?"

Frank cleared his throat and glanced at Stella. "Yes."

"It's still very much in the experimental stage," Stella said in her tipsy drawl.

Frank glanced at her again and said, "It's shown remarkable promise."

"There are a few things that need work," Stella said. "The electricity."

"Oh," Charles said. "What do you do with electricity?"

Frank turned to him, his confidence rising as he faced a sympathetic listener. "I use hypnosis to bring the subject into the dream state. We then enter the dream together, in a manner of speaking. With my guidance, they bring it to a different, better conclusion. The electrical . . . impulses . . . are only for waking them up when things go the wrong way."

"And that always works?" asked Charles.

"Almost always. They soon learn to connect the aversive electrical stimulus with the unwanted dream, and—"

"He even built a special machine for shocking people," Stella said. "It's the size of a steamer trunk. Isn't that brilliant?" Her tone might have been sarcastic, but it was ambiguous enough that I wasn't completely sure.

"Is it dangerous?" I asked.

"Of course not," Charles said. "Frank's very well-known in his field. And it doesn't really hurt, I'm sure," he added, looking to Frank for confirmation.

"Oh, it hurts quite a bit," Stella drawled. "Wouldn't you say, Frank?" Without waiting for his answer, she continued: "But he's only writing about it now. He's stopped using it altogether, and he's not going to go back to it."

Frank looked uncomfortable. "I didn't say that," he answered quietly.

This seemed to surprise Stella. She glanced up from her fish. "I see. Then you're just taking a break for the winter." Frank didn't respond. Stella raised her eyebrows. "Because you left it at home," she added.

Frank, his voice still quiet, said, "It's in the largest trunk in our cabin."

"You said that was full of books."

Frank put down his fork and looked at her steadily. "Well, it isn't." He turned to Charles and me and said, in a more conversational tone, "But Stella's right that I am mostly just writing at the moment." He glanced at her as if to convey that there was nothing for her to be upset about. "A welcome break."

"From all his success." Stella's tone was dry.

"I cured people," Frank said tightly.

"Almost everybody." Stella picked up her tumbler and swirled it, ice clinking, the whiskey long gone.

Both of them seemed moments away from lunging across the table and stabbing the other with a fish knife. "Shall I serve the next course?" I asked.

Frank looked at me as if he had forgotten I was there. "I'll do it," he said.

FIVE

"WELL," I SAID. "IT SEEMS LIKE MR. ARKEL THINKS VERY highly of both of you, inviting us here so you can finish your projects. That's something we can all be thankful for."

I thought, *I hope that's true.*

"Here's to Mr. Arkel," said Charles, raising his glass.

After we had toasted, I cleared my throat. "Stella was telling me you know a bit about him," I said to Frank.

"Yes, we're very curious," said Charles. "We don't know anything, except the family name, of course. Very pleased to get an invitation from one of the Arkels."

"I heard something odd—" I began.

Charlie knew I wanted to bring up the women in Clayton. "Now, Annie," he said.

Frank laughed. "Heard the rumors, have you?" he asked, as he whisked my untouched plate away. "About the secret underground chamber?"

"The—what?" I glanced at Charles, who didn't seem to know what Frank was talking about, either.

Frank stacked the used plates in a compartment of the trunk. "Pure fiction, all of it," he said, sliding the top of the compartment closed. "The man loves to start rumors about himself."

This made Charlie smile. "Likes to get a rise out of people," he said. "A man after my own heart."

I still wanted to ask Frank what he thought about the missing girls. "I was wondering—" I began.

"Excuse me," Stella interrupted. "Frank, what underground chamber?"

Frank glanced at her. "I said it was just a story."

"But I want to know what you're talking about."

Frank turned to Charles. "You must have heard it already," he said.

"No," said Charlie. "Tell us."

"Well," Frank said, "supposedly he's got some sort of collection of mechanical dolls or something in his basement. The truth is," he said, turning to Charles and me, "he's got a hobby of designing automata, like the ones you've seen at penny arcades— you know: a glass cabinet with a fortune teller inside, waving her hand over cards. I gather he's a bit secretive about his designs, so rumor turned it into something nefarious. Some story about him having a locked room full of life-sized dolls underneath the house, which he retreats to, to"—he turned from the trunk, where he was pulling a fresh plate from a different drawer, and waved his free hand dismissively—"commune with them. I understand he starts those stories just to see if people will fall for them and be shocked."

"Life-sized automata? A secret room underground? You never told me *any* of that," said Stella.

"Because it isn't true," Frank said tersely.

Who was this man? What had we gotten ourselves into? I remembered the skinless hanging figure I'd glimpsed through the trees. "Is it deer-hunting season?" I asked Frank suddenly.

"What's that—hunting season? I daresay. Why?"

Charlie smiled. "Annie saw something on the drive out here that spooked her."

"It was hanging by its legs from a tree," I said. "But it was only a deer, right?"

"I'm sure it was. Mr. Arkel loves to hunt," said Frank.

I admitted what was gnawing at me: "It didn't really look like one." The proportions had been wrong—the limbs too thick.

"It could have been another animal. He likes to have game imported. Not much to shoot on a small island like this otherwise."

"What does he import?" asked Charles, interested.

"Elk, bear, whatever he wants."

"A bear. Maybe that's what it was," I said.

"I heard he even had zebras and a tiger brought in once," Frank said.

"Why not, if he can afford it?" said Charles approvingly.

"Indeed," said Frank. "When he decides he wants something, he gets it. Take the canning strike last year. You read about that?" It seemed none of us had. "Well," he said, "his fruit cannery workers demanded some extreme changes, and when Mr. Arkel declined to give in, they had a . . . well, you might call it a tantrum."

Charles absorbed this, eager to learn about our host. "A tantrum, eh? Is that the official psychological term for it?"

Frank laughed. "No. Though you might call it a kind of mass reversion to infantile ideation," Frank said. "Not being able to understand the reality of running a business, thinking they're entitled to things that aren't possible, simply because they want them. The way a young child has no understanding of, or interest in, whether its father can afford to buy the toy it desires—it simply knows that it *wants*. But that is the mentality of the common factory worker, after all. If they had more developed minds, they'd be in other lines of work."

I glanced at Stella to see if she agreed, but I couldn't tell. I probably should have kept my mouth shut then, but I couldn't help saying, "What about domestic servants? Are they infantile, too?"

Frank looked surprised. "I'd say they don't tend to show that same sense of deluded entitlement. They don't often go on strike, for example."

"That's true," I said. "I've never even heard of domestic staff striking. Yet they work so hard. When I read about the movement for the eight-hour workday, I sometimes thought how for domestic servants, it would practically cut their days in half. No one would give it to them. Yet they keep on working."

"It's a good thing they don't demand it. You'd have to hire twice as many servants," Stella said. "Think of the trouble and expense."

"Go on about the canning strike," Charles said. "I'm curious how Mr. Arkel handled it."

"Well," said Frank, "what do you think they did when they couldn't get what they wanted? They went and locked themselves in the canning plant. Barricaded the whole place up. Said they wouldn't allow the factory to operate until Mr. Arkel did what they wanted. *Chapon à la crème*," he added parenthetically, as he set the last of the four plates in front of us.

"It's chicken with cream sauce," Charles told me. I tried to smile appreciatively, although, even with my limited French, that was already obvious.

He hadn't been to college, but he spent a lot of time in libraries, and he had finished high school, which I hadn't—I'd started working for his parents when I was fourteen. I was always aware of our difference in education, but I would have appreciated him not putting it on display tonight.

"What did Mr. Arkel do then?" I asked Frank, who was pouring the next wine.

"Imagine this," Frank said. "There were a hundred workers

in the plant. The workers posted guards with guns around the border fence to keep anyone from getting in and opening up the plant."

"You mean scabs," I said.

"What?"

"Isn't that what they call strikebreakers?"

"Oh, yes, I suppose it is. Anyhow," Frank went on, "when Mr. Arkel saw that, he said, 'So that's how you want to play it, is it?' And he hired *two* hundred armed Pinkertons."

"Just like that Homestead Strike back in the nineties," I said. "Only wasn't that three hundred armed guards against something like five thousand workers?"

"Yes, and the Pinkertons lost that one, so they had to send in the state militia. Mr. Arkel wasn't going to let it get to that," said Frank.

"But did Mr. Arkel really need to hire twice as many Pinkertons as workers?" I asked.

"Yes, that sounds rather excessive," Stella agreed.

"He didn't *need* to. He was making a point," Frank said.

"What point?" I asked.

"That he doesn't have to do something in a certain way just because someone else did," Frank said, with surprising vehemence. "That he didn't have to follow rules just because somebody tried to force them on him. No one tells Mr. Arkel what to do." He glanced at Stella as if daring her to argue. She looked away, uncomfortable, and Frank stalled, seeming to realize that emotion had entered his voice. He shook out his napkin and sat down.

"So the workers backed down?" Charles seemed interested in the story and seemed not to be sharing my increasing dislike for the man whose island we were on.

"Not at first, surprisingly," Frank said. "There was a big showdown. Two Pinkertons were killed, along with half a dozen workers. But in the end, Arkel won. That's not even the best part of the story. You'll never guess what he did after."

"What?" Charles was riveted.

"He didn't stop at not giving the workers higher pay and shorter hours. In fact, he told them they could have their jobs back only if—listen to this—they were willing to accept *half* the salary and *longer* hours."

"And . . . did they?" I asked, with a sinking feeling.

Frank smiled. "They had no choice. Little town in upstate New York. Nothing else around but miserable rocky farms." He raised his glass. "A shrewd man."

Charles clinked glasses with him; neither seemed to care that Stella and I didn't join in.

"What's more remarkable is that his business became even more successful after that. Today you see his labels on the shelves at every grocery. The strikers tried to bring him down, and he not only beat them, he got stronger."

I glanced at Charles to see if his admiration was at all qualified. Maybe he'd ask about the living standards of the workers? But all he said was "A shrewd man indeed! This chicken is quite good, by the way."

"The best food. The best wine," said Frank. "*Non est potestas Super Terram quae Comparetur ei.* No power on earth compares to him. That's from Hobbes—*Leviathan.* You know it?" Without waiting for us to answer, he went on: "Written during the English Civil War, you know, when society was falling apart. Hobbes believed the only way to keep order was to put one strong man in charge and give him absolute power. He believed humans don't have an innate urge toward the *summum bonum*, the greatest good; that if allowed to make their own rules, they'll just look out for themselves."

"Oh, now, do you believe that?" Charles asked. "Why, if everyone looked out for themselves, I'd never have gotten any writing done. I have the good fortune to be married to a girl who looks out for our *summum bonum.*" He smiled at me. "Many times she's kept me fed and clothed while I worked. And I look out for her. When my book is published, I'll buy her anything she wants. A big aviary for her birds: a paradise under glass where they can be safe and warm forever."

I knew it was the wine making him talkative, but it was nice to hear. I smiled back at him.

Frank and Stella exchanged unreadable, heavy glances.

"Maybe you're overlooking the fact that you each benefit selfishly from the arrangement," Frank said.

Charlie shrugged, putting a forkful of chicken into his mouth.

"According to Hobbes," Frank continued, "we don't have any choice but to pursue our self-interest."

"'For what is the heart, but a spring?'" said Stella. "Didn't he write that?"

"Yes," said Frank. "You see, according to Hobbes, we're all automatons who just mechanically pursue what we want. No conscience. No souls."

"Everyone has a soul," I said. The others turned to me. The attention made me uncomfortable. "I mean . . . I always thought so."

"I've never known you to go to church, Annie," Charles said.

"I don't go because I can't believe all of it. The Athanasian Creed, for example. 'The Father is made of none; neither created, nor begotten. The Son is of the Father alone; not made, nor created . . .' How could I believe those things when I don't even know what they mean?"

"You have it memorized, yet you don't believe," said Frank, with curiosity.

I had never tried to put it into words, but Frank's interest, combined with the drink, the warmth, the relief of being fed a good dinner, made me willing to talk. "I think it's because my father was an atheist. He was—" I searched for how to describe him without giving away that I'd grown up so much poorer than anyone else at the table. "He was irreverent," I said finally. What I really meant was that when I was a child, I'd heard him many times cursing Jesus in very graphic and personal terms, especially when he was drunk, which was often. "I don't see how the God of church could approve of him."

"Your position doesn't make sense," Frank said. "Logically, you could just decide that your father was a sinner, and go on with your belief without any inconsistency."

"I guess I'm not logical." I didn't know how to explain that it was impossible to write my father off. He had spent so much of his life miserable in this world. I refused to let go of the hope that there was another where he might find happiness.

"Yet you're certain everyone has a soul? Why?"

"It's just something I know, the way I know I . . . *am*. Or the way I know love exists."

"Love is a subjective feeling," said Frank, "so of that, your experience is proof enough. Though that doesn't explain what love *is* . . . whether it's purely a mechanical function, as Hobbes argues—"

"I'd like another drink, Frankie," Stella said suddenly.

Frank looked at her. "Haven't you had enough?"

"Maybe," she said, with uncharacteristic acquiescence.

I cleared my throat in the awkward pause. "Stella mentioned that you saw Mr. and Mrs. Arkel driving by in their motorcar," I said to Frank.

"Mrs.?" said Charles.

"Apparently he remarried," I said.

"Yes," Frank said. "He was extremely upset after his first wife died. I'm glad he's found happiness."

"Good for him!" Charlie agreed.

"Young, too," said Frank. "In her twenties, and I'd say he's about sixty."

"Replaced his first wife faster than a flat tire," Stella muttered.

"Why should it matter?" asked Frank. "It doesn't matter to the first wife. She's dead. The dead don't hang about watching, judging. They're gone."

"All right, Frankie," said Stella.

"No, it's not all right," Frank said, growing heated again. "It's important to acknowledge: They're gone. They can't hurt anyone or be hurt. One has to get on with life."

I wondered if he was right, that the dead were gone. It hadn't felt that way on the boat, when I had thought of Mary. When that old, heaving darkness opened up below me.

The table lapsed into silence. There was plenty of food to occupy us, and soon the conversation started again and turned to lighter subjects: how much work Frank and Charles would get done, the fact that my birds were looking well. (They were quiet, but still on their perches, not on the floor of the cage.) The mood in the room rose slowly as we worked our way through a full seven courses, from soup through dessert and cheeses, each with its own wine selection; and finally, at the end, coffee, which, like the food, had somehow been kept nice and hot. By then, the atmosphere had completely mellowed. We drank our coffee as we watched Frank tidy up.

"There are cold things in there for tomorrow's breakfast and lunch," said Stella.

"I can't imagine ever needing to eat again," I said. I hadn't spoken for a while, and the feel of the words in my mouth made me realize I was a little drunk.

Stella smiled at me in a way that made me wonder if that was obvious. She glanced at her delicate gold wristwatch and said, "Bedtime," stubbing out her cigarette as she did. She stood and kissed the air by my cheeks and, less enthusiastically, Charlie's, and she and Frank headed off to their cabin.

Before going to bed, I checked on the birds one last time. They were huddled together on one perch, subdued and quiet. It was so hard, sometimes, to know what they were feeling. I missed their loud chatter, which Charles said sounded like rusty door hinges—but it meant they were happy, even if I couldn't understand exactly what they were saying.

He saw me staring at them and put an arm around me. "Don't worry so much," he said.

"What if the travel and the cold gave them a shock they can't recover from?"

"I daresay it's good for them to have an adventure, after living their entire lives in an apartment in the Bronx." He kissed my cheek. "The break'll do you good, too. You won't have to lift a finger the whole time we're here. Not one blasted thing for you to do, unless you decide to start helping old Frank set the table." He nudged me with his shoulder in a joking way. "He's a bit henpecked, don't you think? Did you see how Stella orders him around?"

"I like Stella," I said.

Charles made a noise, a kind of snort.

"What?" I said.

"I didn't say anything."

Later, as we were lying in bed, side by side, I said, "You really don't think there was anything to that petition? Those women at the docks in Clayton?"

"That's still on your mind, eh? That old lady saying, 'Something's not right on that island,' like in a ten-cent mystery novel."

"I just can't stop thinking about it," I said.

We were silent for a moment. "Now," Charlie said, "if you want real mysteries, look in that trunk over there." He gestured toward the trunk that held our notes, which stood against the wall of the bedroom. "There are questions no one has been able to answer. Flesh, butter, blood, falling from clear, calm skies . . ."

The back of the Forts' house, a blue sky, a warm sensation on my cheek—

No, I wouldn't think about that.

"Charlie, are you sure about those theories? The invisible beings in the sky, just . . . throwing things on us?"

"I explained it as well as I could at dinner."

"It's just a little hard to imagine."

"Any explanation is hard to imagine." He pulled the covers up around him. "When my book is finished, it will be clear to everyone, even the most obtuse people."

"I'm not obtuse."

"I didn't mean you," he said, but I knew he did. I never came out and questioned his theories, but he'd often noticed that I didn't follow his convoluted flights of reasoning, and he'd long ago decided that, though I loved him and was often his only audience, intellectually I was no better than the stupid masses.

"Once a sufficient number of people acknowledge them," he went on, "then we'll find a way to prove their existence. Maybe we'll contact them via airships."

"Airships?"

"Yes, I've got lots of good ideas about how to do it. I'll tell you more about it tomorrow."

"I'd like that," I said, wanting to end the night on a friendly note. "Charlie? If you really think they exist, what do you think they're like—those beings?"

"My hope and belief," Charles said, "is that they are benevolent, if a bit mysterious. Like Mr. Arkel. Good night, darling."

SIX

CHARLES WAS SOON SNORING HEAVILY, FULL FROM SEVEN courses of wine, fish, fowl, meat, cheese, nuts, and sweets. But I had been battling my nerves and had barely touched many of the dishes. Lying beside him in the dark, I found myself reaching for a state of mind I used to savor as a child, between waking and sleep, when I was not exactly dreaming, but my imagination was more vivid than during the day. It was in this place that I'd been visited by a benevolent spirit I called King Nyx.

When I was about nine, my father had given me a black tin bird. It was dented and scratched, rescued from some trash can, but became my favorite toy. It was about the length of a child's hand, with a long, pointed beak and wheels instead of feet. Wound with a key, it rolled forward, its joined wings squeaking as they moved up and down. This toy somehow melded in my imagination with the idea of King Nyx.

IN THE SCHOOL LIBRARY I'D discovered Smith's *Dictionary of Greek and Roman Biography and Mythology*, with its tantalizing vision of a sky, earth, and underworld crowded with deities, all with their own interests: light and dark, love and war. I relished the paragraphs, savoring the words in my mind. *Nyx, Nox or Night personified . . . subduer of gods and men . . .*

I could picture the tin bird turning its head so the dented side was away from me and I could see the deep blue glass eye. I recalled the clear, calm voice, neither masculine nor feminine: *Remember you have a test in arithmetic today,* it might say. *Practice your multiplication tables.* Things my mother might have said if she were alive.

Other times, King Nyx would appear with her subjects, which she sometimes referred to as her children: the handful of chipped and grimy penny dolls that I kept in a cigar box under my bed. They followed her through rambling narratives in which they journeyed through the woods or along the banks of streams, stopping at night to gather under her tin wings; they traveled on by day, always looking for something . . .

How often I'd tuck the toy under my pillow and will myself into that half-conscious state where I could visit her and see those soothing pictures, or hear the mundane advice I craved. Sometimes I sat on my bed holding her, stroking the sharp edges of those wings, that dented head, amazed that she could be so small yet contain something bigger than me.

I was a child, but King Nyx was an adult. I remembered the morning I reached to feel her reassuring shape with my fingertips and she told me, *You're going to have to wake your father up for work today.*

I knew my father did not always wake up on time if he'd been out late. By the time I was seven I'd learned to do my braids and get myself to school. School was not always pleasant, but there were big windows and lots of light and things happened on a schedule that you could predict. I needed this like air. But it had never occurred to me to worry, before that morning when I was ten, about getting my father to work.

When King Nyx told me to wake him, it was like a match

struck in a dark room. I saw an area of my life that had been all around me but invisible: my father needed help.

The landlady would serve meals for an extra fee, and we didn't have that every month, but my father usually paid the separate and smaller coffee fee. I brought his cup downstairs, filled it, went back, and shook him until he woke to drink. He got to work. From then on I added getting his coffee and shaking him awake to my morning routine.

On the days when it didn't work, I'd lean back, close my eyes, and hear the calm voice: *Never mind. You did your best. Get yourself off to school.*

IF ONLY I HAD SOMETHING like that now, I thought. I tried to tuck my hand under Charlie's body, but when it was wedged beneath his back, it felt crushed by his sleepy weight, and I pulled away. For years, Charlie had been my calm voice of reason. King Nyx had deserted me back when— No, I wasn't going to think about that.

But I couldn't help it. "Back when Mary left," I whispered aloud to myself in the dark.

Unable to sleep, I lit the lantern on the bedside table and turned the wick down so the flame burned low. I got up and stood looking at the big trunk that held all our notes. Clues to the real mysteries, Charlie had said.

I opened the trunk and looked at all the notebooks and papers, which I had tied in neat stacks and cushioned with crumpled newspaper so the bundles wouldn't shift during the journey. It was hard to believe that in just a few months, all this would finally result in a book, a real book that would be published. I was glad to see that I'd packed well and everything was still in order.

I took out some of the bundles and put them on the writing desk, one after another until I found the one I was looking for, one I hadn't been sure I should bring: the one that contained my own notebook. I needed to remind myself of the time when I had filled those pages, alone and frightened. Before Charles rescued me—and loved me.

I untied the string and took out the notebook, looking at the marbled cover, once black and gray, now faded with age to a greenish, mottled color like lichen. There was a white rectangular label with scrolled designs around its edges, and the words COM-POSITION BOOK in the shape of an arch at the top. Under that, it said, "Name: _____," and in that space, Mary had written, "The Damned."

I looked at the pen strokes. She had made them with her own hand, all those years ago. Twenty-three years now, wasn't it.

I remembered the day she gave me the notebook. It was in June, on a Sunday. We had the afternoon off, and after we finished our morning tasks, she convinced me to take a walk.

She'd only been working at the Forts' house for two weeks but had somehow already found a trail I had never seen, one that ran up a hill a quarter mile behind the Forts' house.

"I can't believe you've never been here before," she said as we entered the bright green early summer woods. I was twenty-three then, and she was only sixteen, but she had a knowing smile that made her seem more worldly. "Do you never just go out walking?"

"No, I like to stay put," I said.

After we had continued on the leafy path for a few minutes, she turned to me and said, "Anna, I asked you to come out here because I want to talk to you about something."

"What?"

"It's those nervous attacks," she said.

I'd just been beginning to enjoy the walk, but now my mood darkened. I knew she was referring to what I thought of as the hornet swarms that had begun pursuing me in the past weeks, ever since I'd been promoted to parlor maid and general head housemaid. Because we shared the attic bedroom, she'd been there when I'd run to my bed during an attack.

"Remember," she said, continuing along the path on the hillside, without looking at me, "the day I came in and you were cutting yourself with scissors?"

"Yes?" I didn't understand why she was bringing it up. It was over; why talk about it?

I had discovered that I could sometimes get the hornets away by rolling myself tightly into the covers. I always tore off my apron and uniform and tossed them over the back of the chair first, so they wouldn't wrinkle, and dove under the blankets in my shift and corset, but that day I felt as if I would suffocate if I didn't get the feeling away immediately, and threw myself onto the bed fully dressed, not even able to think about what I would do about the wrinkles after. It was as if a cloud of buzzing, stinging insects was pressing in around me, so thick and close that my chest could not expand enough for me to get air. But this time the weight of the covers didn't still them as it usually did, the physical sensation driving away the imaginary one. This time, they felt trapped in there with me, buzzing against my skin, burrowing deeper as I twisted my body left and right, trying helplessly to get away from something that now seemed to be inside my body. Then, without warning, as I rolled sideways, I felt a sharp, bright pain at my waist—and for a second, the swarms were gone.

Sitting up, I pulled out the pin I'd stuck in the band of my apron earlier and forgotten about. It had given me a tiny point of relief.

I pricked my waist again through the fabric. The effect was real. It was as if the sensation created a funnel into which some of the hornets fell, concentrating their stings into a single point of pain that I could stand—and that I could control.

But it wasn't enough. I stood up and grabbed my sewing scissors from the basket by the dresser, opened them, pushed up my sleeve, and pressed the point of a blade into my skin, to see if a bigger jab would give me more relief. It did. I dragged it forward, creating a furrow in which beads of blood appeared. Then again. And again.

That was when Mary came in.

She grabbed the scissors from my hand and wrapped her arms around me tightly. It had been years since I'd felt an embrace like that. My father must have done it when I was very small—comforted me. But even before I'd moved out at fourteen, his touch already communicated helplessness and resentment; he knew he was losing me. I could not remember the last time I had ever been *held*.

Although she was only doing it to stop me from getting the scissors again, the pressure of her arms did what the covers couldn't, calming me. I could breathe. When she loosened her grip, I pulled her arms back around me. I breathed in her smells of wheat and wind and sunshine as she squeezed me tight again.

The next time I had an attack, she saw me head for the stairs and followed me, and up in our room she put her arms around me right away.

I'D BEEN GRATEFUL AND TOLD her so. That didn't mean we had to go on talking about it.

"What exactly brings on those attacks?" she asked now.

"I don't know," I said shortly. I couldn't put words to the frightening, nonsensical feelings that came over me for no reason and sent me to my room: a conviction that Mr. Fort's locked study was full of birds I heard as I passed in the hall; that a crumbling brown substance my scrub brush found between the floorboards was blood, so much blood. Worst of all was that the voice of King Nyx, which I'd trusted as a child, had become part of the darkness, hissing awful words in my ear, like: *It is blood* or *They're dying in the dark* . . .

And sometimes when I put the silver coffee urn on the table in front of Mr. Fort or hung one of Mrs. Fort's dresses in the closet, the reflection of Mr. Fort's impassive face began cracking into an animal snarl, or a bloody hole opened in the fabric of the dress.

I knew my mind creating these horrible things meant I was unwell.

Mary was quiet. I watched her back as she walked up the path in front of me. She was wearing the same white blouse and full striped cotton skirt she'd worn two weeks before when she'd come to inquire about the housemaid position. When the previous head housemaid, Betsy, had left suddenly in late May, with an ailment, I'd been promoted to head housemaid, and we needed someone to fill my old position. Mary had been the best applicant, quick and alert and eager for the work. Yet I'd noticed that her street clothes did not fit very well, as if she had lost a lot of weight, and the hem of the skirt dragged slightly on the floor. She wore the same clothes now. They were the only ones she had.

After a bit, she said, over her shoulder, "That first time when you had the scissors, when I asked what was wrong, you said something about hearing birds."

"Birds?" I said sharply. My irritation came from the fact that I knew exactly what she meant, and it embarrassed me. I'd convinced myself I'd heard a kind of screeching sound coming from a closet that, to be honest, I wasn't supposed to be near, as it was in Mr. Fort's study, where only Mrs. Fort herself was ever allowed to clean. In those first days after I'd been promoted to head housemaid, some perverse curiosity, or maybe a desire to rebel, made me take the key from Mrs. Fort's bedside table and enter, and then I'd scared myself imagining I heard noises from the closet, like a girl in a fairy tale who enters a forbidden room where a gruesome secret is being kept.

"Remember saying that, about the birds?" Mary asked. "I wondered what that meant."

"I was just talking nonsense, Mary. Honestly. Couldn't you tell?"

"But were you?"

"Of course," I said firmly.

After a while, she said, "You don't think . . . Mr. Fort could have anything to do with your attacks, do you?"

As she said it, she stopped walking and turned to me. Sunlight and shade dappled her pale face. Her dark hair was cut unevenly, so she couldn't put it up neatly, and some locks hung around her face. Where had she come from, this pallid, disheveled person?

"Let me tell you something about Mr. Fort," I said. "He may be a little hard to get along with, but everything is orderly in his house."

"I've noticed," said Mary.

"There's no chaos."

Not like where I grew up, I thought, living in cheap rented rooms with a father who was always out of work, and not even the memory of my poor dead mother, because she was gone by the time I was three. It all came back as I said those words to Mary: the shared bathrooms down the hall reeking of stale piss—and the odor of cabbage, always, boiled cabbage.

"So you don't mind how strict he is?" asked Mary.

"And what do you think would happen if he wasn't?" I asked. Before she could answer, I said, "I've seen what that's like. I'll take strict over that, any day."

Mary had begun walking again. "Look," she said. "There's a set of steps going up the side of the hill. See? It looks like it will take us right to the top."

I hesitated. "We have to be back before dinner."

"We don't. It's our afternoon off."

"But then what would we eat?"

Already two steps up the stairs, Mary turned again and smiled, opening the canvas satchel that hung from her shoulder. Inside were some bundles wrapped in napkins. "I took food from the kitchen."

"You *stole* it?"

"Just bread and cheese."

"Cook will be furious. And what if she tells Mr. Fort?"

"You know she won't tell him," Mary said. "He'd kill all of us."

"Don't be so dramatic," I said.

"She'll keep her mouth shut."

We continued climbing the stairs, which were made of stones and packed earth. Whoever had made them had not tended them lately. Some stones were crooked, some missing, some sliding downhill.

Why *was* I still following her? Of course, even if we turned back right away, the chances of being able to put the food back without Cook noticing were small. She'd either noticed it missing already or she would soon, and there was nothing to do about that except hope she didn't say anything.

And it was a pleasant afternoon for a picnic.

I hung for a few minutes suspended between irritation and grudging gratitude that Mary had gotten me out of the house.

I'd be sure she didn't steal again. She'd learn, I told myself. Things were done a certain way in that household, and it was best to go along with the rules. As long as you did, you were protected. Part of a well-oiled, efficient machine. I concentrated on keeping my breath regular as I climbed the steep steps, unwilling to let her hear me pant. She seemed to take them easily.

"You'll get used to how Mr. Fort is," I said eventually.

We paused at a small landing where the dark earth was veined with tree roots. Mary leaned against a tree. "He threw a glass of milk against the wall yesterday, you know," she said. "In the breakfast room."

I limited my reply to "Yes?"

"It shattered to bits," she said.

"You cleaned it up, I assume."

"I had to," she said. Then: "Is that normal?"

"It's not as if it happens every day," I said. "But yes, part of the job is handling that kind of thing at times."

"He said the milk was sour."

I stopped. "You . . . didn't give him sour milk . . . did you?" I asked, sick guilt rising in my throat, as if I myself was responsible.

"Of course not! Cook showed me what milk to bring out. And he wasn't even drinking it. Mrs. Fort was. He was reading the newspaper. Saw something he didn't like about the price of sugar." Mr. Fort ran a grocery wholesale business, so news items about such things could affect his mood.

"If he was reading the paper, and Mrs. Fort was drinking the milk, how did he come to throw the glass?" I asked.

"He put down the paper and told Mrs. Fort he could smell that the milk she was drinking was sour," Mary said. "Said he could smell it all the way across the table."

"But you're sure it wasn't?" I asked again.

"Absolutely, and Mrs. Fort told him so, in a very quiet and polite voice, and do you know what he did? Got up, grabbed it out of her hand, and smashed it against the wall. Said it was *his* house and *his* milk and *he'd* say if it was sour or not."

"He gets that way sometimes," I said. "You just have to keep your mouth shut and clean up the mess. In return, you get to live in a big, efficient household that runs on his money. It's worth it."

What I didn't say was how much I had admired Mr. Fort when I'd first arrived at fourteen, after living with my hapless father, who could never even manage to hold on to a rented room or a job, let alone run an entire successful business and own a big, light-filled house, with two maids and a cook.

Mr. Fort was never sad. He never failed to get what he wanted. He never doubted himself. Even when he was wrong. There was something appealing about that. In his house, what he said and thought was, by definition, correct. That was what it meant to be in charge.

Other conceptions of right and wrong meant nothing to him. He didn't believe in any version of God. If he had, I was sure he would only have looked down on Him for remaining weakly invisible, behind the scenes; for not being clear and direct about what He wanted.

Mrs. Fort was a regular churchgoer, and his attitude must have bothered her; but she knew she was lucky he even tolerated her going, so of course she didn't complain.

"He *gets that way*? And you think that's okay?" Mary asked.

Seeing it through her eyes made me uncomfortable. I'd admired him at fourteen, but now, at twenty-three, I did have to admit that his ways could be difficult. Still, I found myself defending him.

"No one's perfect. Someone still has to lead."

Mary was silent. The steps had gotten smaller and rougher until they'd disappeared, and now we were just walking on a narrow path. Then she asked, "Do you ever think of leaving?"

"No! Where would I go?"

"There's a whole world out there."

"You don't understand where I'd be if I hadn't taken the job at the Forts'," I said. "They saved me."

"So everyone outside is the unsaved, then?" Mary asked. "The damned?" She laughed.

"That's a little much."

We were approaching the end of the path, where there was an area of bare rock at the top of the hill. When we got to it, she pointed. "Look," she said. "There's the Forts' house."

"I've never seen it from this far away," I said. It looked dignified and neat, with its yellow paint and white trim and the green lawn around it. It also looked smaller.

Mary glanced at me. Suddenly she said, "Are you ever sorry you quit school?"

"No."

It wasn't that I hadn't liked it. I'd especially liked the school library and the librarian, Miss Klatcher. Many afternoons I'd lingered there, not wanting to go back to whatever rooming house my father and I were living in.

Whatever else could be said about that yellow house down in the valley, it did look the way a home was supposed to. I had one, now.

"Want to know a secret?" said Mary.

I turned to her. She still seemed too thin and small in her oversized clothes, but, I noticed, there was nothing frail about her—her face shone with determination and intelligence.

"A secret?" I said.

She hesitated, choosing her words. I felt my heart expand into the silence. I'd never had a friend to share secrets with before.

I'd help her with the blouse and skirt, I thought. We could sit down together and take them in so they fit properly. I could show her how to pin her hair up better while we waited for it to grow out. I thought: *This is friendship.*

"I left school, too," Mary said.

I was confused. "But in the interview, you said you graduated from Public School 21 on Clinton Avenue," I said.

"Well, I didn't. And I didn't take this job to support my sick aunt on First Street, either. I don't have a sick aunt, or any family in Albany, and I've never lived here. I lied about all of that."

I was just starting to feel like I knew her, and now she was telling me that everything she'd told me was false? "What do you mean?" I asked. "Where did you come from?"

She gestured out across the clustered houses and green trees below us. "The Realm of the Damned," she said dramatically. She laughed again, but I didn't.

SEVEN

"NO, REALLY, WHERE DID YOU COME FROM," I SAID, MY mouth dry. Who had I let into our household?

"Don't have another attack, now," she said, pulling my hand away from my throat. "I'm here. You're okay."

"Tell me the truth."

"The truth," said Mary, "is that I ran away from a boarding school. A place in Massachusetts called the Forest School."

"Massa*chu*setts?"

"Come on, it's not Mars."

"Where in Massachusetts?"

"A patch of woods south of Williamstown."

"A patch of—?"

"It was one of those little experimental schools out in the middle of nowhere, you know—no corsets, equality of the sexes, vegetarianism, that kind of thing."

She said it like I'd know what she was talking about.

"Vegetarianism?" I said. "No *corsets*?"

"That part was fantastic. We had a big garden where we grew

our food, and lessons outside in all kinds of weather, so we could commune with nature."

I was still reeling from finding out she'd lied to me; on top of that, she apparently came from a foreign world that existed just over the state border, where people acted in completely alien ways.

"Where would anyone even get ideas like that?" I said.

"Ever heard of the transcendentalists?"

"No."

"The Swedenborgians?"

"No!" Why was she talking about these weird-sounding things as if some normal person would know what they were?

"Ever hear of a novel called *Little Women*?"

"Yes," I said, relieved that she had finally said something recognizable.

"The author of *Little Women* was Louisa May Alcott," Mary said. "Her father was Bronson Alcott."

"Okay. So?" I wanted her to get to the truth about her past—or maybe to an apology for lying—but she seemed intent on giving me a lecture.

"So," Mary said, "the man who founded the Forest School, where I went, was a follower of Bronson Alcott. Alcott had founded a utopian community years ago, called Fruitlands. Unfortunately, it didn't last through its first winter. The Forest School was supposed to be like that but better. It was run on ideas from the transcendentalists and Swedenborg—"

"So what!" I crossed my arms and turned away. I didn't care about any of that.

"You asked where they got their ideas."

"If it was so wonderful and free," I said after a moment, "then why did you run away?"

At first, she didn't answer. I turned back, to see if she was angry, but she was looking off into the distance over the valley.

"Mr. Haskins."

"Who's that?"

It was windy at the top of the hill, and I watched the breeze pick up the short locks of her dark hair that had come loose from her hairpins. She'd said it was uneven because she'd been sick and had had to cut it, but now I wondered if that was a lie, too.

"He was the art teacher and also the drama teacher," she said. "Because the school was so small, he did both. I liked painting and acting, so I spent a lot of time with him. He cast me as Hamlet in our yearly Shakespeare production—"

"You? As Hamlet?"

"That's right. He said I was better than any of the boys. 'O God,'" she said, "'I could be bounded in a nutshell and count myself a king of infinite space, were it not that I have bad dreams.'"

"'Which dreams indeed are ambition,'" I answered.

She gave me a quick smile. "He told me I was the most brilliant student he'd ever taught," she went on, "and I believed him."

"Why wouldn't you?"

"I wouldn't have," Mary said, "if I'd understood how the world actually worked."

I was a maid, not so naïve about the way the world worked. I had an idea where the story was heading but waited for her to go on.

She said, "You get it into your head that things could be a certain way, but they aren't."

"What actually happened?"

"He asked me to pose for him," she said. "In the nude. And I said yes."

I felt a flush of anger, at him, but also her. "Are you stupid?"

"I was, yes, that's what I'm trying to tell you," she said, her face reddening. "It was just, we talked about art all the time, and I thought that's actually what he was asking."

"You said yes. To posing in the nude. For a man."

"There are such things as artist's models," she said. "We had some come to our drawing classes."

"And take their clothes off?"

"Of course."

"Well—if that's what all you progressive students did, then why *shouldn't* you have done it?"

"Those were professional models, not students. But I thought it *was* actually what he wanted. To draw me. Maybe he even thought it was what he wanted. But once I got there, he wanted something else."

"I hope you said no to that."

"I did. But after that, he just kept trying to get me alone. Every day he'd ask to see me after class, like he always used to, but now he'd be trying to put his hands on me."

"Oh, God, you *are* naïve," I said. "I don't care if it was a progressive school full of vegen-borgians or whatever you call it, why would you think he *wouldn't* put his hands all over you after you let him see you naked?"

"I'm telling you— Oh, never mind." I thought there were tears in her eyes as she turned away again and looked out over the valley. "It wasn't my fault."

"Yes it was. You're old enough to know men can't control themselves. If you expect them to, you're living in a fantasy world."

"Okay. I was. I was living in a fantasy where I was his favorite student because I was really talented, I had a future on the stage." She crossed her arms, the large shirt bunching above them.

"So you ran away?"

"Eventually he showed up in my room in the middle of the night. He was angry. He said he couldn't stand dishonesty. He said I'd led him on." She paused. "I didn't mean to, but evidently I had." She stopped again and looked away, as if trying to decide whether to say more.

The breeze picked up again, blowing between us. I waited. Finally she shook her head. "He was in my room and I was scared. I don't even know how I got him to leave . . . "

"You were lucky."

She met my eyes. "That's when I knew I had to get away from the school. I knew he'd come back, and I didn't think I'd get that lucky again. I asked my friend John for some of his clothes. I cut my hair short in the dark with his scissors. That's why it's all ragged." She touched the loose ends that hung around her face.

"Then you ran away."

She nodded. "I snuck into someone's hayloft to sleep that night. Stole a hatchet out of their barn for protection."

"How long were you out there? Before you came to us, I mean."

"About two weeks. I walked every day, just trying to cover distance. I don't think I went in a straight line."

"How did you eat?"

She shrugged her bony shoulders. I had assumed she was naturally thin, but now realized I'd been wrong.

"Why couldn't you go back to your parents?"

"They would have said the same as everybody—that it was my own fault."

"But you *could* have gone home," I insisted. "Why didn't you?"

"Shame." She rubbed a fold of the striped summer skirt, a little too long for her, between her fingers. "I took these from a clothesline. All the hope I had for my future, and now I'm nothing but a—" She stopped.

"A housemaid?" I said. I was aware of a dull, damp hurt in the center of my chest. I'd thought Mary was like me. But now I knew she was different. She had an education; she'd thought she was going to be someone.

"I mean, do you like it?" she asked. "Being in service?"

"It's the best job I could get," I said.

Mary surprised me by taking hold of both my hands, there on the windy hilltop, under the blue June sky. "You can be whatever you want, you know," she said.

For a second, I felt a thrill, but then I pulled my hands away.

"But you couldn't," I said.

"We'll see." She glanced down at the faraway yellow house. "I know this place isn't the whole world. I can leave."

"You just got here," I said. "You can't leave."

"Maybe you'll come, too."

"I can't imagine what I'd do anywhere else," I said.

"Well, start to imagine it. Let your mind go outside those four walls. Out into the Realm of the Damned." She smiled.

It was that night she gave me the notebook.

NOW, IN THE DIM LIGHT of the lamp, in the cabin's bedroom, with Charles snoring a few feet away, I ran my fingertips over its cover, remembering.

I saw her holding the pen in her hand that night, the look of concentration on her face, as she wrote in neat, self-assured letters, "The Damned."

"For your mind to wander in—even if you yourself never get outside this house," she said.

"I wouldn't know what to write," I said, taking it. I'd never had a notebook full of blank paper with no specific purpose— English composition, for instance, or recording the price of cleaning supplies.

"Write anything," she said. "It doesn't matter."

"Anything? What about what I had for breakfast?"

"Why not? Or what you thought about while you ate."

I laughed. "I always think about what I'm going to do next: dusting, unclogging the carpet sweeper, checking if we're running low on floor wax."

"You could write that. But I'll bet you think about other things, too."

An image flashed into my mind: the cigar box in which I'd kept the black tin bird and its subjects, the half-naked penny dolls. I remembered how, in my childhood, when King Nyx wasn't giving me advice, she used to lead her doll army on rambling imaginary adventures that went on and on, like following a stream . . .

But I said, "No, I don't really ever think about anything else." I put the book on top of the dresser.

Maybe corsetless Swedenborgians sat around writing their thoughts. Maybe they didn't have to work for a living. Maybe they just ran around in the woods naked, painting each other, and then came home to be fed and cleaned up after by someone else. Someone like me.

Even if I could be like them, would I want to?

A FEW DAYS LATER, we were lying in our beds on opposite sides of the attic. The room was dark and airy. It had been a warm day, but the night was cool and the open windows on either side let a breeze come through; it smelled of blossoms and honey.

"Have you written in that composition book?" Mary asked.

"No," I said.

"Why not?"

"Just haven't gotten around to it."

"What do you think about in your spare time, Anna?" she asked.

"I don't have spare time. Especially now that I'm head housemaid."

"When you did, then," she said.

I almost told her to be quiet, that it was time to sleep, but I didn't. The chance to enjoy the feel of the breeze and, most of all, to really talk to someone about something other than chores and duties made me answer her.

"I used to make up stories about a toy bird. I called it King Nyx."

"*King* Nyx? Nyx is a god*dess*, you know."

"Yes, but 'King' is a better title than 'Queen,'" I said. "I know she's a goddess. 'Nyx, Nox or Night personified . . . subduer of gods and men . . . daughter of Chaos . . . mother of Dreams . . .'"

Many times I'd run through those familiar words from Smith's *Dictionary of Greek and Roman Biography and Mythology*, to soothe myself and invoke King Nyx, in that space between sleep and waking.

"Maybe you could write those stories in your notebook," Mary suggested.

But King Nyx was not the same as she had been when I was a child, and I didn't know how to explain that. She had spoken in my mother's voice from a realm beyond the rational, from a place more powerful than the daytime world. That's how it had seemed then. But now I was grown up and I saw things differently. I valued the bright, the orderly, the logical.

"So this King Nyx," said Mary, "is a toy bird. And the protagonist of stories."

"They weren't exactly stories," I said.

I remembered King Nyx leading her subjects along a stream bank, wheels creaking, the pale broken dolls limping behind her, on a long, slow journey to—where? Some sunny, grassy clearing where they all could rest. I remembered her calm, clear voice when she spoke to me on the mornings when I couldn't wake my father: *Go on to school, Anna. You did your best.*

"It was more like I used to talk to her in my head." I realized I was whispering.

"You mean pray to her?"

"Maybe."

What had happened to the voice that used to comfort me, that now whispered frightening words, like "blood" and "danger"?

In the awkward silence, I added, "It sounds stupid, I know."

Instead of agreeing that it was stupid, Mary said, "I used to have a friend I talked to when I was little. She seemed so real . . . like I was talking to a ghost or a spirit."

The night was more than breezy; a wind was picking up, and it rustled the fresh early summer leaves outside the windows and gusted into the room.

"Do you still have that toy bird?" Mary asked.

"Yes." I had put the cigar box containing the bird and the dolls under my bed when I arrived at fourteen, nine years ago, and it was still there.

"I want to see it tomorrow," said Mary.

"It's nothing to look at."

I could hardly admit it to myself, but the things in that box had once held the power of religious artifacts for me. If I showed her, Mary would only see a dented toy and some cheap, grimy dolls. And maybe I would, too.

"Do you ever feel," I said, "as if hour to hour, day to day, you're walking on ice, and if you take a wrong step, you could fall through into something . . . " I stopped.

"Something what?"

I had no words for the churning, cold place just under the surface of life that I sensed so strongly that I could feel it in my throat, in the roots of my teeth. "Like chaos?" I said.

We fell silent, the wind gusting through the attic room. Heat crept to the surface of my cheeks. She thought I was crazy. I tried to come up with other things to say, but anything I could think of would only make it worse.

After a few minutes, Mary murmured sleepily, "'Nyx' backward is 'skin.'"

I smiled, turning toward her in the windy dark. "You're crazy, too," I whispered.

She didn't seem to hear, but after a few moments she said, with a hint of surprise, as if just realizing something: "Una was real."

"The spirit friend you used to talk to?"

"Do you believe in ghosts, Anna?"

"I don't know. Maybe."

"I do," Mary said. "I think they find us for a reason. I think they come to settle things."

A SOUND FROM SOMEWHERE OUTSIDE the cabin brought me back to the present with a jolt. Charles was still snoring—the sound hadn't woken him—but it was a heavy thud, too loud to have been made by a small animal like a skunk or raccoon.

Were there bears? Frank had said Mr. Arkel brought animals to the island to hunt.

I stood frozen next to the writing desk, wanting to creep back into bed and press myself against Charlie's warm, familiar back and tell myself I'd imagined the noise.

Then: another thud, loud and distinct.

I turned to the bed. "Wake up!"

Charles let out a big, meaty snore. I shook his shoulder until he grunted. In the dim light of the lantern that sat on the desk on the other side of the room, I could just barely see him blinking resentfully.

"There's something behind the cabin."

Charles blinked again. "What?"

"I think it's a bear."

He groaned and rolled over. "Leave it alone." His voice was a thick, sleepy mumble.

"Charlie!" Fear rose in me, the sense that something bad would happen if I could not get him to listen. "Charles!" I heard the sharp edge in my voice as I shook him again, then backed off when I saw the way he was looking at me.

"What?" I asked, though I already knew. He had heard the edge of hysteria.

"Annie. *Your response is out of proportion to the facts.*"

Dr. Jacobson's words, part of my diagnosis. Charles groped for my hand and squeezed it. "It's all right," he said. "It's all the changes. It'll be all right. Remember what the doctor said. Let's say it together: *There is no danger*— Come on, say it with me."

I could hear Dr. Jacobson saying it, soothingly, firmly: *Remember you are safe. Your response is out of proportion to the facts. There's no danger except in your mind.*

"There is no danger. There never has been. It's only in my mind," I murmured into the dark.

I held my breath and listened for the sound again, but I didn't hear it.

Charlie looked at me with an expression of genuine tenderness and concern. He squeezed my hand again, and I squeezed his.

"You can go back to sleep," I said. "I'm okay."

"You go to sleep, too." He watched me as I got under the covers. I closed my eyes and turned away.

Charles began snoring again almost instantly. How could he be so comfortable in this place? He had such faith that now that he'd found somebody who believed in his book, everything had to be all right.

It was after he was asleep that I heard the smashing sound, like something being hit with a heavy object. I turned sharply to see Charlie's reaction, but there was none.

It seemed to come from the same place, behind the cabin.

If it was an animal, it couldn't be anything smaller than a bear. And what could it be doing?

Smash. It came again. Metal and splintering wood.

EIGHT

BUT IF THE SOUND WAS SO LOUD, THEN WHY WASN'T IT waking Charlie? Was I imagining it?

I pulled the comforting blanket up around my neck and tried to soothe myself by imagining him saying, *Shh, it's nothing.*

No. There *was* something out there. I pushed the warm covers back, walked to the window, and raised the sash.

The air outside was cool and frosty, and there was just enough moonlight to see. Over by the discarded trunks, at the margin of the woods, half in moonlight and half in shadow, was a hulking, hairy shape. It *was* a bear.

Then it straightened, and it was unmistakably a human, in a fur cape. It raised its arms, a large stone in its hands, which it brought down hard on the edge of the trunk—

Smash.

That was the sound I'd heard. The person hunched forward again to examine the trunk. Then they straightened and brought down the stone once more—*smash.*

This time, there was a distinct cracking sound. The figure pulled the broken latch from the trunk, then raised the lid.

Pale hands pulled out the drawers impatiently. A tablecloth was yanked from one and thrown on the ground. A loaf of bread tossed on top of it. And more food: oranges, sliced meat.

I could see the back of the figure's head more clearly now—a mass of long, matted hair.

Could it be one of the missing girls? If so, what was she doing here?

I remembered the days when I was new to the Forts' house and Charlie was still young, and his father, as punishment, would lock him or one of his brothers in a particular windowless closet, sometimes for hours, occasionally for whole days. I would help the free brothers sneak food into their laps at dinner to bring the prisoner, the boys and I sometimes hardly touching our own meals, so that the one being punished often ate better than us.

Was this person possibly bringing food to the missing girls? Could they be locked up somewhere? Was this one living wild out in the woods? She certainly seemed to be, with her matted hair and ragged clothes.

She crouched on her heels and pulled the corners of the tablecloth together over the food, then slung the bundle over her shoulder as she stood. For a second, her face turned partially toward me.

For that second, I forgot how to breathe.

The face I saw in the gray half-light was Mary's.

When my lungs started working again, I gasped. The girl was already moving away from the trunk. At the sound, she turned fully toward me.

Mary.

No. Impossible.

I slammed the window shut and leaned against the wall, one hand pressed to my chest. It felt like my heart would escape if I didn't hold it in.

It couldn't be. The girl looked to be about sixteen—the age Mary had been when I last saw her. But the real Mary, if she was still alive somewhere in the world, would now be a woman of almost forty.

I tried to control my breathing.

It wasn't her, of course. But then why did my mind and my heart, galloping uncomfortably under my hand, insist that it was?

"Old enough to know better, but not old enough to look out for herself," Mrs. Fort had said the day after she ran away. "I'm afraid for her."

One of the things that tortured me after she left was the terror that she would die, or already had.

That, combined with the feeling that she *couldn't* die—not that it was impossible, but that it was inconceivable.

By the time she left, I had known her for only one summer, yet our friendship—the only real one of my life—had more than changed me.

I had never shared my thoughts with anyone the way I had with her. I had always felt I was nothing but a haphazard collection of daydreams masquerading as a person; she made me feel real. Her leaving felt like the undoing of everything: earth, water, light. Birds, wind, hilltop picnics—they all dissolved into a cold, gray churning.

When she was gone, my life without her was a place I couldn't reenter.

It was this that had led to what Dr. Jacobson later explained was hysterical catatonia—my inability to leave my bed in the Forts' house, even to cross the room and let someone in. I would have had to move the dresser to do that, because I'd pushed it in front of the door. Mr. Fort had been on the verge of hiring a man to break it down when Charles arrived home from traveling and asked if he could have twenty-four hours to get me out. His father was not open to negotiations unless they benefited him, but he saw that this one might save him the cost of repairing a door, so he agreed.

Charlie had spent twenty-three of those hours sitting with

his back or shoulder to the door, eating small meals his mother brought, occasionally sliding a piece of toast or some apple slices under the door, and talking to me, first loudly so I could hear him from my bed across the room, then lowering his voice as I moved across the floor to talk from the other side of the door.

He told me about his travels, how he'd hopped freight trains, worked his way across the ocean to England on a cattle boat, slept in the woods. I got lost in his words, imagining his experiences. He said he had lived without his father's money for a year and liked it. He'd been free. He told me that he wanted to be a writer. It was what he wanted more than anything. He kept up a steady, soothing, sometimes monotonous stream of talk, and in this way distracted me and calmed me.

When I asked why he was helping me, he said, "You've been helping me since we were kids. Now it's your turn." It was true: when I'd arrived at fourteen, Charlie, the middle of three brothers, was only twelve, and in addition to helping sneak food to whoever was locked up for punishment on any given day, I'd tended many bloody noses and raw patches of skin after encounters with Mr. Fort's hand or belt. Charlie had been silent for a minute, then said simply: "I've loved you since then, Annie." I knew: I had seen it in his eyes for years, but had never dared to put a name to it.

By the end of the twenty-four hours we were both sitting on the floor, leaning toward each other, cheek to cheek except for the door between us.

Aside from my weeks at Dr. Jacobson's immediately after that—and the days I'd boarded in the hotel laundry years later—we had not left each other's side since then.

I had to wake him now. He was the only one who could help me.

But how could he help this time? I had seen Mary's face, as clear as anything. I had seen what—*if* it was real—could only be a ghost. Charlie launching into a monologue would not help tonight, as it had then. I'd been so lonely and untethered, and the dense, one-sided conversation had been like a big blanket, wrapping me and anchoring me.

Charlie wouldn't believe I'd seen Mary. He'd say the story about the missing girls and my thoughts about Mary in the afternoon had placed her in my mind, that was all. He'd tell me to go back to sleep and would wrap his big arms around me, squeeze me—

My chest seized; I struggled to breathe.

"Remember you are safe," I whispered to myself in the dark. *"Your response is out of proportion to the facts."*

Charlie's imagined words, so well-meaning, were smothering me. Panic pressed a pale, cool hand against my chest. Pressing . . . harder . . .

I wasn't worried about being safe. That wasn't the problem. I was worried about—what?

Mary. Yes, Mary in rags in the woods, stealing leftover food, her hair a mass of felted knots, a dirty bearskin hanging from her shoulders. A child without a proper coat on a cold night.

Once she had been sixteen and I had been twenty-three and I couldn't help her; now I was forty-six but somehow she was still sixteen; what if now I could help, what if—

I pressed my own palm hard against my chest, trying to dissipate the feeling of the ghostly panic-hand. I couldn't wake Charles. I wouldn't talk to anyone who would tell me not to help her.

Or, even worse, that she didn't exist.

She doesn't exist.

How could I possibly help? I couldn't go out in the middle of the night, looking in the woods. I might walk all night and never find a trace of her.

She doesn't exist.

The thought circled back like a piece of a tune stuck in my head.

Doesn't even exist.

No, Charlie wouldn't say that. He'd say I'd seen a real girl—that was plausible enough—but not Mary.

But if Dr. Jacobson were here, he would say it, the thing I didn't want to hear: that I'd hallucinated.

"Hallucinations can be a symptom of hysteria, Anna." I could hear the doctor's reasonable, even voice. I could smell his slightly lemony, soapy scent, I could see the seam in the shoulder of his white coat, which I had stared at so many times to avoid his eyes. Sunlight through lace curtains, the stillness of those airy rooms, a sense of scrupulous hygiene. If only I would agree with him, I too could be a resident of this calm, clean world. If only I would agree I had hallucinated . . .

Ah, there it was. Ever since the first thought of Mary had come to me in the afternoon, I'd known it was on its way:

The Event.

Even now, I couldn't remember the Event directly. The vagueness of the term was a protective wrapper, a way to handle it without touching it. It was a white-hot exploding star I had shrunk, through sheer willpower and rigorous mental hygiene, to fit inside those two little words.

But even through that wrapper, I could feel the heat.

A warm splash on my skin.

When I told Charles, when we sat on the floor with our heads leaning against the door, *he* believed me.

Splash on my eyelashes. I wince.

But Dr. Jacobson said it was a hallucination.

Standing in the cabin now, in the dim light of the lamp, I could no longer remember the words I'd used to describe it to either of them. I must have sounded crazy—

Ah, don't let it come back now, I thought, but it came:

Standing in the weedy part of the yard behind the Forts' house. Daisies and wild mint.

The yellow house, red roses, white trellis, white curtains bellying out a window in the breeze, gray slate roof, and above it a clear blue sky, without clouds.

I pressed my fingertips to my eyelids, willing my breathing to slow.

The yellow house . . .

"Would you say your thoughts were disordered, Anna, in your last weeks of employment at the Forts' house?" Dr. Jacobson had asked, that day in the room with the lace curtains.

"Of course." I'd been eager to sound practical, healthy, to be on the doctor's side. The side of sanity.

"Why is it so difficult, then, to admit that you might have hallucinated?"

A warm splash on my eyelashes.

"I . . . I don't know."

The splash: I felt it.

"But you admit rain doesn't fall from a clear sky. And you said the sky was clear that day."

Gray slate roof, blue sky.

"I'm positive, yes."

"And yet—?"

Warm splash. I wince.

"It was on my face. I felt it."

Spray of red spots across white daisy petals.

There:

I touch my face, look at my fingertips—blood.

"It was blood, Dr. Jacobson. It fell from the sky."

"A clear sky, Anna?"

I touch my face, look at my fingertips—blood.

Blood.

"A clear sky, Anna?" he repeated.

I didn't answer.

"You admit then your thoughts were disordered, and yet,"

he went on, "you persist in saying that you saw blood fall from a clear blue sky."

I stayed silent. I didn't want to hear him debate anymore, with that calm, authoritative voice, what I knew I had seen.

Anyone who saw the two of us in that room would have no trouble deciding who was correct, who was sane. The doctor sat on a straight-backed chair in his crisp white coat, his notebook on his lap. I, disheveled in my old housecoat, lay on the daybed or sat with my shoulders hunched, afraid to meet his calm, knowing eyes.

Eventually, I'd said he was right, it wasn't possible. I must have hallucinated.

But after I got out, Charles, by some miracle, believed me, even when Dr. Jacobson hadn't, even when I had trouble believing myself.

CHARLES. HIS BREATHING WAS EVEN, his snores quieter now. He slept just a few feet away, in the bed. He'd stayed with me all those years.

By the faint moonlight filtering in through the window, I saw on the desk the notebook Mary had given me. I picked it up and opened it. There was the first entry I had ever written, the week after she ran away. I hadn't looked at it in over twenty years.

I could only make some of the words by the low flame of the lamp, but from memory I knew what it said:

> *The Scientific American Supplement* no. 23, June 3, 1876. Bath County, Kentucky. "SHOWER OF FLESH FROM A CLEAR SKY . . . On last Friday a shower of meat fell near the house of Allen Crouch . . . Mrs. Crouch was out in the yard at the time, engaged in making soap, when meat which looked like beef began to fall around her . . . Mr.

Harrison Gill, whose <u>veracity is unquestionable</u> . . .
says he saw particles of meat sticking to the fences
and scattered over the ground."

How much those words had meant to me: "veracity is
unquestionable."

I'd copied the passage into my notebook on the Sunday after
Mary left. There had been double the work to do, that first week,
when there wasn't yet a replacement, and its relentlessness kept
me tethered to sanity—barely. On my first afternoon off, I went
straight to the Albany Free Library and sat in the reading room,
piling scientific journals around me on the table: decades' worth
of *Nature*, *New American Scientist*, *Popular Science News*.

As a child I had found solace in the school library, a place
that was predictable, stable, quiet. I'd built walls of books and
anchored myself in the safe territory behind them with bits and
pieces of lines I memorized, took home, repeated in my mind.
Later, when I arrived at the Forts', it was material I found on
Mrs. Fort's nightstand: the Book of Common Prayer or a pamphlet she brought home from her Oxford Movement–influenced
church. From all of these I took scraps and shreds and made a
kind of nest, which I wove around myself when I felt anxiety
coming on or at night to fall asleep.

*Nyx, Nox or Night personified . . . daughter of Chaos . . . mother
of Dreams . . . one uncreated and one incomprehensible . . . begotten
before the worlds . . . to thee do we send up our sighs, our sighs . . .*

Then, after Mary left, it was Science I turned to instead of
religion. *A shower of flesh from a clear sky . . . a red substance, the
color of blood . . .*

I remembered the relief as I set down each word. If flesh
really fell from a clear sky in Kentucky twenty years ago, then
blood could have fallen in Albany in May. I wasn't crazy. Such
things were possible. The *Scientific American* said so.

I had spent hours at the table that day with my notebook,

science journals piled around me. That day, I had only found the one entry. But I knew there must be more. I stuffed old volumes into the bag I had brought until it wouldn't hold anymore, covered them up with some sewing, and walked out casually. No one would miss decades-old issues of the *Northeastern Meteorological Society Quarterly* if I kept them for a week or so.

That night, I didn't sleep. I read. Stretched out on the floor of the room I had shared with Mary, I went page by page, line by line.

> *American Journal of Science*, vol. 42, 1842. "Last June our respected correspondent, Mr. W. H. Blake, of Boston, sent us an account of a shower of yellow matter which fell on board a vessel in Pictou Harbor, on a serene night in June, and was collected by the bucket full and thrown overboard; . . . It was found . . . to give off nitrogen and ammonia, an animal odor . . .

Below that, I'd written:

Serene—animal odor

No clouds, no wind to explain the fall of the substance. A substance of animal origin, like the flesh that fell on Mrs. Crouch in Kentucky.

And then:

> *Popular Science News*, 35–104. "Prof. Luigi Palazzo, head of the Italian Meteorological Bureau, reported that upon May 15, 1890, at Messignadi, Calabria, a red substance, the color of fresh blood, fell from the sky. Upon examination in the public health laboratories in Rome, it was found that it was, in

fact, blood. The most probable explanation of this terrifying phenomenon is that migratory birds (quails or swallows) were caught and torn in a violent wind."

Underneath that, I had written the single word "Birds?"

It could have been birds, I'd thought that cool September night in 1895, lying on my stomach on the rug on the floor of the attic bedroom, in my nightgown, reading by the light of a small oil lamp. It wouldn't make any sense for it to be birds, because the sky was cloudless, and there was no wind, but maybe, just maybe, that's what it had been. The important point was that I had not hallucinated.

I could trust my own eyes. I knew what I saw.

What happened was something so wrong that it subverted the natural order of things, and that was terrifying, but not as terrifying as feeling I could not trust my own eyes.

AND IF I HADN'T HALLUCINATED THEN, I wasn't hallucinating now. I *had* seen Mary tonight, outside our cabin.

Her voice in our dark attic room, twenty-three years ago: "Do you believe in ghosts? I do. They come to settle things."

But settle what? Did she need something from me?

. . . "They come back to settle things."

My thoughts were moving in circles as they used to back then. If it was a ghost, then what should I do? Follow it?

No. Clearly, no. I had to stop thinking about it for now. It may well have been real—I knew what I saw was real—but there was nothing I could do about it now, tonight.

"They come back to settle things."

What was it I used to do to stop these circling thoughts? Mrs. Fort's rosary. That was what helped.

She had called herself "very high Episcopalian." My father had always called religion superstitious nonsense, but I was attracted to the mysterious objects I found in her room, crosses and various linen and satin pieces, which she embroidered or delicately repaired for the altar, with their particular names: corporal, purificator, pall, chalice veil, burse. In her night-table drawer was a pamphlet on how to say the rosary. Since I didn't have a rosary of my own, I used to picture one in my mind, imagine the smooth wood of each bead under my fingers as I mentally repeated the verses I'd memorized from the pamphlet, often lying in bed, saying them like incantations to summon sleep and peace. But now the verses were fuzzy in my memory.

I had to sleep. I knew that. In the morning I could think it all through. I didn't have to tell anyone if I didn't want to. I didn't have to open the subject up for debate with Charles.

Closing the composition notebook, I put it back in the trunk, burying it under bundles of paper and an old reference volume, *Birds in Captivity: Species and Their Care.* I'd memorized the section on monk parakeets, *Myiopsitta monachus*, long ago, but had brought the book along for the security it gave me.

I climbed into bed next to Charlie and pressed myself against his sturdy warmth. *Hail holy Queen—* How did it go? *Our life, our sweetness and our fruit, to thee do we cry, the poor vanished children of Eve.* No, it was *banished children.*

I kept trying as I bumbled toward sleep. *Oh feathered, heart in heaven* . . . no . . . *Mercy, mercy, feather-dart, to thee we cry the holy name* . . . *child of the blessed fruiting vine* . . .

I WOKE SUDDENLY. IT WAS still pitch-dark. I'd dreamed the birds were dead, frozen lumps on the bottom of their cage.

The birds couldn't be dead. They'd been on their perch just before I got into bed. Still, I went to their cage, where it sat by the stove, lifted the quilt, and peeked in, trying to see them by the faint light that came from around the edges of the stove's door.

They were still on their perch, huddled together, more puffed up but not dead. One of them, Pollux—his head was longer, the white on its crown more pronounced—opened an eye and looked at me. I was pierced with a sadness that surprised me. I made small noises with my lips and Pollux closed his eye.

Smash.

It came from outside: the same noise I'd heard before.

Smash.

It wasn't a ghost. Why had I thought it was a ghost? A ghost couldn't break a lock with a stone.

I went to the window and opened it as quietly as I could. Last time I had gasped, and she'd heard me, and she'd run away.

The air was sharp with the smell of winter coming. The girl in the bearskin was back, hunched over the second trunk, pulling the drawers out as she had from the first one.

Things are going on here which are not right. We have nowhere to turn. That's what the letter said, the one Mrs. Laches had shown me.

Slowly, so as not to make noise, I closed the window. The girl was busy with the trunk. Maybe I could get outside while she was still there.

I slipped on my coat and pulled on my boots, not even bothering to lace them properly. A tickle on my wrist reminded me my bracelet was there; I rubbed the heart-shaped clasp between my fingers for courage. Then I took a deep breath and opened the door.

Standing on the frost-stiffened grass in my overcoat and my loose boots, I felt a silence around me like nothing I'd experienced before. Half of a cold white moon hung in the black sky. There was no wind. A pale rectangle of light lay on the ground near Frank and Stella's cabin, but I was sure they were fast asleep, like Charlie was.

The girl pulled things out of the trunk, unaware of me. It seemed as if she and I were the only people in the quiet, icy, moonlit world.

I crept toward her, the grass crunching under my boots, again rubbing the clasp of the bracelet between my fingers as I walked, to calm myself.

She heard me and turned. Her matted hair hung over her face, but the face that turned toward me in the silvery light was Mary's. Unquestionably hers.

She grabbed the corners of her cloth, picked it up, and ran.

If it had been any other face, I wouldn't have done what I did next. But the decision was made for me.

I ran after her.

NINE

AHEAD OF ME, THERE WERE WHISPERS, THE RUSTLING of footsteps in dry leaves. Two lights bobbing through the woods, far away and receding. Were others there, waiting for her?

Whatever they were, they were getting away. After only a few steps into the dark woods, I lost her. I stood still, my heart pounding as I tried not to breathe, straining to listen.

As my eyes adjusted, shapes emerged: tree trunks, brush. The air was cold and smelled of ice and towering pines and river wind. She must be far away now, I knew. Nevertheless, I kept on walking into the woods.

I should have been afraid, but a protective urge had flared inside me. I noted, almost with detachment, that it overrode my other feelings.

How many times I'd lain in bed in the dark, that first year, safely by Charlie's side, listening to the rain and wondering if Mary was out in it, if she had anything to eat, if she was even alive.

I wasn't going to let this girl go. I had seen Mary's face.

Although I knew it was impossible, that didn't matter. It had happened.

I was going to help her. I wasn't going to lose her again.

I bumbled forward until I glimpsed a clearing through the trees. It was more illuminated than the woods around it because of the lack of branches overhead, and it was full of shapes that looked like crooked headstones.

As I got to the edge, I saw that this was exactly what they were. It was an old cemetery, partly overgrown with brush and tall grass. At the far end lay what looked at first like a section of low stone wall, but then I saw that it marked the foundation of a now-gone structure, probably a small church or chapel that had once stood there. Brush grew inside the foundation. The whole world stood quiet and still in the cold moonlight. Could this be where she had gone?

Suddenly, a movement made me realize that a person was sitting in front of a dark bush, on the foundation wall. She was too much in shadow for me to see her clearly, but from her general shape, I thought she was not the same girl I had followed into the woods. She seemed to be wearing something that was not a dress, but a sheet wrapped around her.

Then she shifted again, and I saw something else: she was holding a bundle—no, it was a baby! She was nursing it.

As she turned her head, the light fell on her face. She looked about the same age as the girl I had followed, but her lips were thinner, her hair pale—she was not the same person.

Were they living out here, the two of them, with a baby? Why? It was too cold for an infant and a young mother no older than fifteen or sixteen to be living in the woods.

I stepped into the clearing. "I want to help you," I said.

She sat up stiffly, holding the baby close, scanning the clearing until she spotted me.

"Hello. I want to help," I repeated.

She stood up; her mouth was a thin, determined line, the baby tight against her. Then she turned and scrambled over the stone foundation to the other side. For a moment her shadow blended again with the brush, and she was gone.

I crossed the cemetery, through the leaning and broken headstones, stumbling over some that were hidden by the long, dry grass.

The foundation was full of a froth of brush, a mix of bare twigs and still-clinging foliage: bushes that had grown up from the basement floor. That was what she'd disappeared into.

"Please don't be afraid," I called. "My name is Anna Fort. I want to help you."

There was no movement or sound from the thicket.

"Please!" There was desperation in my voice.

Then, from somewhere outside the churchyard, I heard a voice, that of a child, surely not even as old as the girls I'd seen, calling, "Help us!"

"Who's there?" My eyes searched the dark beyond the ruined church. The woods began again there, even thicker than what I'd come through. I could see nothing. "I want to help! Where are you?"

"I'm here—!"

The words were cut short by a sound like someone falling down onto dry leaves. Or being pushed.

"Where?" Without thinking, I headed into the dark. Who had stopped the child from calling out? Who had pushed her?

"Where?" I called, stumbling forward. "Say something!"

I groped my way forward, blind. Nothing, nothing.

I tripped. My boot laces, tied sloppily, had come undone. Catching myself, I realized I'd gone far from the clearing and was surrounded by darkness. Not even the moonlight could get in here. The boughs of fir trees blotted out the sky. It occurred to me that whoever had stopped the child from speaking knew I was here. Maybe was even waiting for me. I could hear no sound of any kind—no struggling, no voices. I could see nothing.

My heart was already racing; now my arms tingled with panic. What was I doing? I had no idea who could be holding the child, how many of them there were. They could be armed. I was one woman alone, in an unbuttoned overcoat and a flannel nightgown and half-laced boots. No one would even miss me until morning. No one knew where I was.

In fact, *I* didn't know where I was. Even if I could find the clearing, would I be able to get back from there?

I stumbled back in the direction I had come from, tripping over my boot laces again. I bent to tie them. Groped my way forward again. There was only darkness.

Then—so vivid that it seemed to come from outside myself—I heard the clear, familiar voice that hadn't spoken to me for years, the voice of King Nyx, saying, *Stop.*

I did.

Turn right. Walk that way.

Again, I did what it said.

And there was the clearing again.

I passed the ruined church and stood among the headstones. "Now what?" I said out loud. But there was no answer. I searched the graveyard, which, in the moonlight, looked dense and colorless, like an etching. There was the place where I'd entered it. I headed that way.

Then, the voice again: *Yes. Here.*

I was on a deer path now, the same one that had led me there. I kept going; I wasn't sure for how long. Time seemed to bend and flicker. But finally, a light appeared through the woods: the cabins!

I hurried forward, relieved, anxious sweat cooling under my coat. Just as I got to the edge of the trees, where the brown, broken weeds began behind the cabins, a scream shattered the silence.

It was a man's voice, muffled, guttural. It was coming from the Bixbys' cabin.

A rectangle of light still lay on the grass below their window. The curtains were closed, but not all the way. I got close, pressed my face against the glass so I could see through the space between them.

Frank and Stella were in the middle of the cabin's main room. He was in shirtsleeves and suspenders. His face was transformed: he was no longer the nervous man who'd served us at the table, but full of anger.

Stella sat in a chair in front of him, her arms behind her. It looked as if they were tied to the seat back. But her face was strangely calm, even unemotional. Frank paced the room, pausing to shake his head and push the sweat-dampened hair out of his eyes. In one hand he carried a revolver.

He crossed the room one way, then the other, then threw his head back and let out another half-throttled scream like the one I had just heard. It was a sound of pure frustration. One hand grasped his hair as if he wanted to pull it out. Then he went back to pacing. The revolver stayed limply held at his side. Stella's expression didn't change.

Finally, he stopped in the middle of the room and said, in a voice so loud I could make out his words through the window, "It's got to work!"

Still, Stella said nothing. As if infuriated by her lack of response, Frank stepped forward and slapped her.

I let out a sound of surprise. But they remained unaware of me, Frank focused on Stella. Her head had turned from the impact of his hand, and she stayed that way, looking off to the side, as if she didn't want to see him. That was her only reaction. This seemed to anger him even more, and his shoulders heaved as if he wanted to hit her again.

Finally, she turned to look at him and said something I couldn't pick up. Her cheek was red, mascara running from the corner of one eye. But her manner was calm and direct, which again seemed to infuriate Frank.

He lifted the arm with the revolver, but then his other hand grasped it, as if it belonged to someone else, and he flung the gun across the room. Then he raised his clasped hands toward the ceiling, his eyes lifted as if in prayer, and slowly he sank to his knees, his body folding forward onto the floor, his sweaty head in his hands. His shoulders shook as if he was sobbing.

For the second time that night, I debated waking Charles. I decided I had to.

I ran back to our cabin and shook him as hard as I could. "Come!" I said, pulling on his arm. "Something's happening over at the Bixbys' cabin. Frank has a gun."

"Egh, what?" Charlie said thickly, blinking in the lantern light. "The Bixbys!"

He must have heard the urgency in my voice, because he got out of bed and followed me to the door.

I led him toward their window. I couldn't hear any sounds now. Shoulder to shoulder, we put our faces to the glass to look through the gap between the curtains. The wooden chair still sat in the middle of the room. It had leather straps hanging down from the back. It was empty.

"They were there," I said.

"I have no doubt you're right," Charles said. He reached for my hand and squeezed it in what I could tell was meant to be a comforting gesture, but it made me impatient, and I pulled away.

"It looked like he wanted to kill her," I said. "What if he did kill her?" Hysteria was in my voice again.

"We would have heard a gunshot."

"You don't always! Not if the muzzle of the gun is right up against the body!"

"Honestly, Annie," Charles said. "You've been reading too many crime novels." I could hear that he was concerned, too, but was trying to calm me down.

"Please," I begged, "let's go knock on the door. Maybe she needs help." I noticed light coming from another window of their cabin, around the corner. "I think they're in the bedroom," I said. "You go back. I'll look over there."

"No," Charles said firmly. "I'm not leaving you here by your-self. Let's go together."

We headed around the side, keeping away from the cabin wall so we could get a view into the Bixbys' bedroom window. I was surprised to see Frank standing right next to it, looking out, a pipe clamped in his mouth. He was disheveled, his sweaty hair flopped forward onto his face, one suspender hanging loose. I held my arm out and Charles bumped into it and stopped.

"He's right there," I squeaked.

"I see him," Charlie said.

"But where's Stella?"

Charles put his big, soft, firm hand on my arm. "Remember: count to ten, and breathe," he said. More of Dr. Jacobson's advice.

"It's not helping," I whispered.

"Stay here," Charles said firmly. "I'll go talk to him."

I stood still, pinned in place. I was grateful to him for taking charge, for his certainty. No doubt Stella was just fine, and he'd find out she was fine, and I'd be able to calm down.

He walked slowly to the window and knocked on it lightly. Frank looked startled, then raised the sash. "Charles. Everything all right?"

Charlie cleared his throat. "Actually, I just came to see if everything was all right with you. Anna thought she heard . . . a sound or something. Anyway, I promised I'd check."

"Oh." Frank laughed uncomfortably and pushed the hair out of his face. "Yes—everything's quite all right. She must've heard the nightmare. No point trying to hide it, I guess. I suffer from them. 'Physician, heal thyself,' and all that." He sucked air through his teeth, running his fingers through his hair again. "I haven't found the key yet, you see. Not for myself. You'll likely hear more. Not a damn thing I can do about it, I'm afraid."

"Sorry to hear that," said Charles. "Any way we can help?"

Frank shook his head. "I'm on my own with this. Thank you."

My indignation rose as they talked. What I'd seen was not a nightmare. And it was not something Frank was going through alone. Yet Charles seemed to believe him.

Frank closed the window and Charles came back to where I was standing in the dark. I felt his warm hand again on my arm and moved away impatiently in a way that surprised him.

"It wasn't a nightmare," I said. "I saw the two of them in the main room. He had her tied to a chair. He had a gun."

When we got inside our own cabin, Charles stopped and looked at me. "You're sure about that?"

"Yes!"

He began taking off his coat and boots.

"You're sure it couldn't be the old . . . ?"

"It's not the hysteria, I'm telling you," I said, my voice cracking, undermining my words. "I *saw* it."

"I believe you," he said, reaching out his hand. "I've always believed you."

"Then why did you act like you believed Frank when he said it was a nightmare?"

Charles was already getting into bed. "That's different. You saw it one way, he saw it another," he said, rolling over.

I didn't know how to answer this. Frank had lied. Or at least he hadn't told the whole truth. But Charlie's confidence in him was like a wall I couldn't get past.

"Did you see Stella?" I asked. "Was she in the room?"

"Sleeping behind him," Charlie said.

I wanted to be satisfied by this, but I still worried. What if she hadn't been sleeping, but . . . dead? No, that *was* hysterical. She couldn't be.

"Why were you out there in the first place, anyway?" Charlie asked. "Just to spy on them?"

"No . . ."

"Why, then?"

I couldn't tell the whole story, about seeing Mary, about going after her alone. But I had to tell him something. "I saw lights . . . in the woods," I began.

His drowsiness disappeared. "Eh? What kind of lights?"

"They were moving," I said, which was truthful enough. I just didn't mention that they were (I was sure) lanterns being carried by girls or by someone deep among the trees.

"Moving lights? In the woods?"

"I'm sure they weren't supernatural," I said quickly.

"Nothing is *super*natural, Annie," Charlie said. He was excited now, sitting up, ready to lecture me. "All is natural, even that which Science can't explain. Take the spherical lights in the ravine in Russia in the summer of 1880, reported in *L'année scientifique*—" He was in his element, reeling off names and dates he kept filed in his head. "Luminous bodies near Toronto in 1913, moving with 'peculiar, majestic deliberation'—that's from the *Journal of the Royal Astronomical Society of Canada*. All perfectly natural—and all unexplained."

"I don't know if those lights were like that," I said lamely, but he was not even listening. He'd gotten out of bed and was opening the window.

"Were they over that way?" He leaned out, scanning the woods, not seeming to notice the ransacked trunks that were almost right in front of him.

"I think they were that way, yes, but . . . "

"It must have been an extraordinary sight, if it made you go outside." He turned to look at me with new appreciation.

"It was," I said faintly, wishing I could back out of the story, but not knowing how.

"You didn't try to follow them, did you?"

"I did, a little bit . . . but I lost them."

Charles looked out again. "I don't see anything now, but I wouldn't be at all surprised if they come back. The false beacons of Durham in the winter of 1865 and '66, you know, appeared over several weeks, to many people—that's according to the London *Times*. I always wondered if one day I'd get to witness the things I write about." Then, his voice hushed with surprise, he said: "It's why he invited me. It must be." He turned to me, his face bright. "Mr. Arkel wants me to investigate. Why else would he choose me, of all people? A man with my eccentric interests, why would one want me, unless one shared those interests?"

He closed the window and came back to sit on the bed. "Maybe the missing girls are part of it, too."

"I thought you didn't even believe in them."

"You know perfectly well that such things do happen. Take the disappearance of the crew of the *Mary Celeste* in 1872, for example. Or the crowd that vanished from on the quay of Lisbon during the earthquake of 1755."

How had my stupid remark caused all this? I'd meant to say something that would stop him from asking questions. Instead he was more excited than I had ever seen him. How had he gone from skeptical and rational to this in just a few minutes? But so many strange things had happened since we got that unexpected invitation, since we arrived on this island . . . it did almost seem that anything could be true, that maybe neither of us had any idea what was or wasn't.

Charlie tried to settle down again, head cradled in the big down pillows. He pulled up the blanket and clasped his hands happily on his chest. "I've found someone who values my work, Annie. I don't expect you to be as excited as I am," he said generously, turning to me. "But soon you'll see. You will."

He lay lost in his thoughts, as I was lost in mine.

Stella wasn't dead. I knew she wasn't dead . . . I realized with a start that the room was cooling. I got up to see if the birds were chilled. They looked the same, huddled on their perch. I put more wood in the stove and moved it around with the black iron poker until the fire flared. Charlie mumbled a sleepy thanks. Eventually, I managed to sleep, too.

TEN

LATER, I EMERGED FROM A THICKET OF SLEEP INTO darkness. I had dreamed about Mary, for the first time in years. In my dream I was in the cemetery I'd found that night, and she was standing on the church foundation. Flames licked at the edges of a big bush that stood behind her. She had matted hair, like the girl I'd seen by the trunks, and she was wrapped in a sheet, like the girl with the baby. A caption over her head, written in ink on the air, read "MARY-IN-THE-WOODS."

She spread her arms, as if in blessing, and said, *I'm right here,* in the clear voice of King Nyx.

I woke up, unsettled. I tried to remember other details. It had been raining, or something had been falling from the sky—small living creatures—insects? Had there also been the sound of a piano? The faint images faded like starglow in the hard light of my waking consciousness.

Mary had asked me to run away with her that night. Begged me. She kept saying, "It's dangerous here." And this had something to do, I recalled—trying to pull it from the jumble of things that had happened around my breakdown—had something to do with my telling her about the blood that fell on my face that afternoon in May.

It was strange how different people reacted so differently to the Event. Some I didn't tell because I already knew how they'd respond—Cook, for example, wouldn't have believed me for a second.

Dr. Jacobson said it was part of my breakdown, a simple hysterical hallucination. Charles understood it, along with my notebook entries, as evidence of occurrences that Science could not explain.

But before them, Mary was the first one I ever told. It was early September. We were in our room in the attic. Her face had transformed in the candlelight, with fear. Something she couldn't communicate. Something I remembered thinking of as insanity.

She said she was leaving. That she couldn't stay another day, couldn't wait to look for another position, even wait till the morning to tell Mrs. Fort she was going.

I remembered being torn between the desire to protect her and the knowledge that leaving the stable job and home I'd had for nine years would be madness. Neither of us had savings—I because of sending money to my father, Mary because she'd only started that summer. Running away with her would have meant sleeping in haylofts, stealing food. I'd never be able to return— the Forts would never take me back if I left without notice.

So I watched helplessly as she climbed out the attic window with a pillowcase over her shoulder. That was the last I saw of her.

She was crazy, I told myself. She'd run away before, and now she'd done it again.

In bed that night after she left, I heard King Nyx's voice hissing: *She was right.*

Right about what? Right to leave? This voice had once comforted me, but over the whole past summer had whispered only disturbing, meaningless things: *It's blood between the floorboards!* Why?

This, on the night Mary left, was the last straw.

"No," I said aloud to King Nyx in the dark. "I renounce you! Go!"

I was determined to stay in the world of light and order and sanity.

I realized that night that I should never have told Mary about the Event. For her, it must have shattered normalcy as she understood it. It was a terrifying breach of reality. But why run away? Had she thought she could run away from *that*?

I, on the other hand, understood it not as a refutation of reality, but simply an anomaly, one dropped stitch in a vast, mostly intact fabric.

My research in the library that Sunday confirmed that the fall of blood had not subverted the natural order of the universe, that the world was exactly as I had always understood it, with the exception of some unusual phenomena—flesh or blood occasionally raining from the sky—that I had not previously known about.

But God, I thought, lying in my bed next to Charles, how had I let her go that night? I was an adult. She was a broken child. It was unforgivable that I'd stood and watched her slip away, through the window of our room, into the darkness.

In my dream, Mary-in-the-woods, in her white winding sheet, had spread her hands and said, in a calm, clear voice, *I'm right here.* It had felt like a blessing.

Mary said ghosts came back to settle things. I thought now: *Maybe her ghost came to me in that dream. Maybe to bless me. Maybe to tell me that although I could never repay the debt, it could be forgiven.*

But then what about the person I had seen last night at the trunks? Did that mean she was not a ghost?

I opened my eyes with a jerk. The dark was dissolving. The wild birds had woken outside, their thin cries of triumph sharp as bare black twigs and thin, shining icicles: *We're alive! Still alive!*

The bedroom was filling with light. It was cold. The stove must have gone out.

The stove! I threw the covers off and rushed to the twins' cage.

They were on the floor again, sitting in the chopped straw, puffed up, and wouldn't look at me. I wrestled the stove door open and used the poker to find the embers under the ash. I took bark and newspaper from the kindling box, blew until I got a flame, fed it till I got a larger one, and put the wood in.

These actions brought back, as if they leapt from the stove through the open door, more memories, this time from early in our marriage: the stove in our apartment in Hell's Kitchen, when we were so poor after Charlie's father disowned him for marrying me. It had been a coal stove, but when there was no money for coal, we'd burned a stool, then a rickety side table, and then a child-sized rocking chair that was loose in the joints; filled with hope, we had bought it from a junk shop. I remembered Charles stomping them all apart with his big worn boots, both of us too miserable even to care what our neighbors thought of the noise.

When there was nothing left to burn, I went to work in the laundry in the Beekman Hotel. The hours were so long that the laundresses had to board in a basement room crammed with bunks, hot with steam and smelling of laundry soap. Charles stayed home working on the book he promised would lift us out of poverty, but it didn't. Eventually, through the help of a friend, he got a newspaper job, and we climbed out of that place into our comfortable apartment on Ryer Avenue in the Bronx.

When Charles was fired, I saw the specter of that life return. He said he'd never work for a paper again—he wasn't going to be muzzled; he was going to finish his book and tell the truth. We'd just have to give up our place and go back to something cheaper. We couldn't keep paying for the upkeep of my parakeets; they would all have to go.

That was what we'd been planning when the letter from Mr. Arkel came, out of the blue, and unexpectedly opened another path. Charles could finish his book here, we'd use the last of our money to pay rent on our apartment through the winter and into the spring, and we'd have no other expenses, except paying Mrs. Binns, the veterinarian's assistant, to take care of the nineteen birds I wasn't bringing. When we got back, there would be no more worries. Mr. Dreiser said he was sure of it, and that was what gave us the most hope. Doors would open, he said. Money would come.

But was it worth it? Risking Castor and Pollux's lives? Putting ourselves at the mercy of this mysterious, strange man?

Things are going on here which are not right. That's what the letter said.

What was going on?

I slammed the door shut on the roaring flame and looked over again at Castor and Pollux. They were shaking their ruffled green heads and sneezing, maybe from the smoke or ash that had gotten into the air while I was building the fire. I moved them gently away from the stove, to one of the chairs by the dinner table, but then worried that the cage was unstable and they would be too cold. My eyes stung with frustration.

And Stella! I had almost put the scene from the Bixbys' cabin out of my mind. I wanted to see her, wanted to see that she was all right. I remembered her expressionless face, a single streak of black mascara on her red cheek, her calm manner. She hadn't struggled, had not seemed afraid. If only I could get to her, my questions could be answered.

The light changed from grayish orange to a clear morning brightness. I dressed near the stove, then propped my hand mirror on the desk in the bedroom to put my hair up. There was my familiar face, always looking a bit older and more serious than I expected. Charlie called it a dear face, and I thought of it as a serviceable one; that had always been enough for me. I wondered how one managed to look glamorous, like Stella, and if it would be worth the effort. Judging by how Frank had treated her last night, maybe not.

Outside, the air was sharp and cold. The grass was still frosted, but not as stiff as the night before. I could see everything more clearly than I had when we'd arrived: our cabin, the Bixbys' and the one that stood between, and two more, arranged in a loose row at the edge of the orchard, with its gnarled, unkempt trees. Long grass and withered apples lay among them. Everything was gray and brown, with an occasional surprise of yellow here and there, on the trees or on the ground: November colors. The sky was blue and streaked with clouds.

When I knocked at the Bixbys' door, there was no answer. I stood there for a few minutes, then knocked again, louder. Still nothing.

My pulse quickened. *Don't be stupid*, I told myself. *It's not as if she's dead. She wouldn't be dead.* Yet I could not get myself to calm down. I decided to go around to the bedroom window.

Its curtains were drawn, and I couldn't see inside. I felt now that I had to get to her, that it was urgent. Almost involuntarily, I found myself banging loudly on the window with the flat of my palm.

The curtains were yanked open and the sash raised so fast that I almost fell forward. Frank, standing there in striped pajamas, looked shocked.

"I'm sorry," I faltered, trying to collect myself. "I thought you would be up." As if that was any reason for me to pound on their bedroom window.

"We weren't," said Frank, looking at me with his keen blue eyes. "Are you all right? Your face is flushed."

"I'm absolutely fine," I said, flustered, touching my cheek. "I just—I wanted to ask Stella something." Why wouldn't he move out of the way so I could see her?

"She's sleeping. Can't you ask me?"

"No, it's a female question." What was I saying? That was what had popped into my head.

Frank gave me that shrewd, unsettling look again, as if he knew something I didn't know about myself. Then he turned to the bed, and as he did, I could see Stella. She stirred slightly: asleep, not dead.

"Darling," he began.

"No, don't wake her," I said quickly. "I'll ask later."

Frank turned back to me. "Are you sure? I got a sense of urgency from your . . . knocking."

"I'm sure. Thank you."

Before I could go, Frank surprised me by saying, "Anyhow. You and I are both up. Let's have coffee. I'll put the kettle on."

His face showed no shadow of either the anger I'd seen through the window or the harried, almost haunted expression he had had when we were all together.

"Well?" He smiled, and I realized I had been studying his face without answering. I smiled back automatically. "You look tired," he said. "Let's sit out on the porch. Coffee and cold morning air are both good for the nerves."

He could have been irritated with me for banging on his window like a crazy person, but instead he was being kind. Grateful, I smiled again.

"Is that your professional opinion, Doctor? I guess I'd better, then."

As I sat beside him on the cabin's porch, looking out at the abandoned orchard, I did feel calmer. The events of the night before seemed to belong to another world. I almost felt I could decide, if I wanted to, that none of it had happened. I could choose this reality—the bright, frosty morning, the smell of the coffee, blue steam in the air, the cup in my hands, warm and solid.

In any case, whatever I had accidentally seen through the window was their business, not mine. That seemed clear now.

I would try to get Stella alone later, though, and just check that she was all right. And as long as she was, I wouldn't ask about what had happened. Maybe it was some private sexual game. I had heard stories of such things. Or maybe they were rehearsing for a play. If they wanted us to know about it, they'd tell us, and if they didn't, there was no reason to bring it up.

But as for the girl at the trunk, ghost Mary . . .

There was no rational cast I could put on that. I *knew* what I had seen. Didn't I?

As I traced the night's events in my memory, from the half-lit area behind the cabins, to the ruined church, to the blackness beyond, they seemed less and less plausible. The girl behind the cabin had been so clear, but that voice in the blackness later, saying, "Help us!"—was I sure *that* had been real?

Frank was gazing at the orchard. He turned to me, one eyebrow raised, as if interested to hear whatever I was going to say.

"Frank," I began. "Did you hear anything outside last night?"

"Hear anything? Why, did you?"

"I did," I admitted.

"An animal?"

I hesitated. "It wasn't an animal."

"No?" He cocked his head.

I hadn't meant to tell the whole story, but now the words came quickly, as if they wanted to escape before I could stop them. "I saw a girl taking things from the trunks. She was wearing a bearskin cape. I think she was one of the girls who— Oh, I didn't tell you about that."

I stopped, flustered. I could feel my cheeks heating. I had meant for the detail about the bearskin to make the story more specific and believable, but now I realized it had made it sound crazier. On top of that, I couldn't remember whether Frank knew about the ladies at the dock and the missing girls. Hadn't I only mentioned it to Stella?

Frank set his cup down on the arm of his chair. "Tell me about what?" he asked. There was quiet encouragement in his voice, as if he was talking to a child.

"When Charles and I were at the dock in Clayton," I said, "we met some people." I faltered. His tone, his expression—he was being polite, but he thought I was crazy.

"What sort of people?"

"Three women, with a petition."

"Ah, yes. The one about the missing girls."

"Yes . . . " I remembered then that Stella had mentioned it. She'd said they hadn't signed.

"And maybe you think the girl taking things from the trunk was one of them?" Frank asked gently.

"I don't know."

I had told the story in a rush, interrupting myself and doubling back in a disorganized way. What if Frank was right to think I was crazy? He was a psychologist, after all.

"She was wearing a bearskin, you say?" It sounded impossible coming from him.

"It . . . looked like she was."

"Do you want to go around back and examine the trunks together?" he suggested.

"Yes," I said quickly. Then he'd see—and I'd see—that they really *had* been broken into.

We walked around to the back of the cabins. The two trunks stood open, drawers pulled out, just as I had seen the night before.

"Someone has certainly been here," Frank said, going closer. "The locks have been smashed. This doesn't look like the work of an animal, not even a bear." He held up a bent piece of metal. "It's been hit with something heavy. And the small latches on the drawers have been undone. By human hands, I'm sure of it."

Relief washed through me. He believed me.

He bent to examine the things scattered on the ground: napkins, dish covers. He picked something up and held it out. "Weren't you wearing this last night?" he asked.

It was the bracelet with the heart-shaped clasp. My hand flew to my wrist: it wasn't there.

I remembered how I had been rubbing the clasp nervously between my fingers as I approached the back of the cabins. I must have accidentally pushed the lever that opened it.

"It is mine," I said.

As Frank handed it to me, he caught my eye. His were pale blue under his sandy brows. I couldn't read his expression.

"I thought you saw someone out your window."

"Yes—"

"But you were here."

I imagined trying to explain that I'd run out in my nightgown and half-laced boots. That when she ran I followed her deep into the woods. By myself. At night. That I'd found a girl nursing a baby by a churchyard . . . heard a voice calling, *Help us . . .*

"I don't remember being out here at all." I was mumbling but couldn't seem to make my voice any louder.

"Yet you were." He paused. "Do you ever sleepwalk?"

I felt relief then. Sleepwalking was preferable to what I feared he thought: that I was lying or, worse, had hallucinated. "Maybe."

He cast another glance at the mess on the ground and said, "Come on." We walked back to the porch.

"Do you think it might have been a dream, Anna, seeing that girl?"

His voice was kind. I nodded, and he nodded along with me.

"I study dreams, so I understand that they can feel very real." He paused, thinking. "It's warming up a bit. Would you like to go for a walk? Also good for the nerves."

I found I did want to. I felt that staying in his company would keep me in the bright, rational world, and that was where I wanted to be. Part of me was relieved to consign the girls to the realm of the imaginary.

Frank began to head for the woods, but I hesitated.

"Don't want to go?" he asked, looking back.

"I'm worried my husband might miss me," I said, imagining Charlie worrying.

"Oh, he'll be all right." Frank smiled. "He can live without you for half an hour. Come."

ELEVEN

FRANK POINTED TO A PATH LEADING INTO THE TREES. IT was different from the one I had taken the night before. "We're allowed to go this way, toward the water. That way"—he turned and gestured—"is the rest of the island, including the house, and it's out of bounds while we're in quarantine."

Had I been out of bounds last night? I wasn't sure.

"What happens if we go that way?" I asked.

"The fellow with the gun makes you go back."

I remembered Stella telling me the night before about the private detectives who patrolled the grounds, enforcing the quarantine. "Is he dangerous?"

"No," Frank said, amused. "It happened to us the first day. They're just servants, you know. Here to help. Look, there's a nice view if we walk this way—follow me."

As we entered the woods, Frank picked up a long branch and began breaking the twigs off to turn it into a rough walking stick. When he was done, he held it out in front of himself, looked at it approvingly, then offered it to me. I took it, and he found another branch to make one for himself.

"I'm not surprised you had a disturbing dream last night," Frank said. "It's normal to feel out of sorts in a new location, and this place . . . "

"What about it?" I asked, eager for anything else he might be able to tell me.

He shook his head, one corner of his mouth twitching. Finally, he glanced around, as if someone might be there to over-hear us, then at me. "I'll tell you a secret," he said in a low voice. "I've been here before."

"Have you?" I was surprised.

"Stella wasn't here," Frank said. "I came without her, in a professional capacity."

"You mean you treated someone here?" I asked. "For psycho-logical problems?"

"That's all I can say," he answered quietly. Then, at a more normal volume, he said, "Let's go sit out on those rocks. There's a nice view." He pointed to where we could now see the river flash-ing blue-gray through the trees. We came to a stony place where a narrow finger of land stretched into the water. "This is called All Souls Point. We can go sit there," he said, gesturing toward a large boulder out near the end. He watched as I picked up my skirt to make my way among the stones. When the footing got uneven, he took my elbow.

Out on the rock, we were surrounded by water, and silence.

"Better to talk here," Frank said in a low voice. "Because we can see there's no one nearby."

"Who would be?" I asked.

"Oh, those private detectives Mr. Arkel has running around." Frank stirred the river water with the end of his stick. Then he looked up at me. "Our host is a bit odd. An admirable man, as I said. But it might be helpful for you to understand some of his . . . " He hesitated. "Peculiarities. Last night, I said that the rumors about him aren't true. Officially, that's all I know. But privately I can tell you, they're not rumors."

"You mean—he does have an underground chamber full of—"

"Lifelike dolls, automatons, I'm not sure what to call them. Yes. You see, I came here some months ago to treat him for recurring nightmares he was having as a result of his late wife Gertrude's death."

"How did she die?" I asked slowly.

"Hunting accident. I've mentioned that Mr. Arkel is a great hunter, haven't I? Apparently she was horseback riding and strayed into a part of the island where she wasn't supposed to be. Another reason it's a good idea to pay attention to the rules."

"And he . . . shot her?"

"Horrible tragedy. He was plagued by nightmares afterward. Always the same: He saw himself walking into the woods against his will, as if he were a puppet, a marionette on strings. As he approached the area where she died, he fought to wake up, and always did—screaming. He was convinced it was her controlling him, from beyond the grave—and that if he ever reached the clearing where she fell, he, too, would die. It got to the point where he couldn't sleep for fear. Lack of sleep, in turn, brought on feebleness, hallucinations. He contacted me in desperation."

I tried to picture Mr. Arkel looking haggard, with dark circles under his eyes. But instead it was Mr. Fort who appeared in my imagination, hair uncombed, eyes wild in a way I had never seen in real life—he'd been a meticulous, well-dressed man. I pushed the disturbing image away.

"So you cured him," I said.

"I did."

"With your . . . machine?"

"Yes."

"Does it always help?"

"Almost always." Frank's eyes flicked over my face, and I had the feeling that he could see my desperation to be fixed. "But back to what I wanted to tell you. I learned a bit about him while I was here." Frank glanced around again, but there was only gray water lapping against the stones. "He admitted that he did have a room full of these—life-sized figures. He said that they were modeled on people he knew. Some moved—one combed her hair—and another sang by means of a small record player inside the chest cavity. He wanted to know what I, as a doctor of psychology, made of that—what it said about him. I said it meant nothing, of course—it was just a harmless hobby. But privately, I have other ideas."

"What are they?"

"Claude Arkel is a man who can't be crossed. You heard the story of the strike, what happened to the workers. Later, his only son, Horace, dared to criticize how he handled it, and he cut him out of his will—his only heir. Of course, a businessman like him is apt to be strong-willed. But I think with him, it goes further. I think he has a mania for power. You saw his motto on the archway by the dock; it translates to 'No power on earth compares to him.' I realized his dream about being a marionette was an expression of that, too. Because, you see, it's precisely men who worship power who never have enough. Who become fixated on the idea that others are trying to control them. That's what I wanted to tell you: whatever we do, we must be careful not to cross him."

"You don't think," I asked quietly, "that his first wife, Gertrude, could have crossed him before she died, do you?"

Frank looked at me with his keen blue eyes. "I won't venture an opinion. But I do hope," he added, "that his new wife is wise enough not to do so."

"What does it all have to do with those dolls?"

"I believe," said Frank, "that he keeps them because he feels most comfortable surrounded by others who have no will of their own. He sent me a letter inviting me to come back and spend the winter. He said it was to work on my monograph on aversive electrical psychotherapeutic methods, but I suspect he may be struggling again, mentally, and that's his real reason for wanting me here. Certain things he said when I was here the first time led me to believe he might be on the verge of mental disintegration." Frank glanced around, then lowered his voice again: "I think his underground doll collection is an attempt to experience a state of perfect control, something that, to his deep frustration, he has not been able to create aboveground. My concern is that one day he might be tempted to try."

"Try what?"

"Who's to say? He's the king here, isn't he—on his own private island. He'd be stopped eventually, of course, but what might a man do who craves absolute control and has the power to enact it?" There was a faraway yet intent look in Frank's eye, as if he was studying something important in the distance. "What might any of us do?"

"Do you assume everyone would do something awful if they could?"

Frank turned to me as if surprised, and studied my face. "There's something very naïve and innocent about you, isn't there?" he said.

I did not consider myself naïve. I had seen plenty growing up in rooming houses with my father. "I just believe that some people are good," I said.

"Many people are good on the surface," said Frank dismissively. "But if you'd earned a degree in psychology as I have, you'd know that the human mind is like an ocean. The deeper you go, the stranger and uglier the monsters that live down there in the dark. And it goes *very* deep. Indeed, I suspect it has no bottom."

A chill wind came across the water, and I crossed my arms. It lifted Frank's sandy hair and pushed it back from his face, and his eyes narrowed against it.

"I heard," I said, "that the local police are afraid to come here to Prosper Island—afraid of Mr. Arkel. Do you think that's true?"

"Yes," said Frank, stirring the water again with his stick. He looked up at me. "And they're right to be."

I heard the buzzing of anxiety in the distance. To distract myself, I said, "Do you know why this is called All Souls Point?"

"The whole place used to be called All Souls Island, before Mr. Arkel purchased it. Commemorating the day over a hundred years ago when a man named Abel Root discovered it. It's All Souls' Day today, you know. And here we are discovering the island anew, in our own way." He smiled at me. We were silent for a moment, looking out over the water. "They say old Abel gave a pair of oxen to an Iroquois chief for the right to occupy the island for ninety-nine years," Frank went on. "But by the time ninety-nine years had passed, so many of the Iroquois people had been killed or driven away that they never got it back."

"That doesn't seem fair."

Frank shrugged. "To the victor go the spoils. Lots of victors around these islands, then and now. Powerful men. Captains of industry. Men who make their own rules."

I wondered how he could talk that way. Did he see it all as some kind of tennis game, where the winner and loser shook hands after, and then maybe went upstairs to dress for dinner in the grand country house where they were all guests together? Where nothing was at stake that really mattered? I felt his dismissiveness was wrong, but also, I envied it.

"All Souls' is a day to remember the dead," I said. I tried to imagine the families who had lived in this beautiful place before Abel Root came and claimed to discover it. Had they sat where we were sitting, on a warm summer day, looking out across the river? Had one of them swum in the water and then lain here and dried her hair in the sun, thinking of people in her own life she had once loved who she had failed to keep?

Frank seemed lost in his own thoughts. He stared down at the walking stick he had made and picked at a piece of bark on it. Then he looked up at me.

"Here's a curious little thing I learned when I was studying under Professor William James," he said. "Did you know that in certain towns in the north of England, a pre-Christian tradition persists of remembering the dead not in the autumn, but at Eastertide? Women of childbearing age bring eggs to the cemeteries and lay them on the graves, or sometimes bury them. It's a fertility ritual. Supposed to bring a fruitful harvest and lots of babies in the coming year."

This made me think of the shroud-wrapped girl I'd seen nursing her baby on the foundation of the ruined church.

"Penny for your thoughts," Frank said.

"I wasn't thinking about anything," I lied.

Frank gave me another one of those canny looks. He knew something was troubling me. "Do you have children?" he asked.

"Just the twins," I said jokingly, wanting to lighten the mood.

"Twins?" he said, impressed, and I realized with a flash of embarrassment that he didn't know I meant the birds.

"Oh," I said, "I meant my parakeets. Castor and Pollux. They hatched from the same egg. Sometimes eggs have double yolks, you know. Usually the hatchlings are too small to survive. But I nursed them, and they lived."

"Aha," Frank said. "Of course. And you treat them like princes, your bird children. They're very lucky. It's too bad you don't have any real children. I'll bet you'd be a good mother."

I bristled at this—was it really too bad I didn't have "real" children? I hadn't wanted them. But, still flustered from the misunderstanding, I only thanked him.

"Shall we go back?" he asked.

I smiled at him as he helped me over the rocks again. He had an old-fashioned, gallant way about him sometimes. Charles was often too lost in his own thoughts to remember to be chivalrous. Soon we were back in the woods.

"Stella's infertile," Frank said abruptly. Surprised and embarrassed to hear him blurt out something so personal, I couldn't think how to answer. "So we're childless, too," he continued.

"I'm sorry," I said.

"It's probably for the best. I don't think she likes children."

I glanced at his face. He seemed to pull himself with effort away from this train of thought. "So, what do you do with your spare time? What are your hobbies?" he asked.

"Charlie and I like to go to the movies," I offered, glad to have something else to talk about. "We saw an interesting version of Jules Verne's *Twenty Thousand Leagues Under the Sea* last month. It was made a couple of years ago, but they'd brought it back to the movie house we like to go to. It had some *Mysterious Island* mixed in. Have you ever read that book? Some explorers were in a dirigible and it crash-landed on an island where there was a young woman in a leopard skin living in the woods—" I was chattering, trying to get away from the awkwardness.

"I mean," Frank interrupted, "what do *you* like to do? You, yourself?"

"Oh, when I have any time outside of housekeeping and cooking, I help Charlie with his research, mostly. I try to be useful. I really believe it's going to be his masterpiece, this book."

The truth was, I had more doubts than ever, especially after the disaster of trying to explain Charlie's work to Frank and Stella the night before, but I didn't want to say that.

"You're such an old-fashioned girl," Frank said approvingly. "Your interests are helping your husband." He looked at me. "I can see it in the way you dress, too."

I glanced down at my long tweed walking skirt and realized I did look old-fashioned. It was probably fifteen years old. "Well, it's a good, warm skirt. I didn't see the need to replace it, and Charles doesn't mind."

"That's where you're different from Stella," Frank said. "She has to have all the latest fashions."

Without breaking stride, he snapped a dead twig off a tree, a shadow crossing his face.

"That's just a superficial thing, clothes," I said, wanting to defend her. "At heart we're both wives. I'm sure she puts as much effort into helping you as I do into helping Charles."

Frank gave an unhappy laugh and didn't answer.

Why was it anyway, I thought, that wives were supposed to help husbands with their books and never got their names on the covers?

After a minute, Frank said, "Today's a day of remembrance. There ought to be a day of forgetting."

"Yes," I said, "a Feast of Saint Lethe."

If there were, I thought, I'd pray to her to put the memories of Mary back where they came from. Had I chosen to release them by opening that notebook? Had I brought about my own mental disintegration?

Or maybe the thing I'd summoned last night was real.

Frank, seemingly distracted by his own thoughts, hit a tree with his walking stick as he passed. Then another. "Makes a nice loud sound," he said. He stopped and swung it hard, like a baseball bat, and I heard it crack. Then he stomped on it until it broke, and threw the halves into the woods.

The violence of his actions surprised me. But then he turned to me with a face that was calm.

"You look pale," he said.

"I'm fine."

"There's something you're struggling with, isn't there?"

I avoided his eyes.

"Something in your past," he pressed. "Some*one*?"

"I've been thinking about an old friend," I admitted. "Years ago . . . she ran away. I never found out what happened to her."

Frank was silent, and I found myself filling the space with words.

"She wanted me to go with her," I said. "She was only sixteen, not old enough to be on her own. I always wondered if I could have talked her into going back. Maybe she'd still be alive. I failed her."

Frank studied me sympathetically. "Do you know," he said, "it's possible that's why you never had children."

"I don't understand."

"It's called hysterical infertility. Sometimes when we convince ourselves that we don't deserve something, it doesn't happen. Your guilt over your friend could be what's standing in your way." He paused. "That can be cured with hypnosis, you know. I'll bet Charles would like to have a little boy, wouldn't he? Someone to pass his name on to, and his work? Or a pretty little girl? Wouldn't you like that?"

I didn't know how to tell him that I hadn't really wanted children, and certainly didn't now. "I'm forty-six," I said.

"Are you still menstruating?" he asked, with a doctor's bluntness.

"Well, yes," I said, embarrassed.

"I've known women to give birth through their late forties and even, in rare cases, past fifty," he said. "So it's not too late." He must have seen that I looked uncomfortable. "Hypnosis can also bring peace of mind about your friend," he said.

That was something I wanted. "What's it like?" I asked. "Is it sort of like dreaming? Would I see her?"

"Yes," Frank said, "it would feel very much like seeing her. You could even talk to her."

I imagined standing again on that hilltop where we'd had our picnic, the summer sun bright on Mary's face. If I had the chance to see her again, what would I say? That I was sorry? That I had never forgotten her?

But I had forgotten her. Dr. Jacobson had told me to, and I had, almost.

Maybe what I needed was not a Saint Lethe to help me forget; maybe what I needed was to remember.

Maybe then Mary would forgive me.

TWELVE

"WHEN WE GET BACK," FRANK SAID, "IF STELLA'S STILL
asleep, I can try some hypnosis on you. All right?"

I nodded, but then remembering last night's dinner conversation, I said, "I thought you'd stopped doing that."

"Oh, I still do hypnosis. It's just the machine I've stopped
using, mostly." He gave me a quick smile. "As far as Stella knows."

What exactly had they been fighting about? "It's safe?" I
asked tentatively.

Frank scoffed. "Perfectly." He seemed on the verge of saying something else, but changed his mind. "God, that woman,"
he muttered.

"What?"

"I'm sorry." He smiled apologetically. "I shouldn't draw you
into our squabbles. It's just sometimes, she seems to take positive
pleasure in undermining me. It's a shame. We used to get along."

I wanted to ask if he planned to use his machine on me, but
now I worried that the question would upset him.

"This friend of yours," he said, "why did she run away?"

"I don't know," I answered slowly. It had been such a long

time since anyone had asked about the events surrounding her leaving, and they were jumbled in my memory now, like puzzle pieces thrown into a box. "Something upset her. It was something I said."

Frank made a sympathetic sound, as if he understood that this must be painful for me. I looked at him walking beside me in his well-cut tweed coat, with his firm chin, the definite set of his mouth, and I realized I felt about him the same way I'd felt about Dr. Jacobson—that maybe he could help me.

Then came a sudden, unbidden image: of a birdcage, slightly larger than mine, and square, sitting on the grass—where? The Forts' yard in Albany. The cage door was open, and two little green birds hopped up from the floor to the lip of the door to look out, uncertain . . . then lifted off, flying. The sky was gray; it was autumn. I watched them go higher and higher.

"Now I know there's something on your mind," Frank said, noticing that I had stopped walking. "Tell me."

"I just remembered something I did right after my friend left," I said. Frank cocked his head to show he was interested. "*He* kept parakeets, too," I said suddenly.

"Who did?"

"Mr. Fort. Charlie's father. I had forgotten. I think I let them go. Outside. Even though I knew winter was coming . . . and I think they died."

A sense of guilt draped itself over me like a shroud.

I felt Frank's hand on my back and realized he had put it there to steady me. "I see you're struggling with some difficult memories," he said quietly.

"I must have been crazy. I went crazy after she left."

I looked at him as if he could give me some kind of reassurance—that I hadn't been, or that I wasn't now. His expression did not convey either of those, exactly, but there was sympathy in it, as if, whatever I was going through, it was going to be all right.

After a moment, he said, "Come on." He moved his palm from my back and gently took my hand, encouraging me to keep walking. "What was it you said that upset her so much?" he asked.

"I told her about something that happened . . . " I began.

I'd told her about the Event. *That's* what had upset her. Part of me didn't want to tell Frank about it; but another part of me did, very much.

"I was walking behind the house," I said. "It was a clear day in late May. There was a bright blue sky, no clouds."

"Your house?" Frank said.

I shook my head, but didn't elaborate. I wasn't ready to tell him I had been a maid in Charlie's father's house.

I stopped then, closing my eyes, and saw the day again in my memory. The high grass, the white-and-yellow daisies, the sound of Mr. Fort's voice raised in anger. I'd heard it that afternoon, hadn't I? It was not unusual. Everyone got yelled at, especially Betsy, who'd been the head housemaid at the time. It was no wonder she kept her own apartment instead of living with the Forts—at least she had somewhere to retreat to at night. Around the time she left, he was yelling at her even more than usual. I must have heard his voice coming from one of the open windows.

"I was walking behind the house, when suddenly—" I stopped. "It sounds silly," I said, "that's the thing. It sounds impossible."

"What does?"

"I just felt something warm splash my face. And then I could see it on the white flowers near me. Red droplets. I touched my cheek and—blood." I held my hand out, looking at it, remembering. "I know it's hard to believe."

"Where did the blood come from?" asked Frank.

"It came from nowhere," I said. "A perfectly clear blue sky."

"And it was this incident that upset your friend, when you told her about it?"

"Yes. She said the place we were in was bad—evil, she used

that word. She said we had to leave right away. She begged me to go with her. But I didn't. I never saw her again."

"Why do you think she said those things?"

"Because it just . . . didn't make sense, for blood to fall from a clear blue sky. Because it broke the rules."

We were within sight of the cabins now, and Frank stopped just before the edge of the woods.

"What rules?" he asked.

"The rules of reality," I said. "I mean . . . that can't happen. But it did." What was he thinking, looking at me with those inscrutable blue eyes? "Am I insane, Dr. Bixby?" I blurted.

"No," he murmured.

"I know it happened. Charlie . . . "

"What?"

"He believes me."

Frank nodded. I remembered how he'd looked the night before when Charlie was trying to explain his theories.

"It's been documented," I said. "All over the world, throughout history. Really. You can look through the archives of any scientific journal in the world."

"That's what your husband's book is about, isn't it?"

"Yes, I found a few incidents after it happened to me. I copied them into a notebook," I said. "I guess I was trying to prove to myself that I wasn't crazy. When I showed Charlie, he looked in the journals and saw the articles himself. He was fascinated. He's found hundreds since them." I was still afraid that Frank didn't believe me. "It's true. You'll see when you get back. You can go to any library . . . "

Frank bit his lip thoughtfully, holding my gaze. "You're sure?" he asked.

"Yes!"

He smiled and put a hand on my arm. "It's all right, I believe you," he said. "Are you afraid I don't?"

"I . . . I mean . . . " I stammered.

He gave a gentle laugh. "It's all right, Anna. Come on."

Back at the Bixbys', everything was quiet. "Stella's still not up," said Frank, after checking the bedroom. "She drank a lot. I don't think an earthquake would wake her. Let's sit here." He got two chairs and set them facing each other; one had leather straps hanging from the back—it was the one I'd seen Stella in the night before. He held out his hand, indicating that I should take it.

"Don't worry about the straps," Frank said. "I'll explain everything. Just sit down."

He went to the other side of the room, opened a large trunk that sat against the wall, and took out a wooden box, about three feet across and not quite as high. I knew it must be the shocking machine he and Stella had argued about the night before.

"Oh, I'm sorry," I said, embarrassed, not wanting to offend him, "but—could you do it without the machine? Hypnotize me, I mean?"

"I'll explain it all, don't worry," Frank said, setting the box between the two chairs. "It's quite safe and very effective."

"Are you sure it doesn't hurt?" I asked, remembering what Stella had said.

A shadow crossed Frank's face, and I worried that I had angered him. But he only shook his head and said, "It doesn't hurt."

I thought of standing up then and there, making some excuse, anything, saying I had to go to the bathroom, but I sensed this would upset him, and that it would make things worse between him and Stella, if I showed that her words last night had scared me. And then, also, maybe I wouldn't get to see Mary.

"You said I'll be able to talk to her—my friend?" I asked.

"Yes."

I thought again of how she had appeared behind the cabin and how I had felt certain she was real. But now, with the distance of hours, and sunlight, and conversation, it seemed possible that she wasn't.

And yet I felt that either way—whether she was actually a ghost or only a projection of my own troubled mind—the thing I most needed to do was talk to her. Even if it did hurt. Maybe I deserved that, after all.

I held still as he adjusted the box between our chairs and opened the hinged lid. Inside were a dial, some brass levers, and a system of leather straps and curved copper plates with long wires attached to them on one end, and to the box on the other. He bent to adjust the dials, then straightened, holding the copper-and-leather thing out to me. "This goes over your head," he said, "so the plates are touching your temples."

He moved it toward me and put it on, buckling it under my chin. "It's perfectly comfortable once it's on, isn't it?" he asked.

"And it'll be okay," I asked, "when you—do whatever you do with the wires, and the dials?"

"You'll feel a vibrating sensation. You'll notice it, but you shouldn't require anything that would rise to the level of pain. I'll be honest: some people do. But you won't." He went over to the machine and adjusted some knobs. "See this? It doesn't rise to the level of danger unless this is turned to eight. I'll be keeping it at less than two for you. One, maybe one and a half."

"If it's dangerous, why does it go that high, if . . . if that's not a stupid question?" I asked, worried that I was displaying the lack of some obvious knowledge.

But Frank's tone was kind. "Not at all. It's just a holdover from the prototypes, which were built to test the safety limits. Tested on animals, of course," he added quickly.

"How horrible," I said, even though I knew scientific experiments were done on animals all the time.

Frank made a sympathetic noise. "It would be worse if we didn't, though, hmm? If we used it without knowing the limits, human beings could get hurt." He began to turn a crank on the side of the box. "Here, I'll show you there's nothing to worry about."

He flipped a small switch, and I felt a strong tingling from the copper plates at my temples. I put my hands to my head.

"Don't do that," said Frank quietly, prying my hands away. "It will interfere with the treatment. Here." He moved one of my arms to the back of the chair, and I felt the strap going around it.

"Are you sure this is necessary?" I asked.

"It's just easier." He buckled my other arm down. "Don't be nervous," he said sympathetically. "It feels a bit odd, but you'll get used to it. The trick is to forget about this contraption"—he indicated the box—"and focus on your own thoughts. Now." He reached inside his jacket. "A pocket watch works well because it's shiny and easy to focus on. I'm just going to swing it on its chain, like so, and you just keep your eyes on it."

I should tell Frank I won't go through with this, I thought. But there was such calm certainty in his face that I couldn't.

"It will be like seeing her, right?"

"Shh, now pay attention," he said.

I followed his instructions to breathe evenly, to allow my eyes to close. A positive change began to come over me. It was as if some irritating noise dwindled and disappeared. A noise I hadn't realized I was living with until it was gone; a hum of anxiety that had been the background to all my thoughts and experiences.

"Good," said Frank. I wondered what he was seeing. His voice seemed to come from another place, like when you're asleep and someone speaks near your bed, but the dreaming mind imagines them to be far away. "Now," said the distant voice, "are you ready to go back and see your friend?"

"Yes," I said. "Yes, I am."

THIRTEEN

THERE WAS HER THIN, PALE FACE, HER UNEVEN HAIR,
those bright, insistent eyes.

"What do you see?" Frank asked.

"It's Mary," I said, amazed. "She's reaching out her hand."

"Do you want to take it?"

"Yes," I whispered.

"Go on." Frank's voice seemed to be coming from an even
greater distance than before.

IT WAS NIGHT IN THE Forts' big house. Mary stood below me
on the attic steps, holding a candle in one hand, and reaching
toward me with the other.

"Come," she said.

She pulled me to follow her. Together, we descended from
our attic room into the second floor of the house. We passed
three closed bedroom doors: Mr. and Mrs. Fort's room; then the
one that had been occupied by Raymond, their eldest son; and
a third that had once been shared by Charles and his younger
brother, Clarence. Raymond was grown and gone, Clarence had

been sent to reform school, and Charles had gone traveling by himself to see the world. We walked around a corner and down the next set of steps to the first floor. Mary came to a stop in front of the closed door of Mr. Fort's study.

"We're not allowed in there," I whispered. Only Mrs. Fort was allowed to clean it.

"I know," said Mary. She handed me the candle, pulled something from her pocket, and put it in the keyhole.

"What are you doing?"

She showed me two bent hairpins. "I'm picking the lock."

"I can't allow that," I whispered back.

"No one is going to know."

I was head housemaid now. It was my responsibility to stop this. Yet I watched, fascinated, as she worked the lock with the two pins, holding one steady while she moved the other, her ear close to the keyhole.

"Where did you learn to do that?"

"Among the damned," she said, flashing a brief smile. She gave the pin one last twist and opened the door.

I had only been in the study a handful of times in the nine years I'd worked at the Forts' house. In the middle of the room was a huge desk. On it stood a globe, inkwells, stacks of ledgers. To the left was a closet door. Mary went straight to the desk and took something from a drawer.

"What's that?"

She held up a key, then went to the closet.

"You mean you've been in here before?" How was that possible? The last time I'd been here was after Betsy had left in the late spring; I'd seen the door ajar and something, I didn't know what, had made me enter. I left after only a minute.

Mary put her finger to her lips, then used the key to open the closet.

"Remember when you said you heard birds?" she asked.

That was why I'd left the study so quickly, that last time.

"I told you I imagined it," I whispered fiercely.

She held the candle up so it illuminated the inside of the closet. On a shelf at the back stood a square cage in which two green parakeets on a perch, looking surprised in the flickering light.

Brk? said one. *Kr?*

"He keeps this cage here in his closet, in the dark," Mary said.

"But . . . why?" I asked.

"Don't you recognize these birds, Anna?"

"There used to be two just like them in the parlor. But Mr. Fort said they made too much noise and he was getting rid of them."

"He didn't get rid of them. He put them here."

"Why would he do that?"

Mary reached out and touched the cage. One of the birds sidled over to nibble on her fingertip. "To be cruel," she said. "To punish Mrs. Fort, because she begged to keep them. *She* knows they're here. She feeds them, but she's not allowed to take them out. I know she wants to, but you know what he'd do if he caught her."

I did. I had seen the bruises.

"If they bothered him, why go to all the trouble to keep them . . . and why keep them here in his study?"

"They don't make noise when they're in the dark," Mary said. "See, Anna, you talk about how there's order in this house, how it runs like a machine. But there's a price to pay. You've seen—"

Black eyes, broken dishes, nosebleeds . . .

Anger boiled up in my chest. "Get out. This is wrong!" I shooed her from the closet, yanking the door shut behind me. Then we both froze, wondering if the slam had woken anyone. But we heard nothing.

"Out of the study, *now*," I whispered angrily. "You never should have come here."

Mary seemed stunned. "You came, too."

"I did. I stood there and watched you pick the lock. I'm supposed to supervise you, and I failed. I've been treating you like a friend. You're not my friend. You're an employee. I've done something very wrong."

I was surprised by Frank's voice. It sounded as if it was coming from another room. "You haven't done anything wrong," he said, and then I experienced the vibrating at my temples that I had felt before, only much stronger. I made a sound of surprise. "Shh," said Frank. "I want you to remember: You haven't failed. You—can—be—a—good—mother."

His voice was louder now. The words were punctuated with bursts of vibrations that were increasingly painful.

"Stop!" I said.

"No!" Frank's voice was almost angry; and with it came another pulse, the strongest yet.

I cried out and tried to lift my arms, but they were strapped to the back of the chair.

The effort pulled my consciousness upward and made the watery, hypnotized feeling flow away from me like a wave receding on a beach. My eyes opened. Frank was leaning forward, an intent look on his face.

"I'm not hurting you, Anna," he said, his voice quieter, as if he was trying to control it. "Close your eyes. Stay with Mary. Go toward the pain in your memory, and we'll change it. Do you understand?"

I wanted to trust him, to put the ghosts to rest. I *wanted* sanity. I closed my eyes.

"There's Mary again," Frank said softly. "Do you see her? What is she doing?"

She was standing with me outside Mr. Fort's study, and we were arguing.

"Shh!" Mary hushed me. "You're going to wake everyone."

She was holding a piece of paper. Waving it in my face.

"No," I said. "I don't want to look at it."

"Look at it, Anna," came Frank's voice, calm and distant.

Across the top was printed: STATE OF NEW YORK, ALBANY

CITY AND COUNTY. The letters were crisp and black, as vivid as if I were really seeing them.

The date on the paper was May 30, 1895. The next line read NAME, and after that was written, in black ink, "Betsy Doyle."

The head housemaid who'd left after being taken to the hospital—the reason I'd been promoted and Mary was hired.

"It's her death certificate," Mary said. "Why does Mr. Fort have it?"

"She had no family. Put it back."

"You said she had her own apartment. How could she afford to live on her own, on a maid's salary?"

"Why does that matter?"

"Mr. Fort is lying to us. You said she was taken to the hospital for appendicitis."

"Oh Mary, put it back."

"It says here," Mary pressed, "that she died of a self-inflicted wound."

A lump of guilt formed in my stomach, a cold ball of clay. "I know," I admitted. "She shot herself in their bedroom. She was in love with Mr. Fort."

I felt embarrassment—for the Forts, whose peaceful home had been touched by such a sordid event; for Betsy; for myself, caught trying to keep it from Mary. "You understand why they didn't want everyone to know," I pleaded. I saw no sympathy in Mary's eyes.

The scene buckled and fractured like a kicked mirror, and I felt a sharp tingling at my temples and heard Frank's voice saying, *"Remember."*

The grass in the backyard, the yellow house, the red roses on a white trellis, billowing curtains, gray slate roof, and the blue, blue sky. A splash on my cheek. A spatter of red across the white petals of the daisies—

Mary sitting on the edge of the bed, leaning forward, eyes bright with fear, as I tell her about the Event.

Blood from a clear blue sky.

A thing that could not have happened, but did.

Mary with her pillowcase over her shoulder, standing at the open window . . .

"Don't go." My own voice loud in my ears.

"I'm sorry I didn't go with you to look out for you. I didn't protect you."

Frank's voice: "There's nothing to be sorry about." He sent another current through the machine. "You *will*—be a *good—mother.*"

With these words, the current came so strong, it felt like fists punching my head from both sides. I struggled to raise my arms, but I couldn't. It got worse, and when I tried to open my mouth to scream, my jaws felt locked, and no sound came.

Then, as suddenly as it had started, it stopped. My muscles lost their rigidity. Frank's cool, strong hand pressed against my mouth. "Shh! Wake now," he whispered.

He slipped the straps off my head and deftly freed my arms from the back of the chair.

"I didn't get to say good-bye. I want to go back," I begged as he picked up the wooden box with the dials and levers.

"Later." He carried the box across the room, put it back in the steamer trunk, and closed the lid. He slipped his watch back into his pocket as he opened the front door.

"Charles!" he said, in a cordial, welcoming voice.

"There you are, you early birds!" Charlie was standing in the doorway, filling it with his big, soft, comforting frame. He was almost bouncing on the balls of his feet, brimming with excitement. "Listen, you won't believe what I've just found in the trunk."

I stood up from the chair awkwardly, disoriented.

"Did you know there's a typewriter in one of the bottom drawers, provided specially for me to use while working on my book?" Charlie went on. "A brand-new Underwood Number Five. Splendid machine. Just like the one in your room, Frank. Mr. Arkel has thought of everything. Come on, Annie, I want to show you."

I glanced at Frank as I went out. He was looking at me with an intent expression, and when our eyes met, he raised a brow and gave me the slight smile of one who shares a secret.

"And here's something that will make *you* happy," Charlie said, as we went into our cabin. "There are games and novels and playing cards. We've got Jules Verne, H. G. Wells, G. K. Chesterton."

The twins, in their cage near the stove, were both sitting on the bottom again, and seemed to be shivering. It didn't look like they'd touched any of the mix of millet and oats I'd given them earlier. The temperature fluctuations, I worried, must be making them sick.

"And dominoes and Parcheesi!" Charles said.

"That's wonderful, Charlie," I said, trying to mean it. It occurred to me that the birds were definitely going to die. It was just a matter of time.

"*The Mysterious Island.* I'd like to read that," Charles said, picking up one of the books. "Or maybe you would." He handed it to me.

I tried to concentrate, though my mind kept drifting. My parakeets . . . what had happened with Frank . . . and what about Stella? Did I know she was all right, just because Frank had said so?

Less than an hour passed before the sound of typing ceased and Charles emerged from the bedroom. "Think I'll go ask the Bixbys over for breakfast. The missus ought to be up by now," he said cheerfully, heading out of the cabin.

I forced myself to focus on the novel, though I could hardly remember what had happened so far. They were on an island, I knew that much. Like us.

Gideon Spilett, Pencroft, and Herbert attentively examined this land, on which they might perhaps have to live many long years; on which indeed they might even die, should it be out of the usual track of vessels, as was too likely to be the case . . .

At the sound of a hand on the latch, I slammed the book shut, not bothering to mark my place. The door opened and I saw Charlie first, not exactly smiling, but not looking as devastated as someone would who had just learned of a death . . . of course, Frank would probably say she had a hangover and was staying in bed for the day . . . These thoughts flashed through my mind in the second or two before Charlie came in, followed by Frank and, finally—

"Stella!" I said, rising and accidentally knocking the book to the floor. "How are you feeling?"

She looked tired. "Nothing strong coffee can't fix. Why, did I drink that much last night?"

"I didn't mean that," I said, but I caught Frank glancing sideways at Charles with a smirk, which he returned with a quick good-natured grin, as if they both thought she had.

"Look at me," I said. "I haven't even set the table." I found the drawer in the trunk marked BREAKFAST. It was full of more fresh fruit, hard-boiled eggs, and pastries than four people could eat in a week. How could I have forgotten to put the food out? I'd been so preoccupied that it hadn't even occurred to me. Now at least there was one less thing to worry about, I thought, arranging the pastries on a platter. At least Frank wasn't a murderer.

As we ate, Stella was subdued, drinking her coffee and smoking. In the morning light, I noticed how heavily her face was powdered.

After we had eaten, Charles said, "Why don't you ladies amuse yourself with these things while Frank and I put in some work time. What do you say, Frank? It's a relief knowing you two will have something to do, with all these games and novels."

"Oh, yes, don't worry about us," said Stella. "You boys work. We'll amuse ourselves."

When Stella and I were alone, I put away the food, stealing glances at the birds, while she watched me, smoking. I almost asked her not to for the birds' sake, but then I thought: *What difference would it make? I can't stop them from dying.*

"Frankie would have done that later, you know," she said, as I put away the last dish. "Do you want to play Parcheesi?"

"I don't know how."

"Never mind, I don't want to." Stella stubbed out her cigarette in her saucer.

I sat down across the table and was silent for a minute.

"What?" she said.

I looked up. "What what?"

"You're in a brown study, as my father used to say. Mind somewhere else."

It was true; I could not stop thinking about what had happened with Frank. The hypnosis had worked, in that it made me remember Mary. Yet I had not gotten to communicate with her in the way I'd hoped. It had given me no peace. In fact, I felt worse.

The hour I'd revisited was one I had tried to forget. The hour before I told Mary about the Event, the night she ran away.

That was why I'd set the birds free. I'd told Frank it was because I was crazy, but now I remembered it was because I'd found out Mr. Fort was keeping them in the dark closet out of sheer cruelty. Even if it was too cold for them in the wild, maybe that fate was kinder than the life they had been living.

And the death certificate of Betsy Doyle—God, why did I have to remember that? Mr. Fort had been friendly toward her, and apparently she'd taken it the wrong way, fallen in love, lost her mind. Yet for her to take her own life was so extreme, so hard to understand. No wonder I'd chosen to forget that in favor of the gentler story, the one that didn't carry the shame of insanity and suicide.

Charlie had been away that year, traveling, and when he came back—shortly after Mary left—he got the same version of the story as everybody else: appendicitis had sent her to the hospital.

I'd never told him the sad truth. What would be the point?

Stella sat across the table from me, watching my face. I didn't know what to say to her. I closed my eyes and pressed my fingertips to my eyelids.

I'd hoped the hypnosis would put the past to rest, but instead it had stirred it up. I rubbed my temples, still tender from the shocking machine.

I knew, better than most, the multitude of strange things our world contained. I, of all people, should be able to chalk up an apparition as one of many anomalies that happened all over the earth, throughout history—

But those girls *hadn't* been apparitions. They were solid, she smashed the locks on the trunk, Mary did—

But I could not have seen Mary.

"Stella," I said. "Will you come for a walk? There's something I want to try to find."

"Ooh," she said, interested. "Did you decide you want to sneak over and see the greenhouses I was telling you about?"

"No. I . . . took a little walk last night," I said, "and I found something. I thought we could look for it in the daylight." If I could see the ruined church, at least I'd know that part hadn't been a dream.

"You?" Stella asked. "You took a walk? Last night."

"I couldn't sleep."

"After dark, by yourself?"

"You're right, that was foolish."

Stella smiled. "I didn't say that. I just didn't think you were the type. I underestimated you."

I smiled back, surprised.

"So what did you find?"

"I'll tell you on the way," I said, stalling. What if it *wasn't* real?

"You're being very mysterious," she said. "You're sure you don't want to go to the greenhouses? They're supposed to be magnificent, whole orchards of fruit trees under glass."

That was when it came to me: *whole orchards under glass.* The birds. I could take them there. They'd be warm, they could fly . . .

"Let's go to both places," I said. "Are you game?"

"Darling," Stella said with her late-night voice, "I'm always game. Let's dress for hiking and meet outside."

FOURTEEN

I WAS RELIEVED THAT CHARLES HAD THE BEDROOM door closed, so he couldn't see me taking the birds. If he found out I was going to sneak into forbidden territory and try to enter one of Mr. Arkel's greenhouses, against his Mr. Arkel's explicit rules . . . Was I risking our future for the sake of my birds?

Two little green ruffled heads looked up at me trustingly as I bent down to the cage. I had to try to save them. I couldn't let them die.

There was the problem of how to carry them. I couldn't lug the cage through the woods; it was awkward, and anyway, if someone saw us, how would I explain it? I decided on the emergency measure I had used to transport them short distances before. I got a pair of stockings from my suitcase. Then I reached into the cage and gently pressed my finger under Pollux's breast. He climbed on as usual, gripping it with his little feet, hoping for a cracker crumb, but squeaked with surprise when I grasped him in one hand, and with the other wrapped a stocking firmly around him. I set him on the floor for a minute, squirming in his silk cocoon, while I swaddled his brother. The little heads sticking out of the two bundles blinked at me with betrayed, angry eyes.

"I promise it will be all right," I whispered. But how to keep them warm? I unbuttoned my shirtwaist and loosened the top of my corset just enough so I could tuck them between my breasts. They stopped struggling then; maybe the heat and closeness reminded them of when they were tiny hatchlings and I'd bundled them in felt and held them under Charlie's desk lamp. "Just stay quiet," I said. I buttoned my coat partway over them, leaving room for some air to reach them.

When I got outside, Stella was waiting, dressed in trousers and a masculine hunting jacket. A long greenish-black feather adorned her peaked hat. "You're going to hike in that?" she asked me.

"Why not?"

"Have you got sturdy boots under there?" she asked skeptically, looking at my long skirt. I lifted the hem to show her. "Good," she said. "You *have* read the news that we're allowed to show ankles nowadays?"

"You're taking it a bit further than that."

She put her hands in her pockets and shrugged. "This is easier to walk in than that nineties housewife skirt."

Nineties! I looked down at it, and it seemed even older than when Frank had commented on it earlier in the morning. I'd married in ninety-six, bought it a couple years later . . . apparently it *was* that old.

"Anyway," I said, "Charles is happy with how I dress. I don't even know what he'd do if he saw me in that getup." I realized that sounded rude and quickly added, "I mean, *I* like it."

"Of course you do," Stella said cryptically. "Come on. Show me where we're going."

I started to lead her around to the back of the cabins, but when I felt the birds wriggling between my breasts, I stopped to adjust them.

"What's the matter?"

"The birds," I said. "I'm bringing them."

She tilted her head, her sleek bobbed hair swinging sideways. "You're taking them on a walk," she said doubtfully. "Like . . . little doggies."

"No." I struggled with a stuck button. "I want to take them to the greenhouses. They're getting sick from the smoky air in the cabin."

"Couldn't you just set them free?" Stella asked, staring, still not understanding why I was unbuttoning my coat.

"They're monk parakeets, native to South America. They'd die in this cold," I said.

"South America has cold. It has quite a range of climates. What are you *doing*?"

"They're in here." Stella looked baffled, her perfect black eyebrows contracting, as I opened my coat to show her.

She peeked in and saw their little faces sticking out, then drew back and laughed. "You are loony," she said. "You want to go to the greenhouses first?"

"No, the other place first."

"The mysterious one you haven't told me about. Okay."

Behind the cabins, Stella stopped to stare with mixed curiosity and disgust at the open trunks and the mess of things scattered around in the weedy dirt. "What happened here?"

I touched my wrist, remembering how Frank had found my bracelet on the ground. Was it possible *I* had opened the trunks, dreaming, sleepwalking? I couldn't tell Stella what I had seen. Not until I knew for sure if the girls were real. "Come on, this way," I said.

I found the deer trail I had walked on in the night, faint but visible.

"What could be *this* way?" Stella asked. But she followed.

In the woods, I still couldn't work up the courage to say anything. What if she looked at me the way Frank had, with that same knowing skepticism?

We walked for about ten minutes, and things began looking more and more unfamiliar. Maybe I hadn't really been here. Maybe that was my answer.

Then, through the trees, I saw it: the overgrown cemetery.

"Here it is!" I practically ran. I felt the birds slipping between my breasts and pressed a hand against my coat, trying to keep them high enough that their heads would stay up where they could breathe.

We came to the field of headstones and long grass. It was as I remembered: some of the stones broken and leaning, and beyond, the old foundation of a small church with a froth of spiny, half leafless brush growing up from the sunken basement. I led Stella to the spot where I had seen the girl nursing her baby.

There was nothing to indicate that people had been there— but then what, exactly, had I expected to find? I sat down on the foundation in the same place where the girl had been.

"Come on, let's have it," Stella said, sitting beside me and reaching into one of the many pockets in her hunting jacket. She retrieved a silver flask and held it out to me, but I shook my head. Shrugging, she took a swig, then pulled a cigarette case from a different pocket and snapped it open. "There's something you're not telling me. You didn't just go for a stroll and find this place, did you? It must be half a mile from the cabins. Why did you walk all that way in the dark?"

For a while I stared down at my hands, turning the bracelet on my wrist. "I saw someone breaking into the trunks," I said finally. "A girl. Maybe sixteen. Her hair was all matted. I followed her into the woods."

I glanced at Stella. Her usual expression of boredom was gone, her gray eyes intent and serious.

"Why would you follow her?"

"I thought she might be one of those missing girls. I thought maybe I could help."

I wouldn't tell Stella about the girl having Mary's face. That must have been a trick of the light, or of my mind. But the girls were real. I knew it now.

Stella said, not without sympathy, "You see, they're runaways, just like I said. Scrounging for food."

"There was another girl when I got here. And I heard another back there in the woods," I said.

"Did they seem to want help?"

I shook my head. "They seemed to want to run away from me," I admitted. Except for the one who had called out. Had she stopped or been silenced? Or had I somehow imagined that voice in the pitch-dark woods?

"Did it occur to you that maybe they want to be out here?"

"Why would anyone want that?"

Stella shrugged, lighting her cigarette. "They want to be free. You can take the girl out of the streets . . . "

"No," I said. "If they ran away, they were running *from* something, I'm sure of it. One of them was sitting right here, nursing a baby. Who would choose to be out here with a baby? Winter's coming."

Stella smiled grimly, her cigarette holder in her mouth. "A naughty little lady who got herself pregnant, maybe, and doesn't want to face the consequences?" She met my eyes. "Oh, don't look so upset. I'm hardly judging."

"Little lady who did *what?*" I said.

"Got—"

"Herself pregnant? How does one do that, exactly?"

"By being stupid," Stella murmured.

Anger bloomed in my chest, crimson petals spreading, twisting. "What about the boy? Where do you think he is?"

Stella shook her head. "They never have consequences. That's why we can't afford to be stupid. Anyway." Her tone was pacifying. "Tell me what happened when you got here."

"I called to the girl with the baby, but she ran away. Then I heard a voice from over there"—I gestured deeper into the woods—"calling for help. At least I thought I did. But I couldn't find anyone."

"Do you think," she said, looking at me, "they might have been playing with you? Sorry to be so blunt. But you are rather earnest. I'd hate to see that. These girls are criminals, after all. You don't know people like that."

I had, though. I'd lived in rooming houses with them as a child. And later my best friend, my only friend, had been a girl who stole food to eat, and clothes to wear. I didn't say this.

We sat in silence. Stella smoked. Overhead, clouds shifted, and the tarnished November sun shone down. The air smelled of frost. I looked at Stella, her perfectly powdered alabaster skin, her shiny hair, her big, clear gray eyes, which made me think of the rippling river.

"I don't think they're playing with me," I said. Then I noticed, beneath the powder, a faint shadow over her left cheekbone. I remembered seeing Frank slap her the night before. Had he given her a black eye? But no, it matched the one under her other eye: exhaustion.

Then a memory came to me: the first time I—new to the Forts' house—had found Mrs. Fort standing by the counter in the big, bright kitchen with a powdered-over bruise around her eye. I'd asked if she was all right. She said, "Of course I am," in a way that made me feel the question had been childish or stupid. "But your eye." That's when she'd looked directly at me and said, "There's nothing wrong with my eye," in a soft, slightly baffled, pitying tone, as if she was speaking to an insane person.

Other bruises appeared in the months and years after that, but nobody talked about them, not the elderly head housemaid and certainly not Cook, who always said, of everything: "I know nothing about it." She made it clear that she left her real life at home; she came to the Forts' only to work and departed as soon as that was done. "Anything else leads to trouble," she said.

There were closed doors in that household. From the start, I understood that I was not supposed to ask what went on behind them. Another child might have rebelled; might, like the girls in the fairy tales, have been unable to resist trying to enter the forbidden rooms and poke around in the darkness. But I was not that child.

I wanted to stay in that big, bright, clean, orderly house. I not only left the doors closed, but, as I grew up, even stopped noticing that they were there.

When Mrs. Fort had a sprained wrist, maybe she *had* tripped over one of the cats and sprained it catching herself.

When Betsy, the new head housemaid with the long, shiny hair, went on errands with Mr. Fort and came back with angry splotches on her arms—what could I do about it, anyway? It was better not to think about those things.

Not until Mary had someone dared to pick the locks on those closed doors.

NOW, IN THE WOODS, in the cold sunlight, Stella gave me a questioning look. *No need to bring up what I saw through the window,* I thought.

But I was worried about her. And I was a grown woman now.

"I saw you and Frank last night," I admitted. "When I was coming back from the woods, I thought I heard something, and I looked through your window. I'm sorry."

I thought she'd be angry, but instead her shoulders hunched and she suddenly looked tired. "It's just something we do."

"What's that mean?"

She shook her head.

"I saw he had a gun, Stella."

She sighed. "It's not loaded."

"He looked so angry," I said. "Why?"

She touched her cheek where he had slapped her. "He doesn't usually hurt me. Last night, honestly, I almost called for help. But I mustn't. That could ruin everything."

"Ruin what?" I demanded. "Do you put up with all of that just for his—his gratification?"

"It's not a sexual thing," she said. "At least that would be fun. No, it's his treatment. He has recurring nightmares and I have to help him."

"By letting him tie you to a chair?" I asked. But I had let him do the same to me that morning. "And *hit* you?"

"I could explain, but it's so tiresome," she said.

A wriggling between my breasts made me worry that one of the birds had slipped, and I bent my head to check. At almost the same moment, something wet landed with a splat on the stone foundation next to where Stella was sitting. She jumped.

"My God, that's creepy," she said. "Where did that come from?" I stood to see a pale, gelatinous blob.

"It looks like the chicken sauce from last night," I said, disgusted.

"Well, someone threw it at us," Stella said, scooting away. "I think your little friends might want us gone." She dropped her cigarette and ground it out with her boot.

I scanned the trees. "Hello!" I shouted. "Where are you? I want to help you!"

My words fell away, and silence flowed into the space where they had been. The woods were still.

"Don't worry," Stella called, "*I* don't want to help. I'm leaving. Come on," she said to me.

I had to agree that the girls didn't seem to want help. And I had to get the birds to the greenhouse. "I'll come back!" I said.

Something else flew through the air then, and this time it hit the front of my coat and dripped down it. Another blob hit the side of my face.

White-and-yellow daisies splashed with red!

Stella had begun walking; now I overtook her, running, as if I could get away from the memory that came, more vividly than ever, with the sensation of wetness on my cheek. But then it was as if a swarm of hornets or a buzzing thicket of thorns closed around me. I stopped and bent over, gasping. It was no use; I sank to my knees.

"Easy, there," said Stella, her hand on my back. "Slow breaths, now. Come on. In . . . out."

"Oh God, I'm sorry," I said. "I don't understand what's happening. But I used to be—years ago . . . " *This is it,* I thought. *She won't want to be my friend after this. But I have to tell her.*

"I had a breakdown," I said finally. "I was in a sanatorium."

Instead of rejection, I saw new compassion in her eyes. "That's all right," she said. "Lots of people do. Big breath in, now. And out."

"I'm so sorry."

"You're all right now." She pulled me to my feet. "Check your birdies. We don't want them to suffocate in your maternal bosom." She waited. "Okay? Let's go. You still want to take them to the greenhouses?"

"Yes," I said. "If it's the last thing I do. If I'm losing my mind, I want to get them there before it's gone."

"No need to be dramatic," she said. "I'll lead this time. Goodbye, girls, or forest spirits, or whatever you are, throwing leftover chicken at us."

It was then that, to our right, there was a *whoosh* and snapping twigs as something sprang up from the ground in front of us. A birch sapling that had been pinned to the ground somehow now stood upright, an empty noose of wire hanging from it.

"It's a snare!" said Stella.

"What, to catch rabbits?"

"Those little beasts are trying to kill us," Stella said. She reached into her jacket and, to my surprise, pulled out the revolver I had seen Frank holding the night before. Holding it in both hands in front of herself, she turned in a half circle, looking for movement in the woods. "Want to trip us up, do you?" Her voice had a steely edge I had not heard before.

I remembered the pink, glistening, hanging form I had glimpsed through the trees when we'd first arrived. It *had* been a skinned deer, hadn't it?

"Show yourselves," Stella said.

There was a rustle in the bushes. Stella whirled and fired.

"Stop!" I grabbed her arm.

"I wasn't shooting *at* her." Stella pulled her sleeve out of my grasp and straightened her jacket. "They need to know not to mess with us." She began to put the gun away, but a sound behind us made her stop. Someone was coming.

FIFTEEN

IT WAS A MAN. HE WORE A WELL-TAILORED COAT AND was heavy-browed and handsome. He could have stepped out of a magazine advertisement.

"Hello," said Stella coldly, as if she recognized him.

He touched his hat. "Mrs. Bixby," he said.

She turned to me. "This is Detective— What did you say your name was?"

"Southerland."

"Southerland," she repeated. "It's his job to make sure we only go to the right places, isn't it, Detective? And stay out of the wrong ones. This is Mrs. Fort. She arrived last night."

"We know." He had an officious air, but underneath it, I sensed he was nervous.

"Of course. You know everything. Are we out of bounds, then?"

"It's your gun," he said.

"Oh." Stella looked at it. "What about it?"

"I'm afraid you'll have to hand it over. No firearms of any kind are allowed on the island."

Stella's eyes flicked over him. "You have one."

His jacket was partly unbuttoned, and we could see the holster that held his revolver.

"Only the house detectives can have them," he said. "Mr. Arkel's rules." He was holding out his hand. A thick gold ring glinted on his finger. "I can't break the rules."

"It belongs to my husband," Stella said. "You'll have to talk to him about it."

Invoking the authority of a man made the detective back off a little. "All right," he said. "You come with me back to the cabins. I'll talk to your husband. I'm sure he won't want to upset Mr. Arkel."

We headed back on the path. "Nice ring you have," Stella remarked, glancing at Southerland's hand. "Fraternity?"

He grunted and held it up. "Mr. Arkel gave it to me for exemplary service in the strike. I rendered fifteen adversaries incapacitated."

"And what's on it? What do those little words say?"

"It's his motto," Southerland answered. *"Non est potes—"*

"We know it," I interrupted. I was trying as hard as possible to hide my despair at the thought that now we would never get to the greenhouses. I felt the poor birds, wrapped in their stockings, moving against my skin, and tried to project my thoughts to them: *I'm sorry. So sorry.*

Earlier, walking with Frank, I'd remembered an open cage door, two green birds hopping up to the sill of the door to look out . . . then lifting off, flying, flying.

A misguided attempt to help; I had released them into the gray autumn sky, where cold and death awaited. I had wanted to do the right thing this time.

We marched in silence. Every few minutes, I closed my eyes briefly and tried to imagine what the birds were doing under my coat. Were they just squirming? Were they suffocating?

Once, long ago, I'd heard Mr. Fort say that animals couldn't feel pain, "not the way humans do." I couldn't recall the context, but I remembered the tone: as if he was stating a simple, obvious fact.

It didn't sound right, but I was so young, I thought maybe I was the one who was wrong. Only now, as an adult, I knew *he* was. I'd heard my birds chatter with excitement when they saw a peanut, and keen with disappointment when they dropped it; I'd listened to them mumbling comfortably when they were warm and drowsy. It would take an exhausting, convoluted line of reasoning to convince myself they felt nothing, and for what? What could be the point? Unless one wanted to feel better about hurting them.

Stella must have been occupied with her own train of thought, because it was a while before she spoke up, breaking the silence: "So the detectives are the only ones who can have guns. How many of you are there?"

This question seemed to catch Southerland off guard. "There were two," he said.

"Were?"

"Detective Peleus . . . left about two months ago."

He hesitated in a way that made me think there was more to the story.

"Where did he go?" I asked.

Mr. Southerland glanced at us. I saw in his eyes that under his officious mask lurked something else: fear.

"He was fired," he said. "Because he displeased Mr. Arkel. You don't want to displease Mr. Arkel, either—your husband will agree, I'm sure. That's why I've got to take the gun."

"It's not as if he can fire *us*," Stella said. "We're his guests."

Southerland glanced back but said nothing.

"There's something you're not telling us," I ventured, surprised by my own bravery.

"You want the truth?" said the detective. He stopped abruptly and turned to face us. Dread prickled the back of my neck. "Detective Peleus was shot."

"Shot by whom?" Stella asked.

"By Mr. Arkel."

There was a moment of silence that seemed to last forever. As in the trick where a tablecloth is pulled off a table leaving all the dishes where they were, I felt the ground slip away quickly and almost imperceptibly. I went on standing, but something had been yanked from underneath me. One of the birds twitched between my breasts.

"It's not a secret," said the detective. "The staff knows it."

"Was it a hunting accident?" I asked slowly, remembering what Frank had said about Mr. Arkel's first wife.

"No. Pell was in love with Mr. Arkel's new bride, Millicent. I told Pell, I said, 'Give her up, she isn't worth it.' There's two things you don't do on Prosper Island: go where Mr. Arkel says not to go, and touch what Mr. Arkel says not to touch." He paused, surveying our faces with his hard, black-pebble eyes. "That's why I'm telling you to follow the rules."

Stella objected: "That's absolutely dreadful, but having our own pistol hardly seems the same as—"

"Listen," Sutherland interrupted. "Pell"—his voice caught on the name of his friend—"Pell was stupid. He brought it on himself. Lots of men would've done exactly the same thing Mr. Arkel did."

"So a judge ruled it was justified?" I asked.

The detective shook his head. "There was no investigation. Who would investigate? Mr. Arkel'd just say Pell left."

"But you said the staff knows what happened."

"None of us are stupid enough to try to do anything about it."

"Are you saying you're all so afraid of Mr. Arkel that you just gave up without even trying? He killed a man on purpose, and not one of you even tried to report it, to get justice?"

"I told you, plenty of men would've done the same. And Pell knew the risk. What Mr. Arkel did might not have been legal, but you can't say it wasn't justice. In some people's eyes, it was."

"I still don't understand," said Stella. "You're acting like we should be afraid of him, too. But we've done nothing wrong. I came here as a houseguest, not a subject of some little kingdom where Mr. Arkel makes the laws."

"Let's ask your husband," Southerland grunted.

A slight movement under my shirt made me remember the birds. "Yes, Stella," I said, "let's go back."

I LEFT STELLA AND THE detective to talk to Frank while I hurried to my cabin. Charles was still shut up in the bedroom with his typewriter. I tore open my coat and blouse. The twins' eyes were wide, and they were panting, beaks open. I pulled them out, unwrapped them gently from the stockings, and put them back in their cage, where they sat looking stunned and shaking themselves to fluff their feathers.

Charles must have heard me come in, because just as I closed the cage, he stomped in from the bedroom, somehow making a lot of noise even in his old slippers. "Hello!" he said brightly. "Birds all right?"

"I don't know," I said, keeping my eyes on them. "I'm worried."

"You've been worried ever since we left home." He came over and looked at them with me. "I'm sure they're fine. You always take good care of them."

These words didn't reassure me about the birds, but Charlie's presence did have a calming effect. While I was gathering my courage to tell him about what Mr. Southerland had said, he clomped over to the dinner trunk, the birds flinching at the sound of his big feet. "Wonder what's for lunch? Frank said it would be in one of these drawers. Have a nice walk?" he asked, looking back at me.

"Yes."

"Do you have any idea what that detective wants to talk to Frank Bixby about?"

Looking at his face shining with a confidence that I hadn't seen in years—if ever—I understood that I couldn't tell him the whole story, or share my growing sense that we should never have come here. "No idea," I said.

"Why don't you lay out some lunch for us all and then lie down and rest while I work this afternoon?" he said. "That would be good for your nerves. No more exertion today."

"Yes, of course." I glanced at the birds, who were still panting slightly but seemed a bit better. The image of the rosary came back into my mind. I saw, streaming from each bead, a simple, repeated prayer: BIRDS LIVE : BIRDS LIVE : BIRDS LIVE. The same phrase three times, in a widening beam, printed in capital letters in black ink. I closed my eyes, formed the words silently with my lips.

I went through the motions of setting the table and finding things in the trunk to put on it: good bread and butter, cheese and fresh grapes, cold meats. None of the canned fruit on which Mr. Arkel had built his fortune.

Arranging purple grapes on a white plate, I thought that ever since Mrs. Laches had spoken to me, it was as if I had walked off the edge of a map, into unknown territory. Missing girls . . . a chauffeur in a gas mask . . . the flayed animal hanging from the tree . . . the girls in the woods . . . revisiting that dark closet in Mr. Fort's study . . .

"*Anna!*" Charles called. I turned, startled, knocking some of the silverware to the floor. My hands hurt, and I looked down to see that my palms had painful red dents from gripping the table. I rubbed them on my hips.

"I said your name three times," Charlie said. He walked over and took my hands between his own. "What's wrong?"

I gazed into his brown eyes, often so faraway and twinkling

with some privately amusing thought, but now focused and serious. I was used to sharing everything with him, only so much had happened in the past twenty-four hours that I couldn't begin to tell him about. "I'm sorry," I said. "Just all the changes, I guess."

He kissed me and said, "Let's call the Bixbys in for lunch."

AT THE TABLE, CHARLES WAS happy. "Wrote several pages," he said between mouthfuls.

The rest of us ate mostly in silence, preoccupied.

I had to get out of the cabin again, had to get to the greenhouse. How? *Don't go where Mr. Arkel says not to go . . .* But what other chance did my twins have?

I had to stop thinking. Turning to Frank, I said the first thing that came to mind: "So you gave it to him? The revolver?"

Frank glanced at Stella, then away.

Stella said, "He could have refused, but he didn't."

"That would have contradicted Mr. Arkel's wishes," Frank said quietly. "Besides, the detective wouldn't have known about it if he hadn't heard a shot." He looked pointedly at Stella.

"I told you, a crow was annoying me," she said. I realized she hadn't told him about the girls. In some unspoken way we had agreed not to tell the men.

Charles said, through a partially full mouth, "Is that what he wanted to see you about? The gun?"

"Yes," said Frank.

Charles shrugged. "No need for it anyway. We're in no danger with the detective patrolling everywhere." He didn't seem to notice Frank and Stella glaring at each other. "Just doing his job, looking out for your well-being," he added as he forked another piece of cold chicken onto his plate.

After we'd eaten, Charles said, "Frank's going to show me some of his research. After that, I think I'll lie down for a bit and read, then try to write a bit more. What a fine day! Nothing to worry about but my work." He smiled at me, then stood up and stretched luxuriously, seeming unaware of everyone else's mood. Frank got up silently.

"Don't worry, we'll clean up," Stella said when they were almost out the door.

Frank met her eyes, his mouth a thin line, as if to convey that he was purposely not doing it. I remembered how he had cleaned up the night before and seemed so deferential. Something had shifted.

As soon as the door closed, Stella took out her cigarette case. "I'm just going to smoke first," she said.

I was thinking about the birds—wondering how I could get them to the greenhouse now. When I glanced at Stella, her head was in her hands.

"Are you all right? I asked. "Frank seemed angry."

"He's always angry."

"He seemed different. Leaving you to clean up. He did it last night."

Without looking up at me, Stella said, "He says he's had enough of me. It happens every now and then."

"Is that what happened last night, when he hit you?"

"He's frustrated that the cure he invented isn't working. He's taking it out on me. It'll pass. The thing about the gun didn't help. He never did like that I kept it away from him during the day. But I don't think he realized I was carrying it around loaded. Then I went and lost it."

"Why *were* you carrying it?"

At first, Stella didn't answer. Then she said, "For protection."

"Protection?"

"It was probably silly," Stella said. "What *would* he do to us? But Mr. Arkel is a strange man. And, if you want to know the truth, Frank has learned a few things about him. He's been here before."

"He told me," I said, feeling vaguely guilty. "We went for a walk this morning."

"Here I promised Frank I wouldn't mention it, but it looks like he did."

I studied her face. She looked tired, and older than she had in the woods, when her cheeks had glowed with exertion, but she had a gravity now that gave her a different kind of beauty.

"He said it's dangerous to cross Mr. Arkel," I said. "Just like Mr. Southerland said."

Stella hesitated. "He didn't only kill that detective, Pell. He also killed his first wife. The one who died in the spring, Gertrude. He shot her."

"In a hunting accident," I said. "Right?"

Stella shook her head. I understood. I'd suspected it ever since Frank told me about her death. I just hadn't wanted to admit it to myself.

The early afternoon light filtered through the cabin's windows and seemed to hang in the still air. I was aware of feeling trapped.

"Why did he shoot her?" I asked, my throat tight. As if there might be good reasons and bad reasons, and I needed to know which it was.

"She confronted him about the girls in the school, that's why. He was having affairs with them."

"The girls in the School for Domestic Service? You knew that and you didn't tell me?"

"What difference would it have made?" Stella finally took a cigarette out of the case she had removed from her pocket earlier. "Did you think he wasn't? You think men don't have affairs with their maids?"

"That doesn't make it right," I said.

"I never said it did." She tapped the cigarette against the table, then fitted it into the short tortoiseshell holder.

"It's got to be why they left," I said. "To get away from him."

"It certainly explains the baby," she said.

I remembered the girl cradling the infant in the cold moonlight: her small, pale face, her round cheeks. "She was a child herself," I said. Frank had said Mr. Arkel was sixty. "That's not an affair."

"Old enough to have a baby is old enough to know—" Stella began.

"You think she had a choice? A young girl saved from jail, working for a wealthy man, you think she could have just said no?"

Stella looked at me intently. "You're right," she said.

I took a breath, trying to calm myself. "So his wife, Gertrude, found out and confronted him, and he shot her."

"Not exactly," said Stella. "According to Frank, she'd known for years. They had an understanding: he kept his affairs private, and she didn't ask questions. But one day about six months ago, one of the trustees telephoned saying she'd gotten a letter from one of the girls. The trustee was concerned and wanted to talk to them. And that's what Gertrude Arkel was livid about—not what he was doing. About their private business going public."

"That must have been Mrs. Laches," I said. "The woman with the petition at the docks. She showed me that letter."

Things are going on here which are not right.

"And I guess no one investigated that either, any more than they did when he shot the other detective?"

"It was a hunting accident," Stella said drily.

"You mean there's some question," I said, still holding out hope. "A chance it wasn't on purpose."

Stella shook her head. "He admitted it to Frank. He wasn't ashamed. He . . . he enjoyed it," she said. "His nightmares weren't from guilt, because he didn't feel any. He thought they were really Gertrude visiting him from beyond the grave, seeking revenge. Every night forcing him one step closer to the place where he had shot her."

"And when he got there, he thought he'd die," I said, remembering Frank's words. "But Frank cured him of the dreams."

Stella nodded. "But Frank thinks he's disintegrating mentally."

I remembered Frank saying that was why he thought Mr. Arkel wanted him here.

"Do you think Frank can help him?"

"I don't know." Stella's eyes glinted with worry, but she blinked it away and lit her cigarette with her gold pocket lighter. "I don't think Frank does, either." She snapped the lighter shut and put it on the table.

"Then why did he come? If he thinks Mr. Arkel is so dangerous?"

Stella held the cigarette in her mouth and inhaled, closing her eyes. Then she said, "Writing his monograph is his only chance to get back on his feet professionally, and Mr. Arkel offered him the chance to do it."

"What do you mean, back on his feet? After what?"

"He ran into some trouble back home," said Stella vaguely, pulling a plate toward her. She absently tapped ash onto a partially eaten sandwich.

My stomach revolted. "I have to go," I said, standing up.

"Where?"

"To the greenhouse," I said. "I still have to get my birds there."

"Are you sure?" Stella asked. "After . . . everything?"

"I'm responsible for them," I said. "You don't have to come."

"You can't go back out there alone."

"You can't stop me," I said as gently as I could.

"I mean," she said, pushing her chair back, "I'm coming, too."

I looked at her, surprised, and started to say something, but she waved it away. "I refuse to be intimidated by that man. I think he *wants* us to be scared. So I'm not going to be. Let him get his sick amusement somewhere else."

"You think that's what it is to him, amusement?"

Stella didn't answer, but hooked her arm through mine. I was overcome for a second, not just with gratitude that she was coming with me, but from the feeling of—it was so silly—just the feeling of having a friend. I hadn't, really, since Mary.

Charlie loved me, but that was different. He would have laughed at my desire to get the birds to the greenhouse. He felt it was his job to point out when I was *taking things too seriously*, one of his euphemisms for the kind of thinking Dr. Jacobson had warned about. When I'd left the sanatorium, all three of us—Charlie, the doctor, and me—had appointed my husband guardian of my mental stability. Of course, if I'd had a choice, I might not have picked Charlie for that role, with all his eccentricities, but maybe love isn't a choice.

"One thing," Stella added. "We're not going anywhere near that churchyard or those runaway girls. They don't want us, and who knows what we'd bring on ourselves if we got mixed up with them."

I almost argued, but stopped myself. "Of course," I said.

I knew that once the birds were safe, I'd have to figure out how to help the girls. I hadn't been strong enough years ago, when Mary needed me. But maybe I was now. And Stella didn't have to be part of it. It was my battle.

"You're not going to squash those poor birds into your cleavage again, though, are you?" she said. "Can't you put them in your pocket or something? They're liable to suffocate. No offense. You're womanly." She patted her shirt. "Not like me. But you weren't meant to be an incubator for parakeets."

I remembered how the birds had been panting. "What else can I do? I can't bring the cage, and I can't put them in my coat pockets—they're too narrow and deep."

"I have a drawstring opera bag I think is the right size. You can put them in there with their little heads sticking out. Then I'll carry them in my hunting jacket. How does that sound?"

Hers was a man's jacket with many large, wide pockets with

flaps that could easily be opened to give them air. It was the perfect solution. I felt so grateful that I hugged her without thinking. She seemed surprised, then returned the squeeze. "We make a good team," she said.

Soon we were outside the cabins again. "The boys don't seem to care what we do, do they?" Stella said. "So happy with their little projects."

We decided to cut straight through the apple orchard this time, as it was the shortest way to the house. As we set off through the brown orchard, the November air was crisp and frosty. It felt good to be away from the cabins—as if some of my anxiety stayed behind in the sooty air and couldn't cling to me out here. The sunlight was strong and clear, and the sky above the dark, twisted branches was very blue. We crossed out of the orchard and into the woods, with no sign of anyone.

We came to a long, low stone wall. It was mossy and half tumbled down, and it wound away in either direction through the woods. Even in this brown and chilly month, the island was a strangely beautiful place.

Stella went to one of the low places in the wall and stepped over to the other side. Then I heard her scream.

SIXTEEN

SHE STOOD JUST ON THE OTHER SIDE OF THE LOW STONE wall, frozen in mid-stride, staring at something on the ground.

I climbed over the tumbled stones. Then I froze, too.

A man in a dark coat was lying there, facing away from us. One arm was stretched awkwardly above his head. He was motionless.

"It's Detective Southerland," Stella breathed.

I tried to keep my voice even. "It can't be. We just saw him."

Stella didn't move. I made myself walk around the body.

It was him. The detective lay half on his stomach, face twisted to the side, eyes open. His skin had a bluish cast. His revolver lay under his dead right hand.

"Look." I pushed his coat aside. A crimson stain bloomed on his shirt. "Oh, I don't like this." I stood up so fast my vision blurred.

"Easy," said Stella, holding my arm.

In spite of her firm grip, I felt as if I had stepped off the edge of solid land and was sinking through water.

"Why did he shoot him? Why did Mr. Arkel shoot *him*?"

"I don't know," Stella said.

"He told us Mr. Arkel's a murderer!" Hysteria rose in my throat. "Mr. Arkel found out somehow and killed him!"

Stella gripped me tighter. "Stay calm," she said firmly. "Here's what we're going to do: we're going back to the cabin to tell Frank and—"

"No!" I pulled away. "Give me the birds."

"Wait," Stella said. "Think this through. If he did shoot Mr. Southerland, it couldn't have been more than an hour ago. He still could be walking around the woods. He could be anywhere."

She didn't say what I was thinking, and what she must have been, too: that if the detective's death did have anything to do with him talking to us, then Mr. Arkel could be looking for us, too.

"I need to save my birds," I said. "If he's after me, I have to get them to the greenhouse first."

"Okay. Okay." Stella pulled the beaded bag from her pocket. The twins struggled in the sudden cold light, alarmed and trying to escape. I held them against my chest, pressing their bodies, trying to calm them.

"Now that you have them, will you come back to the cabins, just for a minute?" she said, her tone cautious. "Then we can go to the greenhouse after."

"When?"

"Later," she said.

I could tell she was lying. She had no intention of going. Instead of answering her, I started walking fast, keeping the birds against my chest.

"Anna—" Stella trotted to catch up to me.

I didn't want to debate. I went faster. I was going to get them there.

"It's okay," Stella panted, "you—don't—have to run."

"You can't stop me."

"Slow down!" Stella reached for my shoulder. "Slow—down. I'm still coming."

I saw that she was telling the truth this time. We walked for a few minutes. Then she said: "You're crying."

I'd hardly noticed the tears spilling from my eyes, streaking my cheeks. "The birds are cold," I said. My voice was steady; I wasn't sobbing, just producing tears, endless tears. "They're going to die."

"Let me put them back in my jacket, where it's warm, okay?" she said, reaching her hand out. "We'll get them to the greenhouse."

Reluctantly, I gave them to her. Stella tucked them into her pocket, showing me their faces one last time before closing the flap. Then she pushed something into my hand: a lace-edged handkerchief. As we walked, I pressed it against one eye, then the other, till the tears stopped.

A rustling in the leaves startled us. Stella clapped her hand to her mouth, before we both saw the squirrel race away, up a tree. She laughed shakily. "We're panicking. We can't panic. Let's talk about something."

"Like what?"

"Anything. Distract me. Where did you and Frank walk this morning?"

"Out to the stony point," I said. And then, because I felt I should have mentioned it already, I added, "Frank offered to hypnotize me when we got back. Because I was having trouble with memories of my friend."

Stella's pace slowed. "Hypnotize you how?"

"By swinging his watch . . . and also hooking me up to his machine." As I said it, I felt guilty. She had clearly not wanted him to use the machine here. Yet I had let him do it.

"You didn't say yes, did you?"

I nodded, feeling stupid.

Stella stopped, grasping my shoulder. "Don't ever let him do that to you again. Do you hear me?"

"Why not?"

"You think Mr. Arkel has a problem? I'll tell you someone else who has problems—Frank. It's no surprise they get along."

"What do you mean by that?"

"Stay away from that machine. That's all."

Stella wouldn't say more. We resumed walking, in silence now except for the rhythmic swish and crunch of our boots on the fallen leaves, putting distance between ourselves and the blue-gray corpse of Detective Southerland. We should have closed his eyes, I thought. I pictured them: open, dry, staring through the dark trees under the bright, empty sky.

We came to a rise, and when we got to the top, we could see the house. Between it and us, there was a dip in the land. It stood on a low hill. It was sprawling, chaotic, filling the November landscape, pale walls and gray-green roofs, gables and spires dwarfing the black bare trees and dark green firs under the bright sky.

"We're seeing it from the back. The greenhouses are right there," Stella said. She pointed to a large glass-walled structure that stood apart from one wing of the house, with gardens in between. It was all sinuous curves of green-painted iron and what must have been thousands of individual glass panes. The main part was round, with a roof that rose to a point in the middle. Narrow, parenthesis-shaped wings curved out from either side.

Stella pulled a small brass telescope from another one of her pockets and handed it to me. "Here," she said.

I raised the telescope and looked. First everything was blurry; then an infinite number of tree branches came into view. I scanned back and forth, up and down, until I caught the wall of a turret, and from there I found the greenhouses. A jumble of green leaves pressed against the glass from inside, as if they wanted to get out.

"It'll do," I said, lowering the glass.

"That's what you have to say about a mansion the size of a small city—'It'll do'?"

"I meant the greenhouse, for the birds."

Stella took the telescope. "You don't even care about the house, do you? I hope your little friends appreciate that we're risking our lives for them."

I knew they didn't, but it occurred to me that if I had never bought that first pair in the pet shop years ago, if I had never bred them, even if I hadn't sat up all night next to the tiny twins begging them to stay alive, these two would already be free—bodiless souls, unbound even by time or space, let alone a small steel cage. This was the very least I owed them.

"Come on," I said. "Let's get this over with."

There was a lawn around the whole mansion, but the woods came closest at the corner where the greenhouse stood, so that we'd only have to cross about fifty feet of exposed grass. By this time, the sun sat lower in the sky, but it was still bright.

"Should we make a dash or walk slowly like we belong here?" I asked as we got to the edge of the woods.

"Slowly," she said.

We crossed the grass. A garden surrounded by a low wall stood next to the greenhouse, and as we walked, I thought I noticed something moving near a tall rhododendron, disturbing its dark, shiny evergreen leaves, but when I put my hand on Stella's arm and pointed, there was nothing there.

We arrived at the greenhouse, and I saw a narrow space between the glass wall and the shrubs on the outside. I squeezed into it.

"You're going to have to come out of the greenery and walk through the door if you want to get in," Stella whispered.

"That door is so exposed. I was hoping there was a window back here we could go through," I said, edging along the wall.

"You're going to get leaves and spiderwebs all over you."

"I don't see anything that looks like it opens," I said, examining the glass panes that made up the wall.

"The door is unlocked!" Stella said, keeping her voice as low as possible. "I just opened it. Come out of there."

I went to her, and she held the door open for me. She pulled a twig out of my hair as I passed. "Let's try not to look like escaped lunatics," she said. I glanced at her face, framed by her straight, neat hair, and at her peaked hat, which had stayed at the same perfect angle throughout our walk. She certainly didn't look like a lunatic, but I must have. Maybe I should have been back in the sanatorium—would have been if we hadn't been stuck out here on the island. Why did she even bother with me? I guessed she didn't have many other choices at the moment.

Inside, the greenhouse was warm and smelled of living plants and damp earth, with a tinge of decay that said the place was full of life in all its stages. Trees with huge leaves, each one longer than we were tall, leaned into the path that led from the doorway. They brushed our shoulders as we passed. Along the walls at knee height ran mottled green copper pipes, some of them dripping at the joints. Through the leaves I caught sight of empty terra-cotta containers stacked upside down, and a potting table next to an old white sink. The floor under our feet was brick, half obscured by moss and soil that had spilled or washed out from the bottoms of the pots.

"I hear crickets," I said. "Listen."

"I hear them, too," said Stella.

"They always come into basements in the fall," I said. "I'll bet all the crickets on the island come here. I'll bet they can live forever in here."

"I don't think bugs can live forever, darling," Stella said. "But come on. Where do you want to let your birds go? Then we must hurry and leave."

"Let's go toward the middle, quickly," I said. "I want to see if there's water, and things to eat. Maybe once we get moved into the house, I can ask one of the staff to look out for them . . . Maybe she can help me get them back when we're ready to leave in the spring." I wondered if I was lying to myself. I couldn't really know if they'd survive until the spring, or even until next week. I was doing what I thought was best for them, but it was only a wild guess.

I took a curving path that was made narrow by leaning palm

trees and prehistoric ferns to a place where it opened out, and found myself in the middle of the main greenhouse. Whereas the edges of the greenhouse felt crowded and dim, this area was full of light, open and manicured like a small artificial park. In the center stood a hill of rock, with a grotto in it from which a waterfall flowed into a pool. The pool then spilled into a narrow stream, which snaked twenty-five feet or so before disappearing under another, smaller rocky mound. The banks of this artificial stream were lined with flowers in every color, bright in the afternoon sunlight pouring through the high glass ceiling overhead. Around the edges of the open space stood trees in huge pots, many bearing fruit: oranges, pomegranates, others I didn't recognize.

Stella was right behind me. "It's the Garden of Eden under glass," she said. "I think your birdies are going to like it here. Look, a couple of sparrows."

Two little brown birds, who must have found their way in by accident, pecked at a piece of fallen fruit under a tree. I reached over and lifted the flap of Stella's pocket. She jutted her hip toward me and I reached in to pull out the soft velvet beaded purse. The twins seemed calmer here in the warm air, with its odors of earth and greenery.

"Birds," I whispered, holding them up, "do you like it? You can fly. There are trees. You don't know trees," I said as the realization struck me. "You were born indoors."

I had denied them freedom all their lives. I wasn't even giving it to them now—just an artificial, miniature version of it.

I gently loosened the drawstring and unwrapped Pollux from the stocking. I set him on the rim of a huge pot. He shook himself to fluff his feathers, then just sat there, not sure what to do, as I unwrapped his brother. I set Castor down next to him.

"Fly, birdies," Stella said, waving her hand. "We have to go."

"Prettybird," said Castor, in a surprised, creaky voice, as if remembering that he could talk. I had hardly heard either of them make a sound since we had left the Bronx.

"Oh!" Stella said.

"They've been too scared to speak," I explained. "They're normally very noisy."

"Pretty*bird*," said Pollux, as if replying to his brother.

"Bird," said Castor. "Bird, bird." Then, in a deeper voice: "*Breathe*. Breathe *in*. Out."

"He sounds like a scratched phonograph record being played too fast," Stella said.

Pollux answered with a series of clacking noises.

"That's typewriter keys," I said.

"I'm glad I didn't hear all this for the first time in the middle of the night," Stella said.

"Oh, they don't speak at night, they—" I began, but Stella wasn't listening; she was waving both hands at them now.

"Fly free!" she said.

Castor, wanting to get away from her hands, jumped up to a low branch of a shrubby tree. Pollux followed. Then they looked at me, as if asking what to do next.

"Will they be all right?" I asked Stella.

"Of course They're in paradise." She was already backing away and pulling her cigarette case out of her pocket in preparation for getting outside.

"Go on," I said to the twins. "It's a good home for you. There's water and things to eat and other birds."

As if he was tired of listening, Pollux turned away, then lifted off into the air, and his brother followed. They landed on higher, smaller branches of the trees we stood near, then went somewhere else from there. I followed them with my eyes until I couldn't see them anymore.

"Come on," said Stella. "We have to go." She pulled my sleeve. A small object on the floor caught my eye, and I picked it up.

"It's a key," I said. It was bent on the end in a particular way that was familiar. "I've seen this before. It looks just like the key to a thing I used to have, a toy bird."

But that was impossible. As impossible as having seen Mary behind the cabins.

"King Nyx," I whispered. It was the first time I had spoken the name aloud since the windy night when I had talked to Mary in our attic bedroom.

It couldn't be the same key. And yet—

"King what?"

"King Nyx. It's the name of—"

"Never mind. We have to go."

I put the key in my pocket. At the door, I stood, listening. The afternoon was advancing, the shadows among the huge leaves deepening. I made the kissing noise that I used back home to call the birds. They didn't appear. But then, from somewhere deep in the greenhouse, I heard, like a grainy recording of Charlie's voice played at the wrong speed, "Breathe *in*. Out. Prettybird!"

"That's going to give some gardener a shock," Stella said.

Outside, we stood again in the narrow, prickly, hidden space between the shrubs and the greenhouse wall while Stella lit a cigarette. The air was noticeably chillier than when we'd gone in. I was surprised at the pleasure it gave me. I inhaled deeply and felt something I had not expected: a sense of relief.

I couldn't know that the birds would be okay. But I had done the best I could, had done what I'd come to do. I felt as if I, too, had been released, as we walked into the cold autumn afternoon.

Passing the garden again, I looked over to where evergreen rhododendrons and other loose, half-bare shrubs spilled over the low brick wall. "Stella," I said. "What's that?"

Without waiting for her answer, I walked toward the white scrap I saw hanging in one of the shrubs. It was a strip of dirty cotton that had been knotted onto a twig.

As I pulled on it, straightening it out, I saw something written on it in faint, smudged letters, as if the words had been scratched there with the end of a burnt stick.

They said: HELP US.

SEVENTEEN

"ANNA, WE HAVE TO GO," STELLA SAID, BUT I IGNORED her. Because over the wall, inside the garden, I saw another, similar scrap of fabric lying on the weedy gravel path, weighted with a stone.

"It's a trail," I said, climbing over the wall. "One of the girls must have left these." I bent to pick up the second scrap among the crushed oyster shells that served for gravel on the path.

"The girls," said Stella, "threw things at us and tried to catch us in a snare."

A clear, familiar voice spoke in my head, then: *This is different.* It was the voice of King Nyx.

"This is from the one who called to me in the dark," I said. "I know it is. She *wants* help." I went back to where Stella stood and held out the scrap with the words on it.

"I don't trust it," said Stella. "It could all be part of a trap— the girl who called to you, these things, all of it."

"Why would the girls want to trap us? That doesn't make sense."

"What if it's not them," Stella said. She lowered her voice: "What if it's Mr. Arkel? Did you consider that?"

"How could it be?"

"I've been thinking. What if they didn't really run away from the school? All you know is that the remaining girls wouldn't say where their friends were. What if the 'missing ones' are still working for him? What if the girl last night was *trying* to lure you out of the cabin?"

I started to protest, but she went on:

"Frank told me Charles was going on about some mysterious lights in the woods."

"Those were girls with lanterns."

"Your husband didn't seem to think so. He's planning to go out after dark and look for them."

I remembered how excited Charlie had been when I'd mentioned the lights, and how I hadn't admitted I'd seen the girls.

Stella said, "All I know is, if someone *is* trying to get you two out in the woods, they're doing a good job. And if the girls are trying to ask for help, they're doing a very bad job. Throwing last night's chicken at us!" She shrugged with disgust at the memory of the lumps of congealed sauce.

I looked from her face to the words scrawled on the dirty scrap of cotton.

HELP US.

I couldn't drop this on the ground and go back home.

"They're in danger," I said. "The more I know about Mr. Arkel, the more sure I am. I have to find them."

Stella looked into the garden. "There's another scrap of fabric over there," I said, pointing toward it. "And I see another beyond it. They're meant for us to follow."

"I can see that," said Stella. "I just don't think we should."

But I was already headed into the garden, and when I turned to look, Stella was climbing over the wall, cigarette clenched in her teeth.

How had she not given up on me? At any time she could turn

and go back, but some mysterious force was making her stick with me. Friendship. Maybe that's all it was.

The way led us deeper into the wild-looking garden. There were big rosebushes with a few ragged blossoms still clinging deep among the thorns, where the frost reached last. We came to an oval fishpond with mossy edges, with pale orange fish moving sluggishly beneath the lily pads in the ice-rimmed, murky water. Several paths branched away from there. A scrap tied in a leafless bush indicated the one to take.

The garden went on and on. The path was covered with old leaves and detritus. Every time we rounded a curve, I thought we must have reached the end, but instead we saw another fork, and at each one, a marker. Most were white cotton, but there was also a torn piece of lace, a pale blue hair ribbon.

We wound through clusters of shrubs, past low spreading trees and stands of brown stalks that had once been flowers, with twisted yellow leaves and dry seed heads.

There was a dreamy feeling here, as if time had stopped or we had slipped into a narrow space between the ticks of a clock, and instead of moving forward from minute to minute, we were moving perpendicular to time, dropping down, down into another world.

Sometimes a statue surprised me, half hidden off the side of the path. A lichen-spotted huntress, bow in hand, gazed out from behind unpruned branches with blank, white eyes. A startled sparrow took off from her flowing marble hair. In another place stood a wolf, its fur spiky, head lowered, mouth half open in a snarl. Two more brown sparrows sat beneath its low marble belly and didn't fly away, but just looked at me, curious.

That was when I heard something I did not expect: the sound of a piano. It was faint but distinct. The music was swirling, modern.

Stella stopped. "Debussy," she said, almost whispering. "'Reflets dans l'eau.'"

"What does that mean?"

"'Reflections on the Water' . . . " She, too, seemed to feel the dreamlike quality of the place.

"Where's it coming from?" I asked.

"I don't know, but it isn't far away. If we keep going, we're going to run into whoever is playing. We should go back," Stella said.

I knew she was right. But I looked at the blue hair ribbon and imagined it tied to the end of a pigtail. I thought of Mary rummaging in the trunk, her hair matted to felt. "I can't."

Stella glanced at the sky. "Once the sun sets, we'll barely have enough light if we hurry—I'm not staying a minute beyond that. If you haven't found the end of the trail by then, we'll have to come back tomorrow. All right? At least the person at the piano can't sneak up on us," she added. "We can hear him. He can't hear us."

"You speak French?" I asked as we continued on the path.

"I was in the middle of getting an education," Stella said, "when I got pregnant."

"You have children?" I was surprised, remembering what Frank had said earlier.

"No." Stella looked away and seemed to study the path under our feet, the gray-and-white bits of broken shells and the small weeds pushing through. "I miscarried," she said shortly.

"Oh."

"There was a lot of bleeding and I had to go to the hospital," she continued, her voice matter-of-fact. "Whatever they did when they patched me up—I never got pregnant again."

So that was what had been behind Frank's disapproving comment about Stella's infertility. He was a crueler person than I'd realized.

"I'm sorry," I said.

"It's all right. I don't know that I wanted children anyway."

We seemed to be getting closer to the source of the music.

Then it stopped and there was silence. We kept going in the same direction, past a fountain: a naked young man spotted with lichen. From his cupped hands a stream of water poured without stopping. "You'd think they'd have turned the fountains off by now," Stella said. "Won't they freeze?"

As I got closer, I noticed stubby horns on the boy's forehead, and a slight, knowing smile on his face.

The pianist started again, and this time the piece was familiar.

"Debussy again," Stella said. "'Clair de lune.' That means 'Moonlight.'"

The music was so strange and beautiful that it seemed to lift us out of the mazelike garden, to someplace above it.

"'*Et sangloter d'extase les jets d'eau, / Les grands jets d'eau sveltes parmi les marbres,*'" Stella said. "That's the poem that inspired it."

"Say it in English."

"'*And they sob in ecstasy, the jets of water, the great jets of water, slender among the marble statues.*'"

"Life in the midst of stones," I said. "Like the water pouring from that boy's hands."

"That was Pan," Stella said.

"I know. God of the wild places." It seemed to me the wilderness was creeping back into this garden, in the weeds that grew on the path and the dried seed heads spilling their seeds into the leaf litter.

We came to another fountain: two marble nymphs, their foreheads and smiling lips spotted, like the boy, with gray-and-green lichen. They were holding hands, the same way Mary and I had on that day long ago, at the top of the hill, when the wind blew the uneven locks of hair that had escaped from under her hat, and the city of Albany, and the green countryside beyond it, lay spread out behind her. I had said my job at the Forts' house was the best I could do, and she had taken both my hands and said, "You can be whatever you want."

I hadn't believed her; instead I'd thought of how she'd wanted to be an actress, before she had to run away from school, and never got to be. I'd said, "But you couldn't."

And what had she said then? Had she answered me, had she dropped my hands and turned away? I couldn't remember now.

This fountain was dry. I stepped forward onto the apron of cobblestones that surrounded it, and suddenly jets shot up from around the girls' feet, taller than them, speckling their faces and tunics with dark splashes, scattering cold drops on me, too. I moved back, surprised, and the jets disappeared.

Stella came up behind me. "I've read about these. Trick fountains. You step on a certain stone."

I moved forward until I found it again. *The great jets of water among the marble statues.* Life amid the stones. Memories I'd tried to silence filtering upward through the present . . .

The nymphs, with their lichen and the dark patches where the water had soaked them, seemed happy, holding hands in this neglected place, with a grip no one could break. I imagined the house one day falling to ruin, the garden going back to wilderness, the statues toppling, broken by the elements, but those marble hands might stay clasped for eternity.

"Anna," Stella said, and I realized I'd been standing there for some time, my face cold where the water had splashed me.

"Come on," she said. "Look."

Ahead, the path opened up into a section of the garden that had been designed in a Japanese style. A few brown leaves floated on the still, black-and-silver surface of a man-made pond. At its edge, among massed evergreen azaleas and weeping trees whose names I didn't know stood a small pavilion-like structure with three walls, open in front. It was unlit and seemed to be filled with some dark objects or piles of things, which I couldn't quite make out.

The music had stopped and there was no breeze, no sound of

birds, just silence. I looked for another scrap of fabric to tell us where to go next, but saw nothing.

"Do you think that's where the markers were leading us?" I asked. "To that pavilion?"

Just then, the inside of the structure, which had been dark, was illuminated with electric light. Inside was a large, black mounded shape.

What was it? It seemed to move or shift. Then the music started again: the same piece we had first heard, eerie and modern. That's where it was coming from.

"There's someone in there," Stella said quietly.

"No," I said, "I think it's some*thing*."

"Whatever it is, it's moving," Stella said. Then: "Oh no, get back here."

But I had come too far to turn back.

The crunch of footsteps on dry leaves told me Stella was following.

"It's something under a sort of heavy rug." I looked back at Stella.

"I'm not touching it," she said. "You can."

The rug or blanket was glossy and black. I reached out, tugged, and it came off all at once in a heavy, slinky pile.

For a few stretched-out seconds, we were frozen, staring at what I had uncovered. It was a life-sized doll, a woman in a long blue dress and a fur wrap, with long, dark hair, sitting at an upright piano. Thick eyelashes fringed her glass eyes. Her silk dress was a dark sapphire, trimmed in black and elaborately embroidered with black glass beads. Her body shifted as her wooden hands moved over the keyboard. Her fingertips didn't touch it; the keys moved by themselves, playing the notes.

"It's his wife," said Stella, her voice muffled by her hands, which were pressed over her mouth.

"What do you mean?"

"His wife, who was with him in the motorcar. I told you, we saw them the first day. She's wearing the same dress and wrap."

"You mean he had this—thing—made to look like her?"

Stella shook her head. "I don't like this one bit. Come on." She grabbed my sleeve. "We're getting out of here."

"Wait." I noticed something in the automaton's mouth, the corner of a brown piece of paper between the polished wooden lips.

"Oh sweet Jesus," Stella said, "don't *pull* on it."

It wouldn't move. I had to pry the mouth open with my fingers while Stella watched. A note, folded into tight squares, was jammed inside it.

I unfolded it and read:

> I HAD TO SHOW YOU THIS. HIS NEW WIFE:
> MISSING 2 MONTHS. HE MADE THIS DOLL IT
> LOOKS LIKE HER. I THINK SHE IS DEAD.
>
> THE OTHERS WANT TO STAY BUT I WANT OUT.
> MEET ME HERE TOMORROW RIGHT AFTER DAWN
> PLEASE I NEED YOUR HELP

Fear rippled in Stella's gray eyes. "We have to go, Anna," she said. "Now."

"Wait," I said. "What if the girl who wrote this is still here? Maybe we can find her without coming back tomorrow. Hello?" I called, stepping out of the pavilion. "Hello!"

"Shh!" Stella pulled on me. "We can't help her if *he* finds us first. Do what the note says—come back tomorrow."

I knew Stella was right. Through the bushes, I spotted a low brick wall. "That must be the edge of the garden," I said. "That will be safer—less chance of being seen if we're in the woods."

Once we were outside the garden, the relief was palpable. Stella led the way and we followed the wall, keeping it in sight. Eventually it would lead us back to where we'd started.

"At least we can tell which way is west," Stella said, raising her face toward the sinking sun.

"I hope we get back before dark," I said. "Stella, if we make it in time to see the chauffeur bringing the dinner trunk, I think we should tell him everything."

"What do you mean?"

"About the girls in the woods, Southerland being shot, that thing in the garden."

"Absolutely not," Stella said. "I don't trust him for a second."

"But we've got to try to get word to the police," I said.

"He'll never go to the police. He works for Mr. Arkel. Besides, do you really think they can help us?"

"The ladies at the dock said they wouldn't," I admitted. "But that was two days ago—it seems like years ago. Now we've got three missing girls, and not one but *two* dead wives, *and* two dead detectives. Four dead and three missing—that's seven people—they can't ignore that."

Stella counted on her fingers. "Three girls who the police don't believe are missing in the first place; one late wife already known to have died in a hunting accident; a second wife, Millicent, who may not be dead at all—all we have is a scrawled note, and we don't even know who wrote it. Then we have one detective who was fired two months ago—Southerland said no one's willing to speak up about him. And Southerland, who definitely *is* dead—which we know because we found his body, but instead of reporting it, we decided to sneak into Mr. Arkel's greenhouse with a couple of parakeets, and then go walking all over Mr. Arkel's garden when we weren't supposed to. How do we explain all that?"

"It doesn't sound good when you put it that way," I had to admit.

"We have to tell the boys," said Stella. "Frank can be such an insufferable prick, but I think he'll know what to do. At least he knows Mr. Arkel better than any of us—he has some insight into what goes on in his mind."

"And he's a respected doctor," I added. "If he goes to the police, they'll listen."

"He'd never do that."

"Why not?"

Stella didn't answer. We were walking fast, trying to beat the setting sun. The late afternoon light was thick and golden brown. It didn't seem like we would make it. I wanted to be safely indoors, with Charlie and Frank, eating a good meal like we had last night. I wanted *not* to tell them, wanted to forget everything I had been through between then and now. It would be so much easier to pretend to live in a world where such things didn't happen.

We walked on, our boots crunching on the fallen leaves. "It's going to be dark before we get there," Stella said. I knew she was right. "Talk to me," she said. "Distract me."

"I'm afraid Mr. Arkel is going to kill us."

"Try again."

"I hope Charlie can get his crazy book written."

"His what?" Stella said.

"It means so much to him—"

"His 'crazy' book, you said. What a relief. I thought you believed all his theories—about invisible ships and whatnot—and that I had to humor you."

"Oh God, no," I said. "I mean," I backtracked, "it's not crazy. I shouldn't have used that word."

"It's all right."

"No, it's not." I felt I'd betrayed Charlie. "He has an eccentric sense of humor. Not everyone understands. But he's very smart. And Theodore Dreiser believes in him. You know Theodore Dreiser?"

"It's all right," Stella said again. "I know you love him." We walked in silence for a few more minutes. Then she said, "So it's not true about all those weird things like—like blood falling from the sky?"

"That part's true," I said. "He gets those from scientific journals."

"Then what are the scientific explanations?"

"That's the problem—they don't ever make sense. Charlie's right about that. Take the red rain that fell in Newfoundland in 1890. There was a theory that it was red sand from the Sahara, picked up by whirlwinds. But how could it travel so far, from the Sahara all the way to Canada? That was the best the scientists could come up with. There are so many cases like that. Charlie's right about the scientific explanations not holding water. I just don't agree with his explanations, either."

"So you're saying there are some things *no one* can explain."

I thought about it. "Maybe even if someone gave us the answer, we wouldn't understand it."

I remembered holding the twins' cage on my lap on the train from Albany, speaking the names of the towns we passed so they could hear a familiar voice as they sat in the dark under the quilt. *Herkimer, Deer River, Carthage.* Places they would never see, named in a tongue they didn't understand. They knew a few of my words, like "cracker" and "peanut," and I knew a few of theirs— the *chrrr* of greeting, the keening of disappointment—but that was all. They'd been mine all their life, yet we still understood so little about each other.

It was almost too dark to see now. "I think we're still going in the right direction," said Stella brusquely, but she didn't sound very sure. She began to hurry, and I scrambled to keep up.

"Scientists *always* say things were picked up by whirlwinds," I pointed out, trying to fill the silence. "Frogs, eels. But why only frogs and nothing else—no leaves or rocks? In a town in England in 1894, frogs fell from the sky. In Allahabad, in India, in 1834, it was dry dead fish. And *only* fish. How does a whirlwind explain that?"

I was out of breath, trying to keep the words going.

Stella stopped short, and I almost ran into her. "Hey. Over there. Do you see it?"

A faint light through the trees.

"We made it," I breathed. I felt hysterical laughter ready to bubble to the surface, and pushed it down. "We really made it."

"Dinner and firelight and a good stiff drink," Stella said.

We came out of the woods into the grassy clearing in front of the cabins. The lights were on in both of ours.

I felt suspended for a moment in the very last of the inky blue light, which was just leaving the sky above the brown and moss-green world. The cold, bent, sepia grass was barely visible under our feet. To our right stood the neglected, broken apple trees, their gnarled branches reaching up, silhouetted in the fading dusk.

"It's so quiet." My voice was hushed. Stella, ahead of me, seemed to float in the half-light. She opened the door to the cabin where Charlie and I were staying, and beyond it, in the warm lamplight, I saw the table laid for dinner.

She moved toward it and picked something up, then stood looking at it. When I got to the door, she turned to me. She held out a paper with writing on it, big loose letters.

"Anna," she said, "they're gone."

EIGHTEEN

Dears—

Tonight's trunk has been brought in and the table set for you. We have been moved to other temporary quarters. You are to stay here. We look forward to seeing your lovely faces at the end of our quarantine, in two weeks.

There was no signature. It was on a single plain sheet of good, heavy, cream-colored writing paper.

"That's the paper that's in the drawers of our writing desks," Stella said. "I suppose Charles wrote it."

"It's not his handwriting," I said.

Stella took it back. "It's not Frank's, either."

We looked at each other. "Mr. Arkel took them," I said.

"Or lured them out," said Stella. "I told you. Those girls work for him."

"No, I don't believe the girls are on his side," I said.

I looked at the table neatly set for two: silverware, linen napkins, crystal wineglasses glinting in the lamplight. "But they must have been lured somehow. There's no sign of struggle. And Charlie would never leave me on purpose."

"No, something is very, very wrong." Stella set the note down. "But they'll be okay. They're fit, strong men."

"Mr. Southerland was a fit, strong man." I could hear the edge in my voice. "We went where we weren't supposed to. It's my fault." I hardly realized I'd turned to leave until Stella stopped me. "I have to find Charlie," I said, pushing her away. "I can't just sit here while he's out there somewhere!"

"We're not going back out in the dark." Stella closed the door firmly and steered me toward the table. "Sit. You need a drink. So do I."

I knew our chances of finding Charles and Frank in the dark, with no idea where to look, were next to nothing. We'd only be exposing ourselves to whatever—whoever—was out there.

Stella went to the new trunk, which stood open, a fresh decanter of whiskey on the top shelf, next to the artificial flowers.

As she picked it up, something occurred to me. "That comes from Mr. Arkel. It could be poisoned for all we know."

"Don't be silly." She poured out two tumblers, handed me one, and clinked hers against it. "Tell you in a minute." She threw her head back. "Not poisoned," she said, setting down the empty glass.

I took a tentative sip. "Tastes okay."

"It certainly does." She reached for the decanter again.

"Stella, I'm scared." I put my glass down.

"Drink steadies the nerves."

"I want to keep my head clear. You should, too."

She ignored me and started on her second glass. "Damn it," she said, "I wish I hadn't left the detective's revolver out there."

"I wonder if yours was near the body, too. Or maybe in his pocket."

"Well. We don't have either of them."

I looked around the room. "Fireplace poker," I said, going over to where it leaned against the wall behind the woodstove. "Pointed tip. Sharp hook."

"You think that's going to protect us?"

I had to admit I didn't.

"There aren't even locks on the doors," I said.

Stella sat with her drink in her hand, still in her hunting jacket, staring at the poker I now held across my lap, with the private, stricken expression of someone reading the tragic final pages of a novel.

"We're sitting ducks," she said.

Then I had an idea. "The furniture. We can pile it against the door. And what about the windows?"

"We could jam sticks of kindling in them so they won't open," Stella suggested.

I put the poker down. "This table against the door first," I said.

I removed the long-stemmed, fragile wineglasses, and Stella helped me push the dinner table across the room. This seemed to improve her mood. "I'll do the windows next," she said.

I went to the bedroom to see what was useful there. The big steamer trunk stood against the wall, full of Charlie's notes. On the desk was a stack of typed pages. The typewriter still had a piece of paper in it. I pulled it out.

> The great difficulty that authoritativeness has to contend with is some other authoritativeness.

"He'd never have left his work behind," I said, sitting heavily on the bed.

"You're all right," Stella said, sitting beside me. But she said it because she could see I wasn't. I put my hand to my throat, which felt tight.

"It's one of those—attacks," I said. It was hard to get the words out. "The ones—that sent me—to the sanatorium."

"What helps?"

"The doctor said to breathe—I can't."

"I could slap you," she offered. "Maybe throw water in your face?"

"My friend—used to wrap her arms around me."

Stella's slender arms were surprisingly strong. I felt embarrassed but grateful. "Harder."

She gave a squeeze so tight it was almost painful. "Better?"

"A little."

Stella held on for a bit. She smelled of smoke, hair oil, whiskey, and some complex, expensive cologne. The constriction in my chest and throat slowly eased. After a few seconds, she let go and stood up.

"There. You're all right now."

I nodded. "Thank you."

"We can't get hysterical," she said, straightening her jacket. "It won't do. Not at all."

We cleared the dinner table completely so we could lay the writing desk on it. We shoved the steamer trunk under the table and all the chairs against the table's legs, all of it against the door. This gave us something to think about besides wondering what had happened to our husbands, and whether they were okay.

Only the bed stayed where it was: it was too big to get out of the room. We laid the tablecloth over the covers and put out the easiest food—bread, cheese, fruits. But neither of us could eat much.

"Getting drunk's not going to help," I said as Stella downed another glass.

"Shh," she said.

"What if they . . . ?" I couldn't finish the sentence.

"They're alive, I can tell you that much." Her words were beginning to slur.

"How do you know?"

"I just do," she said. "One, they haven't done anything wrong. Not like us. And two, he wants them here for a reason, okay. He wants Frank because he's losing his marbles."

"Frank said that," I agreed, remembering our conversation in the morning.

"Yes. Frank might be a—well—but he knows some things. He does. So that means Mr. Arkel wants Charles for a reason, too. And if he wants them, then he's not going to kill them. Right?"

"Then why take them?"

Stella shook her head. Still, I guessed we were both thinking the same thing: It was to punish us. For trespassing, for uncovering the doll, or for finding out he was a murderer. We couldn't tell how much he knew, what he'd seen or heard. But we'd given him more than one reason to be angry, and if the detective and Frank were right about him, then even one was too many.

"Finish your drink," said Stella. "Just one, for your nerves. You can't have another attack. I can't handle it."

I took another sip. It did help a little.

"What could he want Charlie for?" I asked. Stella shrugged. "Charlie said maybe he wanted him to investigate . . . something."

The lights in the woods, that's what Charlie had meant, because I hadn't admitted I knew they were lanterns. But what if he was still right? What if there *were* unexplained things happening? *Things are going on here which are not right,* that's what the letter had said. It could mean anything.

"The girls will know," I said aloud. "When we meet them tomorrow morning. They'll know what's going on."

Stella had crossed to the other side of the room, where the dinner trunk still stood with the decanter on it, and now turned to me with surprise. "You still want to do that?"

"What else can we do?" I asked.

"Go to the dock, look out for boats," she suggested. "Flag someone down."

"No one's around in this season. We could wait for hours."

Stella frowned. "You're right."

Both of us were silent. I didn't want to argue. If I had to, in the morning, I would go alone.

"I talked about Charlie's work to distract you in the woods," I said. "Now it's your turn. Tell me something to take my mind off this. You said you were in the middle of getting an education when you got pregnant. Where?"

"Radcliffe." She came back to the bed and sat on the edge. "Got some of the same professors as Harvard, but they'd give the ladies' version of the lectures."

"What's the ladies' version?"

"Take out the bad words." She laughed. "Not tell the whole truth."

Stella was drunk enough that I thought she might answer questions she wouldn't have earlier.

"Why did Frank seem so—almost scared of you last night?"

Stella stared at her glass and I thought she wasn't going to respond, but then she said, in a flat voice, "Because I know what he did." She looked at me. Her large gray eyes didn't seem cold, as they had at first. They seemed very tired. "I found out his secret."

"What do you mean?"

"About his machine," she said. "He likes causing pain."

I remembered that morning, the increasing strength of the shocks, how Frank wouldn't stop until he'd heard Charlie at the door.

"He found a career where he can do that and call it science," Stella said.

The thought that he had tricked me into it, not to help me, but for the pleasure of hurting me, made me queasy. I picked up my glass again.

"You mean it doesn't actually help?" I asked.

"Sometimes it does. That's why he gets away with it," Stella said. "But after the abortion—" She stopped and took a breath. "I told you I had a miscarriage . . . "

"But you didn't."

She shook her head. "Frank's the one who botched it. He was a medical student. Anyway. He did something wrong and . . . there was a lot of blood. He said I almost died."

"Did you go to the hospital?"

"Can't do that," Stella scoffed. "You'd get arrested. Because they can tell, you know?"

"Oh."

"I had a bad week recovering, and he had to take care of me. He acted like it was my fault." She stared into her glass. "And then I got kind of . . . " She shrugged.

I looked at her, sitting there on the edge of the bed, her shoulders hunched as they had been in the churchyard when I'd told her about seeing her and Frank through the window. Last night she'd seemed so confident, but now I saw there was something fragile about her.

"Kind of what?" I asked.

"You know . . . couldn't really get out of bed. Or eat."

Like when I had locked myself in my bedroom at the Forts' house, after Mary left.

"That must have been hard," I said.

Stella looked away. "Melancholic schizophrenia, that's what Frank said it was. He got a justice of the peace to come marry us so it would be easier for him to manage my treatment. I thought he would help me. Then, as soon as the papers were signed, he took me to Danvers."

"What's Danvers?"

"The state asylum. Lunatic asylum."

I'd heard about those places. Where they chained patients to the walls.

"Oh, Stella," I said.

For me it would have been the Hudson River State Hospital in Poughkeepsie, but Charlie saved me. He'd paid for me to go to Dr. Jacobson's sanatorium, with its bright rooms and lace curtains. I'd often wondered what would have happened if he hadn't.

"What was it like there?" I asked.

Stella set her glass on the floor and patted her pockets, looking for the cigarette case that was on the bed beside her. I handed it to her.

"Once I saw orderlies taking out a dead body," she said, clicking it open. "One of them said, 'She's better off now.'" Stella stood and lit her cigarette. "Better off dead."

"Why did Frank take you there?" I asked. Surely he could have afforded better.

"He worked there. He could keep an eye on me. I remember one time, waiting to see him, outside the room where he was treating someone." Stella picked up her whiskey glass and paced over to the window. "I heard screaming." She looked back. "They let him have the ones they'd given up on. The hopeless cases. So even a slight chance of a cure was enough to justify anything."

Dread congealed in my chest. "What does that mean?"

Stella looked at the window. It was too dark to see anything outside. She could only have been seeing her own reflection.

"Another time, I overheard him talking to one of the other researchers. You want to know what he was collecting data on?" She didn't wait for me to answer. "He was studying what was survivable. How high the current could be . . . "

"Before they died?"

Stella was silent.

"You're not saying he killed them?"

Stella rattled the ice in her glass. "Yes."

"On purpose? You say it like it's normal!"

"Don't you understand?" said Stella. "In a place like that, it is."

I stood up from the bed and began clearing away the food we'd laid out. "Not to me," I said.

"You were in a private sanatorium. I'll bet there were nurses in starched aprons and tea in china cups. That's not what it's like at Danvers."

"You're right," I said, piling up dishes, "there was tea, and a garden, and I'm sorry you had such an awful experience, but that doesn't make killing people 'normal.'"

"I wish I could go back to being naïve," Stella said.

I turned to her. "For your information, I've seen plenty."

Roses on a trellis, gray slate roof, clear blue sky.

I paused, pushing the images away, then picked up the stack of plates and carried it to the trunk.

"You said Frank was scared of you because you know his secret. But it doesn't sound like those patients dying was a secret."

Stella paced away from the window, then back. She glanced at her reflection, then pulled the curtains closed. "There was someone else," she said.

She turned. In the flickering lamplight, her eyes were rimmed with red. She had eaten even less than I had, and had drunk a lot more, and was still drinking. I felt a strange end-of-the-world atmosphere, as if things were being said now that would never be spoken at another time, because we knew we might not get another chance.

"Some of the board members at Danvers got wind of what he was doing and didn't like it. They told him to stop. But he couldn't. Two more of his patients died. They asked him to leave," Stella said. "He knew he had a problem. We both thought being away from Danvers would help. He set up a private practice in our home. He had paying patients who expected results, and he did all right. Then, a few years ago, on a rainy day, there was a young woman. I met her at the door and showed her the treatment room. She said her husband didn't know she was there. I had a bad feeling right away. Maybe because she was sort of innocent-looking, his type." Stella stopped and closed her eyes. "I said, 'Frank, be careful.' He said, 'I'm always careful.' I put a drinking glass against the wall so I could listen. She talked about a dream where her husband was trying to hurt her. She thought it was her fault, having that dream. She couldn't bear for him to touch her, and he was getting frustrated. Said she was willing to try anything. Frank hooked her up to the machine . . . I thought of opening the door . . . but instead . . . " Her voice went flat. "Instead, I told myself I was acting crazy. I made myself go shopping." She paused. "When I got back, she'd gone. That's what Frank said, and I wanted to believe him, so I did. Until last week."

I couldn't get the words out to ask what had happened then. In a way, I didn't want to know.

Stella sat down on the bed again. "I found a tobacco tin in the basement," she went on. "Inside it was a ring and a lock of hair. I *knew* they were hers." She looked up at me, her eyes redder, ugly with strain. "He admitted she died, but said he didn't do it on purpose. That she must have had a heart condition."

"Do you believe that?" My voice was hoarse; it felt like a long time since I had spoken.

"If only he had been honest . . . but he got scared and tried to cover it up. He took the body to the basement, and—" Stella stared at her latest cigarette, smoldering in her hand, untouched. Her cheeks were a damp mess of mascara and clumped powder.

I handed her one of the napkins I'd been about to put in the trunk. She took it but just sat there, squeezing it. "He got a surgical saw . . . the pieces had to fit in the barrel with the lye."

"The . . . *pieces?*"

"After the lye there were still, sort of, lumps. He dumped them in the river . . . "

My horror turned to anger. "Why, *why* didn't you go to the police?"

"Oh, I did," Stella said. "After Frank confessed everything, I waited till he was out and took the tobacco tin to the station. Told them the whole story. I even told them her name, but she must have given a fake one, because they had no record . . . There was no body, because of what I told you. When I showed them the tin, they told me my husband had a mistress. They said to go home and forget it."

"But they looked for other reports of missing people, anything that might match. They tried to help you," I insisted.

"They laughed at me, Anna."

I couldn't shake my anger. "Every day you go around acting normal you're covering for him."

How could she marry someone like that in the first place? I thought.

Then I remembered how I had allowed, had *wanted* Frank to hypnotize me, to shock me. Even after I'd seen him slapping Stella. Even after he'd hurt me with the machine, still I'd begged him to give me another chance to see Mary through his magic.

"I believe it was an accident," Stella said. "He just shouldn't have covered it up."

"You said he liked causing pain."

"That doesn't mean he intended to kill her. He felt so guilty. Who would bring that on himself? He said he was planning to tell me, it was just hard. He wants to get better, and I'm trying to help."

"That's what you were doing last night."

Stella nodded, patting her face with the napkin. "In our ritual, I play the part of Viola. That was her name. He hypnotizes himself to be back on that afternoon, and he tries to change the ending . . . to stop before he hurts her."

"And when he doesn't, it's your fault?" I asked, remembering his rage.

"The nightmares *are* my fault. They started after I confronted him and called him a murderer."

"Killing people didn't give him nightmares, but being confronted about it did?"

"No, he knows he has a problem. He thinks he can get better here, writing up his past experiments."

"But he brought his machine," I said. "He lied to you."

Stella put the stained napkin down on the bed. "When we find him, when we all get out of here, we'll get a good doctor, someone we can trust, and I'll tell him everything."

She put her glass down on the floor heavily and looked up at me with bleary eyes, shadowed underneath by the last traces of mascara and exhaustion.

"You've drunk too much on an empty stomach," I said. I handed her a roll I hadn't yet put away. "Eat three bites of this. Then bed."

Twenty minutes later, Stella came out of the bathroom in the shift I had lent her. "You look like a wedding cake," she said, flipping up the ruffles on my white flannel nightgown. Then she bent and gave my cheek a smoky, whiskey-smelling kiss.

I reached to put out the lamp, but she stopped me.

"Don't. I don't want to be in the dark."

NINETEEN

IT TOOK ME A LONG TIME TO FALL ASLEEP. WHEN I DID, I dreamed we went back to the garden, passing the lichen-spotted sculptures, the gray-green-mottled nymphs with their clasped hands, the stands of dead flowers.

When we got to the place where the pavilion had been, it was instead a much smaller, grassy area, which I recognized as the backyard of the house next door to the Forts' where piano music could often be heard, as the girl who lived there practiced at all hours. There was a small fountain, not like the ones in Mr. Arkel's garden, but impressive to me when I was younger. Mary sat on its edge, in her evening uniform, black with a white starched apron over it, smoking a cigarette, something I had not seen her do in life. The water behind her frothed like the falls in Normans Kill, where my father had taken me for a picnic when I was little, one of our few happy outings. Under her feet, the earth heaved as if things were moving under it, like playful cats under a blanket.

———

I WOKE IN THE THIN gray light. It took me a second to remember that the person breathing next to me was Stella, and that Charlie was missing.

I had to get to the garden to meet the girl who'd written the note. She'd know what was going on here, what we should do.

I went to the bathroom, passing the empty, open cage. I hoped the birds were warm and safe in the greenhouse. I couldn't know.

Then I tended the fire in the stove. What if Stella was right that our enemy was not only Mr. Arkel, but the girls as well? What if they were the ones who had lured Charles and Frank away, had written the note saying they'd been moved? But the handwriting was nothing like the messy scrawl on the paper I had found in the mouth of the automaton.

I shook Stella, who groaned and turned away. "Please wake up."

Stella pushed herself up on her elbows. "Oh, God," she said. "I need aspirin."

I found some in the dinner trunk and brought it with a glass of water. Stella held her head in her hands. She had not washed her face well the night before, and it was somehow touching to see it all messy, with dark smudges and patchy white powder, in the thin morning light.

"The note said to be in the garden just after dawn," I said. "It's time to go."

"You keep saying that, and I keep going with you."

"You can stay," I said, but Stella climbed out of bed. She sat on the edge, bent over. "Really."

"No. Not staying here alone," she muttered.

It took time to move all the furniture away from the door, and the sun was well above the horizon by the time we got into the biting air. The sky was a pale, cold blue. I carried the fireplace poker.

"We have to pass the body on our way," I said. "When we do, we'll take the detective's gun for protection."

Stella agreed. We walked fast, partly to keep warm. It didn't take us long to get to the stone wall. We weren't at the right part, so we walked along it, looking for the place where the body was. "Here," Stella called.

But when I went over, there was nothing.

"This is the spot, I'm positive," said Stella.

"Then it's gone," I said.

"Obviously."

"How? How can it be *gone*?" I said.

Stella held her pocket lighter to a cigarette, her hands shaking. "I don't know."

I moved the leaves with my foot, trying to see if the gun was still there somewhere, but it wasn't. There was nothing to do but go on. A minute later we passed a thicket of brambles and bare scrub that stood against a trio of boulders. That was when I heard it—the voice that had called to me from the darkness behind the church.

"Help us."

"Where are you?" I asked, heading around the bushes to the other side, where the voice had come from.

Stella grabbed my arm. "Don't."

I wrenched myself away. But when I got to the other side, no one was there.

But something caught my eye: on a large boulder with a somewhat flat, mossy top lay a small, pale object. I walked closer to see, and Stella followed.

What I had thought was moss turned out to be a crumpled green handkerchief, and on that lay a small naked doll. One of its arms was broken off above the wrist.

I *knew* it was one of the dolls I had kept in the cigar box under my bed, one of the subjects of King Nyx.

But it couldn't be. I touched the key in my coat pocket, the one I'd found in the greenhouse, the one I'd felt sure was the same one that wound up King Nyx. I thought of the girl at the trunks, turning toward me in the moonlight, with Mary's face. Now this. All of it was evidence of something very, very wrong with me.

Stella passed me and reached for the doll.

That was when I noticed the bent sapling. "Stop!" I said.

It was too late.

In a split second the sapling snapped upright and Stella was on the ground. She let out a kind of yelp. I saw the rope around her ankle. She had stepped into a snare like the one we'd seen before, and it had jerked her feet out from under her. I bent to help, and just then heard a person approaching through the dry leaves behind me. Before I could turn to see who it was, something was thrown over my head—something like a sack.

I felt rough hands everywhere, pulling, shoving. I heard Stella shout, a short, inarticulate syllable. I fell, then was yanked to standing again. My wrists were tied. Light faintly penetrated through the fabric covering my face. Something hard poked me in the back. It felt like the barrel of a gun.

"Move," said a hoarse voice. It was a girl's voice.

Hands pushed me forward. I walked. It was awkward, and I stumbled several times; but the hands—of two people? three?—kept me from falling.

"Where are you taking us?" said Stella from somewhere behind me.

A sharp hiss from behind hushed her.

I didn't know how long we walked—ten minutes? twenty? Eventually, the hands stopped us.

"Get over there," said a new voice, another girl, and someone shoved me until I was sitting down. I felt hands on my ankles, tying them together. Then my hood was lifted.

There were three of them. Their hair was wild and matted, their faces dirty. Their clothing was mismatched and improvised: boys' trousers, torn and filthy, rolled below the knee; battered boots; woolen stockings full of holes; a short toga made from a bedsheet.

There was a circle of logs around a campfire; I was sitting on one, which was draped with a dirty zebra skin, and Stella was nearby on another. The girls stood looking at us. A little way beyond them stood a tent made of a patchwork of canvas boat sails and animal-skin rugs: leopard, elk. Someone's plunder, repurposed. Off to the side of that lay a pile of refuse: ashes, orange peels, bones.

A fourth girl stood with the others, her back to us. A bearskin hung from her shoulders. Its empty hind legs dragged on the ground and had picked up twigs, scraps of dry leaves, and burrs.

The girl turned around, and my breath caught.

The same thin, curving mouth. Dark eyes I thought could swallow me. *Mary.*

The head of the bearskin hung over her shoulder, its forepaws clamped in its mouth, which was tied shut with twine, forming a kind of clasp. At her side was a spear made out of a hunting knife tied to the end of a staff, which she held nonchalantly, as if it was something she carried everywhere.

Even her expression, the way she pressed her lips together; even the way she lifted her hand to push away a lock of dirty hair. *Mary.* Not more than sixteen years old, the same age she had been twenty-three years ago when I'd last seen her.

I said her name, and she froze. All the girls did, as if my voice had cast a spell.

Mary was the first to speak: "How do you know my name?"

Stella looked from her to me, surprised. When I didn't answer, one of the girls walked over to me and nudged the cold muzzle of a gun against my cheek. The girl holding it was about Mary's age, maybe a little younger. She had full cheeks and a blunt nose and was wearing a huge white petticoat tied with string into an improvised dress and, over that, a man's coat I recognized as belonging to the dead detective.

"Tell her how you know," she said, in the same hoarse voice I had heard before. "Go on."

I looked from the girl with the gun to Mary and met her eyes. "You don't know me?" My voice sounded small and strange.

She seemed scared. "How would I know you?"

"We were friends," I said. She kept on shaking her head. I felt as if I were falling.

"You ran away . . . in eighteen ninety-five."

She stared at me, uncomprehending. Then her eyebrows lifted. "Oh," she said. "My God. Are you talking about my *mother*?"

Relief thawed the faces of the other girls, and the earth seemed to gather itself under me as everything became clear.

"You're her daughter? Mary Lyre's daughter?"

"You knew my mother—what, in Albany?" she asked at the same time.

"Yes, Albany," I said.

Stella looked from the girl to me and back again. "Really?" she said, as if the whole thing was a story I was asking her to believe. "How is that possible?"

How *was* it possible? Not only had my friend not died all those years ago—she had not frozen in a hayloft or been stabbed in a back alley—but she'd grown up to have a daughter. That in itself was a miracle. But that her child, so much like her, should be standing in front of me now, on this barely populated island just south of the Canadian border—I'd have been less surprised if she *had* turned out to be a ghost.

"She named you after herself," I said, my throat tight.

"Yes."

"But how did you get *here*?"

"I could ask you the same. I already know about your husbands being invited by Mr. Arkel. But I would never have guessed one of the wives knew my mother. As for me, I was born on this island," she said.

"Then you mean your mother is—is here?" I asked. "Now?"

Mary's expression made me regret the question. I had touched on something painful. But why?

"Is she . . . okay?" I finished lamely.

"Look, we've got to talk about that," said Mary. "That's why we brought you to our camp."

"I thought you lived at the ruined church," said Stella. "Or was that another set of wild girls throwing chicken at us yesterday?"

"We sleep there," said Mary shortly, "because the cellar room has a door. Here is better for talking."

The girl with the gun said, "Why tell them all that? They don't need to know it."

Mary silenced her with a look. "They're our allies now, Poppy."

"They haven't said so," said Poppy.

"I'll take care of that," said Mary. Then, turning to us: "We were bound to meet sooner or later, either on your terms or ours. I decided it would be ours. I know Sam left you a note." She nodded toward the girl in the rolled trousers, who looked to be the youngest, maybe fourteen. "I caught her heading out to meet you this morning, and she confessed."

Sam had blond hair and her blue eyes held an expression of surprise, like the eyes of a cat. "So you were the one," I said. "And was it your voice night before last, asking for help?"

Before the girl could answer, Poppy interrupted. "Yes," she said, "and it was me who shut her up."

"Why?" I asked.

"We didn't want to be found," Mary said.

"She did," I said, looking at Sam. She was twisting her index finger into her tangled blond hair.

Mary said, "She's worried because winter's coming. But she doesn't need to worry because we're doing fine. The room off the church basement is underground. It stays warm enough."

"Is that where you've got Charlie?" I asked. "In your underground room?"

"Charlie?" Mary exchanged glances with Poppy. Their confusion seemed genuine.

"Our husbands disappeared yesterday afternoon," Stella said.

Sam blinked her wide eyes and looked like she was about to speak, but Poppy cut her off. "We've got nothing to do with that."

"Then it was Mr. Arkel," I said. "Look, I don't know anything about you, but we *must* be on the same side. You don't need to have us tied up—we want to help you, and maybe you can help us. Tell us what's going on."

Mary tilted her head, studying me, while the black glass eye of the bear's head, just below her chin, gazed blankly through her knotted hair.

"We'll let you go if we can work out a deal," said Mary.

"What kind of deal?" Even though Poppy was holding the revolver, I wasn't scared. I was more aware than ever that these girls were so young—lost children. "We're ready to help. Figure out how to get you shelter and food—"

"That's not what we need," Mary said. "We're doing fine."

"Scrounging leftovers from our trunks."

"So?" she retorted. "It's good food, and you weren't eating it."

"What will you do when those are gone? We're only supposed to stay in those cabins a couple of weeks."

Poppy waited to see if Mary would answer, then, when she didn't, said, "We know that. We're familiar with the quarantine rules. We'll figure something out. It's not your concern."

The fourth girl had been silent, sitting a little apart from us. She had pale reddish hair and was wearing a garment made out of a sheet, with a wool blanket draped over her shoulders. I realized she was the one who'd been sitting on the ruined church's foundation, nursing her baby. "Where's her child?" I asked.

"Don't tell her. She's too nosy," Poppy said.

Mary ignored her. "Asleep in the tent. And how'd you know about Ginger's baby?"

"I saw her and the baby the first night, when I followed you into the woods."

"Of course. But why on earth did you follow me at night, all by yourself?" asked Mary. "You must have really wanted to catch me." She was looking at me with new intensity, trying to figure me out.

"It's your face," I said. "You . . . your mother meant a lot to me. You said you'd tell me about her."

Mary looked down at the end of her spear, twirling it in the dirt so it made an indentation, as if she would drill down to some layer beneath the surface we stood on. She didn't answer.

TWENTY

THE SUN HAD CLEARED THE CLOUD BANK AT THE EDGE of the sky, and the day was warming. Smoke rose from the fire in the morning light. The strange patchwork tent was grimy with soot and mud. The girls smelled like they desperately needed baths.

"Listen," said Mary, "we ran away from the school in the spring. Well, these three did; I wasn't a student there, but I went with them."

"That's why there are four of you, when Mrs. Laches only said three students were missing," I said.

"*That woman,*" Mary spat.

"Are you the one who wrote to her?" I asked.

"Yes," Mary said tersely.

"Aren't you a little fickle?" Stella said. "Writing for help, then saying you don't want it."

"That was six months ago," Mary answered. "We needed it *then*."

"But people have been trying to help you," I said. "Mrs. Laches tried to get permission to visit, but Mr. Arkel wouldn't let her. She tried to get the police to investigate. You're wrong if you think no one's been trying."

"I know all of that. Clover told us how that busybody rowed over last week and asked about us."

"Who's Clover?"

"One of the girls who stayed back. They all know we're here, but she's the one who keeps in touch. There's a storeroom where we can leave notes for one another. Sometimes we meet. But it's risky."

"If they all knew where you were, then why wouldn't they tell Mrs. Laches when she rowed over here?"

"They promised never to tell. Besides, do you realize the trouble they'd get into if it came out that they know?"

"She could have rescued you!"

"I told you, we needed that when we were living in the house. Now we've rescued ourselves. We've made a life here. Anyway, this whole thing was her fault."

"Mrs. Laches's fault?" I asked. "How?"

"As soon as she got my letter, she could have come here like I asked, but she didn't. Instead she telephoned Mrs. Arkel."

"Wasn't Mrs. Arkel the school's director?" I asked. "Why shouldn't she telephone her?"

"I was stupid not to realize things would end up how they did," Mary said.

"It's not your fault," Poppy said fiercely. She turned to me. "She was trying to help. It's not her fault Mrs. Arkel did what she did."

"How do you mean?" asked Stella.

"I mean," said Poppy, "she already knew what was going on and she never lifted a goddamn finger to stop it." Poppy spoke without taking her eyes or the gun off us. "She didn't care about us. All she cared about was that someone from off the island wanted to come here. Pry into her business. When we wouldn't tell who wrote the letter, she punished *us*. Then she laid into her husband—not for what he did, but for letting the secret out."

That was what Stella had said. He was "having affairs with" the girls. Not that they probably had any choice in the matter:

they were young women with no one looking out for them. That explained Ginger and her baby.

"He was taking advantage of you," I said. "And no one would help you."

"Gertrude Arkel could have," Poppy said. "I know she could have stopped it anytime if she wanted to, but she didn't. She deserved what she got."

"You mean when he killed her," I said.

"That's right," Poppy spat.

"I'm sorry," I said. "About everything. Him taking advantage of you. No one helping. None of that should have happened."

More lives derailed by men who did whatever they wanted. The same story over and over and over.

"I really thought," said Mary, "that we could get help from someone who wasn't part of his little world. I was too stupid to realize she'd pass the complaint right back to the Arkels. But it's all right now. We got away."

"But look how you're living," I pointed out. "Getting away isn't enough. You have to get off the island."

"Where would we go," asked Mary, "four girls with no money and a baby? We have connections in the house. We've got a good hiding place. I can look out for us."

Sam chewed her blond hair, her wide eyes staring into the fire. Without changing her expression or looking at Mary, she said, "You did look out for us. But things are changing."

"That doesn't mean I won't still take care of you, Sam."

"How are things changing?" I asked.

"No one was trying to find us before," said Sam.

"It's true Mr. Arkel was preoccupied with other things before," said Mary. "After he shot Gertrude, he couldn't sleep, kept to his room. He was losing his mind. So he wasn't trying to find us. Then he met his new wife, and I think he forgot we even existed. But yesterday—" She stopped. "It . . . was my fault."

"No it wasn't," said Poppy.

"What wasn't?" I asked. "What happened yesterday?"

Mary sighed. "His detective, Mr. Southerland, saw that someone had broken into the trunks behind the cabins. He traced us from there. And he almost caught Sam."

I realized he must have seen the looted trunks when he'd come to take Stella's gun. We'd led him straight back to the cabins, and he saw the mess. Maybe Mary had left tracks, or maybe he just followed the nearest deer trail; either way, it had ended with finding Sam.

"He was trying to grab her," said Poppy. "He had a gun on her. I saw another one sticking out of his pocket."

Stella's revolver, I thought.

"I grabbed it," said Poppy, examining the weapon in her hand, "and I shot him with it." She looked up at me with a tight grin.

"*You* shot him," I said.

"So that explains how he died," Stella said. "But why did his body disappear later? Where did it go?"

Poppy said, "We didn't need Mr. Arkel finding it. I got Sam home safe, then I went back and hauled the carcass out to the river."

I studied Poppy's face, her dark eyes and her sad, tight mouth. "Want to know what it feels like to kill someone?" she asked. Before I could reply, she said, "Nothing, that's what. It was easy."

"Because you were protecting someone you cared about," I said. I felt at once fiercely proud of her and unsettled by the strength of my emotion. I wondered if I could have done the same.

"What about the other revolver?" I asked. "The one he was carrying—you took that, too?"

"No, that was gone when I went back for the body," said Poppy. "Someone else must've got there first and took it." That meant there was someone else on the island with a gun now. Who?

"Could you maybe put that thing down now?" said Stella. "I promise we're very nice ladies, and it's making me nervous to have it pointed at us."

Poppy glanced at Mary, who gave a slight nod.

Stella exhaled with relief. "Now if you could just untie me, so I could have a cigarette . . . "

Mary ignored this. "After Sam almost got caught, that's when she decided she had to try again to talk to you. That's why she snuck out to the garden and left the trail."

"Sam," I said, "your note said he killed his new wife. How do you know?"

Again it was Mary who answered: "It wasn't just Detective Peleus who disappeared the night he was shot. Millicent did, too. Mr. Arkel said she was ill, that she had to take her meals in her room. But there were too many things that didn't add up. He said his valet would take care of everything for the two of them. Imagine: a valet putting away her underthings when they came up from the laundry, or brushing her hair! It didn't make sense. On top of that, she only ever appeared when she took drives with him. Nobody but Mr. Arkel and the chauffeur saw her up close. When we found that doll, we realized it wasn't really her he'd been driving around with—it was *that*."

"So you're telling me he killed *both* his wives," I said, "as well as his new wife's lover. You're telling me he's murdered three people."

Poppy laughed bitterly. "Why is that funny?" Stella demanded.

The girls glanced at one another. Then Mary said, "He's done more than that."

"What do you mean?"

"It wasn't just that he was taking advantage of the girls. That had been going on since—well, since before I was born. But a few years ago, something happened that made him . . . worse. It was the strike at his canning factory. He put it down—violently. But he was still humiliated. There was so much about it in the papers. People saying he was just an idiot with family money. It came out that Arkel's Canned Fruit had never made a profit—had been bleeding money for years. He took it out on everyone."

"But the ones he took it out on the worst," said Poppy, "were Daisy and Alice."

"Those are students at the school?" I asked.

"Were," said Poppy. "Daisy—he threw her down the stairs before Gertrude Arkel could get her off to an unwed mothers' home."

"She was pregnant, you mean."

Poppy nodded.

I looked with new understanding at Ginger. What had he done, or threatened to do, to her? She hadn't made it to an unwed mothers' home, either. Had she had her baby at the school or out here in the woods, attended by children like herself?

"Daisy was fourteen," said Sam quietly. Her fingertip was red where she had tightly wound her hair around it.

"Stop that, Sam," said Mary, reaching out to pull her hand away. "Your finger's going to fall off."

"What about Alice?" I asked. "What happened to her?"

Mary looked at the indentation in the ground made by the end of her homemade spear. "She got scared and tried to run away."

"Like you."

"Except she got caught." Mary said. "He caught her in the woods. He always takes his rifle when he goes to the woods."

There was a cold knot in my stomach. "You're not saying . . . "

"He shot her," said Mary curtly.

"But that doesn't make any sense," I insisted. "He wouldn't just go out in the woods and shoot a person, a human being. That's murder."

I felt that old tightness in my chest, and fought it. Maybe it should not have come as a surprise, after all I had heard. But the cumulative effect of all the deaths I'd learned of was too much. I had left the normal, rational world, where murder was something I read about in the papers, and slipped into some dark place beneath the surface, where it was everywhere.

It is *normal*, Stella had said about the deaths at Danvers. In a way, it made sense that such things could happen in a place like that.

But at Danvers, Frank had eventually been stopped. Maybe there was no one who could stop Mr. Arkel. *He's the king here,* Frank had said. *What might a man do . . . ? What might any of us do?*

Did Frank sense that Mr. Arkel was, like him, capable of killing just because he could? Was that the real reason Mr. Arkel had invited him back, was this the bond they shared?

Ginger got up abruptly and went to the tent, where her child was sleeping. A heavy silence fell over the campsite. I reminded myself to breathe, tried to focus only on the girls. Sam's fingertip was bright crimson and swollen. Poppy sat expressionless, holding the gun.

Mary said, "To you and me, it's murder. To Mr. Arkel, maybe it was just sport."

I had to get the girls off this island.

"I understand why you asked for help," I told Sam, "and I'm going to help you." I turned to Poppy and Mary. "You have to let me."

"Look, Sam's too young to understand, but we aren't," said Poppy.

"Understand what?"

"Fairy tales aren't real. We're on our own. That if you met her in the garden and took her away like you wanted, she'd only have ended up somewhere worse." I started to speak, but Poppy interrupted angrily: "What were you going to do, anyway? Take us home, darn our socks, and bake us pies?"

"You have to realize," said Mary. "They were already 'rescued' once, from juvenile court, and brought here. It was supposed to be a better life."

"But that kind of life doesn't happen for girls like us," said Poppy. "Sam's just too young to get it."

My frustration was turning to anger. "Listen," I said. "Winter is coming, and you're out here dressed in rags, and this one"—I indicated Ginger, who stood beside the tent now with her child bundled in her arms—"has a little baby! You're on an island with a man who could find you at any moment, and kill you. You were lucky it was Detective Southerland who found you two, Poppy. Next time, it could be Mr. Arkel. Yet instead of accepting help, you decide to hold us here at gunpoint—all because you don't believe in fairy tales."

I looked again at Ginger, who was silent. Her baby was wrapped in a thin-looking, dirty blanket. I wished I had the quilt from the birdcage—I'd take that baby and wrap it tight and warm.

Mary caught my eye. "We didn't bring you here because we don't believe in fairy tales. We did it because I need your help. I was afraid you wouldn't want to help us—that I'd have to threaten you. And I was prepared to do that." She twisted the spear end in the dirt again. "That was before I found out my mother was your friend . . . " She looked up at me. "Because the thing is this: I want you to help me find her."

"*Find* her?"

When Mary had hesitated to say where she was, part of my mind had accepted the fact that she was dead. After all, that was what I'd feared for the past two decades.

"You mean your mother is alive?" I half swallowed the last word. It was too much to hope for.

"Look," said Mary, "I don't know what . . . gods or fates are responsible for bringing you here. Maybe it was chance. Regardless, you're the right person to help us. We need someone who can break into the house." Stella started to object, but Mary went on: "I won't let the girls try. The risk if Mr. Arkel finds them is too high. But for you it's different: you're guests. That's what I was going to ask you, even before I knew you were her friend. And now that I do know—well, I hope you'll agree to do it, that's all."

"We're guests, so you think we can *break in*?" Stella asked.

"Listen," Mary said, "we don't know exactly why you were

invited, but we know it's not out of generosity. That's not how he is. The servants' theory is there's some way he hopes to benefit from your husbands' research. Whatever the reason, he wants something. That means he needs you. If he catches you in the house, he'll be upset that you've broken the rules, but he won't harm you."

"You seem awfully sure of that," Stella said skeptically. Her voice sounded brittle with anxiety.

"You're not the same as the rest of us on the island. You're not . . . " Mary trailed off.

"Not *his*," Poppy finished.

Mary's eyes were on me, and I saw the weight of the question in them. "Will you help?"

She'd said she planned to force us if we didn't agree, but it seemed clear there was no real way for her to do that. In the end, it would be our decision. I shared Stella's doubt that it was safe, yet the idea that there was even a chance that I could see Mary again was too much.

I started to say yes, but the word caught in my throat when I glanced at Stella's face. It was tense and white.

"Look," she said, her voice tight, "would you mind terribly just letting me have a cigarette?"

"Be quiet," said Poppy, gesturing at her with the gun.

But Mary said, "No, Poppy, give her one."

While Poppy squatted to pat Stella's pockets, I met Mary's eyes. "Tell me everything," I begged. "Where is she now? How did she come here in the first place?"

Mary drew a breath. "She came when she was my age. She'd run away from the place where she worked as a housemaid—"

"Yes."

"When she was on her own, she got arrested for trying to steal a sack of apples. She couldn't pay the fine, so she was sentenced to jail time. But the judge liked her and gave her the choice to come here instead. To turn her life around."

"The cigarette case is *there*," Stella interrupted, trying to point with her chin, as Poppy reached into one after another of her many pockets.

"Anyhow," Mary went on, "I was born five or six years later. Somehow she convinced him not to send her away, like he did the other girls. She said it was because she made herself useful, indispensable. Eventually, she became his personal secretary and he let her handle everything—correspondence, investment decisions. She was his right hand. She told me the best way to keep me safe was to make sure he couldn't live without her. But she also always told me to stay away from the girls in the school. She didn't want me to end up like them . . . like her."

"Oh, God, just untie me so I can do it!" Stella said to Poppy, who had found the pocket lighter but was not managing to strike a flame.

"Never mind, I got it," said Poppy, holding out the flame. As Stella inhaled the smoke, her body realigned visibly with relief.

"But you did end up friends with the girls from the school," I said.

"When I was little, there wasn't anyone to play with. I was so lonely. Once I got to be the same age as the students, I went behind her back and started talking to them. I remember when I realized how he treated them. I remember when Daisy got thrown down the stairs, and everyone just acted like it was normal. And when Alice . . . got tracked down in the woods." Her voice dropped on the last words, as if she didn't want to hear herself say them. "I knew I was safe," she continued, "because of my mother. He couldn't do those things to me. But I couldn't stand seeing what happened to them. I had to do something. When Ginger got pregnant . . . I just couldn't let it happen to her. I went to my mother for help and admitted they were my friends, told her everything. I said, 'Mr. Arkel can't live without you. If anyone can change things, you can.'" Mary stared at her spear, drawing an X in the dirt, tracing it over and over, angrily.

"I always thought if it came down to me or him, she'd choose me. But she didn't help. She said that's the way of the world and I might as well get used to it." Mary used her foot to smudge the X and looked up at me. "The one thing she did do was give me the name of one of the trustees to write to, but she said I must never, ever tell where I got the name—"

"But what happened to her?" I asked. "You said you wanted help finding her. Tell me where she is."

"I'm getting to that. After the girls and I ran away into the woods, she begged the ones who stayed back at the school to tell where I was, but I'd made them promise not to. They told me she was upset, but I didn't care."

I felt a pang at the thought that she had abandoned her mother too, like I had.

"You were angry," I said.

Mary nodded.

"But yesterday, after Detective Southerland almost got Sam, I decided it was time to talk to her. Find out how much Mr. Arkel knows—whether Southerland acted on his own or whether Mr. Arkel knows where we are. So I met Clover in the storage room last night. I asked if she could arrange for me to see my mother in secret. That's when she told me . . ."

"Told you what?"

"My mother often works in Mr. Arkel's study. Since Mr. Arkel has been keeping to himself during the last two months, she's been handling everything on her own. So when the servants noticed the lights on late at night recently, they didn't think much of it. But normally they see her during the day, giving orders and supervising things. When I met Clover, she said no one had seen my mother in the past two days, and that the lights in the study had been on all night. You have to understand, she's the one who manages everything. The butler and head housemaid report to her. They never go a whole day without seeing her. They checked her room, and her bed hadn't been slept in. Then the butler got a note from Mr. Arkel. It said my mother had taken ill and no one was to bother her. Exactly the same thing he said about Millicent. And if she'd taken ill, she should have been in her bed. None of it made sense. And I *know* my mother would never just disappear like that."

"And when he said that about Millicent . . . she was . . . " I couldn't say the word. "So you think he may have done something to her, too. You don't know if she's alive."

The ember of hope I'd briefly felt sank in my chest now, cold and black.

"She once told me," said Mary, "that her secret was that she never, ever did anything to displease him. She gave him credit for every success, blamed someone else for every failure. She never disagreed, never asked for anything, never did anything he could object to in any way."

"Until she slipped you the address of the trustee," Stella said.

"He can't have found out. I never told," she said.

"But maybe someone guessed," said Stella. Mary looked stricken.

"Look," I said. "With a man like that, there's always something. He was going to lose his temper eventually. That's how it was when I worked for Mr. Fort." I half swallowed the last word, realizing too late that I'd just given away the secret I'd been trying to keep from Stella since we met. She looked at me with surprise. "That's how Charlie met me," I muttered. "I was his maid."

I wasn't able to read her expression, but I couldn't afford to care about it now. "You asked for my help," I said to Mary. "You must think there's a chance she's alive."

"She'd been going in and out of Mr. Arkel's study. Ever since the night he shot his wife and her lover, two months ago, he'd been in there day and night, except when he went out for drives. He even slept on the sofa in the study. She spent hours working beside him and she also brought him meals, fresh clothes. The day she disappeared, the first parlormaid happened to see her go in. No one ever saw her come out."

"So you think she could still be there," I said. "Alive."

"Yes," said Mary.

And what did all this mean for Charlie and Frank?

"You said you could help us find our husbands. Where do you think Mr. Arkel took them?"

"I wish I knew," Mary said. "I don't think anyone in the world can say what's in that man's head—except maybe my mother."

"We'll find her," I said.

"You'd have to go to his study," Mary began.

"We'll find her," I said, "and she'll tell us what to do about Charlie and Frank."

I looked to Stella for confirmation, but her face was blank, closed.

"What do you mean 'we'?" she said, and I realized what a leap it had been to assume that she would undertake this risky mission for my friend, a person she didn't even know.

"But, Stella," I said, "she could have the answer to where Charlie and Frank are."

"Could have, *if* she's not one of the people who took them, *if* she's findable, and alive."

Stella was right: even if we succeeded in finding Mary, that wouldn't guarantee any help for our husbands.

She must have thought my silence was reproachful, because she went on: "You've done nothing but go on one harebrained mission after another. You're the reason we got ambushed—"

"But," I interrupted, "what other chance do we have?" She was right to think it was crazy. I knew that. "I have to try," I said, my tone almost apologetic. "I have to."

"Fine, go. I'm staying."

TWENTY-ONE

POPPY UNTIED OUR HANDS, AND SITTING AROUND THE fire, the girls shared some fresh water from a spring. They tried to share their food—bread and oranges and hard cheese they'd taken from the trunks—but they didn't have much, and neither Stella nor I had an appetite.

"There's a way in from the greenhouse," Mary explained. "That's how you'll get to Mr. Arkel's study. In the middle of the main greenhouse there's an artificial rock hill with a grotto and a waterfall—"

"We've seen it," I said.

"I know," said Sam. "I heard you talking about going to the greenhouse. That's where I got the idea to leave the trail into the garden."

Poppy gave Sam a thin but approving smile. "You notice a lot, don't you, kid?"

"I saw something else, too," Sam said quietly.

"What's that?"

"Their husbands."

My heart jumped. "Where? Why didn't you say so?"

"I tried," said Sam, and I remembered Poppy cutting her off before. "I saw them a ways out from the cabins. They were walking. I think they were looking for you," she told Stella and me. "They were saying it was getting dark and they were worried."

"Do you think they got lost?" Stella asked.

"No," I said. "*Someone* left that note."

"Did you see anything else, Sam?" Mary asked.

Sam shook her head.

"It's hunting season," Ginger said suddenly. She held her baby close, a grimy bundle with a cherub's face.

"What do you mean?" Stella asked. But we both knew what she meant. Maybe Mr. Arkel had found them. Maybe he had left the note to cover it up.

I thought that Ginger's shadow against the tent wall, a muddy tiger hide, flickered as if a cloud blew past the sun, but there was no wind. For a moment the campsite seemed unreal, like a diorama seen through glass.

Ginger spoke up again, saying, in her low voice, "We built this campsite when we thought he wasn't looking for us. We thought it was safe." She glanced back at Mary. "But I don't think it is anymore. Sam's right. We need to get off the island."

"We have to find Mary first," I said, my voice sounding like it was coming from far away. "She'll explain everything. She'll help find Charlie and she'll help us get away from here. Tell me how to get into the house. Tell me what to do."

THE SUN SET, AND THE last of its light disappeared around five o'clock. The cold, high moon began its descent, and by twelve, when it was time for me to go, the sky was completely dark except for a few stars visible among the clouds, icy and small, blinking through the vast black distance of space.

Mary led us with a kerosene lantern through the woods. Stella was behind me, coming to see me off. Sam, Ginger, and the baby had gone back to the safety of the room off the church basement, which had a door to close against the night. Poppy brought up the rear with a second lantern. One of the lights I'd seen through the trees on the first night, the mysterious lights Charlie said he wanted to follow. Before he disappeared, he'd thought he was on the verge of catching something he'd chased all his life: an answer.

After we had walked about twenty minutes, we stopped at the edge of the lawn surrounding the greenhouses.

Poppy had drawn a map on a torn piece of brown paper. "Remember," she said, handing it to me, "when you come out of the tunnel, you'll be in a room off the wine cellar. If you hear anyone, wait there till they're gone."

Mary handed me her lantern. "Turn the flame as low as you can," she said.

"And here," Poppy muttered, "take this." She pushed something into my other hand, and I realized it was the fireplace poker the girls had wrenched away from me when we'd been caught. "And mind you don't leave the cellar until one o'clock."

I was just wondering how I was going to know the time when Stella slipped something into my pocket in the dark. Holding the poker and lantern in one hand, I felt to see what it was.

"Your wristwatch," I said.

"It's the least I can do," said Stella. She slipped her cool hand into mine and squeezed it.

"One more thing," said Mary. Her thin, tired face was lit from below by my lantern. I looked at those familiar dark eyes. If I succeeded tonight, I would see them again in her mother's face.

"You're going to pass the room where he keeps the dolls," Mary went on. "You might be tempted to go in and look. Don't."

"Isn't it locked?" I asked, remembering that Frank had said so.

Poppy gave a short laugh. "A normal person would have a normal lock on the door. Mr. Arkel . . . "

"You'll get in," said Mary, "but it'll lock behind you. We learned that after he built the room. One of the scullery maids tried to sneak in for fun. He found her the next day. She wouldn't say what happened, but when she got out, she wouldn't wait in the house for the next grocery boat to take her off the island—she sat out on the dock a whole day and night until it came."

Stella's eyes met mine, and she shook her head in a silent *No*. Her meaning was clear: *Don't go.*

I was afraid, too, but the fearful part of myself floated above me now, as if in the basket of a balloon. Although it waved and shouted at me to turn back, I ignored it. "I have to," I said quietly.

I turned and left the edge of the woods, and crossed the grass in the faint light of the stars that dusted the open patches of sky. The hothouses stood ahead, silent and full of secret green life, the glass of the roofs barely reflecting the watery glow of the stars. Were Castor and Pollux sleeping there now, among the branches of the fruit trees?

Inside the door, I paused to inhale warm air in which growth and rot mingled, a scent as soft and thick as moss. A lone cricket, startled into silence when I'd opened the door, started chirping again; then another joined it.

The lantern threw out a sphere of light, protecting me from the green-black dark.

On the narrow path, huge leaves crowded in, brushing my wool coat, my cheeks. The sound of the waterfall led me to the center, where the path opened out. I emerged from the thicket of huge plants. Starlight shone into the open space through the hundreds of glass panes overhead. I walked parallel to the curving banks of flowers, their jewel-like hues grayed now in the faint light.

The pool at the head of the stream was fed by water spilling out of the cave in the rocky mound. The waterfall was about four feet tall, and the cave from which it issued was also about that tall, so its top was about eight feet above the greenhouse floor. I lifted my lamp to look into the cave and noticed something

I hadn't the first time: a marble statue of a woman in flowing robes, half hidden by vines.

Behind the waterfall is the mouth of a tunnel, Mary had said. Yet even as I got close, I couldn't see anything but the dense greenery that grew around the base of the rock mound.

I crouched to run my hand along the ivy-covered wall behind the waterfall till I came to a place where the vines gave way.

It had to be the tunnel mouth. I could edge my way in there. It was low and I had to bend, but I was able to push through.

Once in, I had to crouch awkwardly in the low space. The walls were made of steel struts and concrete, with patches of dark mold. The floor slanted down. After a few steps the tunnel was tall enough to stand in. It was warm at first, like the greenhouse. But soon the concrete ended and the walls became packed earth, framed at intervals by thick wooden support beams. The tunnel sloped more steeply, and the air chilled.

The walls became still rougher, the floor more damp. Then, gradually, it began to slope upward again. I knew I must be getting closer to the house. And then, up ahead, the tunnel narrowed to an irregular opening, through which I could faintly see a stack of wooden crates. This had to be the room off the wine cellar. There was just enough space for me to squeeze through the opening and out from behind the crates.

I stood in a small, rough chamber that could almost have been an animal's burrow; it looked like it had been dug out of the earth, its floor and ceiling curving to meet each other. Aside from the stacked boxes, there was nothing in it. It was here that I was to wait until one o'clock.

I took Stella's watch out of my pocket and held it in the lamplight. It was about a quarter past twelve. Still forty-five minutes to wait. I had kept the watch in my pocket to protect it, but now I fastened it to my wrist. Then I extinguished the lamp. It didn't make sense to risk someone seeing the light if I didn't need it.

In the dark, with my back against the cold wall, I realized how tired I was. I had slept very little the night before, and not at all since waking in the cabin before sunrise.

I closed my eyes, and instantly a dream flashed in front of me, fully formed, as if it had been waiting, like a star invisible until darkness falls.

Silhouetted against an orange sky, I saw black trees and an angular black shape that I recognized as King Nyx. She was not in the form of the tin toy but was larger and messier somehow, resembling a pen-and-ink drawing I had come across in some book, of a crow fighting with another crow in a stormy, chaotic sky.

Tell me if Charlie is okay, tell me if Mary is alive, I said.

An uneasy wind stirred the black feathers; I sensed restlessness and fear.

Then, without warning, I was somewhere else: alone in a sunlit place, near water. I heard the insistent tapping of a telegraph. *If only I knew Morse code, I could tell what it says,* I thought. Then: the sound of a gunshot.

I gasped and opened my eyes, heart racing. How long had I slept? I fumbled for the matches and lit the lamp. The long black minute hand on Stella's watch stood close to the small black V now. It had barely been ten minutes.

Breathe, I thought, hearing Charlie's voice in my head. *Breathe in. Out.*

Where was I? In a strange upside-down world where nothing made sense. Against all odds, I had landed on the same island where my lost friend had been living for years. But I didn't know whether she was all right, or even alive. I didn't know whether my husband was, either. What if both were dead? I had lived without Mary for years, but how could I live without Charlie?

My hand in my pocket touched something small and hard. I wrapped my fingers around it: the tin key I'd found in the greenhouse, the one that looked so much like the key that had wound up King Nyx, the black tin bird with blue eyes that had once reigned over the pale, stiff dolls in the cigar box under my bed.

If only I could find the real key to all of this. The one piece of information that would change the story from an assemblage of mismatched parts into some kind of whole.

Maybe the story would never be a purring, smooth-running thing, like the automobile that had carried Charlie and me when we'd first arrived on the island. Maybe real life never made that kind of sense. At least, not to imperfect human eyes. We were small and tangled in it all; we'd never get a view of the whole machine.

But sometimes, we understood some things, in a crude way—didn't we? We heard a faint echo of the universal order. Enough to get us from one end of our mortal years to the other. Though we might be chauffeured by a crumple-headed praying mantis with goggle eyes and a rubber-hose proboscis, yet still, could we not pray . . . clumsily maybe, nonsensically, but still, could we not pray . . . together . . . ?

I was sliding into sleep without realizing it, my thoughts trailing off into nonsense, the floor tilting slowly under my body, until a sharp pain—the back of my head hitting the wall—jerked me awake. I looked at Stella's watch again. Almost one o'clock. Time to go.

I unfolded the map and looked at it again, memorizing it. It showed parts of the three separate floors I would have to navigate: *Sub-Basement*, *Basement*, and *Main Floor*. I was in the sub-basement now and had to go from *Wine Cellar* through *Storeroom*, *Storeroom*, *Storeroom*, *Stairs*. More chambers, more stairs. Corridor past *Main Kitchen*. Last *Stairs*. *Passageway* alongside *Smoking Room*, *Gun Room*, into *Sitting Room*. Then, finally, to the room labeled MR. ARKEL'S STUDY.

TWENTY-TWO

I SLIPPED INTO THE WINE CELLAR. BEYOND THE EDGES
of the sphere of light from my lamp, endless rows of bottles stored
neatly in their cells melted into darkness.

Next came the storage rooms. These must have been the source
of the girls' odd assortment of supplies. There were chandeliers in
crates, heaped rugs and cushions. A stuffed grizzly bear on its hind
legs, ten feet tall, mouth open, poised to attack, sawdust leaking
from a seam in its back. A suit of armor, its visor raised to reveal
the emptiness inside. There were piles of velvet drapes and the towering, dusty skeleton of an elk; there were daybeds, vitrines, tele-
scopes. There was a pair of huge mirrors leaning in such a way that
they faced each other, creating tunnels of dwindling portals into
fragmented storage rooms, receding into infinite distance.

The walls of the rooms were traversed by steel and copper
pipes of varying thickness, which every now and then gave off
a sound of rushing liquid; there were also cables that must have
carried electricity. The veins and nerves of the house.

There seemed to be no end to the series of rooms, and for a
few tilting moments I thought I'd stumbled into a dimension of

repeating chambers like the one in the mirror. I stopped to check the map, but I had lost track of how many doorways I had passed.

Then, a new level: a few steps leading up into the next row of chambers. Finally, up ahead, I saw the stairs to the servants' level.

I was in a narrow passage, and the stairs were at the end. I squeezed past several wooden boxes the size of coffins that were stacked against a wall. I paused and saw they were shipping crates, lids pried off, empty except for sawdust. In the lamplight, I read an address label—TO: MR. CLAUDE ARKEL, PROSPER ISLAND, ALEXANDRIA BAY, NEW YORK, UNITED STATES OF AMERICA. Above it, another label, which read: FROM: and then a string of Cyrillic letters I couldn't make any sense of. Beneath them, in smaller type, were the words PETROGRAD, RUSSIA.

Near the boxes was a door. Although I had passed through several underground rooms, they had all been open; this was the first closed door I had seen.

I knew what it had to be: the room of dolls. That's what the packing crates were for—they were the right size and shape to hold life-sized figures. Frank had said Mr. Arkel's hobby was designing the dolls; this mysterious Russian address must be where they were constructed, then shipped to him.

Mary said the door wouldn't be locked. If I opened it, I could peek in. It was only if you *went* in that the door locked behind you.

It was a chance to look inside Mr. Arkel's mind.

I reached for the knob. It turned, I pushed on the door, and, lifting my lamp, leaned in.

The air felt stale; there was a sense of something arrested, trapped. Rows of chairs filled the small room, facing away from the door, most of them empty. A couple were occupied by human figures, sitting absolutely still. A woman in a large hat. Another without a hat, who listed slightly to the side, her pose awkward and unnatural.

The chairs faced a raised platform at one end of the room, on which seemed to be another, larger chair, though it was too far from my light to make it out in the stagnant, malevolent darkness.

So this was the room where, as Frank had said, Mr. Arkel went to experience the state of perfect control he longed for. Yet it seemed a sad, cramped place, a stuffy solipsistic hell.

I backed away from the door, and it swung shut. For a second I stood catching my breath, as if I had been holding it underwater.

I turned toward the flight of stairs at the end of the corridor; the map said it led up to the servants' level. Heart racing, I climbed the steps out of the sub-basement.

Here, instead of bare plain walls, I found wood paneling and framed photographs: maids and footmen posing in front of the house, gardeners in a greenhouse.

There was something else I stopped to look at: a big black panel, more than six feet across, framed in oak, on which the name of each room was printed in gold: MUSIC R., LOUIS XIV R. They were tiny and the board was huge. Stella had said there were over two hundred rooms, and they seemed all to be represented here.

I had heard about call boards in big houses, with rows of bells connected to bell pulls in each room, and this looked like a modern, electrified version of those. Under each room name was a gumdrop-shaped piece of glass that looked as if it would light up to tell the staff which room they were wanted in. Next to the board was a telephone. I wondered if the house had its own telephone network, too.

Mr. Arkel ruled over his employees in his orchards and his canneries, but this was the real heart of his empire. Endless rooms, servants who could be summoned at the touch of a button. He had only to think of something he wanted, and he could make it appear.

How could a man be so starved for power that even this was not enough to satisfy him?

Non est potestas Super Terram quae Comparetur ei. From the outside, it looked like he controlled everything. But inside, there must be a bottomless need. *The deeper you go, the stranger and uglier the monsters . . .*

Mary must have thought she'd found the key to surviving him—Mary, who had been so loyal she wouldn't even speak up to save her own daughter. *She made herself indispensable*, Mary had said, and maybe that had saved her. He'd had no choice but to spare her, and had locked her up in the study. Imprisoned, but alive.

I passed the servants' dining room next. Through the open doorway, I saw wooden chairs lined up neatly alongside a big table. Then came the kitchen, which stood dark and empty. According to the map, I had to cross the kitchen to get to the servants' stairs, which went up from the other side.

The tiles on the floor were black and white, like the squares of a chessboard. I crossed cautiously, pausing to listen for sounds, but I heard nothing except the faint shuffle and hiss of embers settling inside the big wood-fired stove.

On the other side, more stairs. I made it to the top, and found myself in a narrow back corridor. Its plainness indicated that it was only for the servants' use. I looked at the map again, studying the heavy pencil marks on the brown paper. At the end of this hallway I would find a door leading into what was labeled *Men's Wing*, a series of rooms ending with Mr. Arkel's private study.

The men's wing consisted of a wide, short passage with framed etchings on the walls: manly scenes, hunting and mountain climbing. I was grateful for the carpet that ran down the middle of the parquet floor, since it muffled my footsteps.

The ghost of cigar smoke hung in the air, along with the scents of wood and leather and wool, a pleasantly masculine mix of smells. The passage ran past the billiards room, smoking room, gun room, just as the map said, ending in a parquet-floored foyer that had, on my right, a door opening to the outside, and straight ahead, my goal: Mr. Arkel's study.

I crossed the shining, blond floor with careful steps. The study door was closed, and I was certain it would be locked. Faint light shone from under it. Other than that, the house was dark. Only this room was lit.

Someone was in there.

I went to the door quietly and stood, holding my breath, listening, then put my ear against it. Nothing. I lowered my eye to the keyhole.

In my limited field of vision, I saw a wall painted dark red. The wall was almost hidden by all the animal heads. Even through the keyhole, I could see many: local creatures like deer and black bears; and exotic ones: a tiger with fangs bared, a zebra, ears alert. The spaces between the large animals were filled with smaller ones: a badger, pheasants mounted whole with wings outspread. There was no sign of a living person in the room.

There was a big desk, facing the wall to my left. But its large, high-backed chair was angled in such a way that if anyone had been sitting there, I would not have been able to see them.

The surface of the desk was cluttered, judging by the bit that was visible: papers, open books.

A pale shape might have been the curve of a finger. But it was motionless.

I fought the urge to leave. Maybe I had learned enough. I could return to the girls and tell them Mary wasn't there. If there was someone sitting in that chair, I was certain they could not be alive. The room felt too still, too silent.

And yet. I had come so far, through basement rooms and dark corridors, and, most of all, through the long stretch of years wondering what had become of Mary. After all that, I might be within a few feet of her. Even if she was there, dead, I could glimpse her face again. I could know. Even if she couldn't be helped now, if I opened that door, I'd know that I'd tried. Maybe that would put her ghost to rest.

I reached into my coat pocket for the two bent hairpins Sam had given me, along with a lesson in lock picking, which she'd demonstrated on the door in the ruined church's cellar. A useful skill for someone who has keys to nothing in this world, she'd said.

Before she'd shown me how, I had never seen anyone do it except Mary, so many years ago, on the night we snuck into Mr. Fort's study. That night, I'd turned away from the things Mary wanted to show me. Closed the closet door on those poor birds, ready to shut them forever in the dark, because that's what Mr. Fort had wanted. Tonight would be different. Tonight I would open the door, and I would not leave until I saw everything.

I inserted the two pins as quietly as possible into the lock, ready to drop them at the slightest sound. But there was none besides the ones I made. Pressing my ear against the door, I listened for the faint click of the tumblers falling into place. In less than a minute, it was done.

I held my breath and closed my eyes. Then, leaving the lantern on the floor and holding the iron poker, I slowly pushed the door open.

Still nothing moved but me. There was a fireplace in the wall to my right: black, cold, and dead. Above it was a wall of weapons, new and antique: curving sabers, flared blunderbusses, solid old muzzleloaders covered with scrollwork. At the center was a rack to hold two rifles crossed in an X. But only one was there; the other rack was empty. I wondered if that was where Mr. Arkel hung a favorite hunting rifle. If so, where was it now?

I moved tentatively over the thick Persian rug toward the desk. I still couldn't tell if there was anyone in the chair. But if there was, there was still no indication of life. I went around to where I could see.

I squeaked, unable to restrain a throttled yelp of surprise. Whatever I had expected to find, it was not this.

At the desk sat a figure just like the photograph of Mr. Arkel I had seen in the one magazine article I'd found. He had the same brushy mustache and hard little eyes. But it was not him: it was a doll.

As if my entrance had triggered some mechanism inside it,

the head turned with a sudden, jerky movement. I stepped back, raising the poker. Then, with a faint click, the eyelids blinked. Glassy eyes turned to me. I heard them roll in their sockets.

How did it know I was here?

He must be in the room, controlling it, I thought, looking around. This was the final trap the hunter had set, and I was the prey. More than a way to capture me—which he could have done at any time—it must be meant to bewilder and terrify. He was watching from some dark place, enjoying it.

But if so, he did not show himself. The only sound was that of an unseen clock. My racing heart vibrated in the silent spaces between the ticks, the small, efficient *crunch* of tiny gears, like footsteps on a gravel path, walking, second by second, into an unknown future.

One thing was clear: Mary wasn't here. I had come so close. To the island where she lived, into the same house, into the very room where she had spent so many hours—and at the last minute, Mr. Arkel had stolen her.

I was nobody to anyone in the world but Charlie, and I knew it. Yet it felt as if everything on the island had happened specifically to lead me to this moment. The fact was, no one could have devised a more perfect plan to torture me.

What could hurt me more than to let me believe I could find Mary, only to discover at the last moment that she had been murdered by this horrible man?

Seeing her escape from the house of one autocratic, violent man—because that's was what Mr. Fort was—only to wind up with another, infinitely worse. Wealthier. More powerful.

That she had nearly cracked the code this time, had managed to raise a daughter and make a life for herself, only made it crueler.

In the end, even though she had made herself useful, killing her was probably nothing to Mr. Arkel.

My eyes swept over the silent watchful heads of the animals, the gilded furniture, the busy, fussy rug. Was he behind the walls or the ceiling, safe and smug, observing me?

"Where are you?" My voice seemed to balloon in the silence. "Come out. You killed her, but you're afraid of me?"

The only answer was the relentless, regular ticking of the damn clock.

"I want my friend," I shouted, first to one wall, then another; to the ceiling, to the fireplace. "I want my friend!"

The last word hung in the air, a beating heart in the dead room: *friend*. Not a spouse or a family member. Someone to whom I was connected by love and nothing else. A word that a man like him could never understand.

I raised the poker again, higher, and slipped into a space between the clock ticks, between the seconds, into a place that pulsed red and was bordered by frantic scribbles of ink-black rage. I felt the blood pound through every vein, I heard the *crack* of the doll's ugly head. The splintering of wood, the thump and tear of stuffing and fabric, the tinkle and crash of objects on the desk: the inkwell and the glass in the silver picture frames and the brass bulldog and the fountain pens. The heavy grunt of leather-covered ledgers, the whisper of paper disturbed, scattering, drifting to the floor.

Without knowing how I got there, I found myself sitting on the rug like a child. I tried to catch my breath under the gaze of the heads on the walls. The zebra, with its gentle, curious expression, had eyelashes so long and thick I could see them from where I sat. They reminded me of the ones on the doll in the garden. The zebra must have died in pain, I thought, but then her face had been arranged in this peaceful expression. I imagined a man's hand holding a thick fringe of artificial lashes, gluing them to the dead lids.

The clock made a different sound: a whirring, then a creak. It was ornately carved, with a peaked roof. A door in its front snapped open, and a small, bent man moved into view. Another door opened on the opposite side, and a bell came out, moving on a track until it met the man, who struck it with a mallet: once, twice. Then he slid away backward and the little door snapped shut.

That was all: Nothing more than parts of a machine. *Machina mundi*, the machine of the world. No kind deity presided over it.

Even in my worst moments, I had never completely lost the belief that above that darkness there was some place—even if it was very far away—where the air was always lit by the sun and a warm presence hovered, intelligent, winged, protective, guarding *something*. Not our little mortal lives—even if a benevolent God existed, it was no guarantee against tragedy. But guarding *something*, an embryonic hope at the center of the world.

But what if this was all? This cruel, controlling man, a parody of the divine, as much unlike a real Creator as the automatons were unlike humans—what if he, and others like him, were really in control, sitting atop their piles of money and laughing down at us? What if there was nothing else, what if anything above him was an illusion, an elaborate painted ceiling that—like everything else—he owned?

Breathe, came Charlie's voice in my mind.

The clock. The black numbers on its face. It had struck two.

I was sure it hadn't been an hour since I'd left the cellar. Did the hours move differently here? Did Mr. Arkel have his own personal version of time? I pushed my sleeve up to look at Stella's watch. It was not yet one-thirty. That was the truth, I told myself, no matter what Mr. Arkel's clock said. There were some things beyond the reach of his power.

I scanned the room again. If Mr. Arkel was watching me from somewhere, he had made no move to harm me. Maybe he was waiting for something.

What, then?

Then I had to go on.

Retrace my steps. Tell the girls I had been to the study, and what I had found.

He might get me on the way out. He could strike at any moment.

But I *would* go back to the girls, because I had promised.

TWENTY-THREE

BACK ACROSS THE PARQUET FLOOR, INTO THE CORRI-
dor, past the gun room, smoking room, billiards room.

How would I tell Mary I had failed to find her mother, that
she wasn't in the study, that she had really disappeared? None
of the servants had seen her; she hadn't been in her room. The
study was the one place they'd thought she might be, their one
last hope. Mr. Arkel's note said she had taken ill and no one was
to bother her. *Same thing he said about Millicent,* Mary had said.
And in reality, he had killed Millicent.

When I told her that her mother wasn't in the study, she'd
know the truth that I was sure of: her mother had been murdered by this man, this man who owned everything we could
see and touch, even the land we stood on, and could never be
held accountable.

How could I tell her that Mr. Arkel had won, that he would
always win, and we could never stop him?

I stepped through the doorway into the plain servants' passageway and went to the servants' stairs. A few steps down, I
realized there was a light on in the kitchen.

How had I been so stupid, making so much noise in the study? Someone had heard me, and the servants were awake.

Or Mr. Arkel had been watching me the whole time. The kitchen was where he'd wanted me to be caught all along. I remembered how, on my way up, the lantern light had caught the glint of butcher knives in a rack. Stella had said Frank cut Viola's body into pieces and stuffed them into a barrel. The kitchen would be the perfect place for murder and its aftermath.

With a feeling of inevitability, I continued down the stairs. Was a band of footmen waiting at the bottom? Or Mr. Arkel himself, ready to stage some final torture?

Part of the black-and-white floor came into view, and I stopped. What I heard was not the sound of many people, or even the tense silence of one man waiting; it was the leisurely, small noises of someone puttering around a kitchen at night.

The back of a pair of legs came into view: work pants cuffed above felt house slippers. I ducked my head to see the rest of the man. He stood at the stove, his back to me. He wore a nightshirt partly tucked into his pants, suspenders hanging down. He was tall and broad-shouldered. He was stirring something in a pan.

No one was waiting for me. No one had even heard me, or the servants' quarters would have been on alert. Instead, a footman had been unable to sleep and had gotten up to make warm milk.

I had two choices: I could wait for him to finish, or I could go back the way I came, to the foyer by the study, with the door leading to outside.

Maybe, I thought, I could get to the woods from there, but I was unfamiliar with the layout of the grounds. Choosing that door could mean spending the night lost in the woods.

No, I would wait on the stairs until the kitchen light went out; then I would go down and back the way I had come.

I tucked the iron poker under my arm and reached for the lantern I'd set down, but the poker tipped forward, hitting the lantern, which fell, went out, and clattered loudly down the steps.

In that instant, I knew the man would come for me and that it would take him only seconds to get up the stairs. By all logic, I should have run back to the foyer outside Mr. Arkel's study. But something turned me away from the dark and sent me down the stairs instead. Poker in hand, I tore across the kitchen, hoping to outrun him, ready to hit him if he tried to stop me.

He was still staring at me when I was halfway across the floor; it took a second for him to realize I was not one of the servants, but someone who was not supposed to be there. Then he lunged and grabbed my right arm, so the poker in that hand was useless.

I tried to pull away but, like a dog tied to a stake, only swung myself in a half circle. This brought me within reach of the stove, and I grabbed the pan and flung the milk at his face. He yelped, recoiled, and loosened his grip enough for me to escape. I was across the kitchen and in the hallway before he started moving again.

Knowing he'd gain on me, I looked around frantically. One of the doors leading off the hallway was ajar. I was almost there, but the man was too close. I made one big, hopeless jump for the opening, knowing he'd get me first.

To my surprise, a flat, heavy object came flying out of the doorway, shining in the faint light from the kitchen. It clattered to the floor and slid past my pursuer.

He and I both turned, but before I could see what it was, the door opened wider and someone yanked me through, slamming the door behind us and turning the lock. Stella! The man rattled the knob while the two of us leaned against the heavy wood, panting in the dark.

"I don't know who you are, but you'd better make it easier on yourselves and come out," the man said. "You don't want me to have to drag you out."

He waited for us to answer. When we didn't, we heard him walk away.

"He's going to get the key," I hissed.

"You're welcome," said Stella.

I heard a click and scrape as she held up her gold lighter. I saw by its flame that we were among mops, brushes, dusters—all familiar tools. But this was not like any supply closet I had ever seen: there must have been a dozen of everything, and it was as big as the whole apartment Charles and I had shared in Hell's Kitchen.

"What are you doing here?" I whispered.

"Sacrificing my best whiskey flask to save your life," Stella said, and I realized that was what she'd thrown to distract the man.

"But how—"

"I couldn't sit there waiting for you, not knowing if you were okay. I'm sorry for what I said. You were right that this was our only chance to help them. I shouldn't have let you risk it alone. What happened? Did you get to the study?"

There was no time to tell the whole story. "She wasn't there," I said, the whispered words sharp on the back of my tongue.

"And our husbands . . . ?"

"I found nothing."

Stella gave my arm a quick squeeze. "The girls will have an idea what to do next. Maybe their little friends can help, the ones who stayed. We'll find them."

"We have to get out of here first," I said. "But the way back to the tunnels is the same direction that man went." I pressed my ear against the closed door. I couldn't hear him anymore. Where had he gone? We might have seconds to sneak out, or he might be waiting nearby, ready to grab us.

I opened the door cautiously. Down the corridor, I could see the stairs I had come from; they led down to the passage with the room of dolls. Just past the stairs was an open door with light spilling out—probably the head housemaid's office, where the man had gone for the key.

"Let's run for it," I whispered. If we were quick and quiet, we could slip down the stairs before he came out of the office.

We moved fast. The man appeared at the doorway just as we plunged into the stairwell. I'd never gone down stairs so fast in my life, the man thundering behind us, too close. At the bottom, I careened into the coffin-like crates stacked against the wall. Stella grabbed me as I stumbled. A box hit the floor, landing between us and the man. In seconds, he'd be on top of us.

There was no time to think. I grabbed the knob and pushed open the door to the room of dolls, dragging Stella in.

"Hey!" The man was almost at the door when I slammed it.

He went completely quiet. He didn't rattle the knob as he had before. It was as if he'd been surprised into silence.

It was pitch-black. I could hear Stella breathing close to my ear: "Where are we?"

TWENTY-FOUR

STELLA AND I STOOD IN ABSOLUTE DARKNESS. WE HEARD
the man outside walking away.

Then silence.

"We're not where I think we are . . . ?" Stella whispered.

"Yes," I said quietly. "The doll room."

For a minute Stella didn't say anything. Then: "He's gone." I
heard her reach for the knob and turn it. Again and again. Faster.
Rattling it, panicked.

"The door won't open!"

"I know." My voice was shaking.

"That's why they said *don't go in!* Why did you?"

"He was about to catch us!"

I was nauseous with fear. Somehow in the confusion I had
dropped the poker, adding to my sense of vulnerability. The
blackness was so complete that we could have been anywhere—a
bank vault, a tomb.

"What do we do?" I said.

Stella took a steadying breath. "We should feel our way
around the walls," she said. "See if there's another Light!"

"I don't think there is."

"Do you have a better idea?"

"Someone will come for us," I said. It was more a prayer than anything. "They know we're here, they'll get us out."

Stella took my arm and started walking to the left, close to the wall.

"Who'll get us out?" she asked.

"That man—the servants."

"You do realize he's going to tell Mr. Arkel," said Stella.

We fell silent but continued inching along the wall. Around the corner to the next wall.

"There are dolls in here. I looked in before I went upstairs."

"Ugh," said Stella. "What did they look like?"

"I only saw two, from behind. I couldn't really tell. And a lot of empty chairs. Facing a kind of stage. I think it had a big kind of throne on it. I couldn't really see."

Stella sucked in her breath. She took hold of my hand and placed it on cool, smooth wood. "This?"

It must have been the armrest. But it felt like—

"It's an arm! With a hand!" I said, pulling away.

"The whole thing's made of limbs—ugh." Stella stepped back.

I could picture it: a big throne made of intertwined arms, legs, feet, maybe torsos. Lacquered, lifelike, like the doll in the garden. "Oh God," I said.

From a couple of feet away, Stella made a sound like *whoop*, then said "Oh!" I groped my way toward her and she clasped my hand excitedly. "Come! It's a door."

I felt a heavy velvet curtain that hung at the back of the dais. Behind it was solid wall—until there wasn't. My hand pushed into a recessed doorway.

"Does this open?" I breathed.

We shoved the big curtain aside awkwardly. I held it away from the door while Stella felt for a knob. Then I heard it turn and click.

Stella pushed the door gingerly. The small space it opened into was also dark, with the exception of a thin line of light under a door on the opposite side. We stumbled forward. My fingers found a handle. I leaned against the door, and it swung open.

We spilled into a cavernous room, with a ten- or twelve-foot ceiling. The dolls' room had felt like being enclosed in granite; this was open, echoing. The walls were of white tile, and though where we stood was dim, brightness filtered through from somewhere at the far end and glimmered on the tile.

All around stood tall shapes shrouded in burlap, some reaching nearly to the ceiling, and huge heavy planters of ceramic and terra-cotta. Some were empty; others held plants, pale and lanky, straining toward the electric light at the far end.

Footsteps sounded from there.

This must, I figured, be a storage room for the greenhouses, a place to stow discarded and half-dead specimens out of the way; there must be another door for servants to go in and out. That meant the person who was in here could be a gardener, someone who could help us.

Or it could be Mr. Arkel.

I remembered the rifle hanging on the study wall, and the bracket for another that should have hung there, crossing it—that was empty.

I looked at Stella. "I'm not afraid," I said, as much to myself as to her.

The burlap-shrouded trees and the big pots threw long, dramatic shadows on the floor and over our faces.

The faint clinking and shuffling from the other end was amplified by the tile walls.

Stella's hand gripped mine. We walked toward the sound, skirting clumps of potted shrubs, crates of earth, tangles of pothos escaped from a dozen pots, tendrils creeping toward the light.

With every step the light became stronger, overwhelming

even, turning everything in its path into chopped-up black shadows and glare.

We passed a half-built grotto, similar to the one in the greenhouse but showing raw edges of artificial rock, scaffolding, and plaster. On the other side I stopped, taking in the sight.

There was an open space, bordered by a fence woven of living willows. We were looking in through an arched willow gateway that grew from soil mounded on the floor. The plants here were green and thriving. The main light source was seven or eight huge black lamps on stands. They looked like the kind that were used in theaters or for filming motion pictures. Their beams were aimed at the growing things: topiary shapes, small trees, flowering vines.

At the back of this fenced-in area stood a construction maybe ten feet tall and twice as wide: an enormous black bird, wings spread, feathers iridescent in the light. They were made of pleated silk; they shimmered green, blue, and deep purple. The bird's head was cocked, and it seemed to gaze down on the figures collected under its wings. There, standing, sitting, lounging, were several life-sized dolls. They must have been the former occupants of the empty chairs in the first room. There were a dozen or so, in various poses: holding hands, sitting on overturned planters, stretched lazily on a bench. They were clothed like Greek nymphs in colorful tunics and chitons, their faces shining with lacquer, hair loose and long, crowned with flowers and leaves. All girls, all so young.

They made me think of the grubby, broken dolls I used to keep in the cigar box. It was as if I had walked into my own dream, only it had been interpreted by another mind, a dark, distorted one. The girls were posed to look appealing, but the effect was sad and disturbed: children under a spell.

In front of this group stood an enormous chair that, like the fence, was woven of growing willows, green leaves curling among the canes. It stood not in soil, but in a shallow puddle on the tiled floor, and living roots spread from its legs out into the water. The chair was empty.

To our left were two topiary shapes that had once been animals—horses, maybe—but now sprouted green leafy spines that blurred their outlines. A figure detached itself from the darkness between them and stepped into the light.

It wore an ugly canvas gas mask, connected by a hose to a metal canister that hung on its chest, like the one worn by the chauffeur when we first arrived. He was lean and short—could it be the same man? But instead of an oilskin coat and woolen scarf, he was, incongruously, dressed in a black doublet, hose, and boots, with a fur mantle and a heavy cape, as if he had just come from some bizarre production of *Hamlet* in which the prince was preparing for a mustard gas attack.

The eerie face turned in our direction. Was this Mr. Arkel? If so, he was not the portly, aging man I had imagined, but wiry and surprisingly youthful in his movements.

He went toward the throne, moving through the sharp, off-kilter shadows. A short path of stepping stones lay in the puddle, and he walked on these, turned, and lifted his cape to sit. A long dagger at his belt knocked awkwardly against the leafy arm of the chair.

"What do you want with us?" I asked, standing as straight as I could. "Do you want to see us afraid? Because I'm not."

It was a lie, but it was all I had.

The figure lifted its chin and regarded us with eyes hidden behind huge, insect-like goggles. It bowed slightly, as if to acknowledge my words.

Hands reached to the back of the canvas hood and pulled it off.

And there was the familiar, strangely calm face of my old friend.

TWENTY-FIVE

"MARY," I SAID.

She sat looking at us from the throne of living wicker. She was not as painfully thin as she had been years ago, and her restless quality had solidified into something muscular, a confidence in the way she sat, in spite of the hair that hung in her eyes, messed by the mask.

Around her lay the puddle, its surface reflecting the glare so that it looked like liquid light rippling over the fine, tangled willow roots.

"Anna," she said.

At the sound of her voice, my eyes itched with tears. After so many years, so many small daily reminders of her, so many nights pricked by worry and regret, here she was, speaking my name.

Stella put a hand on my shoulder. "Where is Mr. Arkel?" she asked Mary.

"Mr. Arkel," Mary said slowly, "is dead."

"Dead?" I said. "That can't be. He invited us here."

"No, Anna," Mary said. "I invited you."

"You—?" I tried to understand what she was saying.

"So it wasn't a coincidence that you two found each other—you made it happen," said Stella.

"But what happened to Mr. Arkel?" I asked.

"He was shot," said Mary, "by Detective Peleus."

"No, no." I shook my head. Nothing was making sense. "He shot Peleus. We heard the story. He calmly found the detective with his wife and killed both of them."

"You heard the story," Mary said. "But the story was wrong. What really happened was that two months ago, Claude Arkel took his hunting rifle and went after his new wife and her lover, *intending* to kill them. But the detective was armed, as always. So, you see, it was a question of who would shoot first. And the detective shot first." Her smile was familiar, but harder, colder than the one I remembered.

"Look here," said Stella, "I don't know what your game is, but you're clearly lying to us. If Millicent Arkel and Detective Peleus didn't die that night, they'd still be here. Which they're not."

"No," said Mary. "I believe they're in New York City. Together, and free, now that Claude Arkel is out of the way." She glanced up with another expression I remembered, a dark glitter of defiance. "And I'm in charge now."

"What does that mean—you're in charge?" I asked, still trying to put the pieces together.

"You seem confused," Mary said, "but really, if you think about it, it's quite simple. I was Claude's right hand for years. In fact, since the strike, I've been completely running his business. He was so upset he tossed it aside, like a child with a broken toy. He'd never made one thin dime of profit, and once everyone found out, he didn't want to play anymore. *I* made it profitable. He was happy to let me, as long as he got the credit. And I always gave him the credit."

Again, that familiar smile, but edged with ice. I realized that where she sat, on the throne, was lit perfectly. Her face was bright and lacked the jagged shadows that lay all around her.

"But Millicent is alive," I said. "If her husband's dead, wouldn't all this belong to her?"

Mary shook her head. "Claude was in love, but he wasn't stupid. He put a clause in the will that she'd get nothing if she was unfaithful. As for the detective, even though he shot Mr. Arkel in self-defense, he knew the case wouldn't look good in court, given that he was having an affair with the victim's wife. Horace, Claude's only son, had been cut out of his will, too. None of them stood to get a penny. That meant they were all willing to negotiate with me."

I remembered Frank saying Mr. Arkel had disinherited Horace. "So you got them to hand the whole estate over to you?"

"We divided it. They were happy to leave the island to me— none of them wanted it. They took their share of the money and left."

It all squared, yet it was so different from what I had thought.

"You look amazed," said Mary, "but really, it's been very easy. I'd done everything for years—talked to his bankers and investors, even forged his signature when he was too lazy to sign things. I just kept on doing what I had been, and no one even noticed he wasn't there."

"What about the staff?" I asked. "Weren't they used to seeing him?"

"He'd gotten reclusive since the strike; even more so after he shot Gertrude. And the man had a cruel, nasty little heart. If anybody did miss him, they didn't say so."

"If you're in charge," said Stella, "then tell us where our husbands are."

Mary tilted her head, and I saw shadows of exhaustion under her eyes. She sighed. "In the far end of the east wing."

"Why did you take them?" I demanded.

"I didn't. They came to the house all by themselves. They

broke quarantine, so we put them where we can keep an eye on them. We sent someone to leave a note so you wouldn't panic."

"I don't understand," I said. "Why would they come to the house?"

"Apparently they were looking for you. Instead, they found Detective Southerland, dead. They came here to report that, and to say you were missing."

"And your response was to lock them up?" Stella said.

"Not me," said Mary. "Tommy—I mean Jenkins. Claude's valet. He's been helping me. He knows everything. Claude treated him . . . well, that's past now." Mary looked at Stella, her voice cold as she said, "Now maybe *you* can explain why you shot my detective."

"She didn't," I said defensively.

"So it was you?" Mary turned to me.

"No!"

"Anna," she said, forcing a level tone, "there's so little time. Tell me the truth. It had to be one of you. No one else here has a gun."

I wanted to tell her about the girls, about her daughter, but I hesitated. In some ways, she was so familiar. Her face, her voice, had lived in my consciousness for over twenty years. And yet I no longer knew her. It was as if we had trespassed in the realm of an angry underground god. Who was she? What would happen if I told her what Poppy had done, and where her daughter and the others were?

"Mary," I pleaded, as if the sound of her name might summon her old self back out of the past. "I can tell you, but promise you won't be angry. Promise you'll try to help—"

"No!" She half rose from her strange throne, shadows shifting and fracturing on the water around her. "Tell me the truth. No conditions. No promises."

"Okay," I said in a pacifying tone. "It was the girls. The runaways from the school. They're still on the island. They're living out in the woods with your daughter."

"Where?" Mary demanded.

"They're just trying to survive," I said. "Your daughter is worried about you. *She* sent me here."

Mary rose fully from the throne and stood on the large flat stone in front of it, her heavy cape swaying, water rippling and glaring between the shadows. "Tell me," she said, slowly, "*where . . . she . . . is.*"

Her voice was cold, but under it was another tone that was desperate, pleading.

"You tell me first," I said, "how to get our husbands back."

Mary's eyes glinted with impatience. "They're perfectly fine. They have books, beer, everything they want. You understand why I had to confine them."

I glanced at the gas mask hanging on her chest. "If you're that worried about quarantine, why did you take off your mask? Don't you think we could have the flu?"

Again, the tired darkness flitted over her face. But instead of answering, she said, "If I let your husbands out, will you tell me where Mary is?"

"Let them out first," Stella demanded.

Mary's face contracted with anger. "Don't try to bargain with me. If you don't tell me—"

Stella blurted out: "Okay. They're living at the ruined church."

Mary's voice was suddenly vulnerable. "My daughter, too?"

"Yes," I said. "Please don't be angry with her."

"She's all right?" Again, the undertone of desperation.

"It depends what you mean by 'all right,'" I said. "Winter's coming, they're scavenging for food. One of them has a baby. They need a proper place to stay."

"They had one," Mary said bitterly. "Until they ran away."

"They did it for Ginger," I said. "They didn't want her to get shot."

"I wasn't going to let him get her."

My eyes traveled over the dolls ranged behind the throne,

under the iridescent black wings of the enormous bird. Mary saw, and turned to look, too. When she turned back, her eyes shone with a hurt I hadn't seen before.

Ever since I'd seen the dolls, a question had been growing in my mind: "Those aren't . . . all . . . ?"

No, I prayed, *Say no.*

Mary nodded. "His victims."

So he'd done worse to the girls at the school than Mary's daughter had told us. He'd done more than throw Daisy down the stairs and shoot Alice in the woods like an animal. He'd killed all of these. Was it possible?

"So many?" I asked, my throat tight.

Stella's face was pale. "Your daughter told us he only shot one girl."

"That's what most people think. The girls in the school, the servants, they know about Alice. She's the one they found out about." Mary paused, looking at me with what seemed like sympathy, as if she realized what it must feel like to be hearing the truth for the first time. "They think the other girls, the ones who 'went away' before poor Alice, were sent to homes for unwed mothers. They weren't."

I waited for the anxiety, the feeling of compression, the buzzing, but it didn't come. Instead it was as if my emotions sensed that they couldn't be any help here and stepped aside, leaving me still and cold.

Mary moved away from the throne, crossed the puddle on the stepping stones so she could stand closer to us. She looked smaller in the bulky cape, with tired lines around her mouth. "No one else knows," she said, "how long ago this started. But I do. I knew all along." She turned. "That is Mae." She pointed to a girl in a blue tunic with straight black hair, frozen in the act of reaching toward a flowering vine. "She was the first. Fifteen years old. Eighteen ninety-five."

"That was over twenty years ago," Stella said.

"Yes," said Mary. "The year I arrived." She walked to the doll and took its stiff hand, lifting it toward a blossom. The girl's fingertip touched the petals; she beamed a frozen smile.

"Mae's death was an accident. At least, as far as I know. He did love hunting, and he wanted her gone, but he hadn't put the two together yet. Gertrude tried to send her to a charity home. But Mae didn't want to go. The girls were treated like sinners there, used as cheap labor. So Mae ran. Claude was out hunting in the woods near All Souls Point, and he shot her." Mary shrugged away the emotion that crept into her voice.

"And you knew? You were a student in the school then?" I asked.

"Not just a student. I was the star." Mary's unnerving calm cracked again as she smiled a little, sadly. In that expression I saw the friend I used to know, the one who'd stood on the hilltop with me that summer day. "Mr. Arkel said I was the brightest he ever had. Just like Mr. Haskins," she said, "who let me play Hamlet." She rubbed her thumb slowly over the fur trim of her heavy cape. "Remember I told you that? 'O God, I could be bounded in a nutshell and count myself a king of infinite space . . .'"

"'Were it not that I have bad dreams,'" I finished.

"I didn't fall for it this time," said Mary. "This time, I knew what he really wanted. I decided to use it to get everything I could from him." Emotion crept in again, and she stopped. "I think he had this first doll made as more of a tribute to her, or maybe even an apology. He let me see it when it was done."

"He showed you—told you?" I asked.

"Yes, he told me his secrets," Mary said.

She turned to a blond doll in green next, stretched out on a bench. Her voice was matter-of-fact again: "It wasn't till a few years later that Irene died. I think she was the first who was on purpose. By that time I was one of the housemaids. But every day, every hour, I was working my way toward more."

Mary looked at me, for what—approval? "What did you do to get *more?*" I asked.

"Whatever I had to," Mary said, holding my gaze evenly. "When I first held my baby in my arms, both of us covered in my blood, I promised her I'd never give up."

"So you just stood by and watched when . . . all those girls . . . ?" said Stella.

"What do you think would have happened," said Mary, coming closer, "if I had tried to stop him?"

Stella didn't answer. Mary turned to me. "You understand. I couldn't have saved a single one. And what do you think would have happened to *me?*"

"Okay," Stella said, "Maybe you couldn't speak up. But why didn't you leave?"

"Because I was less naïve at seventeen than you are, apparently, as a grown woman," Mary said. "I'd already run away twice in my life. Each time, I ended up somewhere worse. As soon as I got here and saw everything Claude owned, I knew I was done with running. From now on, I was going to climb. When my daughter was born, I became even more determined that I wasn't going anywhere but up. On Prosper Island, there was only one way to do that: never, ever cross Claude Arkel."

"Not even when your own daughter asked you to stand up for her friend," I said. "To protect her from being hunted down and killed."

Mary looked suddenly tired. "She told you all that?"

I nodded. "She thought you could help. She said you were the only one who could."

"And you blame me, as she does," said Mary. "You imagine there was a way to stop the killing. There isn't. There will always be victims. The trick is to make sure it's never you."

Mary stood close now. Here, the light threw strong shadows across her face. Fatigue flickered across it: her cheekbones stood out, and her skin was sallow. "I won in the end, though," she said quietly. "I made him the victim."

Her dark eyes were as I remembered, almost black, with something in their depths: a glitter of nervous energy that was at once attractive and frightening, like the lights of a city seen from a high balcony. "I killed him," she said.

"I thought you said it was Detective Peleus who shot him."

"Yes, but I made it happen," she said.

I felt a vertiginous desire to step off the edge, fall into the cool, twinkling, life-extinguishing darkness.

"What did you do?"

"I prayed," said Mary, "to King Nyx."

TWENTY-SIX

I LOOKED AGAIN AT THE CROWLIKE BIRD THAT TOW-
ered above us, wings outspread over the dolls, the images of Mr.
Arkel's victims. Again I had the sense of a dream that was mine
yet not mine, twisted, perverted.

"Is *that* King Nyx?"

"King Nyx is spirit," Mary said matter-of-factly. "That's only
a representation." She took another step closer so there were only
inches between us. I could smell wool, ambergris, grasslands, and
something sharp and feral. In a low voice, she asked, "What's the
worst you've ever wanted something?"

"I-I don't know what you mean."

"When my daughter ran away, I needed help. I had to appeal
to something bigger than myself."

"To kill Claude Arkel?"

"That's right. She ran away the day after he shot Gertrude. I
knew once he was willing to kill his own wife, there'd be no hope
if he caught *her*. I had to stop him from going to the woods. There
was no power on earth that could control him—but maybe there

was power somewhere else. Do you remember what you told me, Anna—how you used to pray to King Nyx?"

I thought back to the windy night we'd lain in the dark in our attic room, when I'd confessed that. I remembered, too, how just before Mary arrived at the Forts' house, King Nyx, the friend of my childhood, had turned on me, begun to show me horrible images: an angry shout, the sound of a gunshot, a dress with a bloody hole in it.

"I stopped all that years ago," I said.

"Maybe that's why King Nyx was free to come to me," said Mary. "I started praying for small things, the night he shot Gertrude: I prayed he'd have crippling guilt, nightmares, weakness. I stayed awake two whole days and nights, and my thoughts gained power—the power of visions." Mary's voice was feverish. "That's when King Nyx came to me."

"And that's when Mr. Arkel started having the nightmares Frank came to cure," said Stella.

"Yes. From then on, every prayer worked. Every one was answered. The dreams crippled him; he couldn't leave his room."

"But those are psychological conditions," said Stella. "They can't be caused by prayer."

"'There are more things in Heaven and Earth, Horatio, than are dreamt of in your philosophy,'" said Mary.

Stella shook her head. "There are scientific explanations."

"Are there?" Mary asked. "Or are they just guesses? No one truly understands the human heart."

"But King Nyx was just something I made up," I said. "Not a god, with the power to affect other people."

"Not to you," Mary said. She began to pace. "But it's true that my powers weren't strong enough. I had to grow, you see. I had to atone for"—she gestured to the dolls, their polished faces shining in the bright electric light—"what I had done. I knew about them all. I let it happen. King Nyx directed me to go to the chamber of dolls and sit in the throne Claude had put there. Did you see it?"

I remembered Stella placing my hand on it in the dark, how it felt like it was made of polished wooden limbs.

"It was an awful thing," Mary said, "a dead thing. I *felt*, then, what I had become. I fell on my knees and prayed: *What do I do to get my daughter back?* That's when I got the vision of this place, the shrine, all of it. I knew the plant storage room lay right behind the room of dolls. King Nyx showed me that I had to make a door, bring them into this place of light and life. When I had done all that, then, finally, she granted my last wish."

"And what was that?" I asked.

"I wanted him to suffer," said Mary. "To love and be betrayed. And it all came to pass. He met Millicent and fell head over heels and married her. And she—" Mary smiled at some private thought. "She was never his, even from the start. But that's a story for another time. The night he found out she was in love with another man—young like her, and strong, and kind, all the things he was not—that was the worst pain he'd ever felt. When he went after them with his rifle, I knew it would be his downfall. You see, he thought a lot of his skills, but what he didn't realize was that he'd never had a fair fight. Everyone had been lying to him for his entire life. Telling him what he wanted to hear because of his family's money. The first real adversary he ever had was Detective Peleus, and he lost. Shot through the heart." She smiled again at the memory. Although I found her expression disturbing, I, too, felt pleasure at the thought of his death.

"After Claude was shot," she went on, "Millie came straight to me. We sat up till dawn making plans. It was the most exciting night. I had what I'd worked and waited for all these years: I was in charge."

"You had everything," I said, "except your daughter. She didn't come back."

Mary looked tired again, pressed her fingertips to her eyelids. "Claude was a great believer in Hobbes. He didn't believe in souls, only the material world. I realized that in my time here, I'd come to see things the same way. I'd figured out how to force the world to bend to my will, but I lost the person I was doing it for—my daughter. I'd lost my soul. And," she said, "I started to have bad dreams."

"Ambition," murmured Stella.

Mary looked up in surprise. "Yes," she said. "Well. I remembered that Frank Bixby had cured Claude, and so I invited him here, hoping he could cure me, too. And I did everything King Nyx asked, all this." She turned to look at the huge black bird. "Isn't she beautiful? I had my man in Petrograd make this."

"That isn't King Nyx," I said. "King Nyx was just an idea, just something I made up."

Mary reached into a pouch that hung from her brass-studded belt and pulled something out. She presented it to me on her open palm.

It was the black tin bird with blue eyes, one side of its head scratched and dented.

I realized I had been clutching the key in my pocket, and I held it up. Mary's face registered surprise.

"I found this in the greenhouse," I said.

"I must have dropped it. You knew I took King Nyx when I left the Forts' house, didn't you?" she asked.

"No," I said.

"I took the cigar box from under your bed. The one you didn't want me to look inside, remember? The night I left, I put it into the pillowcase I stuffed all my things into. It felt like taking a little bit of you with me."

I hadn't realized until that moment that part of the pain I'd carried all those years was separate from my guilt and my worry about her well-being: it was also not knowing if she— the only real friend of my life—had cared for me as much as I had for her.

"You took those things to remember me?"

Mary shook her head. "Not to remember. That I would have done anyway."

I felt the salt of tears at the back of my throat. "When you went away, Mary," I said, "everything sort of fell apart."

"It's all come back together now," she said.

She reached for the key. I felt her fingertips tremble as they touched mine.

Then, as if completing some foreordained sequence in a dream, she put the key in the bird's side and turned it.

It was exactly as I remembered. The tin wings moved up and down, the wheels carried it forward along her open hand. With her other hand, she brought mine up so that the bird rolled onto my palm. Some wild energy that radiated from her skin made me draw back.

"I'm trying to set things right, you see," she said. "I just don't know how."

"Mary," I said. "Why did Mr. Arkel invite Charles to come here?"

Mary shook her head. "Not Charles. You."

"The invitation said Mr. Arkel—"

"Anna," she interrupted. "I already told you. The invitation wasn't from Claude, it was from me."

She had told me. There was so much to take in that I'd forgotten. "But you invited Charles," I insisted. "That's what the letter said—that his work was important, that he could stay here and finish his book."

"Don't you understand?" Mary said. "I sent it to Charles because you would never have come if it was from a strange man to you. I had to find an excuse to invite him. I hired an investigator to locate you, and he turned up that newspaper article Charles wrote, about—what was it? Falling eels or something?"

I was surprised how slighted I felt, hearing her speak so dismissively of Charlie's work. He'd believed that was a truth that had to be reported. He had lost his job over it.

"You mean you don't even care? You don't actually want to support him?"

She pulled her dagger halfway from its sheath, staring at the dull gleam of the blade. "What I wanted was you. But now it's all gone to shit, hasn't it?"

"No, it hasn't." I took her hand from the hilt. "You don't know how I've dreamed of finding you, and here you are."

"But, Anna," she said, "you do realize the police are on the way, don't you?"

TWENTY-SEVEN

"WHAT DO YOU MEAN, THE POLICE ARE COMING?" STELLA demanded.

Mary pulled her hand from mine. "They telephoned two hours ago," she said, "just after midnight, wanting to speak to Mr. Arkel. It seems a body washed up at Clayton."

"A body?" I asked. "Whose?"

"They weren't sure. It had been partially consumed by . . . something. Maybe vultures. But the coroner sat up late examining it, and he found an object that hadn't been immediately visible due to the state of the flesh. On one shredded, chewed-up finger, the corpse was wearing a ring engraved with Claude Arkel's motto."

"That's the detective's ring," Stella said. "He showed us when we were walking back to the cabins."

"That's right," said Mary. "Claude gave it to him for service in the strike, and he always wore it. He was so damn proud of it. Claude could have given him a dog collar to wear and he would have shown it off. But the police thought the ring meant the body was Claude's."

"Mrs. Morton," I said suddenly. "The little old woman at the docks. She said, 'I don't think the police would do a damn thing unless the body of Mr. Arkel himself washed ashore.' Like it was fated to happen."

"I don't know about fate," said Mary. "But it did get them to do something. When Tommy came to tell me the police were demanding to speak with Claude, I got on the telephone and explained that it was the detective's body. I said he'd been let go and he'd left the island, and that Mr. Arkel could not be woken in the middle of the night over a man he no longer employed. I hoped that would hold them off. But I knew they'd come eventually. Clayton is a small town, especially in the winter, and there were already rumors about Millicent, a pretty young woman, appearing so suddenly in Claude's life. People said she was a gold digger, maybe a con artist. And it's true that she never loved him. So I knew other things might have gotten around, too; some of the servants might have been suspicious, talking in the saloon on their days off. I'd just hoped we would have a little more time. But they said if I wouldn't put Claude on the telephone, they'd have to come out. They'd have had to wake the officers and to get the boat here—not to mention, it takes forty minutes to walk from the dock to the house. Taking all that into account, I expect them no later than three o'clock."

I looked at Stella's watch on my wrist. "It's just past two," I said. "That means they'll be here within the hour."

Mary began to pace again, the long dagger in its sheath bouncing at her side, jagged shadows from the lamps fanning around her. Then she stopped, drew the dagger fully, and contemplated the blade in the bright light. I saw that there was a dark, tarry substance on it.

She held it out. "Curare," she said without emotion. "Poison made from a plant known as *Strychnos toxifera*. I have some in the greenhouses. When introduced into the circulatory system—for example, by means of a flesh wound—it causes paralysis of the entire body, including the heart and lungs."

I took a step back. "What exactly are you planning to do with it?" I asked.

She examined the blade dispassionately. "I'm not going back to jail," she said. "This place has been a prison. One I made myself, I know. For years, hope kept me going. But now that's over. Promise me something," she said, looking up at me. "Promise you'll take care of my daughter." Before I could answer, she went on: "God, I had such beautiful plans. Remember Fruitlands?"

"The utopian community that didn't make it through the winter?"

"Ours would have lasted," she said. "We were going to live here safe from the war, and illness, and anything or anyone who would ever hurt us. I was finally going to make up for leaving you all those years ago."

"Make up for leaving *me*? You were the one I was worried about," I said. "You were the sixteen-year-old runaway. I'm the one who stayed in a safe place."

"Safe? You could have been killed."

"Who would have killed me?" I asked.

"Mr. Fort. For being a witness," said Mary.

"A witness to what?"

"To the murder of Betsy Doyle." Seeing my confusion, she said, "The woman you saw being murdered at the open window at the back of the house."

A tingling numbness enveloped me. "What are you talking about?"

"You told me. We pieced it together the night we saw the death certificate. It said Betsy Doyle died of a gunshot wound to the stomach—"

I remembered the hypnosis with Frank. Over the years, I had somehow come to believe the Forts' lie for the neighbors, that it was appendicitis that killed Betsy. Until yesterday, when I went back to that night in my memory and saw the death certificate.

"But she wasn't murdered. It was suicide," I said.

Betsy on a stretcher, blood seeping through a sheet.

"Suicide's not usually a stomach wound, but if you're sure," the *police officer had said outside the house . . .*

"That's what you said when I first showed you the death certificate, Anna. But then you remembered."

Warm wetness on my cheek.

A spray of red spots on white petals.

The yellow house, red roses on a white trellis, white curtains bellying out the window in the breeze, the gray slate roof, and above that a clear May sky, blue, cloudless.

"No," I said. Stark black shadows streaked Mary's face, and Stella's.

"Easy there." Stella held out her arms.

Shadows everywhere, angled, jagged, cutting through my field of vision—the wall of woven willow, the green horses blurring at their edges, turning back into wilderness, the leafy throne with hair-fine roots spreading from its legs out into the glittering puddle. The big black lamps with their blinding glare, which showed every line and smudge of darkness: the hard glare of truth on the faces of my friends. Hands steadied me.

"The blood came from a clear blue sky," I said. But I blinked, and the scene flipped past like images in a stereoscope: the knee-high grass in the backyard that had always been like a wilderness compared to the manicured front lawn. The back wall of the house. The open window. The sound of Mr. Fort's voice raised in anger. Betsy trying to push him off. A struggle. And I hadn't looked away in time.

Betsy's back to me.

The sound of a gunshot, muffled by a human body.

Warm wetness on my skin.

My hand went to my cheek. Stella gripped my arms, supporting me as I stared at Mary.

"Remember," Mary said, "how you used to say it saved you—that place? You believed everywhere else was—what? The 'Realm of the Damned.' You couldn't let yourself see the truth, because you needed to believe in Mr. Fort's rules, his order."

"He killed Betsy," I said. And then I saw his face at the window, noticing me below, saw his cruel, distorted expression. The one I later imagined reflected in the coffee urn. I'd thought there was something wrong with me. *There's blood between the floorboards,* King Nyx had whispered in my ear as I knelt with my scrub brush in the master bedroom. I'd had to choose between her voice and Mr. Fort's version of events, and I'd chosen wrong. King Nyx had told the truth.

There was a loud banging then, and the sound of wood splintering and giving way, from the direction of the doll room.

Mary turned in the harsh light, her dagger in her hand. "That's the police," she said.

TWENTY-EIGHT

A MALE VOICE SHOUTED, "THERE THEY ARE!" IT WAS Charlie's.

Charlie! He hurried through the willow archway and into the lamps' glare. Our eyes met, and his expression mirrored the relief I felt.

"Annie!" he said. "We split off from the police and one of the servants told us to look down he—"

"Stay where you are!" Frank appeared behind him. His eyes were on Mary, and he had a gun.

"I say—" Charles began, but he faltered, surprised at the sight of Frank's expression, an intent anger, like I'd seen the first night through the cabin window.

Frank wasn't more than ten feet from us. He certainly wouldn't miss if he decided to shoot. But where had he gotten a gun? Then I remembered: Southerland's pistol had been missing when the girls went back for the body. He must have taken it.

Frank's eyes flicked over the scene: the grown-out topiary, the strange throne in its puddle, the enormous iridescent bird, the lifelike dolls, and the black lamps blasting light over everything. If he was surprised, he didn't show it.

"The police are here," he said.

"Frankie," said Stella. There was a cautious tenderness in her voice I hadn't heard before, and also, an edge of fear.

Frank ignored her. "They know everything." He was speaking to Mary.

Mary's voice was eerily calm: "What do the police know, Dr. Bixby?"

"They know about you," Frank said. "That you brought us here under false pretenses to be pawns in some game of yours. I don't like that. It's my pleasure to end your delusions here and now."

Mary's voice stayed even: "What delusions?"

"That you have the right to impersonate Claude Arkel, take his property, and control everything and everyone on this island."

"What makes you think I've been controlling things?" she asked almost disdainfully, as if the idea was ridiculous.

The muscles in Frank's jaw rippled with anger. "We don't think, we *know*. It started with servants gossiping in town. There's been talk for weeks. About you telling everyone there was a new chauffeur who no one ever saw, except in that"—Frank used the gun to gesture at the gas mask hanging on Mary's chest"—*that* thing."

She smiled with eerie calm. "But if I hadn't worn it, you'd have known it was me, wouldn't you?"

This seemed to heighten Frank's rage.

"By God, you thought we were stupid, woman." He spat the last word. "Putting those, those dolls in the motorcar, and expecting everyone to think they were Mr. and Mrs. Arkel. The police told me word was all over town; more than one of the servants had figured it out. But what was really going on? Who was behind it? You were the one acting suspicious, but it could have been under Mr. Arkel's orders, and no one was willing to risk confronting him over rumors and theories. Until his body washed ashore. Now we know: you murdered him."

"It wasn't Claude Arkel's body," Mary said.

"Give it up. The game is over. I—we won," Frank hissed. "We found the scene in his study, too—the doll in his likeness, smashed to bits. You can deny it till your last breath, but as a doctor of psychology, I can spot the signs of hysterical rage. You killed him, but that wasn't even enough for you, was it? You had to destroy even the thing that looked like him. Trying and trying to prove that you have his power, which you know in your heart you'll never really have." Frank's voice cracked with anger, and my body felt numb with fear. But Mary betrayed no emotion.

As if he couldn't stop until he got a reaction from her, Frank went on: "You don't like that, do you? Someone who knows your own mind better than you do? Well, I do. I figured you out."

Still Mary didn't react. His eyes flickered over her: her doublet and hose, the heavy cape, the gas mask, the dagger.

"What's the obsession with control?" Frank said, trying, with effort, to regain the authoritative, professional tone he normally used. "You want what men have, is that it?" he asked. "You were probably arrested at the penis-envy stage of your psychosexual development. Not that you would understand what that means."

"Frank, please," Stella said, "that's embarrassing." Her voice betrayed her fear. "Come on, now," she coaxed. "Put the gun down."

"You." He turned on her. "I'm sick to death of *you*."

"Why?" She seemed genuinely confused.

"Don't pretend not to know. I'm sick of living in fear. While I was away from you I had time to think, and I figured it out. Our nightly charades, our ritual, that was your idea, *you* talked me into it. It hasn't cured me, and I figured out why: because you never meant it to. It was your way of keeping me in line."

"*What?*" Stella asked.

"And the threat of going to the police that you kept constantly over my head," Frank went on. "You were *glad* I slipped up with that patient in my office, that young woman—weren't you? It confirmed all the bad things you thought about me, and it gave you an excuse to manipulate me with that threat, to pull my strings, like a puppet."

As he spoke, Stella's husband moved closer to her, and now the gun's muzzle was near her face. He seemed almost to have forgotten about Mary.

Charlie, Mary, and I stood frozen, as if the slightest movement might set off an explosion. I sensed we were all waiting for some sign, something that would tell us that it was the last possible moment to act, that we had to risk it. I prayed the police would arrive before that moment came.

Stella tried. "Frank," she said. "You've had these moods before. We can get through this. We always have."

"No, we can't," Frank said. Color rose in his cheeks, and his eyes were red. "No more."

They stood for a moment, facing off in silence, locked in their own private universe. Then something happened to Stella's face; emotion broke through. It was as if her real self inhabited it fully, not hiding behind rouge and rice powder, or smoke and whiskey. "No," she agreed. "You're right, Frank. No more."

This seemed to confuse him. "What do you mean?" His voice was uncertain, almost vulnerable.

"While we were apart, I got to thinking, too. And I don't want to keep your secret anymore."

He seemed momentarily thrown by this, but then quickly said, "I don't know what you're talking about."

"You just said it. The young woman in your office."

"I *said* I slipped up after . . . You know I did nothing wrong," Frank said.

Stella shook her head. "You've killed people, Frank."

How she had the nerve to confront him when he held a pistol pointed at her, I don't know. He made a slight move, but she went on: "If you shoot me here in front of everyone, it won't help, you know. You can stop me from talking with a bullet, but you won't help yourself. You're a rational man. You see that."

Frank held still, then. He seemed almost hypnotized with horror.

"So," she went on in the same low voice, "if I say out loud, here and now, that some of your patients at Danvers did not survive—"

"That's not a secret," he scoffed nervously. "I did important work there," he went on. "Some patients couldn't be saved. I never lied about that."

"But you did lie about Viola Bennett, the young woman who came to you for private treatment."

"She had a heart defect!"

"I saw the dial on your machine. You left it where it was when you turned the power off. It was set to ten."

Frank had shown me the numbers when he'd had me hooked up in the cabin. It got dangerous at eight, he'd said.

"It was a level you knew could be lethal," Stella continued, "even for a healthy person. She died hooked up to your machine, and afterward you took a handsaw—"

Frank's arm jerked again, a spasmodic, angry movement, but Stella held him with her gaze, which, although fearful, was steady. "Will you shoot me for saying it? What will that prove?" She paused. "You took a handsaw, and a barrel full of lye—"

"I was afraid," Frank interrupted, his voice almost breaking now not with rage, but with something like self-pity. "I did nothing wrong."

There was sympathy in Stella's tone when she replied, "What you just said about pulling your strings like a puppet—that's what Mr. Arkel talked about. You need help, just like he did. Maybe there's a way you can be helped, maybe one of the doctors you worked with at Danvers—"

Frank spoke over her, his voice rising: "Claude Arkel was a better man than ninety-nine out of a hundred you'll ever meet. The only help he needed was being reminded of that, and a fresh start with a beautiful wife, but she betrayed him, like women always do. Viola Bennett's death was an accident, but because I *am* a good person, I felt sorry, I felt scared. Hiding her body was stupid, I admit it. Does that make you happy? There was no victim—the poor woman had already succumbed to her heart condition. But you—you tried to humiliate me by going to the police. You didn't think I knew that, did you? But a friend on the force told me. I know all about how they laughed at you. But you kept threatening me with the law, so I knew you must be planning to see someone else, maybe the state police. They might have taken your side. Maybe they wouldn't be as smart as my friend, who saw you for what you are: a drunk, ugly, ridiculous hag." Then, with a movement so swift no one saw it coming, he raised his free hand and slapped Stella across the face so hard she almost fell.

Charles stepped forward then. "Sorry, old chap," he said firmly. "You'd better give me this." He took Frank's wrist in one of his big hands and reached for the gun with the other. He was taller and heavier than Frank, and he almost succeeded, but he was not prepared for the violence with which the wiry man turned on him and, with a snap of his tennis-strengthened wrist, cracked Charlie in the face with the butt of the pistol and sent him reeling back against a planter, where he slid down to sit on the floor, blinking with confusion.

I started toward him, but Frank turned. "Nobody move," he said, holding the gun up, his eyes darting from one of us to the other.

"I'm all right, dear," Charlie said, rubbing his bloody head. A trickle of red leaked from his mouth. "You just stay put." He struggled to rise again.

"The second you're on your feet, I'll put you back down, by God," Frank said. "You stay out of this. It's between me and my wife." He turned to her. "I've been waiting a long time to have it out with you, Stella," he said. "A long, long time."

A tear streaked Stella's cheek. "Have you? I tried to help you, Frank. I loved you. God knows I tried to stop, but I couldn't."

"You never loved me," Frank said. "You wanted me afraid, and you wanted to control me."

"No."

"No? It doesn't matter to you who's in charge? Prove it, then. Beg for your life."

"Frankie, please—"

"If I really am a murderer, like you think, then how do you know I won't shoot? Even with people watching? Beg, I said. On your knees."

I don't think anyone in the room doubted that Frank was capable of pulling the trigger at that moment.

Stella got to her knees. Frank's eyes searched her face, as if he wanted to take it all in—her pleading, her fear.

Locked in this private drama, he didn't notice that Mary, who had been standing near Stella, had edged around behind him. In a swift motion, she drove the dagger into his back.

Frank dropped the gun with a convulsive movement as he spun to face Mary, her knife still in him. Mary stooped for the pistol. "That's enough," she said, holding it in both hands.

Frank staggered backward, his arms flailing awkwardly. No one noticed until too late that he was reaching to pull the blade from his back. He held it up, his own blood shining on the steel.

"I'm afraid you gave me your dagger," he said.

"I'm afraid it's poisoned," Mary replied. "Forty-five seconds until your lungs are paralyzed and you stop breathing."

Frank's face registered fear before he lunged at Mary. But Mary stepped away easily as he stumbled and fell forward.

She didn't step far enough, though. With one last, desperate reach, Frank managed to plunge the blade into her thigh before he hit the ground. He lay on the floor then, suddenly still, his face frozen, twisted with anger.

Mary didn't make a sound. She pulled the dagger from her thigh. Our eyes met and she saw the fear in mine. "Maybe the poison came off in Frank's body, so that there's not enough left— Ah, no," she said. "I feel it now."

Stella was already at Frank's side. I ran to Mary as she sank to the floor.

I knelt, pulling Mary's head onto my lap, holding her there, everything all wrong, the lights too bright and the shadows confusing, deep and dark as spilled blood.

Senseless words came from my mouth, a confession, out of nowhere. "Mary," I said, "remember the parakeets in Mr. Fort's closet? After you left, I set them free. But winter was coming, and they died. I was trying to help, but they died."

Mary was looking at me, eyes wide, already seeing another, brighter world behind the flimsy curtain of this one. "It's okay," she whispered. Her hand made a small convulsive movement; I grasped it, and she squeezed mine one last time. I kept holding her even after I knew she was gone.

To our right lay Frank's stiff body, his feet in the edge the puddle where the throne sat, water soaking his trousers. Stella knelt over him, her forehead pressed to his, a gesture more tender than I had seen between them when he lived.

Charlie was still slumped against the planter where he'd fallen when Frank struck him. I was aware that he was struggling to rise, and maybe I should have helped him, but I didn't want to let go of Mary. After a few confused tries, he managed to get to me. Tears ran from his nose into his mustache, mixed with blood, as he embraced me, saying, "Anna, Anna," as if by repeating my name he could make everything go back to the way it was.

It was this sad, messy scene that the police found when they charged in.

TWENTY-NINE

AFTER FINDING OUT THAT WE HAD NOT REALLY BEEN invited by Mr. Arkel, the butler, one of the few servants still loyal to him and now the one in charge, insisted that we leave. We were put in guest rooms and given three days to make our plans. They were strange days. Charles had a bad headache, but he looked like he was going to be all right, with lots of ice and aspirin brought by the staff. They had learned everything, in the way servants do, and treated us half like celebrities, half like zoo animals.

Our bedroom was called the Eagle Room because of the painting over the mantel, which showed a pair of fierce-looking birds at their nest high above a river. As we sat on velvet upholstered chairs by the fireplace the first night, Charlie said, "What did you say to Mary just before I got to you? Something about birds."

"Yes, your father kept some in his study."

"I never knew that," Charles said. He kept touching his head as if to make sure it was really in one piece. I decided not to mention how his father had locked them in a dark closet to punish his wife for bringing them home. I wouldn't tell him about Betsy, either. He had too many memories of his father's cruelty to carry already. What was the point of adding more, all these years later?

"Are those the birds you set free before you went to Dr. Jacobson's?" Charlie asked.

"Yes. I wanted to help them, without realizing they'd die in the cold air. They were the same kind I have, monk parakeets. That's why I wanted you to buy me that first pair when I saw them in the pet shop window."

"Annie, are you sure they can't take the cold? I didn't want to argue with you when you were so anxious about them, but . . . "

He went to our trunk full of notes and books, which had been brought to our new room. "Here: *Birds in Captivity: Species and Their Care*," he said. "*Myiopsitta monachus*, page 263." He flipped through the pages, then handed the book to me, pointing to one of the lines, and I read aloud: "'In 1853, a feral colony of escaped parakeets of this breed was established near the town of Schenectady, New York.'" I looked up at him. "That's not far from Albany. If they can survive there, maybe your father's parakeets didn't die."

I remembered Mary's last words: "It's okay." Had she been referring to the birds, or something else?

"I've had this book for years," I said. "How did I not notice?"

Charlie shrugged. "Happens sometimes. Maybe when you were reading it, you were looking for something different. Sometimes we only see what we're looking for. Anyhow, I told you I saw them in the trees by the house that first winter, chattering away. Didn't you believe me?"

I looked into Charlie's familiar, well-meaning face. "I should have," I said. I hugged him, and he looked pleased.

STELLA SEEMED DAZED IN THOSE last days. On the morning after our first night in the guest rooms, I persuaded her to walk in the garden. She'd powdered her face lightly and looked elegant in a matching skirt and jacket that were dark brown, almost black.

"I didn't bring any mourning clothes," she said absently when I complimented her.

We went around to the back of the huge house, past the greenhouses. The cold late morning light flashed off the glass walls and roofs.

I'd talked to the chambermaid who came to tend our fire, Clover; she was close to one of the gardeners and promised he'd put out some millet and oats, and look out for the twins, but as I passed the buildings, I wondered how long they would last now that Mr. Arkel and Mary were dead. He had built them to grow fruit year-round, but surely these extravagant, steam-heated structures were not profitable. Who would inherit them, and what would become of the birds if the gardeners stopped tending them?

"Let's go inside for a minute." I led Stella to the door. She hesitated. "There's no one to stop us now," I said, pushing it open.

The warmth flushed our faces. I went to where we had released the birds: the rock hill with the waterfall and grotto. The place was bright again in the daylight, the flowers along the stream almost garish, like artificially colored candy. I noticed a few signs of neglect I hadn't before: moss furred the brick path, and two glass panels in the ceiling were broken.

THERE WERE A COUPLE OF small benches for observing the waterfall; I sat on one and made the kissing sound I used to call the birds at home, and heard a rustling overhead. There they were, in the branches of a fig tree! "Here, come on," I said, feeling bad that I didn't have the peanuts they expected.

But they wouldn't come; they just sat there looking at me. This had never happened back in the Bronx.

"They're happy," Stella said. "Leave them be."

I'd have to ask Clover to see if her friend could get them out if the greenhouses were shut down. Or at least leave the door open. He could do that, I thought hopefully. But the birds weren't mine anymore, and I realized I would probably never know what became of them.

Outside in the garden, sun shone on the frost-gilded seed-heads and browned grasses, and our footsteps crunched on the crushed oyster shells that paved the weedy path. We went the same way we had before.

"What will you do now?" I asked Stella, after she had been silent for a few minutes.

"Me? Oh . . . get a little apartment, maybe," she said.

"Come live in the Bronx," I said. "Be our neighbor. I can bring you meals so you don't have to cook for a while. You could—"

"No," she interrupted. "Thanks. But I'll stay in Boston, where it's familiar."

"What will you do? You could go back to school."

"I'm too old for that."

"Get married again?"

"Easy, there." She stopped and lit a cigarette. "I don't know what I'll do," she said, blowing out smoke. "It's okay. I'll write to you."

We decided to see if the automaton was still in the pavilion with the player piano. It was. It had been so shocking the first time, seeming to radiate menace, but today in the frosty light I noticed that one set of eyelashes was crooked, maybe falling off, and that the ruffles of the dress were limp with melted frost. "This is the only one I can stand to look at," Stella said.

"I wonder if Mary did this after Millicent left, or if *he'd* had it made already; maybe he was planning—"

Stella made a noise of disgust. "Let's not talk about it." She smoked thoughtfully, then said, "That man was Frank's patient. Frank saw the room of dolls. I keep thinking he *knew* everything and came anyway—because of it. What kind of man would do that?" She closed her eyes. "I really believed that what happened with Viola was an accident. I'd seen the dial, but I thought maybe he panicked when she died, started turning the knob back and forth . . ."

Now that I knew what Frank's nature was really like, and that Stella had seen it early on, I thought, *How could she have believed that?* She'd been aware that he'd killed people at Danvers, that he'd been asked to leave because of it. How could she talk herself into thinking that what had happened with Viola was unintentional? But then, she had tried going to the police and they had laughed at her.

And what about me? I had made myself remember Betsy's death as suicide, in spite of what I'd seen with my own eyes. When everyone is telling you one thing, it can be hard to see something different, even if it's right in front of you. To do so means breaking with the people who make up your world, who keep you safe. It means walking outside the warm circle around the fire and into the dark unknown, the territory of the excluded. Night: daughter of Chaos, mother of dreams.

Yet here we were, Stella and I. Both of us had done it and survived.

I went over to see how the player piano worked. It was electric, plugged into a socket in the pavilion's wall. There was a brass switch on the side, and I flipped it. With a whirr and a creak, the figure's hands began to move over the keyboard, and the music began, the keys going up and down although the wooden fingers didn't touch them. I took Stella's arm and we walked away down the winding path, followed by the stumbling, mechanical rendition of "Clair de lune."

Later, I went to the greenhouse alone one last time, to look for the birds again. I brought their favorite mixture of millet and oats and stood by the artificial waterfall, calling them, but this time there was no response. The sky was a late, deepening blue above the broken panes of the glass roof, and the impossible candy colors of the flowers were tamer in the evening light. I wondered if Castor and Pollux had escaped, or if they had just gone off into some far part of the greenhouse complex where they couldn't hear me.

Why had I bred so many, only to keep them in our apartment, with its heavy drapes, and spend all my time cleaning up
after them? Such a strange relationship: they were my captives
and I their servant. Maybe, I thought, I should set the others
free, too, when I got home.

The next day, I hiked out to the cemetery and found Mary
and the girls. They had a small fire going behind the church
foundation and were standing around looking bored and cold.
The girls actually seemed happy to see me. Mary was subdued.
They already knew what had happened from their friends at the
house. "She told me she was planning to invite you back," I said.
"She loved you." Mary stared into the fire.

"Do you think she was crazy?" she asked finally.

"No more than anybody else. At least she was trying to
do something good. She wanted to make something perfect
for you."

But the way it had all ended, and the fact that the girls were
still standing here now, dressed in rags, the baby fussing in Ginger's arms, showed how completely she had failed. I knew we
were both thinking that.

"Anyway, I promised her I would take care of you," I said,
"and I will. Charlie and I only have a small apartment, but we'll
do what we can to make a home for you."

"Sorry," she said, "I appreciate it, but I can't leave my friends."

"But I promised," I repeated, "and I can't possibly take them
all. We only have one bedroom. Charlie doesn't even have a job
or a publisher for his book."

Mary was holding the bearskin close around her. The wind
had picked up and clouds were moving across the sun, causing
the light to shift over the graveyard, with its yellow grasses.

"Then I can't go," she said simply. I looked into her dark, determined eyes—familiar, but brighter, kinder than her mother's.

In the end, I agreed.

———————

"BUT, ANNA," CHARLES PROTESTED WHEN I told him back in our room. "How will I write with all those people in the apartment?"

In the painting above the fireplace, one large fierce-looking bird brooded over a nest, its mate standing nearby. I wondered if there were eaglets under her or just eggs.

"They can work," I said. "They can help us make ends meet."

He was skeptical. But eventually, reluctantly, he agreed.

The day we left, the same red-faced, bearded man picked us up in the same boat. He didn't speak. I wondered if he already knew everything that had happened, or if he didn't care why we were headed back with all our luggage after only a few days. Maybe, like Cook at the Forts' house, he didn't want to know; maybe his energy and curiosity were reserved for his own private life.

As the boat headed to the mainland, I stood at the starboard railing, with Stella on one side of me and Mary on the other. We watched Prosper Island recede. This time, I had no birdcage clutched against my body. It stood on the floor of the cabin, open, empty.

I decided that when I got the other birds back from Mrs. Binns, I would set them free, too. Maybe in the spring. I'd put food and water out for them in the yard behind our building.

I glanced over to the other side of the boat, where the eight girls from the school stood: the five who hadn't run away, along with Sam, Poppy, and Ginger, with her baby. They were a crowd. How would we ever fit in the apartment?

I closed my eyes and tilted my face toward the cold wind. We would manage.

BACK IN THE BRONX, the girls tried to find employment, to mixed success. They contributed something to the household expenses, but no one was anywhere near being able to afford another place. They slept on the floor of the living room and piled their blankets and pillows against the wall during the day.

Charlie left for the New York Public Library every morning with his briefcase full of notepaper, and didn't come home until it closed.

We'd only been living this way for about a week, though, when a mysterious visitor came to the door. She wore mourning clothes and a heavy black veil. When she lifted it, I couldn't stop a gasp of surprise. It was the face of the doll in the garden. Her blue-green eyes were large, kaleidoscopic, hard to look away from. I saw right away why Claude Arkel had fallen in love.

"Mrs. Arkel," I said.

"Please," she said, "call me Millicent." Her voice was low and slightly husky. Her smile was slow, with a twist in one corner, as if she knew some secret that nobody else did.

I invited her in even though there was hardly anywhere to sit—every surface was covered with the girls' sewing and newspapers and magazines. Up by the ceiling, birds lined the curtain rods, making a racket. Still, I managed to serve tea.

"Your friend Mary," she said, "wrote a letter after she found out the police were on their way to Prosper Island and gave it to her maid to post. She intended to ask you to take care of her daughter and gave me your address. It looks like you have . . . several young ladies living here, though." From the curtain rods, one of the birds kept making the sound of a crying baby. Ginger, trying to rock the real baby to sleep in the kitchen, shushed it.

"Some of her friends came, too," I said.

Millicent smiled. "Mary asked if I would give you something," she said, "to help support her daughter. I see you may need a bit more than I thought."

"Oh, you mean money?" I asked, embarrassed at the excitement that made my heart jump. "Oh, really, we're okay."

"Are you sure?"

She could obviously tell we weren't. "Anything would be a help," I admitted.

Millicent lowered her voice: "How much do you know?"

"About what?" I asked cautiously.

"The death of my late husband."

I picked up my teacup and looked at the ripples inside it. "The police said Mary killed him," I answered, "and since she's dead, the case is closed . . . so I think that's all there is to know."

"Good."

I looked up and our eyes met. Hers held my gaze, as a flame holds the gaze in a dark room. There'd been no articles in the paper except a brief report of Claude's death "from an unexpected illness." The Arkels' wealth had swallowed the rest of the story like the ocean closing over a shipwreck. They probably didn't miss the money Millicent and the others had taken any more than the Atlantic would miss a pail of water.

"Tell me what you need," she said.

A bird screeched as Sam shooed it out of the kitchen. "A larger house," I said.

"And?"

I was silent, remembering Mary in the plant storage room, her face streaked with shadows, saying, *Remember Fruitlands?*

Were such idealistic projects always doomed to fail? Maybe. But then, what were any of us but short-lived experiments? Bumbling along, trying to figure things out, while we were still on this side of the sod, as my father used to say.

"What I'd really like," I said, "is to have a farm. Not a huge one. Just some orchards, a small barn. A farmhouse with room for everyone. And parakeets in the trees all year round," I added.

"You shall have it," said Millicent.

"You really mean—"

"Nothing could be easier."

"I don't know about that," I said. "But it's something I'd like to try."

When she stood at the door, ready to leave, she took both of my hands in hers, the same way Mary had done on that summer day on the hilltop. "Good luck," she said.

THAT NIGHT, AS CHARLES AND I lay next to each other, we could hear rustling, shifting, coughing, and snoring from the girls in the living room. I thought about how I had a secret from him, something I'd never had before. The incident that had started his—our—research hadn't been blood falling from the sky. It had been Betsy Doyle's blood the day she was murdered by his father. I thought again how much Charlie had suffered from that man, who hadn't spoken to him in years. The events of that day were a burden I could carry alone so that Charlie wouldn't have to.

The new secret put distance between us, and yet, in a way, it calmed me; it felt like breathing room. For our entire marriage, I had told him everything I thought, believing that this would protect me from sliding back into insanity. Everything that entered my mind had to meet with his approval before I decided it could stay. At last I had something of my own, a hard truth, small but heavy as a rock, that I carried inside me. A whole structure of truth might accrete around it, I thought, growing slowly like a pearl.

EPILOGUE

September 20, 1933

THAT'S IT. THAT'S THE STORY. It's been fifteen years now, Charlie is dead, and I've finally moved out to the farm that I owned but didn't live at while he needed me.

He never told Mr. Dreiser why the trip to Prosper Island was cut short—they weren't in touch frequently—but he did send Dreiser his manuscript in the spring of 1919, and by early the next year it was on the shelves. Most readers didn't know what to make of it, but he went on to publish three more, and accumulated a small, passionate, very odd collection of admirers, who I occasionally had to make lunch for.

I'd gone to Prosper Island thinking murder was a rarity, and always notable when it happened; I'd left with the sickening sense that it was everywhere: in asylums, charity schools, bedrooms; in barns and kitchens. That it not only lurked beneath the surface of everything, but fed and spread like rot, multiplying uncontrollably once it started.

I was amazed how many people—through luck, willful ignorance, an instinct for self-preservation, or tricks of the mind— were able not to see it, and that I had been one of them. I thought my new understanding of the world was permanent, but time passed and I went back to being someone who only occasionally reads about murder in the paper. It takes effort to remember what I learned that long-ago November.

The girls did a good job with the farm: they grew vegetables, put together a library, kept chickens, sold hay from the fields. I hired a woman to run the place and teach them, a Mrs. Pearson, who'd been fired from another position for getting her students too worked up about universal suffrage and labor rights. I liked her.

When I moved in last year, I saw that the sign Poppy had hung at the end of the driveway years ago was half hidden by branches and very faded. I could just make out the word FRUIT among the leaves. I knew it said NEW FRUITLANDS. That was the name I gave it.

I left the sign there—not fixing it up, but not taking it down, either. It was a reminder of my dreams. It never was a grand utopian community, never anything more than home for a few girls, but they grew up here all right, and Ginger's daughter, Lois, is still growing up.

Sam went on to teach mathematics at a girls' school. Poppy moved out early to work as a nurse, and for a while wrote regularly to ask for money, then stopped and fell out of touch. Maybe a busy, full life took her away, or maybe something else. The other girls had mixed success, as people do. There are two besides Poppy I don't hear from; another three write of engagements and children, illness and jobs, gardens and travel.

As for Mary, she moved to Manhattan as soon as she could, and from there to California. She writes every couple of months. Last I heard, she was living on a ranch with friends, and it all sounded very bohemian—worse, actually, than the corsetless vegetarians of her mother's youth. Her letter was exuberant and a bit disjointed, and the lavender-colored writing paper smelled of men's cologne and tarry smoke I thought might be hashish. She said she and her friends had been up all night working on some sort of screenplay.

Back here at the farm, old Mrs. Pearson is gone, retired, and Ginger looks after the place. I call it a farm, but it's really just a small orchard and a big garden and miscellaneous animals we've accumulated over the years: two goats, a runt sow, three stray dogs, an unknown number of cats who come and go.

I should have done more—made it productive—instead of just running it on the Arkel money, but that would have meant devoting myself to it instead of to Charlie, and I chose Charlie.

The afternoon is mellowing now over the hayfields. Until a week ago it felt like summer, but now there's a slant to the light, a sadness, something different as autumn comes in.

Maybe there's still time to do more with the place. But maybe not. I imagine winter gathering in the high black distance, crystals of ice forming far above the soft golden afternoon, with its odor of fallen apples and the soft buzzing of the little striped hornets that gather to eat them. I saw them in the orchard today, all over the ground, wobbling drunkenly over the bruised, collapsing fruits, delirious with sunshine and sugar as they sensed the approach of killing frost.

Back in the Bronx, fifteen years ago, the night after Millicent came to tell me about the money, I stood at the window and saw snowflakes glittering in the night air over Ryer Avenue. Later, as Charlie and I lay in bed and I thought about all that had passed, I pictured the snow falling, and falling, soft in the light from streetlamps and windows.

I remember that as I slipped into sleep, I saw many things descending from the sky: mica, goldfish, silk. Lifted by winds, carried sideways through the air. Coming to rest on grass, streets, rooftops; accumulating in the corners of the windowsills. The whole world peppered with small gifts, indecipherable messages from some place beyond what we could see. Like me whispering to the birds through the quilt: *Herkimer, Deer River, Carthage.*

Always these little signs, bits of jumbled telegrams, dots and dashes of Morse code thrown up in handfuls like confetti to land every which way, and still, and always, our little minds keep trying to piece them all together.

Author's Note

Charles Fort's *The Book of the Damned* was deemed unpublishable until a friend of his, the novelist Theodore Dreiser, essentially forced it on the publishing house Boni & Liveright by threatening to leave if they turned it down. Boni & Liveright was courting Dreiser at the time, acquiring and reprinting his early works in the hopes that his next big success would be theirs, and so they reluctantly produced five hundred copies of Fort's book, which appeared in bookstores early in 1920. They were rewarded with Dreiser's acclaimed novel *An American Tragedy* in 1925.

Years earlier, when Dreiser already believed in Charles but Charles had not yet finished *The Book of the Damned*, Dreiser went searching for Charles, who had moved since their last contact, and found him looking miserable and disheveled in a filthy tenement. Anna was away supporting the household, working at a hotel laundry where the hours were so long that workers had to board there. Charles couldn't offer Dreiser much, but invited him to come back for dinner when Anna was home to cook.

According to Dreiser's notes, he returned a week or so later to find cheerful candles in the windows, the apartment scrubbed clean, dinner cooking, and Charles in a fresh shirt. This was all Anna's doing.

But he noticed that while Charles discussed the lofty subjects of his research, Anna did not participate. Eating the food she'd cooked for him, the novelist observed that she seemed only dimly aware that she was "part of something magnificent." He was sure she was incapable of comprehending her husband's theories. "This woman cannot think," Dreiser wrote, "she feels."

For this information, I'm indebted to the biographies *Charles Fort: The Man Who Invented the Supernatural*, by Jim Steinmeyer, and *Dreiser*, by W. A. Swanberg.

King Nyx is a fantasy inspired by Anna's life, about a week in November 1918 that never was. A dream of how it might be if lost girls were found, if the owner of a hand sore and chapped from laundry soap had time and space to hold a pen.

Acknowledgments

This novel represents the love, support, and help of many people. Huge thanks to Pete Simon for believing in this book, for his close reads and keen editor's eye; to Gina Iaquinta for incredibly helpful notes; to Bonnie Thompson for her brilliant copyediting; and to everyone at Liveright Publishing. I'm immensely grateful to Lynn Nesbit for her guidance and confidence through the years. Thanks to the Sustainable Arts Foundation for a grant that bought me precious writing time in 2021. Love and thanks to my family, who make me feel anchored, uplifted, and cared for: my parents, Ann and Raimo Bakis, and my sister, Ingrid Bakis-Ray, and also her family: Gracie, Mark, and Peter. Thanks and love also to my friends: Molly Gaudry for the weekly writing check-ins that kept me from giving up, and for the first read of this novel; Charlie Buck for precise and brilliant comments; Priscilla Gilman, Emily Barton, and Lauren Eberhardt for extremely helpful early reads and encouragement; Soyung Pak for our writing weekends at Mariandale and for believing with me, one cold March evening, that a wild turkey was actually a peacock; Charlie Buck, Angela Fasick, Kris Vervaecke, and Lee Montgomery for friendship and writerly encouragement over thirty years (!) since our days in Iowa City; and Florence Lesandro: Love you and miss you. The biggest thanks go to my children, Theo and Charlotte, for changing and expanding my world and my heart, and for being my source of inspiration every day.